Palgrave Studies in Modern European Literature

Series Editors
Ben Hutchinson
Centre for Modern European Literature
University of Kent
Canterbury, UK

Shane Weller
School of European Culture and Languages
University of Kent
Canterbury, UK

Many of the most significant European writers and literary movements of the modern period have traversed national, linguistic and disciplinary borders. The principal aim of the Palgrave Studies in Modern European Literature book series is to create a forum for work that problematizes these borders, and that seeks to question, through comparative methodologies, the very nature of the modern, the European, and the literary. Specific areas of research that the series supports include European romanticism, realism, the avant-garde, modernism and postmodernism, literary theory, the international reception of European writers, the relations between modern European literature and the other arts, and the impact of other discourses (philosophical, political, psychoanalytic, and scientific) upon that literature. In addition to studies of works written in the major modern European languages (English, French, German, Italian, and Spanish), the series also includes volumes on the literature of Central and Eastern Europe, and on the relation between European and other literatures.

Editorial Board:
Rachel Bowlby (University College London)
Karen Leeder (University of Oxford)
William Marx (Collège de France)
Marjorie Perloff (Stanford University)
Jean-Michel Rabaté (University of Pennsylvania)
Dirk Van Hulle (University of Oxford)

More information about this series at
https://link.springer.com/bookseries/14610

Ian Ellison

Late Europeans and Melancholy Fiction at the Turn of the Millennium

palgrave
macmillan

Ian Ellison
Goethe-Universität Frankfurt
Frankfurt am Main, Germany

ISSN 2634-6478   ISSN 2634-6486   (electronic)
Palgrave Studies in Modern European Literature
ISBN 978-3-030-95446-8   ISBN 978-3-030-95447-5   (eBook)
https://doi.org/10.1007/978-3-030-95447-5

This Palgrave Macmillan imprint is published by the registered company Springer Nature Switzerland AG.
The registered company address is: Gewerbestrasse 11, 6330 Cham, Switzerland

This book is dedicated to my family, and to the memory of Michael Hundehege, with love and thanks

Series Editors' Preface

Many of the most significant European writers and literary movements in the modern period have traversed national, linguistic, and disciplinary borders. The principal aim of the Palgrave Studies in Modern European Literature series is to create a forum for work that takes account of these border crossings and that engages with individual writers, genres, topoi, and literary movements in a manner that does justice to their location within European artistic, political, and philosophical contexts. Of course, the title of this series immediately raises a number of questions, at once historical, geo-political, and literary-philosophical: What are the parameters of the modern? What is to be understood as European, both politically and culturally? And what distinguishes literature within these historical and geo-political limits from other forms of discourse?

These three questions are interrelated. Not only does the very idea of the modern vary depending on the European national tradition within which its definition is attempted, but the concept of literature in the modern sense is also intimately connected to the emergence and consolidation of the European nation-states, to increasing secularization, urbanization, industrialization, and bureaucratization, to the Enlightenment project and its promise of emancipation from nature through reason and science, to capitalism and imperialism, to the liberal-democratic model of government, to the separation of the private and public spheres, to the new form taken by the university, and to changing conceptions of both space and time as a result of technological innovations in the fields of travel and communication.

Taking first the question of when the modern may be said to commence within a European context, if one looks to a certain Germanic tradition shaped by Friedrich Nietzsche in *The Birth of Tragedy* (1872), then it might be said to commence with the first 'theoretical man', namely, Socrates. According to this view, the modern would include everything that comes after the pre-Socratics and the first two great Attic tragedians, Aeschylus and Sophocles, with Euripides being the first modern writer. A rather more limited sense of the modern, also derived from the Germanic world, sees the *Neuzeit* as originating in the late fifteenth and early sixteenth centuries. Jakob Burckhardt, Nietzsche's colleague at the University of Basel, identified the states of Renaissance Italy as prototypes for both modern European politics and modern European cultural production. However, Italian literary modernity might also be seen as having commenced two hundred years earlier, with the programmatic adoption of the vernacular by its foremost representatives, Dante and Petrarch.

In France, the modern might either be seen as beginning at the turn of the seventeenth to the eighteenth century, with the so-called Querelle des anciens et des modernes in the 1690s, or later still, with the French Revolution of 1789, while the Romantic generation of the 1830s might equally be identified as an origin, given that Chateaubriand is often credited with having coined the term *modernité*, in 1833. Across the Channel, meanwhile, the origins of literary modernity might seem different again. With the Renaissance being seen as 'Early Modern', everything thereafter might seem to fall within the category of the modern, although in fact the term 'modern' within a literary context is generally reserved for the literature that comes after mid-nineteenth-century European realism. This latter sense of the modern is also present in the early work of Roland Barthes, who in *Writing Degree Zero* (1953) asserts that modern literature commences in the 1850s, when the literary becomes explicitly self-reflexive, not only addressing its own status as literature but also concerning itself with the nature of language and the possibilities of representation.

In adopting a view of the modern as it pertains to literature that is more or less in line with Barthes's periodization, while also acknowledging that this periodization is liable to exceptions and limitations, the present series does not wish to conflate the modern with, nor to limit it to, modernism and postmodernism. Rather, the aim is to encourage work that highlights differences in the conception of the modern—differences that emerge out of distinct linguistic, national, and cultural spheres within Europe—and to prompt further reflection on why it should be that the very concept of the modern has become such a critical issue in 'modern' European culture, be it aligned with Enlightenment progress, with the critique of Enlightenment thinking, with decadence, with radical renewal, or with a sense of belatedness.

Turning to the question of the European, the very idea of modern literature arises in conjunction with the establishment of the European nation states. When European literatures are studied at university, they are generally taught within national and linguistic parameters: English, French, German, Italian, Scandinavian, Slavic and Eastern European, and Spanish literature. Even if such disciplinary distinctions have their pedagogical justifications, they render more difficult an appreciation of the ways in which modern European literature is shaped in no small part by intellectual and artistic traffic across national and linguistic borders: to grasp the nature of the European avant-gardes or of high modernism, for instance, one has to consider the relationship between distinct national or linguistic traditions. While not limiting itself to one methodological approach, the present series is designed precisely to encourage the study of individual writers and literary movements within their European context. Furthermore, it seeks to promote research that engages with the very definition of the European in its relation to literature, including changing conceptions of centre and periphery, of Eastern and Western Europe, and how these might bear upon questions of literary translation, dissemination, and reception.

As for the third key term in the series title—literature—the formation of this concept is intimately related both to the European and to the modern. While Sir Philip Sidney in the late sixteenth century, Martin Opitz in the seventeenth, and Shelley in the early nineteenth produce their apologies for, or defences of, 'poetry', it is within the general category of 'literature' that the genres of poetry, drama, and prose fiction have come to be contained in the modern period. Since the Humboldtian reconfiguration of the university in the nineteenth century, the fate of literature has been closely bound up with that particular institution, as well as with emerging ideas of the canon and tradition. However one defines it, modernity has both propagated and problematized the historical legacy of the Western literary tradition. While, as Jacques Derrida argues, it may be that in all European languages the history and theorization of the literary necessarily emerge out of a common Latinate legacy—the very word 'literature' deriving from the Latin *littera* (letter)—it is nonetheless the case that within a modern European context the literary has taken on an extraordinarily diverse range of forms. Traditional modes of representation have been subverted through parody and pastiche or abandoned altogether; genres have been mixed; the limits of language have been tested; indeed, the concept of literature itself has been placed in question.

With all of the above in mind, the present series wishes to promote work that engages with any aspect of modern European literature (be it a literary movement, an individual writer, a genre, a particular topos) within its European context, that addresses questions of translation, dissemination, and reception (both within Europe and beyond), that considers the relations between modern European literature and the other arts, that analyses the impact of other discourses (philosophical, political, scientific) upon that literature, and, above all, that takes each of those three terms—modern, European, and literature—not as givens, but as invitations, even provocations, to further reflection.

Ben Hutchinson
Shane Weller

ACKNOWLEDGEMENTS

This book was a number of years in the making, beginning before I had even intentionally started work on it, and along the way it has incurred many debts, both intellectual and personal, which I should like to acknowledge here. In bestowing my thanks I shall attempt to be accurate and exhaustive in order to repay the graciousness with which family, friends, and colleagues have supported me, putting up with my peregrinations around Europe over the past half decade or so. However, in keeping with the book's approach, my thanks will remain geographically and historically contingent, although persons mentioned here may have since relocated.

The research and writing of this project occurred in many locations but certainly would never have come to pass were it not for the support of the Leverhulme Trust and the Deutscher Akademischer Austauschdienst (DAAD). I hope this book repays their much appreciated generosity. I am also grateful to the European Cooperation in Science and Technology (COST), the Consortium for the Humanities and the Arts South-East England (CHASE), the Forschungsverbund Marbach Weimar Wolfenbüttel (MWW), the British Comparative Literature Association (BCLA), and the Association for German Studies (AGS) for funding various research trips undertaken during the course of my doctoral studies. Earlier versions of parts of this book appeared as '"Eine Märchenerzählung, die [...] älter geworden ist mit der verflossenen Zeit": W. G. Sebald's *Austerlitz* as a melancholy *Kunstmärchen*', in *Oxford German Studies*, 49:1 (2020), 86–101; '"Un homme marche dans la rue": Parisian flânerie and Jewish cosmopolitanism in Patrick Modiano's *Dora Bruder*', in the *Modern Language Review*, 116:2 (2021), 264–280; and 'Melancholy

Cosmopolitanism: Reflections on a genre of European literary fiction', in *History of European Ideas*, 47:6 (2021), 1022–1037. I am grateful to the editors and the publishers of these journals for their permission to reuse and adapt this material.

At the University of Leeds, I must first of all thank Helen Finch, Stuart Taberner, and Duncan Wheeler for their supervision of the doctoral research upon which this book is based. I would also like to thank Max Silverman for his insightful comments on some material contained in what follows during its incipient stages and Richard Hibbitt for his perspecacity in examining the full work in a later incarnation. I owe much, too, to conversations with Maya Caspari, Ingo Cornils, Daniel Hartley, Jade Lawson, Rebecca Macklin, and Dominic O'Key. At the Goethe-Universität in Frankfurt am Main, I extend my heartfelt thanks to Astrid Erll for welcoming me into her doctoral colloquium and supporting my research, and to Maria Dorr, Magdalena de Gasperi, Pavan Malreddy, Hanna Teichler, and Jarula Wegner for their camaraderie. Beyond Frankfurt, in the diffuse and eclectic collective that is cultural memory studies, I am grateful for the advice and encouragement of Aleida Assmann, Stef Craps, Ann Rigney, and Rebekah Vince. At the Stockholms Universitet, I thank Elisabeth Herrmann and the other members of the German department for the kind invitation to speak at their colloquium and for their generous responses, as well as those of Stefan Helgesson, who also has my thanks. At the University of Kent, I am grateful to Ian Cooper for inviting me to present my research at the Centre for Modern European Literature and Culture, and in particular to Ben Hutchinson for his exacting and generative questions, both then and later, and for his sustained interest in and encouragement of the project. At my former stomping ground of the University of Bristol, I thank Steffan Davies, Stephan Ehrig, Debbie Pinfold, and Francesca Roe for their continued friendship and encouragement far above and well beyond the call of duty.

Staff at the libraries at the institutions mentioned above, as well as at the Universitätsbibliothek in Münster, the Württembergische Landesbibliothek in Stuttgart, and the Deutsches Literaturarchiv in Marbach am Neckar were always unfailingly helpful and I am grateful to them for their assistance on countless occasions. The participants and organizers of the inaugural CHASE Summer School in Comparative Literature at the University of Kent and of the MWW Internationale Sommerschule at the DLA Marbach in 2018 provided an invaluable burst of intellectual stimulation for which I am very thankful. My former co-organizers of the National Postgraduate Colloquium for German Studies—*allen voran* Ellen Pilsworth, Joanna Raisbeck, Maria Roca Lizarazu, and Hanna Schumacher—have been and continue to be a great source of inspiration; I salute them, along with Emma Crowley, Kelsie Donnelly, Laura González Salmerón, Joanna Rzepa, and Jessica Sequeira, my co-conspiritors on the BCLA executive committee. I would also like to express my thanks to Brenda Barnes, Karen Boyland, Janet Kirby, Barbara Leedale, Geoff Park, and Sylvie Pinnington for giving me the tools; to Louise Coley, Judi Creese, and Gail Riminton for lighting the fire; and to Pamela Ganncliffe for keeping it burning.

Stephanie Obermeier, James Sills, Tiffany Soga, Thomas Swinson, and Andrew Taylor enrich my life and inspire me in more ways than I can say. For the conversation and the company, the food and the drink, and for filling our days with more books, films, art, music, and laughter than I could ever have asked for, I am inexpressibly glad. I can never thank Hildegard and Michael Hundehege enough for providing shelter and perspective when it mattered most. And if I were to attempt to list here the multitude of ways in which I am supported, encouraged, and inspired by my wife, Stefanie Hundehege, then these acknowledgements would be longer than the book itself. She is a fountain of knowledge and understanding, and her vitality, wit, insight, and love are written into every page that follows. Our life together is a source of continuous delight to me. Finally, the encouragement, indulgence, patience, and love of my parents, Brian and Lesley, and of my sisters, Sarah, Kate, and Hannah, have sustained me these past three decades and continue to do so. For this, and for so much more, I will be forever grateful to them.

CONTENTS

About the Author

Ian Ellison divides his time as a DAAD PRIME fellow between the University of Kent in Canterbury, their Paris School of Arts & Culture, and the Goethe-Universität in Frankfurt am Main. He holds a PhD in Comparative Literature from the University of Leeds, an MPhil in European Literature from the University of Bristol, and a BA (Hons) in Modern European Languages from the University of Liverpool. This is his first book.

CHAPTER 1

The Late, the Melancholy, and the European

Paris. Spring 1940. It's been persistently cold ever since the previous year lurched into this one, and the walls of 10 Rue Dombasle can't keep it out. Walter Benjamin's heart is failing. In January, it had become so inflamed that its rhythm turned rapid and irregular, the chill of the city air too penetrating for him to be able to walk more than a few paces before exhaustion set in.[1] Huddled in the apartment in the 15ième arrondissement that he shares with his sister Dora, he writes to friends and former colleagues. He petitions them for assistance in acquiring a visa to the United States, which will arrive too late. In a matter of weeks, Paris will fall, and they will be forced to flee before the city becomes a trap whose jaws have closed. Nazi forces have already crossed the French border. Though the year begins so inauspiciously, Benjamin nonetheless completes one of the works for which he will be best remembered: *Über den Begriff der Geschichte*, his theses on the philosophy of history. In an early passage, which is reduced in the oft-cited English translation to render Benjamin's sentences more authoritative and less meditative, he muses that

[1] Walter Benjamin to Gretl Adorno, 17 January 1940 in Walter Benjamin, *Gesammelte Briefe VI: 1938–1940*, ed. by Christoph Gödde and Henri Lonitz (Frankfurt am Main: Suhrkamp, 2000), 382–388. See also Walter Benjamin, *The Correspondence of Walter Benjamin, 1910–1940*, ed. by Gershom Scholem and Theordor W. Adorno, trans. by Manfred R. Jacobson and Evelyn M. Jacobson (Chicago: University of Chicago Press, 1994), 625–628.

© The Author(s), under exclusive license to Springer Nature Switzerland AG 2022
I. Ellison, *Late Europeans and Melancholy Fiction at the Turn of the Millennium*, Palgrave Studies in Modern European Literature, https://doi.org/10.1007/978-3-030-95447-5_1

Die Vergangenheit führt einen heimlichen Index mit, durch den sie auf die Erlösung verwiesen wird. Streift denn nicht uns selber ein Hauch der Luft, die um die Früheren gewesen ist? ist nicht in Stimmen, denen wir unser Ohr schenken, ein Echo von nun verstummten? [...] Ist dem so, dann besteht eine geheime Verabredung zwischen den gewesenen Geschlechtern und unserem. Dann sind wir auf der Erde erwartet worden. Dann ist uns wie jedem Geschlecht, das vor uns war, eine *schwache* messianische Kraft mitgegeben.[2]

Each prior generation, for Benjamin, lived in the hope of future restitution through connection to past revolution and upheaval.[3] Missed opportunities, unrealized aspirations, paths not taken; these moments, these potentialities are never entirely lost to history. Every present is the future of a past, its possible future-perfect. To think with Benjamin is to recognize that that which has never been actualized remains with us, not as a faint echo, but as an insistent call.

At the start of May 1940, Benjamin composes a letter to the author and art collector Stephan Lackner. All modern writers, Benjamin declares in this missive, are fighting against becoming what he calls the 'last European': 'On se demande', he writes, 'si l'histoire n'est pas en train de forger une synthèse ingénieuse de deux conceptions nietzschéennes, à savoir des guten Europäers et des letzten Menschen. Cela pourrait donner den letzten Europäer. Nous tous nous luttons pour ne pas le devenir'.[4] The optimism of the 'good European' becomes fused—even tainted—with the subjective pathos and urgent desperation of the 'last man'. However glibly meant, Benjamin's conflation of these two figures is a tantalizing one, and

---

[2] Walter Benjamin, 'Über den Begriff der Geschichte', in *Gesammelte Schriften I.2*, ed. by Rolf Tiedemann und Hermann Schweppenhäuser (Frankfurt am Main: Suhrkamp, 1974), 693–704 (694). 'The past carries with it a secret index by means of which it is directed to salvation. Doesn't a breath of the air that surrounded those who came before then reach us? Isn't there in voices to which we give our ears an echo of those now silenced? [...] If that is so, then there is a secret agreement between previous generations and ours; then we were expected on earth; then we, like every generation that was before us, are endowed with a *weak* messianic power'. Emphasis in original.

[3] Restitution is understood here, as elsewhere in this study, to be a secular counterpart to the religious concept of redemption.

[4] Walter Benjamin to Stephan Lackner, 5 May 1940, in Walter Benjamin, *Gesammelte Briefe VI*, 442. 'One wonders if history is not forging an ingenious synthesis of two Nietzschean conceptions, namely the good European and the last man. This could give the last European. We all are fighting not to become this'.

one, moreover, which *Late Europeans and Melancholy Fiction at the Turn of the Millennium* takes seriously. As the twentieth century draws to a close, this book contends, it is no longer the case that writers fight against becoming the last Europeans. Rather, they have embraced their status as historical and cultural latecomers. Coming after the Shoah, the end of the Cold War, and the fall of empire, the millennial caesura's simultaneous sense of finality and transition engenders in many literary artists a compulsion to examine the cataclysmic events of twentieth-century modernity in a world where Europe is no longer the centre of a global order. Less concerned with being individual last men in a teleological chain, the European writers examined in this book understand themselves to be the diminished returns of those arriving too late.

Distinct strains of lateness and melancholy found in European fiction written and published around the turn of the millennium vary not only from writer to writer, but also from language to language. This study therefore examines differing incarnations of this historically and geographically contingent mode of writing by specifically comparing a French novel (*Dora Bruder* by Patrick Modiano, 1997), a German novel (*Austerlitz* by W. G. Sebald, 2001), and a Spanish novel (*Sefarad* by Antonio Muñoz Molina, 2001).[5] *Late Europeans and Melancholy Fiction* is the first full-length monograph to bring together works by these three writers for comparative study. Thematically, the three novels examined in this book engage with the catastrophic events of twentieth-century European modernity, including, for instance, the terror of the Occupation of France and the deportation of French Jews in *Dora Bruder*, the traumas

---

[5] All quotations from these novels in this study are taken from the following editions: Patrick Modiano, *Dora Bruder* (Paris: Gallimard, 1997); W. G. Sebald, *Austerlitz* (Frankfurt am Main: Fischer, 2001); and Antonio Muñoz Molina, *Sefarad*, ed. by Pablo Valdivia (Madrid: Cátedra, 2013). Page references to these novels will be cited hereafter in the main body of the text as *DB* for *Dora Bruder*, *A* for *Austerlitz*, and *S* for *Sefarad*. Page numbers for the original French, German, and Spanish novels are given in brackets in the main body of the text; page numbers for the published English translations are given in brackets in the footnotes. These translations are taken from *The Search Warrant*, trans. by Joanna Kilmartin (London: Harvill Secker, 2000), previously published as *Dora Bruder* (Berkeley: University of California Press, 1999); *Austerlitz*, trans. by Anthea Bell (London: Hamish Hamilton, 2001); and *Sepharad*, trans. by Margaret Sayers Peden (London: Harcourt Press, 2003). If page references are absent in the footnotes, then the translation is new, although this usually implies nothing more than a slightly freshened-up version of the published translation, which has been modified in order to take account of what the text is required to mean for the purposes of this study's argument.

of the *Kindertransport* and the concentration camp at Theresienstadt in *Austerlitz*, along with the paranoia and suffering of victims of twentieth-century conflicts and the persecution of Jewish refugees in Spain in *Sefarad*. By comparing three novels in three different languages, this book argues for the emergence of a mode of writing inflected by aesthetics of lateness and melancholy in European fiction published around the turn of the millennium. Moving beyond an examination of their thematic concerns, this study's close reading of the aesthetics, language, and style of these three novels suggests that their backward-facing, tradition-oriented articulations of lateness and their resultant melancholy aesthetics may yet be imagined as collective expression in European fiction of a more optimistic sense of futurity.

The possibility for future cultural renewal is slippery and hypothetical, yet even if not actualized in the subsequent history that is the world's future beyond these novels, its potentiality in this collective of literary works—and, indeed, perhaps in others—remains. A diminished idea, perhaps, yet visible when the objects of this book's gaze are seen in the right light. 'Das wahre Bild der Vergangenheit *huscht* vorbei', as Benjamin notes in the fifth of his theses. 'Nur als Bild, das auf Nimmerwiedersehen im Augenblick seiner Erkennbarkeit eben aufblitzt, ist die Vergangenheit festzuhalten'.[6] *Late Europeans and Melancholy Fiction* attempts to grasp an image, an idea drawn between various works of literature written and published around a significant instant in the recent past. Famously, for Benjamin, 'die Ideen verhalten sich zu den Dingen wie die Sternbilder zu den Sternen'.[7] Neither governing principles nor binding laws, ideas are no

---

[6] Benjamin, 'Über den Begriff der Geschichte', 695. Emphasis in original. 'The true picture of the past *flits* by. Only as an image that, never to be seen again, flashes up at the moment of its recognizability, can the past be captured'.

[7] Walter Benjamin, *Gesammelte Schriften I.1*, ed. by Rolf Tiedemann and Hermann Schweppenhäuser (Frankfurt am Main: Suhrkamp, 1980), 214. 'Ideas are to objects what constellations are to stars'. Walter Benjamin, *The Origin of German Tragic Drama*, trans. by John Osborne (London: Verso, 1977), 34. In its astronomical usage, 'constellation' typically describes a configuration of phenomena in the celestial sphere under specific spatial and temporal circumstances. In Benjamin's more imaginative terms, it emphasizes the transformation of an imaginary outline or pattern out of stars into a 'star-image', or 'Sternbild', to use the German term employed by Benjamin. The use of the verb 'sich verhalten', meaning to behave towards, also imparts more agency to ideas in relation to the objects to which they refer than the English construction 'to be to', such that Benjamin suggests an idea may not only describe but also transform the object of its focus.

more present in the world's reality than constellations are in the heavens. Nevertheless, they still exist as a means of perceiving relations, one moreover which is grounded in history, tradition, and storytelling. 'Nicht so ist es, daß das Vergangene sein Licht auf das Gegenwärtige oder das Gegenwärtige sein Licht auf das Vergangene wirft', Benjamin would later write twice in his unfinished *Arcades Project*; 'sondern Bild ist dasjenige, worin das Gewesene mit dem Jetzt blitzhaft zu einer Konstellation zusammentritt'.[8] Imagining and presenting such a constellation of late European novels is one of the tasks of the present book.

While there may exist a tension between the Benjaminian critique of historicism that rejects the notion of the past as a continuum of progress and the conceptualization of a chain of late and melancholy influence in what follows, it is in precisely such spaces of tension that the mode of writing explored in this book emerges. Drawing on a wide range of literary figures, movements, and traditions, from the Spanish Golden Age, to German Romanticism, to French literary theory and philosophy, to Jewish modernist fiction, this study argues for the emergence of an aesthetic idiom in European novels written and published at the turn of the millennium. Exploring the ways in which certain works of fiction engage with a sense of cultural and historical lateness in their narratives, this study shows that a melancholy perspective on the past emerges in various novels from discrete national traditions within a broader Western European context. Less a pathological phenomenon anchored in the psychological depression associated with the planet Saturn, melancholy emerges, however belatedly, across modern European literature as a philosophical aesthetic mode of contemplation. Combining close readings of novels by three culturally significant European writers with historical and theoretical comparisons within specific national contexts, this study explores the literary influences on—and intertexts of—the works it examines in order to reveal a latent possibility of futurity and resistance to the

[8] Walter Benjamin, 'Das Passagen-Werk: Erster Teil', in *Gesammelte Schriften V.1*, ed. by Rolf Tiedemann (Frankfurt am Main: Suhrkamp, 1982), 45–654 (576 and 578). 'It is not that what is past casts its light on what is present, or what is present its light on what is past; rather, image is that wherein what has been comes together in a flash with the now to form a constellation'. Walter Benjamin, *The Arcades Project*, trans. by Howard Eiland and Kevin McLaughlin (Cambridge, Massachusetts: The Belknap Press of Harvard University Press, 1999), 462 and 463.

obsolescence of the European. Along with readings of three individual novels, and the identification and analysis of a particular constellation of works of European fiction published around the turn of the millennium, this study proposes commonalities across linguistic, territorial, and literary boundaries in Europe. Among these, however, unique distinctions maintain these demarcations, even as the act of reading these novels alongside one another might suggest that such boundaries are overcome. More broadly, this book contemplates how literature might conceive of its own historical and geographical locatedness and its capacity to think beyond itself by making imaginable, seemingly against the odds, something akin to what Raymond Williams might have called an affirmative structure of feeling, the inferred trajectory or formation of an emergent idea at certain point in history.[9] Such a structure of feeling cultivated within and among the novels examined in this book appears acutely aware of its own untimeliness and obsolescence. Yet such obsolescence may prove to be a distraction that obscures how these novels exemplify a wider phenomenon that is traceable in various works of European literature written and published at the close of the twentieth century and the dawn of the twenty-first.

The crux of this study is the extent to which the aesthetic impulse behind the individual texts it examines may be emblematic of something more widespread in Western European literary culture. In other words, despite the conspicuously local and even personal nature of these novels' discrete enactments of lateness and melancholy, do they epitomize a broader modulation, both in form and in temperament, which may have consequences for responses to literary works that test out the language of melancholy lateness against the threat of European cultural obsolescence? While mindful of making the sort of immodest and grandiloquent claim that literary critics and scholars—perhaps most especially, those of a comparative bent—are wont to do in their search for urgency and relevance, this book ventures to suggest that the European novels it examines are by no means isolated in their late and melancholy state, and invites a reassessment of how the aesthetic attitudes of literary works may constitute a counterweight to perceived cultural collapse.

But what makes a European novel European? How is this concept to be reconciled with the distinctly European notion of national literatures? And

---

[9] For further discussion of this concept, see Raymond Williams and Michael Orrom, *Preface to Film* (London: Film Drama, Ltd., 1954).

how do the tensions between the two manifest themselves in literary works? In what ways, moreover, does the period in time in which certain of these works are written affect their aesthetic attitude? What kind of aesthetic practice is immanent to modern European literature at the close of the twentieth century and the dawn of the twenty-first? This book pursues comparative readings of Modiano's *Dora Bruder*, Sebald's *Austerlitz*, and Muñoz Molina's *Sefarad* in an attempt to suggest some answers to these questions. In doing so, it coins the term 'late European' in order to identify, characterize, and analyse a mode of writing that emerges around the millennial caesura in works of European fiction from different but related national and linguistic contexts. Notions of good Europeans and last men thus become subsumed—even sublated—into the category of late Europeans.

The aesthetics of these novels will be the central concern of this study, which has three principal arguments to put forward. Firstly, that late European novels respond in a variety of ways to a perceived sense of European cultural obsolescence and historical lateness. Secondly, that these novels display a distinctly melancholy outlook, such that their engagement with history is inflected by an understanding of the past's fundamental and irrecoverable separation from the present. Thirdly, in the face of such overwhelming negativity, this study proposes that by reading them alongside one another, an aesthetic attitude may be seen to emerge out of these novels' lateness- and melancholy-inflected narratives, one which suggests a potential—however latent—for the re-enchantment and re-invigoration of European culture. As Alfred Tennyson—himself a late Romantic—wrote in 'Ulysses' (1842), "tis not too late to seek a newer world'.[10] *Late Europeans and Melancholy Fiction at the Turn of the Millennium* as a whole, meanwhile, attempts to offer new insights into European literature as a concept. It seeks to position the novels examined in the following pages within a larger narrative regarding the tensions between constructed national literary traditions and a broader imagined European cultural community.[11]

---

[10] Alfred Tennyson, *The Works of Alfred Lord Tennyson*, ed. by Karen Hodder (London: Wordsworth Editions, 1994), 162–163.

[11] For further discussion of this, see Joep Leerssen, *National Thought in Europe: A Cultural History* (Amsterdam: Amsterdam University Press, 2018).

The three novels examined in this study are celebrated literary works within and beyond the national contexts in which they originated.[12] They and their authors have been lauded with literary prizes and are regularly singled out for academic study.[13] It perhaps surprising, then, that *Late Europeans and Melancholy Fiction* is the first comparative study of works by Modiano, Sebald, and Muñoz Molina. As regards the selection of texts for examination, however, this study echoes Erich Auerbach's remark in his *Nachwort* to *Mimesis: Dargestellte Wirklichkeit in der abendländlischen Wirklichkeit* (1946) that his 'Interpretationen sind ohne Zweifel von einer bestimmten Absicht gelenkt; doch hat diese Absicht erst allmählich Gestalt gewonnen, jeweils im Spiel mit dem Text, und ich habe mich auf weite Strecken von ihm führen lassen'.[14] Novels, not theories about them, were

[12] Certain discrepancies exist between the relative international prestige of Modiano, Sebald, and Muñoz Molina. Since winning the Nobel Prize in Literature in 2014, Modiano is probably the most widely known and certainly the most prolific writer of the three. When alive, Sebald had been regularly touted as a potential winner of the Nobel Prize, but today he remains a writer better known in the Anglophone sphere than in his native Germany, even though wrote little in English. Lastly, while Muñoz Molina is highly regarded as a novelist and cultural critic in Spain, beyond the Hispanophone sphere, his international profile is less substantial than those of Modiano and Sebald. The positive reception of recent translations of his other works in the Anglophone world looks set to change this, however, with the English version of his 2014 novel *Como la sombra que se va* (*Like a Fading Shadow*) appearing on the 2018 Man Booker International Prize shortlist.

[13] Patrick Modiano was awarded the Prix Fénéon (1968), the Prix Roger-Nimier (1968), the Grand Prix du roman de l'Académie Française (1972), the Prix Goncourt (1978), the Institut de France Prix mondial Cino Del Duca (2010), the Österreichischer Staatspreis für Europäische Literatur (2012), and, as already mentioned above, the Nobel Prize in Literature in 2014. W. G. Sebald was the recipient of the Fedor Malchow Lyrikpreis (1991), the Johannes Bobrowski Medaille (1994), the Berliner Literaturpreis (1994), the Preis der Literatour Nord (1994), the Heinrich Böll Preis der Stadt Köln (1997), the Mörike Preis der Stadt Fellbach (1997), the Los Angeles Times Book Award (1998), the Joseph Breitbach Preis (2000), the Heinrich Heine Preis der Stadt Düsseldorf (2000), and the National Book Critics Circle Award (2001) and was awarded the Independent Foreign Literature Prize posthumously in 2002. Antonio Muñoz Molina has received the Premio Nacional de Narrativa twice (1988 and 1992), as well as the Premio Planeta de Novela (1991), the Premio Príncipe de Asturias (2013), and the Jerusalem Prize for the Freedom of the Individual in Society (2013). Margaret Sayers Peden's English translation of *Sepharad* was also named as the winner of a PEN/Book-of-the-Month Club Translation Prize in 2004. Regarding academic research on these writers, see the bibliography of this study, which, despite having no pretentions to being an exhaustive list, gives some of an indication as to the breadth and depth of research undertaken on these novelists' lives and works.

[14] Erich Auerbach, *Mimesis: Dargestellte Wirklichkeit in der abendländlischen Wirklichkeit* (Bern: Francke, 1946), 497. 'Interpretations are no doubt guided by a specific purpose. Yet

the starting point of this study and have been its guiding thread through-out. It is in the interplay of the similarities and differences observed among these novels upon first and subsequent readings that the whole idea of late European novels was born.

The variously mediated narratives of Modiano's, Sebald's, and Muñoz Molina's novels indicate a self-consciousness of their lateness and melancholy, and it is central to this study's argument that it is precisely such narratorial self-consciousness that contains the potential to overcome their lateness and melancholy, since it implies a sense of possible futurity and renewal. It is true that these narrators share ambiguous traits with the authors of the novels—in the case of the narrator of *Dora Bruder*, for example, he has even published other novels that share titles of works written by Modiano—but this study's focus throughout is on the fictional figures of the narrators of each novel. It thus refrains from drawing lines of comparison and connection between the biographical features of author and narrator. Such speculations often lead to circular arguments, not least because potential references to the author's biography in the narrator's words 'provoke the reader into a constant *mise-en-abîme*, where identity with the author is reinstated as soon as it is denied', as Helen Finch observes.[15] While such comparisons would not necessarily be invalid or uninteresting, the goal of this study is to investigate what these literary texts as literary texts reveal when they are read as examples of a late and melancholy mode of writing. It therefore confines its critical purview to the fictional works and their aesthetic, stylistic, and symbolic points of similarity and difference. Reading *Dora Bruder*, *Austerlitz*, and *Sefarad* together as works of fiction, this study argues, suggests that there still remains a residual potential for future artistic meaningfulness in late and melancholy European novels that embody a vestigial sense of aesthetic renewal, as well as the possibility for difference to co-exist within commonality.

---

this purpose assumed form only as I went along, playing as it were with my texts, and for long stretches of the way I have been guided only by the texts themselves'. Erich Auerbach, *Mimesis: The Representation of Reality in Western Literature*, trans. by Willard R. Trask (Princeton: Princeton University Press, 1953), 556.

[15] See Helen Finch, 'Revenge, Restitution, Ressentiment. Edgar Hilsenrath's and Ruth Klüger's Late Writings as Holocaust Metatestimony' in *German Jewish Literature after 1990*, ed. by Katja Garloff and Agnes Mueller (Rochester, New York: Camden House, 2018), 60–79 (61).

Emerging at a significant historical moment, and in a particular geographical and cultural milieu, late European novels respond to an established discourse of lateness in European literature, whereby modern literature understands itself not as young, new, and fresh, but as old, late, and exhausted. This sense of arriving after greater literary works and movements is compounded by a perception of coming at the end of an era as the close of the twentieth century looms. The aesthetics of these novels thus appear under an aspect of lateness, and their narrators style themselves as inheritors of a long tradition of canonical European culture at the end of the twentieth century, under whose shadow—striding behind them and rising to meet them—they appear as epigonal latecomers.[16] Epigones, from the Greek *epígonos* meaning offspring, are less distinguished followers, even imitators, of earlier artists, who are generally, in the words of Giorgio Van Straten, 'tasked with concluding itineraries rather than opening up new ones'.[17] Lateness and endings go hand in hand. From the historical perspective that these epigones adopt, the past is always and unavoidably separated from the present in which they find themselves. Intimately related to this, these novels' melancholy is expressed in the irrevocable determination of the present by the past and the simultaneously acknowledged impossibility of reconciling the two across the gulf of history, such that history itself becomes understood as melancholy. Paul Valéry once asserted that tradition and progress are the two great enemies of humanity; in this study, however, they are revealed to be, for better or for worse, two key elements of a constitutive tension within the concept of European literature.[18]

LITERARY LATENESS IN EUROPE

At the turn of the millennium, a 'sense of an ending'—to use the oft-cited eponymous phrase of Frank Kermode's studies in the theory of fiction—was in European culture a particularly heightened phenomenon. For Kermode, apocalyptic thought best encapsulates not only how Western literature organizes narratives, but also how Western culture comprehends

---

[16] See T. S. Eliot, 'The Waste Land, 1922', in *The Waste Land other poems* (London: Faber and Faber, 1999), 21–46 (23–24).

[17] Giorgio Van Straten, *In Search of Lost Books: The forgotten stories of eight mythical volumes*, trans. by Simon Carnell and Erica Segre (London: Pushkin Press, 2017), 98.

[18] See Paul Valéry, 'Orient et Occident: Préface au livre d'un Chinois', in *Regards sur le monde actuel et autres essais* (Paris: Gallimard, 1988), 174.

time and its passing. With the approach of the millennium, he argues, the notion of the apocalypse had become transduced into an insoluble and ongoing crisis.[19] 'Although for us the End has perhaps lost its naïve *imminence*', he remarks, 'its shadow still lies on the crisis of our fictions; we may speak of it as *immanent*'.[20] While the millennium is a largely arbitrary formulation for measuring the passing of time, in a Western European context it is nevertheless a cultural moment freighted with the burden of time that has gone before.[21] The narrators of the three novels examined in this study understand themselves to be late in two principal senses: culturally, coming after great European writers who precede them, and historically, since they are consciously aware that they are writing at the end of the twentieth century. That which is new is bound to define itself in relation to that which already exists. No artistic work exists in isolation and any new work necessarily either draws on or repudiates that which has gone before, thereby marking itself out as a later development—an older instantiation—of artistic expression. Such lateness is understood in what follows as a foundational element of the aesthetics of *Dora Bruder*, *Austerlitz*, and *Sefarad* that is both culturally and historically determined. Lateness—understood in cultural, historical, and aesthetic terms—is thus both a useful interpretative heuristic and an influential matrix for these works.

It is not only novels that were written at the end of the twentieth century that exhibit such lateness. As Mark Fisher cautions, when discussing the sense of terminal exhaustion emerging in European cultural and political spheres towards the close of the twentieth century, 'this malaise,

[19] For further discussion of the millennium as a cultural construct, as well as the fears and hopes invested in this signifier at the turn of the twenty-first century, see, for example, Raymond Williams, *The Year 2000* (New York: Pantheon Books, 1983), Charles B. Strozier and Michael Flynn, eds., *The Year 2000: Essays on the End* (New York: New York University Press, 1997), Christopher Kleinhenz and Fannie J. LeMoine, eds., *Fearful Hope: Approaching the New Millennium* (Madison: University of Wisconsin Press, 1999), and Marlene P. Soulsby and J. T. Fraser, eds., *Time: Perspectives at the Millennium (The Study of Time X)* (Westport, Connecticut: Bergin and Garvey, 2001).

[20] Frank Kermode, *The Sense of an Ending: Studies in the Theory of Fiction* (Oxford: Oxford University Press, 1967), 6.

[21] For further discussion of the concept of 'Eurochronology', see Arjun Appadurai, *Modernity at Large: Cultural Dimensions of Globalization* (Minneapolis: University of Minnesota Press, 1996) and Pheng Cheah, *What is a World? On Postcolonial Literature as World Literature* (Durham, North Carolina: Duke University Press, 2016).

the feeling that there is nothing new, is itself nothing new'.[22] In literary studies, the hour has been growing late for nigh on several decades. Concerns around cultural and historical lateness have constituted signature intellectual formations of the twentieth century as a whole, taking the form of what Peter Boxall has termed 'the perception of late historical conditions' in literary works.[23] Observing that one of the prevailing cultural dominants of post-war Western culture was 'the dawning of an apocalyptic or millenarian mood or cast of thought', Boxall recognizes that conceptualizations of late culture and theorizations of the end of history are symptomatic of how Western culture ushered in the closing decades of the twentieth century.[24] It is under the aspect of what Boxall calls 'a general lateness or belatedness, a vast historical gloaming, a gathered agedness' that late European novels emerge, characterized by a perception of a sustained sense of ending in European culture.[25]

This study prefers the terms 'late' and 'lateness' over 'belated' and 'belatedness', since 'belatedness' suggests normative connotations in cases where an occurrence is delayed (often unintentionally) and takes place after a specific expected moment or juncture, rather than consciously taking place towards the end of a period of time. While Boxall argues that it is predominantly contemporary works of dystopian fiction that express this, the present study makes the case for a more prevalent and, indeed, multivalent understanding of lateness in European fiction at the end of the twentieth century. Boxall's gaze is fixed forward and he concerns himself principally with works of Anglophone fiction in the early twenty-first century, but he nevertheless acknowledges the significant 'co-incidence of late culture and late prose style' in articulating the potential of a new future for the novel form.[26] The millennial caesura inculcates a burgeoning awareness of youth and uncertainty in the Anglophone novels that Boxall examines, which, he argues, may lead to a new understanding of temporality in a globalized world. Unlike in the case of late European novels, however, the writers Boxall discusses deliberately do not attend to the literary traditions from which they emerge. The corollary problem of this is, as Boxall

[22] Mark Fisher, *Capitalist Realism: Is There No Alternative?* (Winchester: Zero Books, 2008), p.6.

[23] Peter Boxall, *Twenty-First-Century Fiction: A Critical Introduction* (Cambridge: Cambridge University Press, 2013), 15.

[24] Boxall, *Twenty-First-Century Fiction*, 22.

[25] Boxall, *Twenty-First-Century Fiction*, 23.

[26] Boxall, *Twenty-First-Century Fiction*, 225.

identifies, the temporal estrangement and even greater sense of being left behind by the inexorability of time's continued passing that results from the ending of a culture whose historical and geographical orientation is so deeply imbricated with 'the late-cultural, millennial logic of the post'.[27] In Boxall's account, there is a definitive moment of finality at the turn of the millennium in Anglophone literature, rather than the ongoing sense of ending in European literature argued for in this study. Boxall's use of the term 'post' also denotes occurring after, whereas the term 'late', in this study's understanding of it, suggests that a final end point has not yet arrived. While it is true, then, that 'late' may be used in English to refer to the posthumous, this study does not suggest in any way that either European fiction or, indeed, the novel form itself is finally dead and buried.

For many scholars across the humanities, the notion of late style—the idea that with the proximity of death the final creative years in the lives of truly great artists are distinguished by a discernible change in tone that both draws on their earlier work and looks forward beyond the ultimate caesura of death to potential future development—has in recent decades become something of an obsession that threatens to verge into cliché. The lack of resolution to the cultural and historical sense of ending that the present study traces also echoes one of the principal thrusts of Edward Said's argument in his posthumously published study *On Late Style* (2006). This text, foundational in many ways for contemporary understandings of lateness in artistic works as a biographical category, holds that late aesthetics must be understood 'not as harmony and resolution but as intransigence, difficulty, and unresolved contradiction', with artists and their works existing beyond what might be considered normal or acceptable.[28] 'Late style', Said argues, 'is *in*, but oddly apart *from* the present'.[29] This implies a distance from the present moment, such that *now* is rejected in favour of taking refuge in *then*, leaving the future obscure. Embodying the tension of a 'deliberately unproductive productiveness going *against*', Said draws on Theodor W. Adorno's formulation of Beethoven's late style as process but not development.[30] In recent years, however, Said's

---

[27] Boxall, *Twenty-First-Century Fiction*, 33.

[28] Edward Said, *On Late Style* (London: Bloomsbury, 2006), 7 and 13.

[29] Said, *On Late Style*, 24. Emphasis in original.

[30] Said, *On Late Style*, 7. See Theodor W. Adorno, 'Spätstil (I): Spätstil Beethovens', in *Nachgelassene Schriften I* (Frankfurt am Main: Suhrkamp, 1993), 180–199. See also Theodor W. Adorno, 'Late Style in Beethoven', trans. by Susan H. Gillespie, in *Essays on Music*, ed. by Richard Leppert (Berkley: University of California Press, 2002), 564–567.

formulation of late style has been criticized as a normative reconceptual-ization of the figure of the genius applied to mostly male artists, who, in Said's formulation, 'acquire a new idiom' in their work and thoughts towards the end of their life.[31] With perhaps the unfortunate exception of Sebald, who died suddenly in 2001 aged just 57, the forms of lateness exhibited by the novels examined in this study are not classifiable in such biological or biographical terms.[32] Nevertheless, to draw on one particular phrase in Said's conceptualization of late style and apply it to literary works, it is the unresolved tensions of late European novels that emerge as key constitutive elements of their aesthetic practice.

Lateness may move beyond the implications of biological senescence to be understood as an emergent category in literary works that responds to a sense of historical and cultural agedness. In this way, an artist's sense of their own ageing and of their historical locatedness coalesce into what Karen Leeder calls 'a spectrum of anxieties: obsolescence, redundancy, anachronism, the sense of always coming after a legitimizing model, but also losing touch with an originating authority'.[33] Like any aesthetic phe-nomenon, late style is for Leeder 'a complex product of the artist's expe-riences as a being *in a particular time and place*, rather than a universal mode or technique that descends on the artist at a certain moment in the ag[e]ing process'.[34] Literary lateness thus expresses both a sense of epigonal inadequacy and the perception of historical latecoming. Leeder suggests that an aesthetic style of lateness may be consciously adopted by an artist at any chronological point in their lives, in order 'to eschew harmony and to be critical of a particular outmoded or obsolescent status quo'.[35] If this is the case, then such lateness has the potential to resist said status quo through what Anne Fuchs calls its 'desynchronization'.[36]

---

[31] Said, *On Late Style*, 6.

[32] As will be considered in greater depth in the third chapter of this study, although Sebald's death was premature, his writing at all stages in his life might be understood as late. See also, for example, Ben Hutchinson, *W. G. Sebald: Die dialektische Imagination* (Berlin: de Gruyter, 2009), 170.

[33] Karen Leeder, 'Figuring Lateness in Modern German Culture', in *New German Critique*, 125 (2015), 1–30 (2).

[34] Leeder, 'Figuring Lateness', 8. Emphasis added.

[35] Leeder, 'Figuring Lateness', 8.

[36] See Anne Fuchs, 'Temporal Ambivalence: Acceleration, Attention and Lateness in Modernist Discourse', in *Time in German Literature and Culture, 1900–2015: Between Acceleration and Slowness*, ed. by Anne Fuchs and J. J. Long (London: Palgrave Macmillan, 2016), 21–28.

A late perspective thereby offers an alternative understanding of temporality that repudiates the ever-increasing speed of hypermodernity under capitalist globalization. In light of—or, perhaps better, under the shadow of—European culture's concomitant sense of ending as the millennium approaches, novels like those examined in this book collectively resist the anticipated obsolescence of European culture in the wake of the catastrophes of modernity as the twentieth century draws to a close by performing a deceleration of their own temporalities through their responses to and engagement with cultural and historical lateness.

The conscious adoption by cultural practitioners of forms of late style is, as Gordon McMullan notes, best understood as an artistic and critical construct that is fundamentally imbricated with European modernity itself.[37] *Dora Bruder*'s investigation into disappearances during the French Occupation, *Austerlitz*'s excavation of traumatic experiences of the *Kindertransport* and the Holocaust, and *Sefarad*'s reimaginings of persecution and exile in Spain and abroad constitute a range of literary responses to question of what it means to live through and after European modernity. As Ben Hutchinson notes in his 'Afterword' to McMullan's and Sam Smiles's volume on *Late Style and Its Discontents* (2016), 'the feeling of being "born late" provides one of the driving forces of aesthetic modernity'.[38] Coupled with an awareness of historical latecoming, debilitating epigonal self-consciousness, this suggests, may yet constitute a generative aesthetic force in European literary culture. Hutchinson's monograph on *Lateness and Modern European Literature* (2016) explores how modern European literature has repeatedly defined itself via a sense of epigonality or senescence as late in an expression of literary modernity's continuing search for legitimacy.[39] Countering the conventional view that modern literature is progressive and new, he argues that backward-looking overdetermination emerges as an unacknowledged generative impulse in European literature from the mid-nineteenth to the earlier twentieth century. In short, the pathos of biological late style is ascribed to the ethos of modern European culture as a whole. If, however, individual artists' late

[37] See Gordon McMullan, 'The "Strangeness" of George Oppen: Criticism, Modernity, and the Conditions of Late Style', in *Late Style and its Discontents: Essays in Art, Literature, and Music*, ed. by Gordon McMullan and Sam Smiles (Oxford: Oxford University Press, 2016), 37–38.

[38] Ben Hutchinson, 'Afterword', in *Late Style and its Discontents*, 235–239 (236).

[39] Ben Hutchinson, *Lateness and Modern European Literature* (Oxford: Oxford University Press, 2016).

style comprises a phase of rejuvenated—even serene or childlike—creativity, what implications does this have for lateness in modern European literature? By reading *Dora Bruder*, *Austerlitz*, and *Sefarad* alongside one another as distinctly late and melancholy works of European fiction, this study proposes a discernible possibility of imagining future artistic development and the potential for cultural revivification. *Late Europeans and Melancholy Fiction* therefore focuses its attention on the turn of the millennium in order to show how lateness persists as an aesthetic driver of European literature beyond modernism and beyond the end of the twentieth century, uncovering, so to speak, a later lateness.[40]

Such an investigation entails understanding *Dora Bruder*, *Austerlitz*, and *Sefarad* not as postmodernist, however, but rather as late modernist works. Although this may seem counterintuitive, given that the period in which Modiano, Sebald, and Muñoz Molina are writing is historically postmodern, there is little in the way of consensus regarding the exact characteristics of the postmodern. The term is regularly used to denote both a temporal historical period and a plethora of stylistic characteristics, but however one chooses to apply it, it is unavoidably defined in terms of its relationship to the modern and to modernism. For Fredric Jameson, postmodernism's predominant elements consist in a lack of emotional depth or meaning along with a loss of historicity.[41] Exhibiting a tendency to refract reality into playful language games, postmodern literature questions the possibility of fiction to adequately represent it, while rejecting the modernist belief in certain universal truths in favour of a deconstructed distrust of any notion of truth itself.[42] The novels examined in this study, however, embrace their historicity, understanding themselves as

---

[40] Elsewhere Hutchinson argues that the scholarly discipline of comparative literature in the twentieth century may be conceived of as a school of 'late reading' and thus as a hermeneutic counterpart to the artistic concept of late style, such that it derives its interpretative force from its consciousness of coming at the end of the tradition of European high culture. In this regard, the present study may be considered an act of *later* reading. See Ben Hutchinson, 'Late Reading: Erich Auerbach and the *Spätboot* of Comparative Literature', *Comparative Critical Studies* 14, no. 1 (2017), 69–85.

[41] See Fredric Jameson, *Postmoderism, or, The Cultural Logic of Late Capitalism* (London: Verso, 1991).

[42] See also Andreas Huyssen, *After the Great Divide: Modernism, Mass Culture, Postmodernism* (Bloomington: Indiana University Press, 1986), Brian McHale, *Postmodernist Fiction* (London: Methuen, 1987), Lawrence E. Cahoone, *From Modernism to Postmodernism: An Anthology Expanded* (Hoboken, New Jersey: Wiley-Blackwell, 2003), and Peter Brooker, ed., *Modernism/Postmodernism* (Oxford: Routledge, 2014).

fundamentally historically implicated and positioned towards the perceived ending of modernity. Moreover, the literary techniques—of enigmatic difficulty, of stylistic self-consciousness, of fragmentedly rendering
the world's banal depravities, for example—that are employed by Modiano,
Sebald, and Muñoz Molina and will be discussed in the following chapters
are certainly reminiscent of modernist writers.[43] Even while the notion of
framing of one story within another, as these three writers do, for example, may be typically considered a postmodern technique, its purpose in
the novels examined here is quite different.[44] Rather than rejecting after a
postmodern fashion any possibility of locating truth in their work, the narrators of *Dora Bruder*, *Austerlitz*, and *Sefarad* are still concerned with the
modernist search for moral truth, the belief that art might, in Jameson's
words, 'transcend a merely decorative and culinary aesthetic, to reach the
sphere of what is variously identified as the prophetic or the metaphysical,
the visionary or the cosmic, that realm in which aesthetics and ethics, politics and philosophy, religion and pedagogy, all fold together in some
supreme vocation'.[45] Not unlike 'high' modernist writers of the early
twentieth century, they push the boundaries of fiction beyond the confines
of realism towards greater self-critique in an indictment of the failings of
realism's conventions to capture the texture of modern experience. The
primary epistemological concern of each of these novels centres around
the extent to which the past can possibly be known and understood. Even
if these novels and their narrators evince a certain scepticism towards the
modernist faith in human progress, they nonetheless extol its sense of
moral purpose. That the narrators of *Dora Bruder*, *Austerlitz*, and *Sefarad*
examined in this study ambiguously resemble the novels' authors is likewise not a technique employed towards postmodernist ends, whereby the
figure of the author is reduced to a linguistic sign within the text to
encourage further ontological scepticism. On the contrary, this serves to
highlight their narrative projects, their historical position, and their perspective on the past. With the breakdown of traditional modes of

---

[43] See, for example, Rebecca Walkowitz's account of Sebald's achieving his 'vertiginous'
prose style by borrowing modernist literary practices in Rebecca L. Walkowitz, *Cosmopolitan
Style: Modernism Beyond the Nation* (New York: Columbia University Press, 2006), 155.

[44] It should be acknowledged, however, that there is a long tradition of literature with
frame narratives stretching back to, perhaps most notably, Geoffrey Chaucer's *Canterbury
Tales* (1387–1400), Giovanni Boccacio's *Decameron* (1353), and *The Thousand and
One Nights*.

[45] Fredric Jameson, *The Seeds of Time* (New York: Columbia University Press, 1994), 80.

transmitting the past to the present, they evince a gravitation towards the category of the modern as distancing from history yet defined by it. While Hutchinson suggests that the narrative of modern European lateness ends in the late modernist period because theorizations of the postmodern render its tensions obsolete, this study contends that this period of late modernism is nonetheless as ongoing as the sense of ending in European literature to which the novels examined here respond.[46] Late modernism is less a specific literary movement or clearly delineated category of works and more of an aesthetic attitude of sustained posteriority that emerges from the works of various authors in various ways at an historical juncture beyond the presumed end of the modernist era. These novels are, in short, the inheritors of Walter Benjamin's aforementioned concern of 1940 that all modernist poets and critics were fighting not to be the 'last European'.

For Hutchinson, the *locus classicus* of lateness in modern European literature is Friedrich Nietzsche's characterization of modern poets as 'rückwärts gewendete Wesen'.[47] Literature throughout modernity emerges as an expression of this backward-facing stance, and over a century later, this still holds true for certain European writers. The perception of lateness in Modiano's, Sebald's, and Muñoz Molina's novels, and their narrators' subsequent understanding of history, echo Nietzsche's concept of modern writers as latecomers and epigones.[48] Although he would later move towards a criticism of modernity as decadent, in his earlier work Nietzsche perceives nineteenth-century Europe to be oversaturated with preceding cultures, which leads him to critique modernity and modern writers as epigonal, encouraging modern man's understanding of himself as a latecomer. For Nietzsche, such lateness and epigonality has both positive and negative implications, however. From a philosophical perspective, epigonality is entirely unproductive. 'Wahrhaftig, lähmend und verstimmend ist der Glaube, ein Spätling der Zeiten zu sein', states Nietzsche; 'furchtbar und zerstörend muss es aber erscheinen, wenn ein solcher Glaube eines Tages mit kecker Umstülpung diesen Spätling als den wahren Sinn und

---

[46] See Hutchinson, *Lateness*, p.331.

[47] Friedrich Nietzsche, *Nietzsche Werke IV.2: Menschliches, Allzumenschliches I*, ed. by Giorgio Colli und Mazzino Montinari (Berlin: de Gruyter, 1967), 145. 'Beings facing backwards'. See Friedrich Nietzsche, *Human, All Too Human: A Book for Free Spirits*, trans. by R. J. Hollingdale (Cambridge: Cambridge University Press, 1996). Cited in Hutchinson, *Lateness*, 4 and 204.

[48] For further discussion of Nietzsche and the 'latecomers' of modernity, see Hutchinson, *Lateness*, 198–213.

Zweck alles früher Geschehenen vergöttet, wenn sein wissendes Elend einer Vollendung der Welt geschichte gleichgesetzt wird'.[49] Nonetheless, Nietzsche considers epigonality and lateness as essential and productive categories for modern poets, who 'müssen [...] selbst in manchen Hinsichten rückwärts gewendete Wesen sein: so dass man sie als Brücken zu ganz fernen Zeiten und Vorstellungen, zu absterbenden oder abgestorbenen Religionen und Culturen gebrauchen kann. Sie sind eigentlich immer und nothwendig Epigonen'.[50] It is, indeed, the imminent expiration of a culture or civilization that, for Nietzsche, is both conducive to and constitutive of epigonal lateness.[51]

Forgetting and burying the past remain but passive and momentary options: 'Die herbe und tiefsinnig ernste Betrachtung über den Unwerth alles Geschehenen, über das zum-Gericht-Reif-sein der Welt, hat sich zu dem skeptischen Bewusstsein verflüchtigt, dass es jedenfalls gut sei, alles Geschenene zu wissen, weil es zu spat dafür ist, etwas Besseres zu thun', Nietzsche writes.[52] In order to overcome the anxiety of arriving at the end of the century and the immensity of what has gone before, therefore, he advocates that modern writers become self-conscious of their lateness and

[49] Friedrich Nietzsche, *Nietzsche Werke III.1: Unzeitgemäße Betrachtungen I–III*, ed. by Giorgio Colli und Mazzino Montinari (Berlin: de Gruyter, 1972), 304. 'The belief that one is a latecomer of the age is paralysing and depressing: but it must appear dreadful and devastating when such a belief one day by a bold inversion raises this latecomer to godhood as the true meaning and goal of all previous events, when his miserable condition is equated with a completion of world history'. Friedrich Nietzsche, *Untimely Meditations*, trans. by R. J. Hollingdale (Cambridge: Cambridge University Press, 1997), 104.

[50] Nietzsche, *Menschliches, Allzumenschliches I*, 145. 'Must be in some respects beings looking backwards, so that they can be employed as bridges to quite distant ages and conceptions, to dead or dying religions and cultures. They are, in fact, always and necessarily epigones'. See Nietzsche, *Human, All Too Human*, 81. Translation modified.

[51] See also Anne Fuchs, *Precarious Times: Temporality and History in Modern German Culture* (Ithaca, New York: Cornell University Press, 2019), 75–77. Fuchs reads Nietzsche's observation as more of a personal diagnosis than a generational one, such that she understands lateness as 'the condition of modern man who inhabits a culture of imitation. A weakened personality that manifests itself in the split between the outer and the inner self afflicts the modern epigone, in whose personality mere remnants of man's individuality are buried without a chance to reassert themselves. Lateness thus designates the condition of a degenerate and emaciated culture that has lost all vigor and power of renewal' (77).

[52] Nietzsche, *Nietzsche Werke III.1: Unzeitgemäße Betrachtungen I–III*, 301. 'Austere and profoundly serious reflection on the worthlessness of all that has occurred, on the ripeness of the world for judgment, is dissipated into the sceptical attitude that it is at any rate as well to know about all that has occurred, since it is too late to do anything better'. Nietzsche, *Untimely Meditations*, 102.

epigonality, making these the preconditions for cultural renewal. 'Selbst
der oftmnals peinlich anmuthende Gedanke, Epigonen zu sein, gross
gedacht, grosse Wirkungen und ein hoffnungsreiches Begehren der
Zukunft, sowohl dem Einzelnen als einem Volke verbürgen kann',
Nietzsche observes; 'insofern wir uns nämlich als Erben und Nachkommen
klassischer und erstaunlicher Mächte begreifen und darin unsere Ehre,
unseren Sporn sehen'.[53] Self-conscious awareness of lateness and epigonality on the part of the narrators of *Dora Bruder*, *Austerlitz*, and *Sefarad*,
along with the melancholy anxiety caused by their historical position, may
then be worked through, such that 'wenn sie selbst als Spätlinge geboren
werden, – [...] die kommenden Geschlechter werden sie nur als Erstlinge
kennen'.[54] As Hutchinson also observes, in Nietzsche's eyes, 'truly strong
moderns will not look to bury the past, but rather to generate the future'.[55]
Rather than attempting to forget the past and ignore one's late historical
position and sense of epigonality, the self-conscious acknowledgement of
these factors—and, by extension, of the melancholy view of the past that
may emerge from them—may suggest the possibility of future innovation.
The rejuvenating serenity of late style, this implies, may yet become realized in the lateness of modern European literature.

Such self-consciousness is an essential foundational element of late
European novels as conceptualized by this study. As works written around
a particular point in time whose narrators are individually self-conscious of
their lateness and their melancholy, this community of literary works suggests that European literature still contains a residual potential for cultural
renewal. If, as Rosi Braidotti observes, 'consciousness is about co-
synchronicity: shared time zones, shared memories and sharable timelines
of projects', then this is *a fortiori* the case for the self-consciousness of the
late narrators of *Dora Bruder*, *Austerlitz*, and *Sefarad*.[56] These novels' narrators display such self-consciousness principally through their explicit

---

[53] Nietzsche, *Nietzsche Werke III.1: Unzeitgemäße Betrachtungen I–III*, 303. 'The thought
of being epigones, which can often be a painful thought, is also capable of evoking great
effects and grand hopes for the future in both an individual and a nation, provided we regard
ourselves as the heirs and successors of the astonishing powers of antiquity'. Nietzsche,
Untimely Meditations, 103–104.

[54] Nietzsche, *Nietzsche Werke III.1: Unzeitgemäße Betrachtungen I–III*, 307. 'Even if they
themselves are late born coming generations will know them only as first-born'. Nietzsche,
Untimely Meditations, 106–7.

[55] Hutchinson, *Lateness*, 203.

[56] See Rosi Braidotti, *Transpositions: On Nomadic Ethics* (Cambridge: Polity, 2006), 95.

insertion of themselves into the narratives they tell, reflecting in various ways on the entangled processes of researching and writing. In *Dora Bruder*, for instance, the narrator periodically interrupts his account of Dora's life and final days not only with references to events in his own life that his investigations cause him to recall, but also with explicit accounts of the process of investigation and construction of the narrative. The narrator of *Austerlitz*, meanwhile, is at pains to mediate Jacques Austerlitz's account of his life by regularly reminding the reader that these are not the narrator's own words through his sustained use of the *Konjunktiv I* to indicate reported speech, as well as markers such as 'sagte Austerlitz' ('said Austerlitz'), which appear throughout the narrative.[57] Sebald himself considers this 'periscopic' form of narration, which he claims to borrow from Thomas Bernhard, to be integral to the aesthetics of his prose fiction.[58] In *Sefarad*, furthermore, the narrator's imaginings of others' experiences of persecution and exile are routinely interspersed with his accounts of being at home, or with his family, or sat at his desk, pondering the stories with which he is working. By layering and mediating their narratives in these ways, the narrators of these novels not only distance themselves from the people, events, and places in history they describe. They also self-consciously draw attention to their acts of periscopic narration and, by extension, to their Nietzschean lateness and epigonality, as well as the melancholy outlook that emerges from this.[59]

Given the time-bound nature of cultural and historical constructions of lateness explored in this study, it may seem anachronistic to draw on Nietzsche's thoughts from the latter half of the nineteenth century to

[57] For further discussion of this in relation to the ethical dimensions of *Austerlitz*'s retelling of Jewish experiences of the Holocaust, see Stuart Taberner, 'German Nostalgia? Remembering German-Jewish Life in W.G. Sebald's *Die Ausgewanderten* and *Austerlitz*', in *Germanic Review*, 79 (2004), 181–202.

[58] See Lynne Sharon Schwartz, ed., *The Emergence of Memory: Conversations with W. G. Sebald* (New York: Seven Stories Press, 2007), 82.

[59] In the case of Sebald's literary project, for example, Anne Fuchs among others argues that the self-conscious reflections of the Sebaldian narrator prevent appropriative identification on the part of a German narrator with his Jewish subject. See Anne Fuchs, *Die Schmerzenspuren der Geschichte: Zur Poetik der Erinnerung in W. G. Sebalds Prosa* (Cologne: Böhlau, 2004), 28–34. As Mary Cosgrove also notes, 'this kind of narrative signalling communicates, on the aesthetic level of the text, how the German must always respect the inalienable difference of the Jewish victim other'. See Mary Cosgrove, *Born under Auschwitz: Melancholy Traditions in Postwar German Literature* (Rochester: Camden House, 2014), 160.

elucidate the aesthetic attitudes of novels written over a hundred years later. Needless to say, the Europe of Nietzsche's day was markedly different to that of the end of the twentieth century. This, however, is precisely why it is not only useful to consider Nietzsche in order to understand these novels' aesthetics, but perhaps essential. Nietzsche warned that 'die Abschliessung der Nationen durch Erzeugung *nationaler* Feindseligkeiten' works against the achievement of a more transnational European ideal.[60] He suggested, as Christian Emden has argued, that a 'community can exist which is both more than the nation state and less vague than humanity'.[61] Yet this future-oriented cosmopolitan philosophy for Europe to exist beyond the limits of nationhood did not come to pass. This finds its echo in the lateness-inflected melancholy of European writers at the end of the twentieth century, since over the preceding hundred years Europe failed to become what Nietzsche envisioned. Not all European intellectuals and novelists desired—or desire—Europe to be fashioned after Nietzsche's ideas. From the late vantage point of the turn of the millennium, however, novels such as *Dora Bruder, Austerlitz,* and *Sefarad* look back at the seemingly irretrievable loss of European optimism in the face of rising nationalism and its ensuing horrors. In doing so, they implicitly mark not only the absence of Nietzsche's vision for Europe, but also the passing away of the notion of 'high' culture following the catastrophes of the early twentieth century. European modernity is tainted and rendered suspect. The marked disappearance of 'high' European culture in its wake is thus registered in late European novels through their understanding of history as melancholy and the past as irretrievable. The optimism of Nietzsche's vision appears to be lost for them.

Following two world wars, the rise of totalitarianism, and the Holocaust, Europe experienced a levelling out of its 'high' culture. As Shane Weller, among others, has argued, the sequence of catastrophic historical events over the course of the twentieth century prompted a radical questioning among European writers and thinkers of the very idea of European culture

---

[60] Friedrich Nietzsche, *Nietzsche Werke IV.2: Menschliches, Allzumenschliches I*, ed. by Giorgio Colli und Mazzino Montinari (Berlin: de Gruyter, 1967), 319. 'The isolation of nations due to engendered *national* hostilities'. Nietzsche, *Human, All Too Human*, 228. Emphasis in original.

[61] Christian Emden, *Friedrich Nietzsche and the Politics of History* (Cambridge: Cambridge University Press, 2008), 286.

itself.[62] The subsequent emergence of the postmodern embodied, as Jameson observes, 'specific reactions against the established forms of high modernism'.[63] While this was to some extent prefigured by the elimination of illiteracy in Western Europe in the early twentieth century, as Béla Tomka notes,[64] it was fuelled by what Andreas Huyssen terms 'modernism's running feud with mass society and mass culture'.[65] In the wake of what Huyssen describes as the 'great divide' between 'high' modernist culture and 'low' postmodern mass culture, late European novels written at the end of the twentieth century register through their late and epigonal Nietzschean echoes this perceived loss of 'high' European cultural ideals alongside the end of great literary movements. The generative potential of these novels' lateness, however, is not exhausted through melancholy reflection and narration. By thematizing the difficult history of twentieth-century Europe through aesthetic attitudes of lateness and epigonality, which resonate across the boundaries of different national literary traditions—be it through *Dora Bruder*'s engagement with the legacy of Jewish writers' troubled relationship to the French and European literary canon, or *Austerlitz*'s apocalyptic late modernism fused with reworkings of the German Romantic tradition, or *Sefarad*'s confrontation of Spain's repeated exclusion from European cultural history and the implications of this— these novels collectively gesture towards the possible future exemplification of a transnational Nietzschean vision of European culture and, indeed, the emergence of *Erstlinge* after *Spätlinge*. From the proximity of ending stems the possibility of rejuvenation. As Ernst Bloch writes on the final page of his three-volume study *Das Prinzip Hoffnung*, 'die wirkliche Genesis ist nicht am Anfang, sondern am Ende'.[66] Conceiving of novels such as *Dora Bruder, Austerlitz,* and *Sefarad* in terms of a literary

---

[62] See Shane Weller, *Language and Negativity in European Modernism: Towards a Literature of the Unword* (Cambridge: Cambridge University Press, 2019), 2–3. See also Shane Weller, *The Idea of Europe: A Critical History* (Cambridge: Cambridge University Press, 2021).

[63] Fredric Jameson, 'Postmodernism and Consumer Society', in *The Anti-Aesthetic: Essays on Postmodern Culture*, ed. by Hal Foster (London: Pluto Press, 1983), 111–125 (p.111).

[64] Béla Tomka, *A Social History of Twentieth-Century Europe* (London: Routledge, 2013), 364.

[65] Andreas Huyssen, 'Mapping the Postmodern', in *New German Critique,* 33 (1984), 5–52 (49).

[66] Ernst Bloch, *Gesamtausgabe 5: Das Prinzip Hoffnung: Kapitel 28–55* (Frankfurt am Main: Suhrkamp, 1959), 1628. 'True genesis is not at the beginning but at the end'. Ernst Bloch, *The Principle of Hope, 3 Volumes* (Cambridge, Massachusetts: MIT Press, 1986), 1376.

community both emphasizes their comparable understandings of their present in relation to the past and expresses the transnational optimism of the very vision whose absence these texts mark. Out of the pathos of lateness and the melancholy of history, then, the potential for more optimistic future cultural renewal begins to emerge.

From Literary Lateness to the Melancholy of History

The novel is, in many ways, a form born exhausted. As Kermode has argued, 'the special fate of the novel [...] is to be always dying' and, indeed, its impending demise has been routinely trumpeted—however absurdly—in many corners for centuries.[67] Alluding to the tensions between age and youth, between the late and the new, encapsulated by the discourse of lateness, Pieter Vermeulen considers declarations of the form's exhaustion to have 'a long and venerable pedigree: they are a crucial part of the texture of a literary history premised on innovation and originality'.[68] Georg Lukács's *Theory of the Novel* (1914–15) notably explores the novel's long history of conceptualizing its own lateness, considering it a form cursed to remain 'nothing but a struggle against the power of time'.[69] Building on Lukács, Vermeulen considers the novel to be 'always marked by melancholic imitations of its own insufficiency, and the lingering suspicion that it is merely living out its own afterlife'.[70] While Vermeulen's argument that the novel 'is constitutively caught up in the question of its own (in)sufficiency' might suggest that lateness and melancholy are supratemporal aspects of the form,[71] *Late Europeans and Melancholy Fiction* seeks to historicize these aesthetic phenomena, contending that novelistic anxiety intensifies with the impending arrival of the new millennium and is exemplified in the concurrent emergence of a late and melancholy mode

---

[67] Frank Kermode, 'The Life and Death of the Novel', in *The New York Review of Books*, 28 October 1965. Available online: https://www.nybooks.com/articles/1965/10/28/life-and-death-of-the-novel

[68] Pieter Vermeulen, *Contemporary Literature and the End of the Novel: Creature, Affect, Form* (Basingstoke: Palgrave Macmillan, 2015), 105.

[69] Georg Lukács, *The Theory of the Novel: A Historico-Philiosophical Essay on the Forms of Great Epic Literature*, trans. by Anna Bostock (Cambridge, Massachusetts: MIT Press, 1971), 122.

[70] Vermeulen, *Contemporary Literature*, 106.

[71] Vermeulen, *Contemporary Literature*, 106.

of writing within European fiction. In the case of works like *Dora Bruder*, *Austerlitz*, and *Sefarad*, latent features of the novel's formal inadequacy such as those identified by Vermeulen are enhanced and actualized by the historical crisis of the arrival of the second millennium, as well as by a deeply felt sense of cultural lateness experienced and articulated within European letters at this time.

In the final decades of the twentieth century, many psychologists and sociologists suggested that the period of anxiety experienced across Europe in the aftermath of World War II subsequently led to a new age of melancholy in Western society.[72] This sense of societal and psychological melancholy was engendered by many potentially catastrophic events pertinent to the post-industrial societies of late-twentieth-century Europe, including growing political and military tensions between the West and the East, terror at the prospect of imminent nuclear annihilation, the threat of economic crisis, environmental disaster, and exponential population explosions. In a literary context, such a sense of melancholy relates to and is reflected in the cultural and historical sense of lateness documented in works produced during this time. If, as George Steiner observes, there is 'a core-tiredness' in Western European culture at the close of the twentieth century, then, he argues, this is undoubtedly because 'we are, or feel ourselves to be latecomers'.[73] With the impending turn of the millennium, Steiner heralds the arrival in European culture of what he terms 'the eclipse of the messianic'.[74] Understood in either a personal or metaphorical sense, the 'messianic' signifies in Judeo-Christian religion and culture a sense of rejuvenation, the end of historical temporality, and the coming of a new world. For Steiner, the events of the twentieth century have done away with this optimism, not so much in the sense of history collapsing into a stagnant present without past or future as François Hartog has conceptualized, but rather such that the present is inundated and

---

[72] See, for example, G. L. Klerman, 'Is this the Age of Melancholy?', *Psychology Today*, no. 12 (1979), 36–42; Olle Hagnel, Jan Lanke, Birgitta Rorsman, and Leif Öjesjö, 'Are we entering an age of melancholy?', *Psychological Medicine*, no. 12 (1982), 279–98; and Anthony J. Marsella, Norman Sartorius, Assen Jablensky, and Fred R. Fenton, 'Cross-cultural studies of depressive disorders: an overview', *Culture and Depression*, ed. by Arthur Kleinman and Byron Good (Berkeley: University of California Press, 1985), 299–324.

[73] George Steiner, *Grammars of Creation* (London: Faber & Faber, 2001), 2.

[74] See Steiner, *Grammars of Creation*, 7–8.

overwhelmed by the history that precedes it.[75] Steiner's notion of the
eclipse of the messianic is therefore far more melancholy in tone than, for
example, Francis Fukuyama's much-derided—and, indeed, later recanted—
thesis of the 'end of history', which, in optimistic Hegelian fashion, heralds the endpoint of mankind's ideological evolution with the apparent
conclusion of the Cold War and the arrival of Western liberal democracy
as the final and ultimate form of human government.[76] For Steiner, however, the darkness of his eclipse, and its concomitant sense of ending, is
ongoing and insoluble. Yet, even while suggesting that the notion of the
messianic may be eclipsed at the close of the century, Steiner nonetheless
acknowledges that 'the forces emanating from the eclipse of the messianic
will find manifest expression', thereby anticipating the potentially generative qualities of lateness and melancholy that this study hypothesizes.[77]

Though hardly unique to European culture, melancholy aesthetics have
enjoyed a long-standing and diverse history in European letters, from the
early modern period, through the Renaissance to Romanticism, and up to
and beyond modernity.[78] Indeed, for Matthew Bell, melancholy may be
understood as 'the Western malady'.[79] Although scholarship on its instantiations in European literature has principally remained confined to discrete national contexts, melancholy may be considered a prevalent
European aesthetic attitude, especially given the evident interconnected-

[75] See François Hartog, *Présentisme simple ou par défaut?* (Paris: Seuil, 2003), or *Regimes of Historicity: Presentism and Experiences of Time*, trans. by Saskia Brown (New York: Columbia University Press, 2016).

[76] See Francis Fukuyama, 'The End of History?', *The National Interest*, no. 16 (1989), 3–18, and Francis Fukuyama, *The End of History and the Last Man* (New York: The Free Press, 1992). Although Fukuyama's vestigially Hegelian view of history and his optimistic endorsement of Western hegemony appear naïve at best with the benefit of hindsight, the suggestion in his work that the future would remain haunted by Nietzschean spectres (300–327) is, this study submits, not so wide of the mark.

[77] See Steiner, *Grammars of Creation*, 8.

[78] For further discussion on the development of melancholy from the perspectives of vari-
ous thinkers, see Jennifer Radden, ed., *The Nature of Melancholy: From Aristotle to Kristeva* (Oxford: Oxford University Press, 2000). For further discussion of how engagement with history in modernist literature in particular is closely entwined with the history of melancholy in European art, see, for example, Sanja Bahun, *Modernism and Melancholia: Writing as Countermourning* (Oxford: Oxford University Press, 2014). For a concise overview of the emergence of melancholy in relation to European rationalism and Enlightenment thought, see Roger Bartra, *Angels in Mourning: Sublime Madness, Ennui and Melancholy in Modern Thought*, trans. by Nick Caistor (Chicago: University of Chicago Press, 2018).

[79] See Matthew Bell, *Melancholia: The Western Malady* (Cambridge: Cambridge University Press, 2014).

ness of national literary traditions in Western Europe.[80] Nonetheless, the term itself is inherently slippery since it has been redefined and reappropriated in many guises over the centuries by religion, medicine, and the humanities, perhaps most notably by Robert Burton in *The Anatomy of Melancholy* (1621–1651). While understandings of melancholy have altered over time, however, its symptoms have remained constant: affected sadness, fear, and a sense of inner crisis; expressions of grief and of a desire for solitude; an inability to act and a loss of interest; longing, emptiness, and the fragmentation of cognition.[81] The figure of the melancholy creative genius, moreover, who always desires to know more than the world will allow, recurs again and again across European art and intellectual history. This is perhaps best exemplified in the seminal study *Saturn and Melancholy* by Raymond Libanksy, Erwin Panofsky, and Fritz Saxl in their analysis of Albrecht Dürer's 1514 engraving *Melencolia I*, which depicts a gloomy angel staring beyond the apparatus of art, alchemy, and geometry scattered before her.[82] If melancholy, broadly defined, constitutes an affective withdrawal from the world, then it is one which, as Mary Cosgrove

[80] For recent examples of studies of melancholy aesthetics in various European national literary contexts, see Ross Chambers, *The Writing of Melancholy: Modes of Opposition in Early French Modernism* (Chicago: University of Chicago Press, 1993); Roger Bartra, *Melancholy and Culture: Essays on the Diseases of the Soul in Golden Age Spain*, trans. by Christopher Follett (Cardiff: University of Wales Press, 2008); and Cosgrove, *Born under Auschwitz*. Recourse to these studies is not to suggest in any way, however, that melancholy aesthetics have an exclusively European provenance. Beyond Europe, the poetry of many Chinese authors writing after the Tang or Song dynasties, for example, as well as the works of contemporary scholars of their poetry, would serve as a corrective to the notion that melancholy ought to be associated exclusively with, or be considered constitutive solely of, any presumed European cultural identity. See, for example, Fusheng Wu, *The Poetics of Decadence: Chinese Poetry of the Southern Dynasties and Late Tang Periods* (New York: State University of New York Press, 1998), 146, and Sylvia Van Ziegert, *Global Spaces of Chinese Culture: Diasporic Chinese Communities in the United States and Germany* (Oxford: Routledge, 2009), 119. For a generation of Israeli writers, too, born between the 1960s and 1990s, who came of age during wars, occupation, and cultural conflict, militarism and conservative state politics left little room for democratic opposition or dissent, such that political melancholy became the defining trait of their work. See, for example, Nitzan Lebovic, *Zionism and Melancholy: The Short Life of Israel Zarchi* (Bloomington: Indiana University Press, 2019).

[81] For further discussion of the symptoms and history of melancholy, see Jonathan Flatley, *Affective Mapping: Melancholia and the Politics of Modernism* (Cambridge, Massachusetts: Harvard University Press, 2008).

[82] See Raymond Libanksy, Erwin Panofsky, and Fritz Saxl, *Saturn and Melancholy: Studies in the History of Natural Philosophy, Religion, and Art*, ed. by Philippe Despoix and Georges Leroux (Chicago: McGill-Queen's University Press, 2019), 284–375.

notes, entails 'a contemplative response to recent history that is embedded in the ancient cultural traditions of writing about and depicting the universal human experience of sorrow'.[83] Drawing inspiration from Benjamin's study of German tragic drama *Ursprung des deutschen Trauerspiels*, his habilitation thesis submitted to the University of Frankfurt in 1925 but not published until three years later, which in parts also engages with Dürer's engravings, Cosgrove observes how, over the course of European modernity, 'melancholy becomes much more than just a persistent and doleful mood [...]. Instead, it stands for the work of culture itself: the quest for meaning'.[84] The emergence of melancholy late European novels after the cataclysmic events of twentieth-century European history—after an apparent end of grand narratives and in the shadow of the Steinerian 'eclipse of the messianic'—thus constitutes a literary response to the burden of engaging with earlier historical events through the affectation of a melancholy aesthetic attitude.

The idea of Europe has long been one of a continent and culture that is freighted with the burden of its history, to paraphrase Valéry's concise summation, which itself echoes the Nietzschean reading of European modernity as an age oversaturated with history.[85] Writing towards the perceived end of an era, it is perhaps unsurprising that the narrators of late European novels should adopt so melancholy an outlook on the past thematized in their narratives. Aleida Assmann, drawing on the work of Hartog and Reinhart Koselleck, describes how the emergence of modernity from the nineteenth century in the wake of both the French and

---

[83] See Cosgrove, *Born under Auschwitz*, 9. Cosgrove's study opens with a comprehensive introduction to melancholy as a performative affected mode, as well as a history of melancholy through Antiquity, the Renaissance, and Modernity, with a focus on its conceptualizations in psychoanalysis, religion, and medicine. The present study follows Cosgrove in consciously preferring the term 'melancholy' over 'melancholia', since, as Cosgrove explains, 'while it was a synonym for "melancholy" during the Renaissance, its [melancholia's] application, in other epochs, has often been restricted to descriptions of disease' (9). For further discussion of melancholy aesthetics in a distinctly Germanic context, see also Mary Cosgrove, 'Introduction: Sadness and Melancholy in German-Language Literature from the Seventeenth Century to the Present: An Overview', *Edinburgh German Yearbook Volume 6: Sadness and Melancholy in German-Language Literature and Culture* (New York: Camden House, 2012), 1–17.

[84] Cosgrove, 'Introduction: Sadness and Melancholy', 9.

[85] See Paul Valéry, *Cahiers/Notebooks*, vol. IV, trans. by Paul Gifford, Robert Pickering, Joseph Rima, Norma Rinsler, and Brian Stimpson (Frankfurt am Main: Peter Lang, 2010), 521.

industrial revolutions encouraged an understanding that with the split between Antiquity and the modern age, between the past and the present, 'wurde Zeit als ein immer tieferer Abgrund sichtbar, der seine Entsprechung in historischem Bewußtsein und zeitlicher Entfremdung hat'.[86] The historical consciousness of the narrators of late European novels, which emerge towards the close of the twentieth century, constitutes a melancholy perspective on the past determined by a sense of loss and separation, of irrecoverability and irreconciliation with history. History itself may thus be construed as melancholy. Indeed, as Peter Fritzsche argues, 'the losses of the past are irreversible; this is what constitutes the melancholy of history'.[87] Writing after the catastrophes of European twentieth-century history and distanced from the past that precedes them, the narrators of late European novels such as *Dora Bruder*, *Austerlitz*, and *Sefarad* confront and attempt to work through the legacy of modernity, partly driven by their late historical location at the century's end. 'The more we seek to persuade ourselves of the fidelity of our own projects and values with respect to the past', as Jameson notes, 'the more obsessively do we find ourselves exploring the latter'; for Jameson, this constitutes 'the latecomer's melancholy reverence'.[88] Such a reverential focus on the past relies on temporal distance and separation from earlier events, which is to say, on a fundamental understanding of one's present as unavoidably and irrevocably separated from the past. Accordingly, these narrators and their narratives are at once separated from and yet remain determined by events that came before them. Melancholy aesthetics in millennial works of European literature thus emerge as intrinsically bound up with a narratorial self-conscious awareness of historical lateness. As Walter Moser argues, melancholy, along with nostalgia, might be thought of as the 'affects' of lateness, although he defines the two terms in contradistinction to one another. If

---

[86] Aleida Assmann, *Erinnerungsräume: Formen und Wandlungen des kulturellen Gedächtnisses* (Munich: C. H. Beck, 1999). 'Time could now be seen as an ever widening gulf, reflected by a new historical consciousness and temporal alienation'. Aleida Assmann, *Cultural Memory and Western Civilization* (Cambridge: Cambridge University Press, 2012), 81. See also Hartog, *Présentisme* and Reinhart Koselleck, *Vergangene Zukunft: Zur Semantik geschichtlicher Zeiten* (Frankfurt am Main: Suhrkamp, 1979), or *Futures Past: On the Semantics of Historical Time*, trans. by Keith Tribe (New York: Columbia University Press, 2012).

[87] Peter Fritzsche, *Stranded in the Present: Modern Time and the Melancholy of History* (Cambridge, Massachusetts: Harvard University Press, 2004), 1–10 (8).

[88] Fredric Jameson, *A Singular Modernity: Essay on the Ontology of the Present* (London: Verso, 2002), 24.

nostalgia expresses a desire to return to the past, then melancholy, Moser argues, is the recognition that this is impossible, that the past and the present cannot be reconciled.[89] Whether it be through ekphrastic contemplation of photographs and abandoned objects in *Dora Bruder*, descent into alternative fairy tale realms in *Austerlitz*, or memories of lost homelands and fleeting moments in time in *Sefarad*, the narrators of novels such as those examined in this study respond to their perceived historical and cultural lateness via a melancholy aesthetic attitude that acknowledges, encapsulates, and reflects the mutual irreconcilability of the past and the present.

The melancholy disconnection between past and present renders history an object of intense scrutiny for cultural practitioners in the present, according to Fritzsche. While this is certainly true in the case of the novels examined in this study, the following chapters propose a fundamentally different characterization for the self-understanding of literary artists and the present they inhabit. 'Insofar as the present was characterized by the new', Fritzsche remarks, 'the past appeared increasingly different, mysterious, and inaccessible'.[90] A reading of the present not as new but as late, however, further underscores the bereft sense of coming after, which is articulated in novels such as those mentioned above, intensifying their conceptualization of history *as* melancholy. Franco Moretti suggests that by understanding that literature '*follows* great social changes – that it always "comes after"', then it is able to not only repeat or reflect the problems of history, but to resolve them.[91] That such resolution should be automatic is perhaps overly optimistic. Qualifying the causality expressed by Moretti, *Late Europeans and Melancholy Fiction at the Turn of the Millennium* proposes that in coming after—or, indeed, later—and being self-conscious of this, novels which exhibit in various ways a melancholy aesthetic and a melancholy perspective on history collectively express a possibility for the resolution of historical problems and the potential for a generative sense of future renewal in literature to emerge.

This potentiality is perhaps best exemplified in Sebald's understanding of his own literary project as 'Ein Versuch der Restitution', as his final public speech at the opening of the Literaturhaus in Stuttgart in 2001

---

[89] See Walter Moser, 'Mélancolie et nostalgie: Affects de la *Spätzeit*', *Etudes littéraires*, 32 (1999), 83–103. Cited in Hutchinson, *Lateness*, 13 and 26.

[90] Fritzsche, *Stranded in the Present*, 7.

[91] See Franco Moretti, *Modern Epic: The World System from Goethe to García Márquez*, trans. by Quintin Hoare (London: Verso, 1996), 6. Emphasis in original.

attests.[92] Such a project holds that the recovery, restoration, and reparation of historical damage may be enacted through fiction, thereby meaningfully moving closer towards the rectification of the catastrophes stemming from what J. J. Long has termed the 'meta-problem' of modernity that haunts Sebald's œuvre.[93] For Long, the melancholy aesthetics in Sebald's work constitute an epiphenomenon of his thematization of this meta-problem. Melancholy may thus be understood as a potentially restorative aesthetic form, a means of recognition and of bearing witness that allows the meta-problem of modernity to be articulated. It is also an active response, both affective and effective, to modernity's legacy of destruction and loss. This study's conceptualization of late European novels draws partly on this Sebaldian notion of a literature of restitution but expands the focus from the reparation of historical calamity to include the potential restitution of literary form and style. If, alongside the restoration of property to rightful owners, the term restitution may connote, as Russell Kilbourn argues, the restoration of works of art, then novels such as *Dora Bruder*, *Austerlitz*, and *Sefarad* may variously be understood to offer recompense to works of European literature and culture, carrying the burden of modernity's damages and thematizing this in their narratives through their narrators' self-consciously melancholy aesthetic attitude.[94]

There is undeniably a distinctly Germanic flavour to the articulations of melancholy referenced in this study, and this is most clearly evoked in another saturnine angelic figure, who acts as a modern counterpart to Dürer's engraving: Benjamin's celebrated Angel of History. Blown backwards into the future by the storm of progress, the *Angelus Novus* presides over the ruins of modernity's failure, fixedly contemplating history while inextricably moving away from it.[95] Such an awareness of the past's

---

[92] 'An attempt at restitution'. See W. G. Sebald, 'Zerstreute Reminiszenzen: Gedanken zur Eröffnung eines Stuttgarter Hauses', *Stuttgarter Zeitung*, 18 November, 2001.

[93] J. J. Long, *W. G. Sebald: Image, Archive, Modernity* (Edinburgh: Edinburgh University Press, 2007), 1. See also, Taberner, 'German Nostalgia?'.

[94] See Russell J. A. Kilbourn, 'The Question of Genre in W. G. Sebald's "Prose" (Towards a Post-Memorial Literature of Restitution)', *A Literature of Restitution: Critical Essays on W. G. Sebald*, ed. by Jeannette Baxter, Valerie Henitiuk, and Ben Hutchinson (Manchester: Manchester University Press, 2013), 247–264 (261).

[95] It is perhaps worth quoting the ninth thesis on the philosophy of history in full to appreciate the scale of the melancholy separation of the past, the present, and the unseeable future Benjamin evokes:

Es gibt ein Bild von Klee, das Angelus Novus heißt. Ein Engel ist darauf dargestellt, der aussieht, als wäre er im Begriff, sich von etwas zu entfernen, worauf er starrt. Seine Augen

irreconcilable and unbridgeable distance from their present lends the narratives of late European novels a melancholy perception of history. If the Benjaminian *Angelus* thus acts as a metaphor for modernity's progress, observing retrospectively the destruction wreaked by Western advancement, then late European novels' echo of this cultural embodiment of the modern and the European endows them with further pathos.[96]

There is, moreover, a brief connection to be made between the present study's historicization of melancholy as an aesthetic and literary mode and the term's use to diagnose a psychopathological condition in

sind aufgerissen, sein Mund steht offen und seine Flügel sind ausgespannt. Der Engel der Geschichte muß so aussehen. Er hat das Antlitz der Vergangenheit zugewendet. Wo eine Kette von Begebenheiten vor *uns* erscheint, da sieht *er* eine einzige Katastrophe, die unablässig Trümmer auf Trümmer häuft und sie ihm vor die Füße schleudert. Er möchte wohl verweilen, die Toten wecken und das Zerschlagene zusammenfügen. Aber ein Sturm weht vom Paradiese her, der sich in seinen Flügeln verfangen hat und so stark ist, daß der Engel sie nicht mehr schließen kann. Dieser Sturm treibt ihn unaufhaltsam in die Zukunft, der er den Rücken kehrt, während der Trümmerhaufen vor ihm zum Himmel wächst. Das, was wir den Fortschritt nennen, ist *dieser* Sturm. ('Über den Begriff der Geschichte', 697–698. Emphasis in original)

A Klee painting named Angelus Novus shows an angel looking as though he is about to move away from something he is fixedly contemplating. His eyes are staring, his mouth is open, his wings are spread. This is how one pictures the angel of history. His face is turned toward the past. Where we perceive a chain of events, he sees one single catastrophe which keeps piling wreckage upon wreckage and hurls it in front of his feet. The angel would like to stay, awaken the dead, and make whole what has been smashed. But a storm is blowing from Paradise; it has got caught in his wings with such violence that the angel can no longer close them. The storm irresistibly propels him into the future to which his back is turned, while the pile of debris before him grows skyward. This storm is what we call progress. (Benjamin, 'Theses on the Philosophy of History', 257–258)

[96] It is interesting to note that, even only a few years after Sebald's untimely death in 2001, theorizations of his work in relation to Benjamin's Angel of History were already being perceived as tired reformulations in some quarters. In an early piece of Sebaldian scholarship, for example, Julia Hell takes the Angel of History as evoked by Sebald in his lectures on *Luftkrieg und Literatur* (1999) as a point of departure but prefaces her essay by warning that she is 'not proposing another reading of Sebald through the lens of Benjamin; on the contrary, I would like to find out what this cultural icon of the (academic) left – by now so worn out, so terribly fatigued – might be glossing over, if not concealing'. In the wake of the reams of subsequent Sebald scholarship engaging with these very notions (which, of course, includes the present study), this statement has acquired a wry ambiguity: is the Angel of History, Benjamin, or Sebald himself understood to be the fatigued cultural icon? See Julia Hell, 'The Angel's Enigmatic Eyes, or The Gothic Beauty of Catastrophic History in W. G. Sebald's *Airwar and Literature*', *Criticism* 46, no. 3 (2004), 361–392 (361 and 380).

individual or society. In a review of a book of poems by Erich Kästner, Benjamin coined the term 'linke Melancholie' ('left-wing melancholy') in order to describe what he perceived as the intellectual shortcomings in political art in the early 1930s. By exposing a moralistic stance in the work of artists fixated on exposing inequality, Benjamin hailed such art as smugly reactive rather than politically engaged in imagining and constructing alternatives, as bearing witness to torments without attempting to transform them: 'er hat von vornherein', he notes, 'nichts anderes im Auge als in negativistischer Ruhe sich selbst zu genießen'.[97] Highlighting political hypocrisy, Benjamin's diagnosis of left-wing melancholy condemns the political left's nostalgia-inflected tendency towards reactionary and conservative attachment to the way things used to be or how they might have turned out had history followed a different course. Melancholy of this left-wing variety consists in a form of progressive political despair and guilt in not having challenged authority in the past, in having surrendered to resignation and disarray in the present, and in mourning the human cost of this and the lack of realizing any utopian ambition. Yet, even here, hidden within this melancholic political tradition, later scholars have argued, the resources for a revitalized challenge to prevailing regimes of historicity may be found.[98] The present study accordingly takes up the investigation of literary and aesthetic manifestations of melancholy's rejuvenatory potential.

The view of history expressed at so late an hour in novels such as *Dora Bruder*, *Austerlitz*, and *Sefarad* gestures towards a way of understanding contemplative melancholy aesthetics in European fiction as offering a form of potential restitution for European literature. Such melancholy— such grief over history and the inability to reconcile past and present in literary works—suggests, when they are read alongside one another, neither a loss of interest nor an inability to act as they might individually articulate, but rather a generative potential to salvage something from the

[97]Walter Benjamin, 'Linke Melancholie: Zu Erich Kästners neuem Gedichtbuch', in *Gesammelte Schriften III*, ed. by Hella Tiedemann-Bartels (Frankfurt am Main: Suhrkamp, 1972), 279–283 (281). 'From the beginning all it has in mind is to enjoy itself in a negativistic quiet'. Walter Benjamin, 'Left-Wing Melancholy', in *Selected Writings: 1927–1934, Volume 2*, ed. by Howard Eiland, Michael W. Jennings, and Gary Smith, trans. by Rodney Livingstone and Others (Cambridge, Massachusetts: The Belknap Press of Harvard University Press, 1999), 423–427 (425).

[98]See Enzo Traverso, *Left-Wing Melancholia: Marxism, History, and Memory* (New York: Columbia University Press, 2017).

wreckage of European literary modernity. In their similarities to Nietzsche's figures of *Spätlinge* and *Erstlinge*, the narrators of late European novels encapsulate the potential of achieving future renewal in European literature through self-consciousness of their lateness and, by extension, of their melancholy outlook on the past. If the mediated or periscopic style of the narrators of the novels examined in this study evinces their self-consciousness of their lateness and their melancholy, then a collective of self-consciously late and melancholy *Spätlinge* suggests the possibility of futurity, that they—or, indeed, others—may yet become *Erstlinge*. In this regard, their conscious self-stylization as melancholy latecomers is key. To see such potential futurity more clearly, it will therefore be helpful to return to the aforementioned corollary figure to Nietzsche's backward-facing modern poets, namely, the 'good European'. Through the ethos of the 'good European', for whom personal stylization and self-consciousness are essential, Nietzsche responds to the emergence in the late 1800s of nationalist tendencies across Europe by rejecting what he describes as the pathological manner in which nationalism had alienated and continued to alienate the peoples of European from each other.[99] Fundamentally, for Nietzsche, being a 'good European' was defined *ex negativo* as being not principally identifiable with or allied to any one particular nationality. Imagining a future community that has left nationalism behind, Nietzsche claims that by being undaunted in presenting oneself as a 'good European', it is possible to exhibit a self-consciously European identity.[100] It is up to each individual, Nietzsche argues, to make themselves and their lives more artistic, more poetic, and more beautiful, thereby enriching the totality of European culture and society. The 'good European' is, as Martine Prange notes, 'the exemplary cosmopolitan practitioner', who exhibits a highly individual praxis of self-consciousness and self-renewal within a collective

[99] 'Dank der krankhaften Entfremdung, welche der Nationalitäts-Wahnsinn zwischen die Völker Europa's gelegt hat und noch legt'. Friedrich Nietzsche, *Nietzsche Werke VI.2: Jenseits von Gut und Böse*, ed. by Giorgio Colli und Mazzino Montinari (Berlin: de Gruyter, 1968), 209. See also Friedrich Nietzsche, *Beyond Good and Evil*, trans. by Judith Norman (Cambridge: Cambridge University Press, 2002), 148.

[100] 'So soll man sich nur ungescheut als *guten Europäer* ausgeben'. Friedrich Nietzsche, *Nietzsche Werke IV.2: Menschliches, Allzumenschliches I*, ed. by Giorgio Colli und Mazzino Montinari (Berlin: de Gruyter, 1967), 319. Emphasis added. See also Nietzsche, *Human, All Too Human*, 228.

of similarly self-conscious practitioners.[101] By virtue of their narrators' self-consciously assumed stance of lateness and melancholy with respect to the past, the novels examined in this study already contain the seeds of possible future renewal. They thus encapsulate a particular form of aesthetic futurity that is located within a national literary context while resonating with others. This is not to argue that the narrators—or, indeed, the authors—of late and melancholy European novels are themselves actively striving to embody the figure of the 'good European', however. Rather, it is to suggest that, when viewed through a Nietzschean lens, it is precisely out of a self-consciousness of lateness and a melancholy perspective on the past in these novels that a form of European literary commonality may begin to coalesce. Read alongside one another, these novels echo Nietzsche's suggestion of the potential for an aesthetic literary community to exist beyond individual national contexts and traditions without being lost in the totality of humanity.[102]

If the novels examined in this study exhibit an engagement with historical and cultural lateness that implies a sense of futurity beyond themselves, then this is not least because lateness is inherently invested with the potential of overcoming itself. Late is not last and time has not run out. Unlike, for example, the Nietzschean figure of the last man, whose conflation with the good European Benjamin both identified and feared among his contemporaries, these novels' narrators do not understand themselves to be the last individual survivors who have grown tired of life, having witnessed everything, and who seek security and comfort in spite of their crippling self-awareness.[103] As late modernists, they

---

[101] See Martine Prange, 'Cosmopolitan roads to culture and the festival road of humanity: The cosmopolitan praxis of Nietzsche's good European against Kantian cosmopolitanism' in *Ethical Perspectives: Journal of the European Ethics Network*, 14: 3 (2007), 269–286 (270). To draw further connections between lateness and the cosmopolitan ethos of the 'good European', it is interesting to note that for Adorno, a key feature of artistic late style is an intense expression of the artist's uninhibited subjectivity or personality, whereby heightened self-expression is favoured above aesthetic norms. See Adorno, 'Spätstil (I): Spätstil Beethovens', 180, or Adorno, 'Late Style in Beethoven', 564.

[102] Nietzsche's conception of the 'good European' as existing beyond nationalism nonetheless does seem to a greater or lesser degree to expand the form of the nation to a supra-national level. For further discussion of this, see Weller, *The Idea of Europe*, pp. 122–128.

[103] For further discussion of the decadent figure of the 'last man', conceptualised by Nietzsche as the negative counterpart to the figure of the *Übermensch*, see in particular the prologue to Friedrich Nietzsche, *Nietzsche Werke VI.1: Also sprach Zarathustra*, ed. by Giorgio Colli und Mazzino Montinari (Berlin: de Gruyter, 1968).

constitute less the culmination of a teleological tradition, than the diminished returns of a generation of late arrivals. Rather than possessing an acute awareness that they are a final incarnation, they are conscious of their late emergence in the shadow of their literary forebears.[104] Accordingly, the narrators' self-consciousness in *Dora Bruder*, *Austerlitz*, and *Sefarad* of their lateness and of their melancholy view of the past constitutes an aesthetic attitude that is more redolent of Nietzsche's 'good European', since this attitude may be understood to exist in various national traditions. A collective of novels—and, indeed, of writers—is thus established, which goes beyond the context of the national within Europe, while the individual novels still exhibit particularities specific to the national literary milieux in which they emerge. Neither 'last men' nor 'good Europeans', they are best understood as *late Europeans*.

EUROPEAN FICTION

In bringing together works by Modiano, Sebald, and Muñoz Molina, *Late Europeans and Melancholy Fiction at the Turn of the millennium* aims to achieve a greater understanding of the commonalities and distinctions among them, as well as the implications of these. Similarities and points of departure reveal how the discrete national expressions of late and melancholy aesthetics may be understood both as an indication of generative potential and as an expression of a fundamental tension in European novels around the turn of the millennium. By synthesizing the vast range of thought and scholarship on lateness and melancholy, not to mention ideas of European culture and literary scholarship from three linguistic and cultural contexts, this study draws on the works and ideas of numerous critics and historians, philosophers and poets, who may not always agree methodologically, let alone ideologically. Taking advantage of the historical perspective afforded by undertaking this investigation two decades into a new millennium, this study draws on all findings that aid the construction of its arguments, thriving off past differences without being restricted by them. Recourse to canonical figures and works of canonical or 'high' European culture, and especially works of 'high' modernist literature, in what follows is justified and appropriate, given that late European novels are determined by their narrators' self-understanding of coming after just such a literary tradition. While such notions of 'high' culture and 'high' literature

---

[104] See Hutchinson, *Lateness*, 46.

are much contested in the current intellectual climate and, indeed, are not without their significant historical and geographical biases, they are necessary and relevant to this study's purposes. For better or for worse, they constitute the source of the late and melancholy aesthetic attitude investigated in what follows.

Having already tracked across the territory of the late and the melancholy, it only remains to attempt to navigate the eddying tides of the European. This study is certainly not an attempt to establish a universal or universalizing theory of European literature; it makes no claims that all novels written around the turn of the millennium in Europe necessarily fall into the category of late European fiction. Nevertheless, it does propose that the particular novels by Modiano, Sebald, and Muñoz Molina which it takes as its objects of investigation are indicative of a broader geographically and historically contingent mode of writing in European literature. In his study of conceptualizations of European literature throughout history from Antiquity to the present day, Walter Cohen advocates that, if respect for difference is undoubtedly a positive thing, then recognition of commonality, cultural similarity, and mutual indebtedness among literary works across time and place is just as significant.[105] The three novels examined in this study are brought together with a view to perceiving the aesthetic, stylistic, and thematic resonances among them as an example of an international and intracontinental conversation. Catherine Brown notes that 'ideally, comparatists bring together works which are capable of conducting with each other a conversation, on one or more topics, which is worth overhearing for what the conversation reveals'.[106] Perfect alignment is never necessary for forms of communication to occur, especially across national and linguistic boundaries, yet there is much to be overheard among these novels.

That being said, the investigations undertaken in *Late Europeans and Melancholy Fiction at the Turn of the Millennium* were not intended to arrive at any sort of foregone conclusion. The tensions out of which European fiction emerges remain constant; indeed, their lack of resolution and its ongoing deferral emerge as a crucial defining feature of late and melancholy European novels. While this study has no pretensions

---

[105] See Walter Cohen, *A History of European Literature: From Antiquity to the Present* (Oxford: Oxford University Press, 2017), 503.

[106] Catherine Brown, 'What is Comparative Literature?', in *Comparative Critical Studies*, 10:1 (2013), 67–88 (83).

whatsoever to being either a comprehensive survey or an exhaustive analysis of all European fiction at the turn of the millennium, it is nonetheless an attempt to understand the nature, function, and forms of certain European novels at a particular moment in their long history.[107] 'Bei Untersuchungen dieser Art', Auerbach notes, 'hat man es nicht mit Gesetzen, sondern mit Tendenzen und Strömungen zu tun, die sich auf mannigfache Weise kreuzen und ergänzen'.[108] Given the lack of unanimity within the different national contexts that make up European literature, any notion of a universal theory is not only implausible but goes against the very constitution of the idea of literature which is 'European'. So, while *Late Europeans and Melancholy Fiction at the Turn of the Millennium* does not herald the emergence of a movement of authors or prescribe any particular literary features, it does attempt to illuminate, describe, and analyse *a posteriori* an already existing conversation between novels in different languages. In delineating the salient characteristics of a selection of literary works that have never before been brought together for comparative study, it thereby reveals a new constellation of European novels published at the turn of the millennium. Although literary fiction has long been a medium for interrogating the categories of the nation and the nation state, by exploring the specificities of late European novels in multiple national contexts this study also interrogates the notion of the European. Over the course of its close readings, it extrapolates ways in which certain novels articulate and embody tensions between the national and the European, as well as between a past seen to be overwhelming and the potential promise of future renewal. Late European novels thus emerge as containers of the constitutive tensions of European literature at the turn of the millennium.

When considering what is meant and understood by the term 'European' alongside the significance of national literary traditions, their incommensurability, and their imbrication, it is key to remember that Europe is a

---

[107] Such an approach shares much in common with the Danish comparatist Georg Brandes's view of comparative literature as a telescope that is able to see further by focusing on specific objects. See Sven Erik Larsen, 'Georg Brandes: The Telescope of Comparative Literature' in *The Routledge Companion to World Literature*, ed. by Theo D'haen, David Damrosch, and Djelal Kadir (Oxford: Routledge, 2012), 21–29.

[108] Auerbach, *Mimesis: Dargestellte Wirklichkeit in der abendländischen Wirklichkeit*, 497 'Studies of this kind do not deal with laws but with trends and tendencies, which cross and complement one another in the most varied ways'. Auerbach, *Mimesis: The Representation of Reality in Western Literature*, 556.

constructed idea, as well as an ideal.[109] Rather than conceiving of Europe and European culture as delineated by clearly drawn lines, divisions, or parameters, then, this study adopts an open view of the 'European' as an imagined category which exhibits many variations within commonalities, since there is in any case no single and fixed *a priori* characteristic that signifies intrinsic 'Europeanness'. One's understanding of 'European' literature and culture necessarily informs and also reflects one's understanding of 'Europe' and vice versa. This is an ongoing process subject to historical and geographical locatedness. Bounded by water to the north, west, and south, and roughly delimited by the Urals, the Caucasus, and the Black Sea to the east, the geographical frontiers of and within Europe, not to mention its cultural boundaries, have shifted and changed much and often since Antiquity. Although the exact origins of the continent's name are uncertain, it is nonetheless pertinent to this study's approach to note that the etymology of 'Europe' is sometimes suggested as a compound of the Greek *euros* (wide or broad) and *ops* (eye or face), meaning 'wide-eyed' or 'broad of aspect'.[110] An inherently capacious concept on the one hand, Europe remains on the other hand an historical, political, and cultural entity containing shared and interlinked pasts and concerns among its constitutive nations.[111] Recalling conceptions of Europe as the *Abendland*, the land of the evening, which is also bound up with the classical myth of Europa's abduction by Zeus and their flight westwards over the sea, Hutchinson also considers it unsurprising that the etymology of 'Europe' is sometimes traced to the Greek *erebos*, or to the Semitic *ereb*, meaning darkness or evening.[112] In this etymological aspect, then, as in so many others, Europe is a continent of variety and contradictions, whose cultural, social, political, economic, and religious tensions have conspired

---

[109] See, for example, Aleida Assmann, *Der europäische Traum: Vier Lehren aus der Geschichte* (Munich: C. H. Beck, 2018) and George Steiner, *The Idea of Europe: An Essay* (New York: Overlook Books, 2015). For a reappraisal of the significance of nationhood in contemporary European society, see Aleida Assmann, *Die Wiedererfindung der Nation: Warum wir sie fürchten und warum wir sie brauchen* (Munich: C. H. Beck, 2020).

[110] For an account of this etymology's curious intersections with the myth of Europa, see particularly the third chapter of Charles FitzRoy, *The Rape of Europa: The Intriguing History of Titian's Masterpiece* (London: Bloomsbury, 2015).

[111] See, for example, Perry Anderson's account of Europe's antecedents, and in particular the retrospective connections between Latin Christendom and the modern Enlightenment conceptualization of Europe in Perry Anderson, *The New Old World* (London: Verso, 2009), 475–504, especially 476.

[112] Hutchinson, *Lateness*, 5.

for centuries to tear it apart, even while it has many times moved towards greater unification. As Perry Anderson observes in his account of the history and development of the European Union, however, 'the demarcation of Europe poses one set of questions for the Union, [and] another for the history of ideas'.[113] Cultural understandings and expressions of the 'European' are neither easily nor neatly mapped onto historical and political realities, such that the very idea of 'Europe' throughout history has been one fraught with tensions and conflicts as well as unity. The recent rupture of relations between the United Kingdom and the European Union is but the latest in a long litany of upheavals.

If the emergence of the modern nation state is a fundamentally European phenomenon, then surely the conflicts between these discrete nations—and their national literatures—is likewise intrinsically European.[114] As Pascale Casanova observes, 'one of the few trans-historical features that constitutes Europe, in effect, one of the only forms of both political and cultural unity – one that is paradoxical but genuine – that makes of Europe a coherent whole is none other than the conflicts and competitions that pitted Europe's national literary spaces against one another'.[115] However, rather than conclude, following Casanova, that the only possible literary history of Europe is one which highlights the rivalries, discrepancies, struggles, and power relations between national cultures, this study adopts a more optimistic stance towards the notion of European literature. While the following chapters remain divided along national literary lines for practical purposes, thereby avoiding any interruption of the flow of arguments and carving up each novel's specificities, this study in its entirety draws together diverse cultural traditions within Europe, shedding light on the intersections and points of departure among them. This does not constitute an attempt at a fully 'denationalized' and deconstructive

[113] Anderson, *The New Old World*, 475.

[114] For further discussion of the nation state as an intrinsically and uniquely European phenomenon, see, for example, Miroslav Hroch, *Das Europa der Nationen: Die modern Nationsbildung im europäischen Vergleich*, trans. by Eližka and Ralph Melville (Göttingen: Vandenhoeck & Ruprecht, 2005). For further discussion of this with relation to national literatures, see J. Manuel Barbeito, Jaime Feijóo, Antón Figueroa, and Jorge Sacido (eds., *National Identities and European Literatures / Nationale Identitäten und Europäische Literaturen* (Berlin: Peter Lang, 2008).

[115] Pascale Casanova, 'European Literature: simply a higher degree of universality?', in *Literature for Europe?*, ed. by Theo D'Haen and Iannis Goerlandt (Amsterdam: Rodopi, 2009), 13–25 (13).

examination of the concept of European literature since, for better or for worse, national traditions still define its parameters.[116] Instead, what follows is a piece-by-piece approach that allows for the emergence of national specificities and particularities, building a collage of European literature from the bottom up, so to speak.

Traditionally, the study of European literature has concentrated on a corpus of literary works originating from Europe's geographical purview, broadly defined. Taking as its subjects the canonical authors and works from discrete national literatures, its exegetic focus has remained principally confined to national literary contexts, downplaying the significance of cross-border exchange, as Andrew Hammond notes.[117] In the latter half of the twentieth century, however, there was in Europe an ongoing attempt at 'salvaging a common European matrix from the debris of two world wars', as Roberto Dainotto observes.[118] Resting on a series of commonplaces that echo across the Western literary tradition, the very enterprise of conceptualizing European literature, he argues, constitutes an 'attempt to *invent* a unity in the face of discord'.[119] While this might bring to mind Benedict Anderson's concept of an 'imagined community', the key difference between that concept and the supranational notion of an imagined European literature is the lack of the institutional and infrastructural framework of support that a nation state itself could provide.[120] In place of that, European literature must, without erasing the specificities of its constitutive nations, languages, and literary traditions, be imagined all the more strongly, bringing together national philologies in comparative literary practices.[121]

---

[116] 'Denational' ways of analysing European literature is a hypothetical theoretical approach proposed by Pascale Casanova, which she claims is not yet extant. See Casanova, 'European Literature', 15.

[117] Andrew Hammond, 'Introduction', in *The Novel and Europe: Imagining the Continent in Post-1945 Fiction*, ed. by Andrew Hammond (London: Palgrave Macmillan, 2016), 1–52 (7–10).

[118] Roberto M. Dainotto, 'World Literature and European Literature', in *The Routledge Companion to World Literature*, ed. by Theo D'haen, David Damrosch, and Djelal Kadir (Oxford: Routledge, 2012), 425–434 (430).

[119] See Dainotto, 'World Literature and European Literature', 432. Emphasis added.

[120] For further discussion of the notion of 'imagined communities' and its relation to national contexts, see Benedict Anderson, *Imagined Communities: Reflections on the Origin and Spread of Nationalism* (London: Verso, 1983).

[121] Dainotto rightly points out that while imagined communities on a national scale have long been established and reinforced through the institutionalization of state-sponsored

In his history of European literature, Cohen offers a useful, albeit somewhat laboured, definition of what it means for literary works to be classed as European literature. The dramatic proliferation of vernacular literary languages in the wake of Latin and Greek in the Middle Ages in Europe constitutes, he argues, European literature's defining characteristics: its plurality and its polyglossia. European literature may therefore be defined, he suggests, as 'the literatures of medieval Latin Christendom's self-constitution as such, of their chosen predecessors, of their successors, of those successors' chosen predecessors, of the cultures deeply influenced by those successors, of their chosen predecessors, and so on'.[122] Such a definition's potentially infinite capacity for extension and inclusion is both one of its strengths and one of its weaknesses, as Cohen acknowledges. As writers' chosen predecessors change, and those of their successors, any definition of European literature remains fluid. Cohen advances the argument that, following Jewish modernist literature in the first half of the twentieth century, the expansionist vocation of European literature ends in a pyrrhic contradiction. Since more and more languages become part of a larger, more global literary scene in the contemporary era, the logic of Western expansionism results in the simultaneous fulfilment and abolition of the idea of European literature.[123] It is on the cusp of such potential dissolution that this study concentrates its synoptic purview. Rather than advocate the inexorable obsolescence and flattening out of the category of 'European literature' around the end of the twentieth century in an increasingly globalized world, *Late Europeans and Melancholy Fiction at the Turn of the Millennium* aims to show that this category may yet prove to be hermeneutically useful when considered with reference to specific national literary traditions within Europe, as well as to the literary heritages explicitly and implicitly

departments, as well as national curricula, school books, and prizes, lamentably 'nothing comparable has ever happened in the case of the European Community. For the recent Union, literature has remained largely marginal if not ignored'. See Dainotto, 'World Literature and European Literature', 433.

[122] Cohen, *A History of European Literature*, 114.

[123] This is a clear inversion of Auerbach's heralding the simultaneous realization and destruction of the concept *Weltliteratur* through mass standardization (see Erich Auerbach, *Die Philologie der Weltliteratur*, in *Weltliteratur: Festgabe für Fritz Strich zum 70. Geburtstag*, ed. by Walter Muschg and E. Staiger (Bern: Francke, 1952), pp. 39–50). It should be made clear, however, that this study stops short of endorsing Cohen's assertion that, in the case of contemporary literature, 'if prose fiction from around the world now draws centrally on Western forms, and especially on the novel, why not see all of it as Western literature?' See Cohen, *A History of European Literature*, 6.

drawn on in particular novels. Of helpful significance for the present study is the implication in Cohen's definition that any understanding of what European literature might mean at a particular moment in time, and which particular works of literature might be understood as European, is predicated upon the contingencies of a work's 'chosen predecessors' and its implied literary lineage, those works and writers that are both explicit and implicit influences on new literary works. Motifs of European culture and history explored in this study, it must be emphasized, are not understood as the sole preserves of Europe. Indeed, the aesthetic elements of lateness and melancholy examined in the following chapters are certainly not phenomena to be associated exclusively with, or understood as constitutive solely of, a presumed European cultural identity. Nonetheless, their mutual articulation at a particular moment in time in the French, German, and Spanish novels examined here is the deciding factor in their being grouped together as objects of study. The comparative research that follows reveals more insights into the composition and inner workings of the greater imagined whole of European literature, of which the national literatures and languages examined here are seen as but a part. Even then, this study is only one version of events, since, as Theo D'Haen observes, 'there can be no such thing as "a" European literary history'.[124] While this study does not consider French, German, and Spanish culture to be synecdoches either of one homogenous European culture or of other national cultures within Europe—neither *pars pro toto* nor *tota pro partibus*—it does intend to make a contribution towards enriching the understanding of what it means to talk of 'European literature'.

As late modernist works of melancholy fiction, it is in many ways appropriate that Jewishness and secular Jewish cultural achievements are significant to all three novels, not only because of Modiano self-identification as Jewish, Sebald's philosemitic affinities, and Muñoz Molina's sustained interest in the biographies of Jewish historical figures across the centuries. The connections between Jewishness and Europeanness bind together the articulations of late European melancholy in the three novels that this book examines.[125] In spite of their evident intimacies, however, the

---

[124] Theo D'Haen, 'Introduction', in *Literature for Europe?*, 5–9 (8).

[125] As Weller acknowledges, 'the very epitome of Nietzsche's good European would seem, then, to have been western European Jews, at least as he conceived then. And yet, at the same time, Nietzsche undercuts this conclusion by arguing that these very same Jews sought above all to be "absorbed and assimilated into Europe".' This would suggest that, from a

confluence of Jewishness and modernist literature has received surprisingly little in the way of scholarly interest until recently. Cohen argues that 'the period between the turn of the century and the beginning of World War II witnesses a remarkable and rather sudden rise to literary prominence of things Jewish and especially of writers of Jewish descent', and this is indeed most evidently the case in prose fiction.[126] Framing his analysis within various contexts, including the Jewish heritage of persecution and vulnerability, the Jewish cultural ideal of learning and literacy, the perceived advantages of secularization for a frequently oppressed minority, and the earlier historical shift in European languages and literatures towards the vernacular, Cohen establishes the conditions of emergence of Jewish modernist literature in the early twentieth century, ultimately concluding that 'Jewishness proves the single most important demographic component of modernist fiction'.[127] If the figure of the Jew was at that time for many Western societies the representative of modernity and the modernist movement, then this fact also goes some way to explaining the relative lack of attention paid to the significance of Jewishness to modernism. As a community of innovative, insecure, questioning exiles, Jewish migrants in Europe, mistrustful of claims of superiority and authority, were much resented, in spite of the massive and consequential contribution they made to cultural and intellectual history.[128] Shortly after the turn of the century, Henry James, for example, upon returning to visit his native New York after a long absence as an immigrant in Europe, famously (and, it seems, unironically) wrote in his travel account *The American Scene* (1907) that the influence of immigrants of Jewish background and their Yiddish language on English was an 'impudence', assuming the inferiority of Jewish writers and intellectuals to be a given fact.[129] Later, the literary critic and

Nietzschean perspective, European Jewry constitutes both the fulfilment and the abandonment of a European ideal. See Weller, *The Idea of Europe*, p. 126.

[126] Cohen, *A History of European Literature*, 406.

[127] Cohen, *A History of European Literature*, 406.

[128] See Chad Alan Goldberg, *Modernity and the Jews in Western Social Thought* (Chicago: University of Chicago Press, 2017) and Scott Spector, *Modernism without Jews? German-Jewish Subjects and Histories* (Bloomington: Indiana University Press, 2017). For another perspective on the decline of and turn towards conservatism in Jewish after 1945, following the flourishing between the age of Enlightenment and the Second World War of the intellectual, literary, scientific, and artistic legacy of Jewish modernity, see Enzo Traverso, *The End of Jewish Modernity?* (London: Pluto Press, 2013).

[129] Cited in Jonathan Morse, 'English Literature of the Twentieth Century', in *Antisemitism: A Historical Encyclopedia of Prejudice and Persecution: Volume 1: A–K*, ed. by

travel writer Rebecca West would observe in *Black Lamb and Grey Falcon* (1941) further instances of resentment of the Jewish people as the embodiment of the modern in the Balkans, for example, just prior to the outbreak of the Second World War. 'Many primitive peoples', she recalls her husband Henry Maxwell Andrews mentioning, in reference to local nationalists, 'must receive their first intimation of the toxic quality of thought from Jews. They know only the fortifying idea of religion, and they see in the Jews the effects of the tormenting and disintegrating idea of scepticism'.[130] The Jewish people are thereby categorized as disturbers of the *status quo* and harbingers of uncertainty and change, with Sigmund Freud, Albert Einstein, and Karl Marx being prominent among many examples of Jewish intellectuals who respectively exploded long held assumptions about the human mind, the cosmos, and society. Antisemitism thus emerges in European and Western literature and culture during the period of modernity as a reaction against the embodiment of modernity by the Jewish people and subsequently as a deciding factor in the neglect of Jewishness in accounts of the development of modernism.

Late European novels encapsulate the European Jewish tensions among cultural difference and national assimilation, the persistent history of antisemitism and twentieth-century genocide. The year 1940, a traditional endpoint for 'high' modernism, takes on a grim and elegiac significance for Jewish modernist literature, as Cohen notes, given that the genocide of the Shoah placed the 'Jewish question' in a new and extreme light. Self-evidently, it also drastically reduced the number of Jewish people in Europe. The significance, however, of Jewish modernist literature lies not in the Holocaust and its aftereffects *per se*. Rather, Jewishness's centrality to modernism 'occurs simply at the moment when Jews become central to European cultural, social, and political life more generally', as Cohen notes.[131] Crucially, he argues, it is not so much the ubiquity of Jewish contributions across many areas of European life and culture that is of the greatest relevance, so much as the fact that—in the case of the novel in particular—this was the first time such contributions were made. Nevertheless, Cohen is mindful both of the question of his historical position looking back on these figures and of the significance of questions of

Richard S. Levy (Santa Barbara, California: ABC-CLIO, 2005), 206–209 (208).

[130] Rebecca West, *Black Lamb and Grey Falcon: A Journey through Yugoslavia* (London: Penguin, 1941).

[131] Cohen, *A History of European Literature*, 412.

national identity to his arguments.[132] 'The potential problem in this remarkably impressive body of writing', he notes, 'is the possibility that the long historical view will fail to do justice to more proximate patterns, particularly if those patterns do not seem to confirm the larger model'.[133] This larger model is what Cohen refers to as 'the teleological distortion involved in looking back through the age of Auschwitz' which 'makes it difficult not to read the culture of early twentieth-century Europe as a prelude to genocide'.[134] In precisely their look back, late European novels constitute an attempt to address the unprecedented Jewish contributions to national cultures within Europe and the notion of European culture more broadly, foregrounding the legacy of this cultural history and attempts to erase it.

Almost without exception, debates around literature written after the Holocaust take as their starting point Adorno's often selectively misquoted denunciation of writing poetry after Auschwitz as barbaric.[135] However, as Gert Hofmann, Marko Pajevic, Rachel MagShamhráin, and Michael Shields emphasize, Adorno would later develop his position in 1962 to argue that, rather than being condemned outright as barbarians, 'die authentischen Künstler der Gegenwart sind die, in deren Werken das äußerste Grauen nachzittert'.[136] Ultimately, the Adornian view does not imply that the Holocaust should remain the epicentre of art, or that it should overwhelm either the art or criticism of it, but rather that it resonates throughout and under the surface of great literary works. While aware of the Holocaust's

---

[132] While Cohen acknowledges 'the ease with which Jewish high culture could be taken for German high culture', he clarifies that 'the roots of Jewish modernism lie in European, rather than specifically German culture', although, of course, German culture and philosophy do play a not insignificant role in the formation of an idea of European culture. See Cohen, *A History of European Literature*, 408 and 410.

[133] Cohen, *A History of European Literature*, 407.

[134] Cohen, *A History of European Literature*, 407.

[135] Written in 1949 and first published in 1951, the original quotation reads: 'Nach Auschwitz ein Gedicht zu schreiben, ist barbarisch'. See Theodor W. Adorno, 'Kulturkritik und Gesellschaft', in *Gesammelte Schriften*, 10.1, ed. by Rolf Tiedemann (Frankfurt am Main: Suhrkamp, 1977), 11–30 (30).

[136] Theodor W. Adorno, 'Jene zwanziger Jahre', in *Gesammelte Schriften*, 10.2, ed. by Rolf Tiedemann (Frankfurt am Main: Suhrkamp, 1977), 499–506 (506). 'The true artists of today are the ones in whose work absolute horror still quakes'. Cited in Gert Hofmann, Marko Pajevic, Rachel MagShamhráin, and Michael Shields, 'Introduction', in Gert Hofmann, Marko Pajevic, Rachel MagShamhráin, and Michael Shields, eds., *German and European Poetics After the Holocaust: Crisis and Creativity* (Rochester, New York: Camden House, 2011), 1–15 (4).

centrality to the thematics of each of the novels it examines, the present study concerns itself primarily with their stylistic and aesthetic aspects, finding them to be more fruitful lines of enquiry to the study of comparative literature. An intense focus on memory, testimony, ethics, and politics during the past two decades has somewhat obscured significant aesthetic and poetic aspects of literature written in response to the events of the twentieth century in Europe in favour of prioritizing the centrality of the Holocaust and memory of it in literary criticism.[137] Today, the Holocaust has 'gone global', as Aleida Assmann suggests, as the paradigm for framing and understanding historical and current traumatic events and artistic works that engage with them.[138] However, Sebald himself, for example, is reported to have commented in relation to Holocaust fiction that 'it's a dreadful idea that you can have a sub-genre and make a speciality out of it; it's grotesque'.[139] This study accordingly acknowledges the significance of the Holocaust for all three novels it examines yet distances itself from conceiving of them as solely, or even principally, works of Holocaust fiction. Instead, they are approached as works that confront the aforementioned 'meta-problem' of European modernity, in which the horror of the Holocaust still quakes, while the critical purview of each chapter is restricted primarily to the examination of the aesthetic and stylistic forms this engenders in particular contexts at a particular moment in time. Writing in the wake of twentieth-century atrocities, Modiano, Sebald, and Muñoz Molina are in any case something more akin to post-Holocaust writers, exploring questions of posterity rather than direct experience. That *Dora Bruder*, *Austerlitz*, and *Sefarad* engage with the past through the thematic framework of the Holocaust and that the narrative strategies they employ to confront the past clearly position these novels within a European literary and cultural tradition, initially invite reading them alongside one another,

---

[137] See, for example, Robert Eaglestone, *The Holocaust and the Postmodern* (Oxford: Oxford University Press, 2004); Michael Rothberg, *Multidirectional Memory: Remembering the Holocaust in the Age of Decolonization* (Stanford: Stanford University Press, 2009); Richard Crownshaw, *The Afterlives of Holocaust Memory in Contemporary Literature and Culture* (Basingstoke: Palgrave Macmillan, 2010); and Robert Eaglestone, *The Broken Voice: Reading Post-Holocaust Literature* (Oxford: Oxford University Press, 2017).

[138] Aleida Assmann, 'The Holocaust – a Global Memory? Extensions and Limits of a New Memory Community', in *Memory in a Global Age: Discourses, Practices and Trajectories, ed. by* Aleida Assmann and Sebastian Conrad (Basingstoke: Palgrave Macmillan, 2010), 97–117 (114).

[139] Maya Jaggi, 'Recovered Memories', in *The Guardian*, 22 September 2001. See www.theguardian.com/books/2001/sep/22/artsandhumanities.highereducation

although their points of connection go beyond thematics. The chapters that follow therefore focus less on the thematic content of the novels and, by extension, the ethical or political implications of this with regard to remembering the past. Rather, this study turns its gaze to the ways in which the novels are written, how they resonate stylistically and aesthetically with one another, and the points of commonality and tension that emerge from such a comparative reading.

Dora Bruder, *Austerlitz*, and *Sefarad*—and also the present study itself—collectively encapsulate an attempt to salvage something meaningful from what appears to be an increasingly obsolescent European tradition and perspective in the hope that it may offer a form of redemption, enhancement, or re-enchantment, along with better orientation and insight. Nevertheless, the question remains as to how comparative research on European literature might engage with the epistemic privilege of European culture and its legacy without replicating and endorsing its biases. In attempting to do just that, this study asserts that a form of literary criticism that acknowledges its troubled legacy is still more worthwhile than either the pretence of ignorance through abstraction or outright condemnation and repudiation. The work of identifying the pathologies of a culture has to be transformed into the more lasting, more compromising, and more patient work of reclaiming it from them. Too often in contemporary criticism the dominant mode of analysis seems to hold that the only serious and intellectually valid pursuit—and, indeed, the only way to interpret works of art or literature correctly—is to articulate the ways in which something is irretrievably deficient. This is not the kind of work this study sets out to do.[140] Although the present study is Euro*centred* by its very nature, it is not intended to be Euro*centric*: it is internal to the history of European ideas, culture, and history, but it does not claim the superiority

---

[140] See, for example, Paul Ricoeur on the 'hermeneutics of suspicion', which attempts to decode hidden meanings in texts as a form of ideological critique, as opposed to 'hermeneutics of faith', which aims to restore meaning, in Paul Ricoeur, *Freud and Philosophy: An Essay on Interpretation* (New Haven: Yale University Press, 1970), 28–36. See also Rita Felski, 'Critique and the Hermeneutics of Suspicion', in *M/C – A Journal of Music and Culture*, 15:1 (2012), www.journal.media-culture.org.au/index.php/mcjournal/article/view/431. For suggested alternatives to such a hermeneutics of suspicion, see, for example, Eve Kosofsky Sedgwick, 'Paranoid Reading and Reparative Reading, Or, You're So Paranoid, You Probably Think This Essay is About You', in *Touching Feeling: Affect, Pedagogy, Performativity* (Durham, North Carolina: Duke University Press, 2003), 123–152, and Timothy Bewes, 'Reading with the Grain: A New World in Literary Studies', in *Differences*, 21:3 (2010), 1–33.

of this culture or attempt to assert its authority or superiority over others. Nor is this study concerned with evaluations of any potentially compromised ethics of European culture. Rather, it constitutes a way of reading that allows for the coexistence of both critique and tradition. A pessimistic view of late European novels would determine them as reliant on aesthetic modes that contradict any collective potential and tarnish the future with the past. A more positive, more optimistic reading, however, would understand them as novels which make use of privileged structures, conventions, and history as a means of representing this and reflecting on it, looking not only to the past but also to the future. Such a reading does the harder work of recognizing the troubled legacy of European literature, and of the concept of Europe itself, without throwing out the proverbial baby along with the sullied bathwater.

If, as Edward Said notes, 'the European novel is grounded in [...] a changing society [...] seek[ing] to construct a new world that somewhat resembles an old one left behind',[141] then the recuperation of forms of writing deemed to be damaged or diminished may constitute a means of resisting the fading of the future in Europe that Aleida Assmann, among many others, has described.[142] This is especially relevant given the sense of the obsolescence of European perspectives described in this study during a time of increased globalization, transnational study, and the re-emergence of debates and theories concerning the notion of a 'world literature', which are as ubiquitous as they are multivalent. These debates and approaches, furthermore, evince a tendency to use the term European as a pejorative shorthand for Western colonialism and elite structures of power, engaging in often oblique readings of literary works in search of hidden imperialist impulses. It cannot be denied that the aesthetic attitude of the novels examined in the present study does draw on a European literary tradition and a legacy of 'high' culture that inevitably brings with it problems of the European canon and broader connotations of Western cultural privilege. Indeed, the present study's exegetic focus on white male writers arguably does little to dispel this, although it is certainly the case that the reductive narrative of dismissing literary figures as simply pale, male, and stale—which is to say, the cliché of the dead white men—belies these writers' and others' significant biographical identities, subjective experiences, and

---

[141] Edward Said, 'Reflections on Exile', in *Reflections of Exile and Other Essays* (Cambridge, Massachusetts: Harvard University Press, 2000), 173–186 (181).
[142] Aleida Assmann, *Ist die Zeit aus den Fugen?* (Munich: Carl Hanser, 2013), 13.

artistic achievements. Caution must be taken also not to set up European culture simply as an obsolete straw man; any object of critique ought always to be taken at its strongest. Great artistic and literary works of European culture undoubtedly exist within an historical continuum of colonial expansion, oppression, and domination. And yet, they also represent a triumph of innovation and ingenuity on the part of those who strove to create them. Even Dipesh Chakrabarty's work on provincializing Europe concludes that such a process of provincialization cannot be 'a project of shunning European thought', which 'is a gift to us all'.[143] A critical perspective on the expansionist vocation of the West—and of its *modus operandi*—is essential, but it would nevertheless be a mistake to regard everything produced by Western European civilization and culture since the late fifteenth century as nothing other than a sustained series of acts of violence. This entails a form of essentialist thinking grounded in the conviction that Western European culture is—and always has been—fundamentally compromised and that if it is doing anything, then it is, by definition, impossible for this to be good. However, as Cohen notes, 'it does not follow that tradition is necessarily regressive, rupture automatically progressive', especially since 'virtually any text is a compound of tradition and innovation'.[144] All forms of art have power structures, and may even disguise barbarity, as Benjamin suggests when he argues in his oft-cited aphorism that 'es ist niemals ein Dokument der Kultur, ohne zugleich ein solches der Barbarei zu sein'.[145] Yet, if this is the case for all acts of writing, then barbaric history can be acknowledged and understood in literary works—and scholarship on them—without automatically entailing the outright branding of the entangled cultural traditions out of which these works emerge as bogus or invalid. Nor does this mean that such works only have a relevance and a reality that is social and political. Works of literature also have an existential and aesthetic reality, which exists in a quasi-sacred relation to their own cultural histories. Deconstructing the canon, and being suspicious of it, is an invaluable pursuit, especially when it elicits an understanding of how the canon and certain literary traditions were constructed and curated in a particular way to push, explicitly or implicitly, certain agendas and ideas. However, this

---

[143] Dipesh Chakrabarty, *Provincializing Europe: Postcolonial Thought and Historical Difference* (Princeton: Princeton University Press, 2007), 255.

[144] Cohen, *A History of European Literature*, 10.

[145] Walter Benjamin, 'Über den Begriff der Geschichte', 696. 'There is no document of culture which is not at the same time a document of barbarism'.

cultural tradition, this established canon, may be added to and extended, without claiming that it and later works that draw on it are of no inherent worth or fundamentally compromised. It is hard—and ultimately misguided—to imagine such aesthetically meaningful and culturally significant works as ineluctably oppressive.

All people—fictional narrators and characters included—are political subjects in history and no human action can be entirely apolitical. However, the problem with the question of whether all works of art are political— and, by extension, whether all acts of writing are political—is the presupposition that the political precedes the creative act of imagination. This study holds that, to the extent that it is a category of art, the novel can never be entirely reducible to a container of ethical or political messages. While it is never possible ever to separate novels fully from the world or from the societies and histories out of which they emerge, they also have a fundamentally irreducible surplus element that exists outside of or beyond the realms of the purely political or ethical. Accordingly, while the thematic content and time of writing of these novels do still play a role in the analysis that follows, this study's intervention constitutes more of an aesthetic investigation, focusing not solely on what is written but also on how. It does not concern itself with evaluating the ethical and moral virtues and failings of the narratives in question, partly since these novels do not attempt to create a mimetic reconstruction of the past, but rather exist as self-reflexive, self-consciously mediated engagements with history. Such an overly evaluative reading of these novels' ethics and morals would also entail understanding them as more than constructed works of fiction, which they so manifestly are. For this reason, the present study also does not engage in speculation about the authors' personal or psychological motivations in writing these novels, preferring instead to focus on the narrator figures of these works of fiction.

Late Europeans and Melancholy Fiction at the Turn of the Millennium focuses on works of fiction from a range of national traditions in order to emphasize their particularly Western dimension as it develops diachronically and operates synchronically in each text. Within European literature the nation is a foundational element and accordingly a comparative project in this field benefits greatly from studying European literature on its own terms. The problems of a nationally oriented approach to literature must not go unacknowledged, however: the erasure of multiple languages and ethnicities within literary cultures, on the one hand, and the implication that languages and cultures move ever forward and unchanging through historical periods, on the other. Nevertheless, the gains afforded by the form of comparative work this study undertakes, which would always be dogged by such questions of cultural difference, far outweigh the limitations of a narrower focus and extreme specialization. The comparative and international focus of this study allows for an approach that crosses cultures, languages, and traditions. This illuminates the similarities and the tensions between notions of the national and the European that are, in spite of its historical use as a shorthand for nationalism, perhaps best encapsulated by Johann Gottfried Herder's concept of the *Volksgeist*, along with his insistence on the protean and contingent nature of literature. Herder's observation that literature 'verwandelt ihre Gestalt nach Sprache, Sitten, Gewohnheiten' understands the people—the *Volk*—in terms of the nation state.[146] However, he is also keen to point out that changes and developments in literature occur not just within nations, but among different nations also. European literature is, after all, an international phenomenon, emerging in the interaction of national literatures. 'The nation state', as Moretti observes, 'found the novel. And vice versa: the novel found the nation-state. And being the only symbolic form that could represent it, it became an essential component of our modern culture'.[147] The national is not at odds with the ideas of the European; they are intimately connected. In a European context, as Kwame Anthony Appiah neatly puts it, 'literature and nationalism were born twins'.[148] Literature thus emerges and takes shape within cartography. If Herder, in championing the notion of the *Volksgeist*, nonetheless saw European expansionism as an immoral catastrophe, his broader concept of *Humanität* also emerges out of this theorization of the nation.[149] For Herder, then, nations and national traditions offer a non-aggressive framework for particularities to be thought through within

[146] Johann Gottfried Herder, 'Resultat der Vergleichung der Poesie verschiedener Völker alter und neuer Zeit', in *Sämmtliche Werke 18*, ed. by Bernhard Suphan (Berlin: Weibmannsche Buchhandlung, 1883), 134–140 (134). 'Changes form according to the people's language, customs, habits'. Johann Gottfried Herder, 'Results of a Comparison of Different People's Poetry in Ancient and Modern Times (1797)', trans. by Jan Kueveler, in *The Princeton Sourcebook in Comparative Literature: From the European Enlightenment to the Global Present*, ed. by David Damrosch, Natalie Melas, and Mbongiseni Buthelezi (Princeton: Princeton University Press, 2009), 3–9 (3).

[147] Franco Moretti, *Atlas of the European Novel: 1800–1900* (London: Verso, 1997), 17.

[148] Kwame Anthony Appiah, 'Boundaries of Culture', in *PMLA*, 132:3 (2017), 513–525 (514).

[149] See also Hans Adler, 'Herder's Concept of *Humanität*', in *A Companion to the Works of Johann Gottfried Herder*, ed. by Hans Adler and Wulf Koepke (Rochester, New York:

a broader collective. As James Hodkinson observes, philosophical and academic thinking of all-inclusive models of *Humanität* such as Herder's were historically also caught up in evolving discussions of nationhood.[150] Parallels between the self-conscious stylization of the 'good European' and the self-consciously late and melancholy *rôle* assumed by the narrators of the novels examined in this study may accordingly help navigate the tricky waters between restrictive *Nationalität* and nebulous *Humanität*. Nevertheless, the interplay between the two is, in this study's view, liberating, as opposed to restrictive, allowing new imaginative space to open up within and among literary works, such that they might be appreciated anew and afresh. Novels such as those examined here, as well as this study's approach, highlight the contingency of such constructed categories as nationality and tradition, even while acknowledging their significance to particular writers and their works.

Adhering to the view that research in comparative literature is best achieved through engagement with works in their original language, this study pays close attention to the formal properties of French, German, and Spanish as employed in the three novels it examines. This close reading provides key insights into the aesthetic and stylistic formulations of works of literature that may be missed in translation. The focus on working with texts in the original language is also in keeping with this study's contention that late European novels emerge in discrete national traditions and contexts around a particular point in time; the only way to test this hypothesis is to engage directly with these traditions and these languages. Wherever possible, this goes for works of secondary as well as primary literature. It may be a vain fantasy to imagine that anyone might have unfettered or privileged access to a piece of writing in its original language, since every act of reading itself arguably constitutes an act of translation, as Steiner, channelling W. H. Auden, asserts.[151] Nonetheless,

Camden House, 2009), 93–116, and Alan Patten, '"The Most Natural State": Herder and Nationalism', in *History of Political Thought*, 31:4 (2010), 657–689.

[150] See James Hodkinson, 'Impersonating an Ideal? Islam, Orientalism and Cosmopolitanism in Political, Academic and Popular Literary Discourses of *Fin-de-siècle* Germany', in *Comparative Critical Studies*, 10:2 (2013), 283–302 (283).

[151] See George Steiner, *After Babel: Aspects of Language and Translation* (Oxford: Oxford University Press, 1975), 28: 'When we read or hear any language statement from the past, be it Leviticus or last year's best-seller, we translate'. For further discussion of this, see Matthew Reynolds, *The Poetry of Translation: From Chaucer & Petrarch to Homer & Logue* (Oxford: Oxford University Press, 2011), 9–11. Steiner's remark echoes W. H. Auden's sentiment that 'To read is to translate, for no two persons' experiences are the same'. See

this study takes the view that working with literary and scholarly sources in their original language might offer a more compound and more meaningful context, as well as closer access to the literary and artistic truths contained within a given text. 'An informed, avid awareness of the history of the relevant language, of the transforming energies of feeling which make of syntax a record of social being, is indispensable', Steiner declares; 'one must master the temporal and local setting of one's text, the moorings which attach even the most idiosyncratic of poetic expressions to the surrounding idiom'.[152] Besides the English in which it is written, the present study limits itself to novels and works of criticism in French, German, and Spanish for the simple reason that these are the languages and literary traditions with which its author is most familiar. Other languages and national contexts may have been considered, should this study have aimed to produce a more comprehensive survey of European literature, but since access to these texts would have been limited either by more rudimentary language skills, by access through translations, or by greater unfamiliarity with other fields of study, any readings of them would have appeared somewhat conditioned or disingenuous in comparison with the other chapters offered here. If this study succeeds in staking a claim within certain linguistic limitations, it will be for others to map the territory beyond its borders.

The force of this study's comparative work necessarily lies in its being a unitary whole. If, however, there remains a tendency over the course of the following chapters to adopt a more tentative tone in place of an authoritative form of absolutist theoretical universalism, then this is not least because the idea of Europe—and of European culture especially—is nothing if not imagined. In place of any empirically provable and universally applicable theory, this study gestures towards an allusive trend or tendency within the cultural imaginary of Europe. Theoretical discourse, for all its febrile urgency, can threaten to suffocate writers and their texts, and so discussions that move away from the literary text must be reconciled with the invaluable work of close reading. While formal institutional spaces such as universities, literary canons, and today's world book market, along with authors' and critics' political and ideological perspectives, may influence literary tastes and practices, caution is needed with theoretical

W. H. Auden, 'Prologue: Reading', in *The Dyer's Hand and Other Essays* (London: Faber, 1948), 3–12 (3).
[152] Steiner, *After Babel*, 25.

models and approaches that rely solely on these to interpret the dynamics of literary works. Much contemporary scholarship evinces a tendency towards reductively extrapolating heavily theorized excursus from literary texts at the expense of their artistry. This results in a discussion of authors and their works as a form of highly abstracted philosophy instead of finely constructed literary works written at a particular time and in a particular place. Attention must still be paid to the specificities of individual literary constellations in their particular historical and geographical contexts.

This study adopts the view that historical circumstances on a macro scale are at least in part the cause or origin of the particular individual works of literature examined here on the micro scale. Yet these novels are not merely acts of mimetic representation. They are also creative, suggestive, and imaginative works. In moving away from a form of literary criticism that addresses texts merely as epiphenomena of Western European expansionism, then, this study not only offers new readings of some of the most culturally significant works of European fiction published around the turn of the millennium but also provides a fresh perspective on what it sees as a collective of literary works whose responses to European cultural lateness and melancholy form the negative preconditions for an optimistic sense of futurity which resists the obsolescence of the idea of European culture, suggesting that forms of aesthetic and artistic value may yet be salvaged from it. This, however, inevitably raises questions of causality, as well as of the intentionality of the novels examined here ultimately to express this. To an extent the performativity of a self-consciously late and melancholy aesthetic attitude in these novels creates its potentiality out of itself, insofar as it enacts its own concerns with the possibilities, as well as the limitations, of aesthetic representation.[153] Its manner conveys its meaning. If literary works may be understood not only as products of historical change, but also as agents of change, then the present study offers itself as a meeting point for these phenomena, revealing meaningful ways in which they map onto the past, but also how they gesture towards European literature's vestigial potential for future change and renewal.

---

[153] The term performativity is understood here following John L. Austin's original definition, which holds that the act of communication enables and entails the consummation of an action. In Austin's own words: 'to utter the sentence (in, of course, the appropriate circumstances) is not to *describe* my doing of what I should be said in so uttering to be doing or to state that I am doing it: it is to do it'. See J. L. Austin, *How to Do Things with Words* (Oxford: Oxford University Press, 1962), 6. Emphasis in original.

Although her work is generally more concerned with philosophy and ethics than with literary criticism, Hannah Arendt—herself an influential figure in Kermode's situating *The Sense of Ending* as a contribution towards a broader anti-totalitarian project—provides a helpful illustration of this sense of literary futurity.[154] According to Arendt, it is 'the revelatory character of action as well as the ability to produce stories and become historical, which together form the very source from which meaningfulness springs into and illuminates human existence'.[155] Her later German rendition of this text is of a slightly different tenor, however, as is often the case with the translations Arendt produced of her own work.[156] She writes of how 'die Enthüllung der Person auf der einen Seite und das Hervorbringen von Geschichten auf der anderen' together constitute 'die Quelle [...], aus der sich in der Menschenwelt selbst ein Sinn formiert, der dann wiederum als Sinnhaftigkeit das menschliche Treiben zu erhellen und zu erleuchten vermag'.[157] To the extent that the verb 'hervorbringen' denotes the act of bringing forth into being, of creating something out of nothing, it also connotes bringing something to the fore, implying a past lineage to that which is brought forward from a place where it already exists. The nuances of Arendt's German formulation thus suggest that the act of writing may also involve reworking stories that have gone before, not simply creating something from nothing, but bringing that which is already there to the fore in a new form. Coupled with the self-conscious personal revelation and understanding that Arendt describes, this evaluation of the emergence of meaningfulness resonates closely with this study's line of argument. Drawing on and responding to artistic works that precede them, the novels examined here express the potential to imagine new future potentialities out of backwards-facing melancholy lateness, constructing new categories to make sense of human experience in literature in a meaningful way.

Hovering between a critical investigation of European writing and a residual endorsement of certain novels' late and melancholy sensibility, *Late Europeans and Melancholy Fiction at the Turn of the Millennium*

---

[154] See Kermode, *The Sense of an Ending*, 56.

[155] Hannah Arendt, *The Human Condition* (London: University of Chicago Press, 1958), 234.

[156] See Marie Luise Knott, *Verlernen: Denkwege bei Hannah Arendt* (Berlin: Matthes & Seiz, 2011).

[157] Hannah Arendt, *Vita Activa oder Vom tätingen Leben* (Munich: Piper, 1958), 316–317.

highlights the significance of the different historical temporalities involved in such aesthetics and their critique. Perhaps inevitably, this raises further questions. Is the emergence of late European novels at the turn of the millennium simply another iteration of an endless sense of ending, or does it mark an ultimate end for European literature, a point of no return? Does it indicate an end to European literature as a viable hermeneutic and critical category? Are these late Europeans also in some way the last? Is, moreover, an implicitly non-late, non-melancholy futurity still possible and, if so, what forms might it assume? Is there time for something new, or is it too late? And will its temporality be as it was in the twentieth century? Can there ever be such an absolute break with the past and an immediate realization of a new historical beginning in European literature? While answers to these questions might prove just as elusive as any *finis* or *telos* of European literature's sustained 'sense of ending', this study hopes to provide a foundation upon which they might be imagined. In unexpected defiance of the millennial moment's sense of historical and cultural exhaustion and obsolescence in European culture, the late Europeans and their melancholy fiction that are the focus of the following chapters collectively constitute a defence of the power of literary works not only to react to the world and history, but also to suggest an unextinguished potential of recasting it.

CHAPTER 2

Detecting Lateness in *Dora Bruder* by Patrick Modiano

Midway through *Dora Bruder*, the narrator recalls how, as a younger man, he came across some antisemitic literature from the 1940s, which inadvertently inspired him to write his first novel. Looking back to the writing he subsequently produced, the narrator reflects on his ambitions:

> je voulais dans mon premier livre répondre à tous ces gens dont les insultes m'avaient blesse à cause de mon père. Et, sur le terrain de la prose française, leur river une fois pour toutes leur clou. Je sens bien aujourd'hui la naïveté enfantine de mon projet: la plupart de ces auteurs avaient disparu, fusillés, exilés, gâteux ou morts de vieillesse. Oui, malheuresement je venais trop tard. (*DB*, 71)[1]

While this statement might initially appear to be merely an innocuous expression of regret as the narrator focuses on his intense desire to react against fascist writers and considers himself to have been somewhat naïve in his hopes of confronting these supporters of the National Socialist regime, his remark also offers an intriguing point of departure for reading *Dora Bruder*. It demonstrates a clear awareness on the part of the narrator

---

[1] 'I wanted my first book to be a riposte to all those who, by insulting my father, had wounded me; to silence them once and for all on the field of French prose. I can see now that my plan was childishly naïve: most of the authors were gone, executed by firing squad, exiled, senile or dead of old age. Yes, alas, I was too late.' (*DB*, 65).

© The Author(s), under exclusive license to Springer Nature Switzerland AG 2022
I. Ellison, *Late Europeans and Melancholy Fiction at the Turn of the Millennium*, Palgrave Studies in Modern European Literature, https://doi.org/10.1007/978-3-030-95447-5_2

of the late historical position from which he is writing, as well as of the national literary tradition in which he sees himself. Looking back on events and figures from the past, he is aware of himself as a latecomer and of the ways in which his engagement with history is contingent on this lateness: he is both determined by and distanced from the past that is the focus of his narrative. Crucially, moreover, it is on the field of French literature where his engagement with authors and literary works of the past will take place.

Dora Bruder is by no means Modiano's first book; it is his twentieth. Like much of his œuvre it concerns a fraught search for vanished persons, relentless sifting through evidentiary documentation, and an at times almost obsessive retrospection. A prolific author, Modiano has to date penned over thirty novels tackling themes of identity and loss. In 2014, he became the eleventh French writer to win the Nobel Prize in Literature for what the Swedish Academy described as 'the art of memory with which he has evoked the most ungraspable human destinies and uncovered the life-world of the Occupation'.[2] His work returns again and again to the city of Paris and the Nazi Occupation of France, exploring the veracity of memories, their maintenance, and their potential recovery when they have been, or appear to have been, forgotten. Frequent authoritarian violence (such as that of the police during the Occupation of France by National Socialist forces during the Second World War), conflicts between parents and children, and meandering searches for a clearer sense of identity against all odds are common thematic features of Modiano's work. His narrators unearth names, dates, and other documentary evidence pertaining to vanished individuals and his plots frequently turn on events that occurred during the Occupation. Over the course of his novels—in particular those known as his 'Modianos', the slim volumes published between the mid-1970s and the present, which feature amnesiac narrators or protagonists in a noirish setting—history is excavated in lyrical, elegiac prose. Of his many works, *Dora Bruder* is often seen to be the apotheosis.[3]

Although the events of the novel are not narrated chronologically, but rather assembled piecemeal and intercut with other reflections, *Dora Bruder* primarily concerns its narrator's recollections of his investigation

---

[2] See https://www.nobelprize.org/prizes/literature/2014/summary/

[3] See Richard J. Golsan and Lynn A. Higgins, 'Introduction: Patrick Modiano's Dora Bruder', *Studies in 20th and 21st Century Literature*, 31:2 (2007), 317–324.

into the history of the disappearance of a fifteen-year-old girl during the Occupation and of his own life. Having come across a notice in an old edition of *Paris Soir* announcing her as a missing person, the ambiguously autobiographical narrator Modiano begins searching for any trace of Dora Bruder in documentation from the time. He is familiar with the neighbourhood where Dora disappeared, although he has often passed by the house at number 41 unaware that it had once been the home of the Bruder family. Learning that one day Dora, for reasons the narrator is unable to uncover, did not return to the Catholic convent school where her mother and father—a Hungarian Jew and an Austrian Jew, respectively—had hidden her in an attempt to conceal her from the Nazi's occupying forces, the narrator recalls a time he ran away from home in the winter of 1960. Later in life he goes on to write a novel based on these historical events entitled *Voyage de noces* ('Honeymoon'), which appears in 1990 and is also the name of a novel written by Modiano himself in 1990. In the years following that novel's publication, however, the narrator continues to research Dora's life, unearthing files about her and her parents. He is able to reconstruct the events of their lives until December 1941, when Dora disappeared. According to a police memo, Dora returned to her mother in April 1942, by which time her father had already been interned. Later Dora was taken to the internment centre at Les Tourelles and then to Drancy transit camp in August, where she was reunited with her father. They were then both deported to Auschwitz where, in February the following year, Dora's mother was also imprisoned. These investigations are juxtaposed with the narrator's ruminations on his family history, particularly his troubled relationship with his Jewish father. During the Occupation, his father was arrested, only narrowly avoiding deportation through a friend's intervention. The narrator recalls how his father once re-enacted this event with his eighteen-year-old son in his former position as the arrested party, reporting the narrator to the police for loudly knocking on his father's door and creating a public disturbance after being sent by his mother to collect maintenance payments owed. This traumatic arrest is a frequent point of reference for the narrator's ruminations on investigating the past, on his father's motivations, and on Dora's experiences during the Occupation.[4] The novel ends with the narrator

---

[4] For further discussion of elements of the traumatic in *Dora Bruder* within the framework of Marianne Hirsch's concept of 'postmemory', see Judith Greenberg, 'Trauma and Transmission: Echoes of the Missing Past in Dora Bruder', in *Studies in 20th and 21st*

walking through the streets of Paris, occasionally feeling an echo of Dora Bruder's presence, traces of which he is still attempting to uncover. He admits to never knowing what she did in the weeks she ran away, where and in whose company she was hiding. By acknowledging that this is as far as he will allow his narrative to go, Dora is allowed a *fugue*, the freedom of her flight: 'j'ignorerai toujours à quoi elle passait ses journées', declares the narrator. 'C'est là son secret' (*DB*, 144–145).[5] The narrator considers this to be a private matter that Dora may keep to herself, upon which neither he nor anyone else will intrude. While the narrator's searching—or at least his account of it—is over, there still exists a gulf between his present and Dora Bruder's past that remains ultimately unbridged.

The present chapter traces how the narrator of *Dora Bruder* consciously positions himself as an epigonal latecomer not only on the field of French literature, but also at the end of a genealogy of Jewish modernist writers. An often neglected yet significant feature of European modernist literature, Jewishness is central to understanding the late and melancholy aesthetics at play in *Dora Bruder*. Its Jewish narrator's investigations into the life and fate of Dora Bruder, as well as his engagement with his own personal history, constitute an attempt to write Jewishness back into a modern European literary tradition in which its significance has long been ignored. The narrator's perceived epigonality as a writer at the end of the twentieth century who is both French and Jewish, as well as European, becomes a means of legitimizing his own work and the traditions out of which it emerges. *Dora Bruder*'s investigations into the past reveal deeply rooted preoccupations with melancholy lateness and are defined by tensions: between a reliance on lateness in order to try and overcome epigonality; between an irreconcilable past and present, the investigation of which locates the narrator at the centre of the narrative just as much as Dora Bruder herself; between presence and absence in the photographs he finds; and between motifs of imprisonment and attempted escape.

Such tensions parallel in intriguing and relevant ways those in detective fiction identified by Roland Barthes in *S/Z* (1970), and a sustained lack of

---

Century Literature, 31:2 (2007), 351–377. This special edition of *Studies in 20th and 21st Century Literature* is devoted to *Dora Bruder* and contains several useful introductory articles to the novel and its writing of history. See also Golsan and Higgins, 'Introduction: Patrick Modiano's Dora Bruder', 322.

[5] 'I shall never know how she spent her days [...] That is her secret' (*DB*, 137).

resolution emerges as a key constitutive element of *Dora Bruder*'s late and melancholy aesthetic attitude. For Barthes, such tensions constitute fundamental principles for many literary works: analysing the enigmas of narrative works, such as a vanished person or an unexplained death, he proposes the 'hermeneutic code' as a means by which narrative puzzles may be distinguished, formulated, and investigated. For Barthes, this hermeneutic code demands closure if a literary work is to prove satisfying, yet its lack of resolution provides narrative drive, such that in the detective novel 'c'est, entre la question et la réponse, tout un espace dilatoire'.[6] This extends itself over the course of a narrative, such as in a work of detective fiction, so that 'l'attente devient la condition fondatrice de la vérité' within the novel to such an extent that 'la vérité est ce qui est au bout de l'attente'.[7] It is under an aspect of lateness, in other words, that detective narrative truth emerges. The structure of straight narratives resembles that of a sentence—subject precedes object, noun precedes verb, and so on—but in the hermeneutic code of narratives like those of the detective novel, resolution is withheld and narrative truth is predicated on 'un sujet incomplet, fondé en attente'.[8] If, moreover, all works of fiction set during the Second World War can, as Margaret-Anne Hutton has observed, be understood as crime fiction to a greater or lesser extent, then this is *a fortiori* the case for later novels that investigate that conflict and its consequences.[9] Though it is not explicitly advertised as such, Modiano's *Dora Bruder* exhibits numerous stylistic features and thematic concerns that recall those of crime fiction. The narrator's desire to piece together the facts of the past and his obsessive raking over every piece of evidence connected with Dora Bruder's life that he can find cast him in the role of an amateur sleuth, searching for traces not only of her and her family, but also of himself and his own father in due course.[10] Indeed, the concept of trace is fundamental

[6] Roland Barthes, *S/Z* (Paris: Seuil, 1970), 81. 'Between the question and answer there is a whole dilatory area'. Roland Barthes, *S/Z*, trans. by Richard Miller (Blackwell: London, 1990), 75.

[7] Barthes, *S/Z*, 82. 'Expectation thus becomes the basic condition for truth'; 'truth [...] is what is at the end of expectation'. Barthes, *S/Z*, 76.

[8] Barthes, *S/Z*, 82. 'An incomplete subject'. Barthes, *S/Z*, 76.

[9] See Margaret-Anne Hutton, *French Crime Fiction, 1945–2000: Investigating World War II* (Farnham: Ashgate, 2013). Interestingly, Hutton notes that 'many of Patrick Modiano's texts would sit comfortably – and productively – in each if not every chapter of this book' (113).

[10] Claire Gorrara similarly uses the term 'detective-historian' to describe Modiano's narrators. See Claire Gorrara, 'Tracking down the Past': The Detective as Historian in Texts by

to the narrative of *Dora Bruder*, as the narrator frequently invokes detective tropes—such as the picking up of clues, the exercising of his powers of deduction—only to subvert these almost immediately. 'Je suppose', 'je devine', 'peut-être', 'il semble que', 'sans que je puisse préciser' (*DB*, 19): such interjections pepper the pages of *Dora Bruder*, emphasizing the epistemological limits of the narrator's investigations into the events of the Occupation. Alongside these constructions, the narrator frequently poses rhetorical questions on almost every page, which serve both to outline the potential course of his inquiries and to emphasize the extent to which the past will ultimately remain at a remove from his present. Perhaps the most prominent example of the invocation and subversion of crime fiction elements comes in the closing lines of the novel where the narrator leaves his investigation unfinished by turning the problem into the solution, according to the unknown and unknowable parts of Dora's life protection from intrusion. This irresolution does not erase the possibility of coming closer to the past; the open-ended nature of the novel's close suggests a future beyond itself.

Aspects of crime and detective fiction may be discerned not only in the narrator's investigation of the history of Dora Bruder and her family, but also across Modiano's entire œuvre. In the case of *Rue des boutiques obscures* (1978), one of his most celebrated earlier novels, for instance, the amnesiac narrator is a detective whose final case becomes a search for his own memories of his activities during the Second World War. Modiano's limpid prose and frequent use of ellipsis in the narrative of *Dora Bruder* also owe much to mystery novels by writers such as, perhaps most notably, the strikingly prolific Belgian author Georges Simenon.[11] Modiano himself acknowledges a profound debt to Simenon's style: 'J'ai beaucoup lu Simenon', he has remarked; 'cette précision m'aide à exprimer des choses, des atmosphères où tout se dilue'.[12] Tellingly, even Modiano's description of Simenon's influence encapsulates a tension between precise expression

---

Patrick Modiano and Didier Daeninckx', in *Crime Scenes: Detective Narratives in European Culture since 1945*, ed. by Anne Mullen and Emer O'Beire (Amsterdam: Rodopi, 2000), 281–290 (282).

[11] See Bill Alder, *Maigret, Simenon and France: Social Dimensions of the Novels and Stories* (London: McFarland & Company, 2013), 8.

[12] 'This precision helps me to express things, atmospheres, where everything comes undone'. Pierre Maury, 'Patrick Modiano: Un Cirque passe', in *Magazine littéraire*, 302, September 1992, 102.

and narrative dissipation. In the novel's opening pages, the narrator remarks that 'je n'étais rien, je me confondais avec ce crépuscule, ces rues' (*DB*, 8),[13] suggesting that the more he wanders the twilit boulevards and arcades of the French capital, the more diffuse and unclear his sense of self becomes. Similarly to Simenon's celebrated detective, the Commissaire Jules Maigret, the narrator of *Dora Bruder* does not so much hunt for clues or examine crime scenes as wander his immediate vicinity and allow the pattern of events and their consequences to unfold before his eyes. While *Dora Bruder*'s narrator is far more interested in documentary evidence than Maigret typically shows himself to be, their mutual interest in observing their surroundings suggests a resigned investigative affinity. Throughout the narrator's account of his investigations, the temporal distance between his present and Dora Bruder's past is continually emphasized. However close he may physically be to where she may once have been, however much he may empathize with her plight, he struggles, with a certain melancholy, to perceive the city in which he moves as the same as the one through which she once ran:

> les lampadaires, les vitrines, les cafés s'allument, l'air du soir est vif, le contour des choses plus net, il y a des embouteillages aux carrefours, les gens se présent dans les rues. Et au milieu de toutes ces lumières et de cette agitation, j'ai peine à croire que je suis dans la même ville que celle où se trouvaient Dora Bruder et ses parents, et aussi mon père quand il avait vingt ans de moins que moi. J'ai l'impression d'être tout seul à faire le lien entre le Paris de ce temps-là et celui d'aujourd'hui. (*DB*, 50)[14]

The tensions which the narrative of *Dora Bruder* attempts to overcome are, as this chapter will show, ultimately constitutive of its aesthetics and it is through this sense of aesthetic irreconciliation that a clearer picture of the novel's late and melancholy nature emerges.

---

[13] 'I was non-existent, I blended into that twilight, into those streets' (*DB*, 4).

[14] 'The street-lamps and shop windows and cafés light up, the evening air freshens, contours sharpen, there are traffic jams at the crossroads and hurrying crowds in the streets. And in the midst of all these lights, all this hubbub, I can hardly believe that this is the city where Dora lived with her parents, where my father lived when he was twenty years younger than I am now. I feel as if I am alone in making the link between Paris then and Paris now' (*DB*, 45).

66   I. ELLISON

Memories and Tensions

That towards the end of the twentieth century a novel by Modiano should engage with and respond to perceptions of literary and historical lateness is perhaps unsurprising. Even as early as 1975, less than a decade after his first novel *La place de l'étoile* (1968) was published, the centrality of time and history to the novel form constitutes a perennial concern in Modiano's work: 'Le grand, l'inévitable sujet romanesque', he declares, 'c'est toujours, de toute manière, le temps'.[15] Grandiose observations such as this threaten to reinforce some criticisms of Modiano's literary style as exhibiting what Alison Finch has described as 'a tendency to portentous generalizations'.[16] Time, however, is less of a subject for Modiano than one of the raw materials of his œuvre; time-keeping and records of the past are frequent and serious obsessions for Modiano's narrators. Historical events, figures, and objects are logged in his novels with regularity and precision, often down to an exact date and time. This provides a scaffolding upon which his narrators may structure their investigations into the history that eludes them. Earlier in his career, Modiano presented himself as a writer obsessed with recovering the losses of the past, echoing the sentiment of his later narrators, perhaps most especially the narrator of *Dora Bruder*: 'moi, j'avais la manie de regarder en arrière, toujours ce sentiment de quelque chose de perdu, pas comme le paradis, mais de perdu'.[17] This sense of looking backwards towards postlapsarian historical loss is crystallized in *Dora Bruder*, as the narrator looks back not only to events that precede him, but also to the literary works and writers of whom he perceives himself to be an epigonal descendant. Through its examination of the sense of lateness in *Dora Bruder*'s narrative and its ensuing melancholy aesthetics, this chapter seeks to dispel any claims of Modiano's portentous generalities by revealing the complexities of the novel's literary legacy in its aesthetic attitude, as well as its influence on the narrator's preoccupations with historical events and his own life. *Dora Bruder* constitutes a distinctly French example of a late and melancholy mode of writing that

---

[15] Jean-Louis Ezine, 'Patrick Modiano ou le passé antérieur', in *Les Nouvelles littéraires*, 2501 (1975), 3. 'The great, inevitable fictional subject is always, in any case, time'.

[16] Alison Finch, *French Literature: A Cultural History* (Cambridge: Polity Press, 2010), 175.

[17] Dominique Jamet, 'Patrick Modiano s'explique', in *Lire*, 1 (1975), 23–36 (36). 'I had an obsession with looking back, always this feeling of something lost, not like paradise, but lost'.

emerges around the turn of the millennium in European literature, which in the Barthesian 'dilatory area' of its narrative holds national and European literary contexts in tension, alongside the dark history of the Occupation. *Dora Bruder* stands out from Modiano's body of work for its more ambiguous fictional status, not least because the text purports to be an autobiographical account of the author's research for another novel. The investigation and deliberation of the fictional or factual status of the novel is one of two principal avenues of research within the significant body of existent scholarship on Modiano and his work, and especially on *Dora Bruder*.[18] Particularly within French literary scholarship, connections are often drawn between *Dora Bruder* and Serge Dubrowsky's concept of autofiction, that chameleon brand of fictionalized autobiography notably found in French-language literature of the late twentieth century. While Claude Burgelin observes that Modiano's œuvre as a whole embodies a 'dissolution' of autofiction, he ultimately concludes that Modiano's novels stand as 'un compromis entre autoportrait (se peindre) et autoprofération (se dire): un autoportrait où le peintre se représenterait en receptacle d'images et en chamber d'échos'.[19] For as much as the narrator of *Dora*

[18] For an indication of the extensive range of scholarship on Modiano's entire œuvre, see John Flower, 'Introduction' in *Patrick Modiano*, ed. by John Flower (Amsterdam: Rodopi, 2007), 7–18. For further discussion of questions of memory and the (non-)fictional status of *Dora Bruder* and other works by Patrick Modiano, see, for example, Colin Nettelbeck, 'Novelists and their engagement with history: some contemporary French cases', in *Australian Journal of French Studies*, 35:2 (1998), 243–257; Akane Kawakami, *A Self-Conscious Art: Patrick Modiano's Postmodern Fictions* (Liverpool: Liverpool University Press, 2000), 121–131; Dervila Cooke, *Present Pasts: Patrick Modiano's (Auto)Biographical Fictions* (Amsterdam: Rodopi, 2005); Annelies Schulte Nordholt, '*Dora Bruder:* le témoignage par le biais de la fiction' and Joseph Jurt, 'La mémoire de la Shoah', in *Patrick Modiano*, ed. by John Flower (Amsterdam: Rodopi, 2007), 75–87 and 89–108; Susan Rubin Suleiman, '"Oneself as Another": Identification and Mourning in Patrick Modiano's *Dora Bruder*', in *Studies in 20th and 21st Century Literature*, 31:2 (2007), 325–350; and Sven-Erik Rose, 'Remembering Dora Bruder: Patrick Modiano's Surrealist Encounter with the Postmemorial Archive', in *Postmodern Culture*, 18:2 (2008), 1–37. In light of Modiano's winning of the Nobel Prize in Literature, Richard J. Golsan and Lynn A. Higgins provide reassessment and overview of Modiano's œuvre, especially given the apparent sameness or repetitiveness of his work. See Richard J. Golsan and Lynn A. Higgins, eds., '"Detecting" Patrick Modiano: New Perspectives', *Yale French Studies* (special issue), 133 (2014).

[19] Claude Burgelin, 'Modiano et ses "je"', in *Autofiction(s)*, ed. by Claude Burgelin, Isabelle Grell, and Roger Yves-Roche (Lyon: Presses universitaires de Lyon, 2010), 207–222 (220–222). 'A compromise between self-portrait (painting oneself) and self-profession (telling of oneself): a self-portrait where the artist would represent himself as a receptacle of images and as an echo chamber'.

Bruder might resemble snatches of Modiano's personhood, sharing some life experiences and achievements, most else is absent. In relating the sufferings of others to his own life, moreover, the narrator of *Dora Bruder* relies, as Susan Rubin Suleiman argues, 'less on a kind of identification than on differentiation'.[20] When he connects, for example, Dora's flight from her convent school with his running away in the 1960s, this is not a clumsy attempt at equivalence; rather, the mundanity of his trials in comparison to the tragedy of Dora's disappearance and the life-threatening terror endured by her and her family reveal both a sense of lateness and inadequacy on the narrator's part. Recalling a trip in a Black Maria police carriage with his father after being reported for creating a public disturbance, the narrator mediates what he knows of Dora's flight and capture through his own experiences. He acknowledges, however, that his own journey was merely 'la répétition inoffensive et la parodie' (*DB*, 99) in comparison to hers.[21]

This sense of later repetition and echo relates to the other significant strand of scholarship on Modiano, which is concerned with questions of identity and appropriation, principally concentrating on the role of forms of memory in the author's novels and their contribution to francophone memory work of the events of the twentieth century. In *Dora Bruder* the narrator resolutely refuses to invent or fictionalize Dora's life outside of what documentary evidence can relate. Dervila Cooke views this as a form of resistance, remarking that 'Modiano [is] concerned to create a sense of consciousness using his own in default of Dora's where necessary, in order to counter in some small way the dehumanization of the Holocaust'.[22] While it may be impossible to access the reality of Dora's life or that of others, Modiano shows that, as Cooke affirms, 'a sincere attempt at representation is always better than silence', just as his narrator's attempt at consolation in Dora's *fugue* is better than nothing.[23] As he wanders through Paris, the city itself stimulates the narrator's thoughts about Dora and her family, yet he also reflects on his own ignorance of their lives and the potential impossibility of knowing more. This is often integrated into extended descriptions of the routes taken on his Parisian perambulations:

---

[20] Suleiman, '"Oneself as Another": Identification and Mourning', 327.

[21] 'A harmless repetition, a parody' (*DB*, 93).

[22] Dervila Cooke, 'Hollow Imprints', in *Journal of Modern Jewish Studies*, 3:2 (2004), 131–145 (143).

[23] Cooke, 'Hollow Imprints', 144.

Vers 1968 je suivais souvent les boulevards jusque sous les arches du métro aérien. Je partais de la place Blanche. En décembre, les baraques foraines occupaient le terre-plein. Les lumières se décroissaient à mesure que l'on approchait le boulevard de la Chapelle. Je ne savais encore rien de Dora Bruder et de ses parents. (*DB*, 29)[24]

Throughout the text the narrator also demonstrates an ethical awareness of the dangers of potentially appropriating the story of Dora and her family, or of inappropriately identifying with them, by insisting that there will always remain an essential element of their lives and histories that remains unknown to him. Although the narrator refers to that which will never be known about the Bruders as 'ce blanc, ce bloc d'inconnu et de silence' (*DB*, 28), he also describes, with reference to printmaking techniques, how certain locations retain a stamp or faint trace of previous inhabitants as a 'marque en creux ou en relief' (*DB*, 29). The technical term 'en relief' suggests sculpted material raised above its background plane, whereas 'en creux' refers to counter-relief where a form appears hollowed out of a background, rather than seeming to emerge from it. In the case of the Bruders, the narrator specifies his preferred term: 'Pour Ernest et Cécile Bruder, pour Dora je dirai: en creux. J'ai ressenti une impression d'absence et de vide, chaque fois que je me suis trouvé dans un endroit où ils avaient vécu' (*DB*, 29). The term 'en creux' in particular, which is central to Cooke's reading, is suggestive, moreover, of a revealing *double-sens* in French since it is an almost perfect homonym for 'encre',̓ meaning 'ink'. The hollowed out imprint of the Bruders' absence therefore not only provides the narrator with space to fill, but might prompt implicitly the writing of a new account of their story. On the one hand, such a 'marque en creux' is indicative of the narrator's respectful approach to his historical sources. Yet, on the other hand, it is a means for him to also acknowledge his conscious invention and new writing in setting down the fictional narrative of *Dora Bruder*. As outlined in the introduction, this study understands each of the works it investigates as consciously constructed works of literature, as novels.[25] This overwriting of the Bruder family's 'marque en

---

[24] 'Often, around 1968, I would follow the boulevards as far as the arches of the overhead metro. My starting point was the Place Blanche. In December, a travelling fair occupied the open ground. Its lights grew dimmer the nearer you got to the Boulevard de la Chapelle. At the time, I knew nothing of Dora Bruder or her parents' (*DB*, 24).

[25] For further discussion of the apparent unclassifiable nature of *Dora Bruder* due to its inclusion of elements of fiction, biography, and autobiography, see Jennifer Howell, 'In defi-

creux' by the narrator's own ink also anticipates a key feature of the particularly palimpsestic aesthetic aspects found in Modiano's novel.

By following the clues left in allusions to other literary works by the narrator of *Dora Bruder* that establish the novel as one emerging from a French literary tradition, as well as one bound up with questions of Jewishness, this chapter detects forms of historical and cultural lateness and epigonality. These are most clearly embodied in Jewish figures encountered by the narrator, whom he perceives to be legitimizing his investigation and his writing. The chapter then subsequently moves to consider the nature of the narrator's melancholy style, which articulates the irreconcilability of the past and present through ekphrastic interactions with photographs that signify both the presence and the absence of the Bruder family, as well as through recurring motifs of attempted escape and imprisonment. If, as Suleiman observes, 'the "melancholy" tone of Modiano's works is not (or not only) a sign of pathology but the result of artistic shaping', then such artistic shaping is the work of a narrator preoccupied with the tensions of a French, Jewish, and European literary heritage.[26] This results in a melancholy separation of past and present that centres on the narrator, even as he tries to bridge this gulf by investigating the life of another, which reflects constitutive tensions in the novel and its aesthetics.

LINEAGE AND PALIMPSEST

With explicit reference to Jean Genet, Victor Hugo, Edgar Allan Poe, and Robert Desnos, a Surrealist poet who was murdered in the Theresienstadt Concentration Camp in 1945, the narrator of *Dora Bruder* embeds his narrative in a distinct literary tradition, but with a clear *décalage* from writers and literary movements that precede him. Many of the references to other works of literature across the novel point to the narrator as an epigone emerging at the end of a predominantly French literary lineage, yet there are also other forces at play in his constructed genealogy, namely, questions of Europeanness and Jewishness. Implicit similarities to the palimpsestic style of Marcel Proust in particular, to whom Modiano has

ance of genre: The language of Patrick Modiano's Dora Bruder project', in *Journal of European Studies*, 40:1 (2010), 59–72. Howell not only reads *Dora Bruder* as an example of 'second-generation Holocaust ekphrasis' (60), but also focuses on the ways in which minute editorial changes in the various editions of Modiano's novel play a key role in the conceptualization of Modiano's novel as an ongoing work of mourning and reconstitution.

[26] See Suleiman, '"Oneself as Another": Identification and Mourning', 341.

often—however superficially—been compared, are indicative of an engagement with a tradition of modern European literature, the key Jewish aspect of which has been routinely marginalized in Western literary history. *Dora Bruder* emerges as an attempt to suture these traditions together from a late vantage point at the end of the twentieth century. Other Jewish figures, such as the brocanteur (a second-hand salesman or bric-a-brac trader), as well as forms of narrative bricolage, contribute to the narrative's sense of lateness, while also pointing to the narrator's ongoing quest for authority and legitimacy in investigating and writing the story of Dora's life and fate. Ultimately, the narrator casts himself not only as epigonal latecomer detective, but also as a literary brocanteur. One such attempt at legitimizing the novel may be glimpsed when the narrator declares that his awareness of the name of the prison in which Dora was held before her deportation to Auschwitz originally came from *Miracle de la Rose* (1946), an autobiographical novel by Jean Genet (*DB*, 138), which recounts his experiences in prison.[27] The narrator of *Dora Bruder* recalls how Genet identified in the voices and the slang of children in Paris a particular 'tendresse attristée' (*DB*, 139).[28] Like Dora, if not her parents, the narrator is a child of Paris himself and he implicitly draws attention to the saddened tenderness in his melancholy narration, as well as to an author writing in prison, which will emerge as another significant motif in the novel. In this brief nod to Genet's work, the narrator establishes himself as a literary latecomer and suggests a self-understanding as an inheritor of Genet's status as a significant figure of French literature, positioning his narrative as a later work while attempting to legitimize it via reference to thematic and aesthetic resonances with its literary forebears.

The narrator's tracing of his work's literary genealogy goes beyond Genet and twentieth-century French literature in a further attempt at bestowing credibility, as well as a sense of melancholy pathos, on his narrative. In the first half of *Dora Bruder*, the narrator recalls reading the fifth and sixth volumes of *Les Misérables* (1862), in which Hugo describes the characters of Jean Valjean and Cosette, pursued by the inspector Javert, crossing Paris by night from the Saint-Jacques toll gate, across the Pont d'Austerlitz, to Hugo's imaginary district of Paris, the Petit Picpus. Charted in scrupulously realistic detail in the original novel, this passage

---

[27] His previous novel, *Notre-Dame-des-Fleurs* (1943), was also written while he was in fact incarcerated.

[28] 'Sad tenderness' (*DB*, 132).

acts as a literary map onto which the narrator of *Dora Bruder* plots his and Dora's movements. The moment in *Les Misérables* when the two fugitives escape by slipping behind the wall of a convent, before they enter Hugo's imagined territory, provides the narrator of *Dora Bruder* with the opportunity to establish an instance of deliberately staged coincidence as he claims that the convent in *Les Misérables* is located at the exact address of the convent where Dora was a boarder (*DB*, 51–52). Quoting verbatim from Hugo's novel, the narrator declares that it is not possible for him to pass this building without thinking of 'l'histoire mélancholique de Jean Valjean' (*DB*, 52).[29] He thereby suggests parallels between his tale and Victor Hugo's monumental account of France in the early 1800s. Hugo's influential presence is invoked, suggesting a threshold between fiction and history, whereby Hugo himself inserts a fictional space into the topography of Paris and Modiano has Dora's convent school become aligned with the fictional building that shelters Valjean and Cosette. This associative leap is central to the narrator's understanding of the practice of writing itself: one of 'les efforts d'imagination, nécessaires à ce métier, le besoin de fixer son esprit sur des points de detail – et cela de manière obsessionnelle – pour ne pas perdre le fil' (*DB*, 53).[30] Although he elevates himself by association to the level of a canonical writer within the field of French letters, by conceiving of himself as a late imitator of Hugo's work he also constructs an epigonal identity whose lateness heightens the pathos of the story he recounts.[31] He cannot pass by these Parisian locales, either physically or mentally, without engaging with the past. Yet he must do so—or feels obligated to do so—via reference to other literary works that preceded his, thus casting himself as an epigonal latecomer.

Other 'histoires mélancholiques' act as a literary lynch pin to hold together the narrative of *Dora Bruder*. With reference to the work of

---

[29] 'The melancholy story [or history] of Jean Valjean' (*DB*, 47).

[30] 'The essential leaps of the imagination, the need to fix one's mind on detail – to the point of obsession, in fact – so as to not lose the thread' (*DB*, 47).

[31] Other French literary figures from the Goncourt brothers, to Gustave Flaubert, to Charles Baudelaire in fact originally criticized Hugo's novel for being artificial, disappointing, and lacking in any sense of truth. This is, perhaps, a veiled reference by the narrator of *Dora Bruder* to the potential futility of his attempting a reconciliation between the past and the present in his narrative, although clearly he holds Hugo in greater esteem than the aforementioned literary figures. For further discussion of their views on *Les Misérables*, see, in particular, Lois Boe Hyslop, 'Baudelaire on *Les Misérables*', in *The French Review*, 41:1 (1967), 23–29.

Edgar Allan Poe, which achieved considerable renown in France through Charles Baudelaire's translations, the narrator further embellishes his literary credentials by referencing the work of a key figure in American Romantic literature—and, indeed, an early proponent of the detective story—while tracing Dora's movements.[32] Describing the building used by the Préfecture of Police during the Occupation, for example, as 'une grande caserne spectrale au bord de la Seine' (*DB*, 83),[33] the narrator of *Dora Bruder* explicitly likens this edifice to the House of Usher. His reference to this house, which splits in two and crumbles into rubble at the end of Poe's tale, underscores the pathos and fragility of the narrator's late perspective on history. In Poe's story, the House of Usher and its environs reflect the mood and relationships of the characters that inhabit it. Similarly, the building used by the Préfecture is spectral, an architectural ghost of the past, yet one which could disintegrate at any moment. The narrator gestures towards significant literary figures, but must simultaneously continue with his own writing, aware of the precarious epigonal position he is in. He declares that his brief mention of the place where Dora lived in his earlier novel *Voyage de noces* was 'le seul moment du livre où, sans le savoir, je me suis rapproché d'elle, dans l'espace et le temps' (*DB*, 54).[34] He places his own literary engagement with Dora at the centre of the narrative. Yet, being in a place that compels him to make reference to other literary works in recording what happens to him, he cannot overcome his sense of epigonal lateness. The fact that his investigations later continued after the publication of his earlier work further heightens the pathos of his epigonality. Though Dora never wrote her own story, the narrator's anxiety about reconstructing it is channelled into references to earlier works that he perceives to be greater than his own. The constitutive tension of his attempts to overcome his sense of lateness while drawing on precisely this in the telling of Dora's life story is thus emphasized all the more.

That being the case, the narrator nevertheless moves closer towards the possibility of overcoming this sense of fragile epigonality, as his references

---

[32] For further discussion of Baudelaire's translations of Poe, see Gary Wayne Harner, 'Edgar Allan Poe in France: Baudelaire's Labor of Love', in *Poe and His Times: The Artist and His Milieu*, ed. by Benjamin Franklin Fischer (Baltimore: The Edgar Allan Poe Society, 1990), 218.

[33] 'A great spectral barracks on the Seine' (*DB*, 78).

[34] 'The only moment in the book when, without knowing it, I came close to her in time and space' (*DB*, 49).

to works by Robert Desnos and Jean Jausion reveal. His attempts at literary innovation and his engagement with his Jewish literary heritage become further entangled as he lists the names and biographies of several writers all of whom disappeared during the Occupation in 1945, the year he was born, thereby implying that he perceives himself to be their successor (*DB*, 92–100). His account of a suspected illness, however, which appears during his presentation of these writers, suggests itself as a physical manifestation of his anxiety and insecurity of his epigonal lateness. Yet on a later visit to the doctor he is informed that there is no shadow on his lung as he had expected (*DB*, 96). This connects to a subsequent appointment with another doctor, during which the narrator is shown a novel by Robert Desnos bearing the same title as the first book the narrator wrote. This is entitled *La place d l'Étoile*, just like Modiano's first published work, and, as the narrator self-consciously confesses, 'je lui avais volé, bien involontairement, son titre' (*DB*, 100).[35] The irony of the narrator's unintentional theft of Desnos's title is suggestive of a certain inevitability to his epigonality: he is left with only imitation and parody even when he does not initially realize or intend it. However, the fact remains that it was only the title of the novel that he inadvertently stole, not the contents. While confined to work within a particular framework of a French literary tradition, indicated by the stolen title, the vestigial possibility of creating something new within this restriction still exists. Another novel entitled *Un homme marche dans la ville* (1945) by Jean Jausion, a man whose Jewish fiancée was arrested during the Occupation to prevent their marriage from taking place (*DB*, 118–120), hints at the constitutive tension between innovation and constraint embodied in the narrator's epigonal lateness, as well as providing another way for him to reimagine himself through the works of others.[36]

It is through more elusive allusions to the work of Marcel Proust, however, that the narrator's constructions of lateness in *Dora Bruder* become more nuanced and complex. Proustian prompters in the novel open up questions concerning the relationship between modernist literature and Jewishness, as well as palimpsests of style and memory that articulate the sense of lateness in *Dora Bruder* and gesture towards the

---

[35] 'Quite unwittingly, I had stolen his title from him' (*DB*, 94).

[36] For more on this, see Ian Ellison, '"Un homme marche dans la rue": Parisian flânerie and Jewish cosmopolitanism in Patrick Modiano's *Dora Bruder*', in *Modern Language Review*, 116:2 (2021), 264–280.

melancholy that emerges from it. Parallels between Modiano and Proust have been frequently made. Notably, for example, when awarding Modiano the Nobel Prize in Literature, the spokesperson for the committee, Peter Englund, named him a 'Marcel Proust for our time'.[37] While memories in Proust's work emerge from sensory experience and the subjective means by which recollections are prompted and enabled, as opposed to the contents and veracity of these memories, *Dora Bruder* is not concerned with the function or structure of remembering or the process by which memories rise in an individual's consciousness. Time is recorded, remembered, and taxonomized as lost in *Dora Bruder*, but there is no 'time regained': the secrets of Dora's *fugue*—the period when she ran away and about which the narrator refuses to speculate—remain undisclosed. Nevertheless, through the motif of the palimpsest, which is key to both Proust's literary style and to Modiano's aesthetics of memory, a complex relationship emerges. Palimpsest is understood here both in the sense of a reused text or a text overwritten by another and in the more metaphorical sense of something altered yet still containing vestigial traces of its earlier form. The image of the palimpsest—a commonplace in much criticism in the wake of poststructuralism—surfaces not infrequently in critical studies of memory, such as in Andreas Huyssen's study of the urban politics of memory, which argues that memory of historical trauma has a unique power to generate works of art as urban spaces that witness social or political traumas are rebuilt and reconfigured into sites of commemoration and monumentalization.[38] However, the epigonal narrator of *Dora Bruder* draws on the often side-lined significance of Jewishness in modernist literature in various figurations of Proustian palimpsest, attempting to suture this together with the tradition of European fiction via the narrative of *Dora Bruder* from his late position at the end of the twentieth century. The functional metaphor of the

[37] See www.theguardian.com/books/2014/oct/09/nobel-prize-literature-winer-patrick-modiano-hailed-modern-marcel-proust. Alan Morris also offers a brief analysis of Proustian themes in Modiano's work, declaring that 'he is set to be the Marcel Proust of the years to come as well'. See Alan Morris, 'Patrick Modiano: A Marcel Proust of our Time?', in *French Studies Bulletin*, 36:134 (2015), 1–3 (3).

[38] For Huyssen, such acts of physical rewriting constitute the urban palimpsest. Focusing on the issue of monumentalization in divergent artistic and media practices, he suggests that the transformation of spatial and temporal experience by memory politics is a major cultural effect of globalization. See Andreas Huyssen, *Present Pasts: Urban Palimpsests and the Politics of Memory* (Stanford: Stanford University Press, 2003).

palimpsest thus acquires a crucial structuring significance *Dora Bruder* and, more specifically, for the traces of lateness in the novel.

For Gérard Genette, the literary style of Marcel Proust in *A la recherche du temps perdu* (1913–1927) is encapsulated in the image of the palimpsest. 'La métaphore n'est pas un ornement', he argues, echoing in the structure of his sentence a passage from Proust's *Le temps retrouvé*; 'elle est l'équivalent stylistique de l'expérience psychologique de la mémoire involontaire, qui seule permet, en rapprochant deux sensations séparées dans le temps, de dégager leur *essence commune* par *le miracle d'une analogie*'.[39] While Genette observes that 'Ce palimpseste du temps et de l'espace, ces vues discordantes sans cesse contrariées et sans cesse rapprochées par un inlassable mouvement de dissociation douloureuse et de synthèse impossible, c'est sans doute cela, la vision proustienne',[40] there is nonetheless a central tension or apparent contradiction in that this palimpsestic structure of the novel ultimately consumes its substance. 'Partie pour dégager des essences', Genette observes, Proust's prose 'découvre au contraire un plan du réel où celui-ci, à force de plénitude, s'anéantit *de lui-même*'.[41] For Proust, then, the truth of reality is not to be found in the people, the events, or the objects he examines *per se*, but rather in instances of their palimpsestic overlapping and the sense of aesthetic and historical profundity that this creates. The palimpsest therefore brings together discrete essences, simultaneously creating something new, while concealing its literary provenance. Turning to the palimpsestic assemblage of *Dora Bruder*'s traces and the narrator's present in the Modiano's novel thus begs the question: what provenance is concealed? For Max Silverman, intertwined memories of the Holocaust and of French colonialism in

---

[39] Gérard Genette, 'Proust Palimpseste', in *Figures I* (Paris: Seuil, 1964), 39–67 (40). 'Metaphor is not an ornament [...] it is the stylistic equivalent of the psychological experience of involuntary memory, which alone, by bringing together two sensations separated in time, is able to release their *common essence* through the *miracle of analogy*'. See Gérard Genette, 'Proust Palimpsest', in *Figures of Literary Discourse* (Oxford: Blackwell, 1982), 203–228 (204). Emphasis in original. For further discussion of this, see also Ben Hutchinson, *Modernism and Style* (Basingstoke: Palgrave Macmillan, 2011), 135–142.

[40] Genette, 'Proust Palimpseste', 51. 'This palimpsest of time and space, these discordant views, ceaselessly contradicted and ceaselessly brought together by untiring movement of painful dissociation and impossible synthesis – this, no doubt, is the Proustian vision'. Genette, 'Proust Palimpsest', 213.

[41] Genette, 'Proust Palimpseste', 52. 'Having set out to locate essences [...], it [l'écriture proustienne] discovers a level of the real in which reality, by virtue of its plenitude, annihilates *itself*'. Genette, 'Proust Palimpsest', 214. Emphasis in original.

Algeria haunt the narrative of *Dora Bruder* in a process that he terms 'palimpsestic memory'. Like Huyssen, Silverman's understanding of the metaphor of the palimpsest is rooted in urban layering. This 'post-war presence of the concentrationary universe' emerges through an 'imbrication of colonial and Holocaust denial', which is subtly indicated by the fact one of the narrator's points of access to a story about the Holocaust and the Occupation is a structure that the narrator recollects as being a barracks for colonial troops.[42] It is striking, however, that no common essence is found between palimpsest of the narrator's present and Dora's past, which are overlaid in the novel; there remains a gulf between them.

Whereas the palimpsestic nature of Proust's work evokes plenitude, in Modiano's novel the palimpsest connotes brevity. Yet behind this palimpsest lies a frequently overlooked literary heritage, which Modiano's narrator attempts to bring to light over the course of *Dora Bruder* superimposing it onto his already established literary lateness and thereby bolstering the significance of both his narrative and the tradition on which he draws. For the narrator of *Dora Bruder* the Holocaust is not a means to explain away the tragic absence of Jewishness from received understandings of modern literature. Rather, it constitutes a motivating factor in his attempt to reaffirm this key aspect of twentieth-century modernism in a European literary tradition. Any 'teleological distortion', to use Walter Cohen's terminology,[43] of Jewishness's significance caused by the narrator's late historical perspective in Dora Bruder constitutes less an act of erasure or a failure to do justice to particularities in the service of a longue durée perspective, than an attempt at literary restitution. His narrative is to a great extent (over-)determined by the events of the past—a characteristic which could, in a nutshell, encapsulate Modiano's œuvre in its entirety—and this also holds true for literary events: the work of earlier writers constitutes the literary heritage that lies concealed behind Dora Bruder's palimpsestic narrative. Yet, if guilty of such teleological distortion, the narrator in fact employs it to other—more inclusive—ends, given that his narrative aims for the restoration of the significance of Jewishness in modern French and, by extension, European literature.

---

[42] Max Silverman, *Palimpsestic Memory: The Holocaust and Colonialism in French and Francophone Fiction and Film* (Oxford: Berghahn, 2013), 111–113 (113).

[43] Walter Cohen, *A History of European Literature: The West and the World from Antiquity to the Present* (Oxford: Oxford University Press, 2017), 407.

One of the defining characteristics of Jewish modernist literature, according to Cohen, is a sense of 'identification between narrator and character that arguably locate[s] the center of the reader's interest not in the plot involving the nominal protagonist but in the reactions to it on the part of the narrator'.[44] This is key to understanding constructions of lateness in *Dora Bruder*. The narrator's palimpsestic assemblage and mediation of his investigations into Dora's story via references to his own experiences is a later embodiment of this Jewish modernist trait, which, as Cohen observes, 'convert[s] what might seem a solipsistic point of departure into a means of reconstructing the social world from the inside out'.[45] This late palimpsestic reconstruction in *Dora Bruder* is further emphasized by Cohen's subsequent comparison of this to Fredric Jameson's provocative claim that, rather than being defined by narrative subjectivity, modernism in fact involves a flight from subjectivity.[46] Dora's *fugue*, her flight from her would-be captors and the time that she evades both them and the narrator, encapsulates just such a flight from subjectivity, albeit one which is expressed in the novel through the narrator's reactions to it: 'j'ignorerai toujours à quoi elle passait ses journées' (*DB*, 144). The narrator's insistence on his centrality in recounting what he knows of Dora's *fugue* and his ignorance of what occurred during it results in Jewishness being emphasized, rather than ignored, through echoes of Jewish modernist literary techniques. Following Proust, the narrator of Modiano's novel—who, like Modiano himself, identifies as Jewish—positions himself as both inheritor to a French literary heritage and to that of an overlooked Jewish modernist tradition. If his allusive engagement with the works discussed here articulates an attempt to suture these aspects together from a late perspective in order to legitimize the narrative being told, then this is simultaneously an attempt to overcome the sense of lateness and epigonality that haunts the narrator. As a Jewish narrator investigating the lives and fates of a Jewish girl and her family via references to works and techniques of Jewish modernist literature, this act of suturing together emerges as a key expression of the sense of lateness in *Dora Bruder*. Even as the narrator desires to overcome it, he is nonetheless reliant on this lateness. By amassing historical and biographical information throughout the

[44] Cohen, *A History of European Literature*, 415.
[45] Cohen, *A History of European Literature*, 416.
[46] See Fredric Jameson, *A Singular Modernity: Essay on the Ontology of the Present* (London: Verso, 2002), 85–86 and 131–136. Cited in Cohen, *A History of European Literature*, 416.

text—even including verbatim extracts from documentary evidence in his narrative (*DB*, 101–127)—the narrator reveals Paris as a further palimp-sest of different lives and histories. Yet there exists a material aspect to this overlayering, which ensures that the abandoned detritus of the *années noires*—including other literary works, recovered letters, newspapers, objects, and photographs—are brought together as a palimpsestic brico-lage that mediates these elements through the narrator's own experience and situation. Through such a bricolage, which is embodied principally by another significant Jewish figure—the brocanteur—in *Dora Bruder*, the narrator's unfulfilled desire to legitimize his investigations and deductions, while attempting to overcome his epigonal lateness, is most clearly evoked.

BRICOLAGE AND BROCANTERIE

Bricolage in *Dora Bruder* centres around the narrator and his interactions with secondary Jewish characters who—not unlike his palimpsestic style—work to bring together disparate objects to create something new. Lateness thus emerges not only as a thematic concern of Modiano's novel, but also as an aesthetic one. Bricolage establishes a key narrative metaphor for understanding the sense of lateness evoked in *Dora Bruder* and further clarifies the narrator's act of suturing together Jewishness and the European literary tradition, while remaining constrained by epigonality. The tech-nique of bricolage itself is modelled after Claude Lévi-Strauss's figure of the bricoleur by whom 'les éléments sont recueillis ou conservés en vertu du principe que "ça peut toujours server". [...] D'autre part, la décision dépend de la possibilité de permuter un autre élément dans la fonction vacante'.[47] Bricolage is thus reliant on a fundamental principle of contin-gency: the narrator immerses himself in the vicissitudes of history so that he may then cut together and order his experiences. As a result, Lévi-Strauss claims, 'une multitude d'images se forment simultanément, dont aucune n'est exactement pareille aux autres; dont chacune, par conséquent, n'apporte qu'une connaissance partielle de la décoration et du mobilier, mais dont le groupe se caractérise par des propriétés invariantes exprimant

---

[47] Claude Lévi-Strauss, *La pensée sauvage* (Paris: Plon, 1962), 27–29. Used elements, items, and objects are collected on the basis that 'they may always come in handy [...] and the decision of what to put in each place also depends on the possibility of putting a different element there instead'. Claude Lévi-Strauss, *The Savage Mind*, trans. by Doreen Weightman, John Weightman (Chicago: University of Chicago Press, 1966), 18–19. Translation modified.

une vérité'.[48] Lévi-Strauss's anthropological theories lend themselves to comparison with the narrative strategies employed by the narrator of *Dora Bruder*, not least because despite its partiality and lack of resolution the novel aims at reconstructing the truth of Dora's life and fate. However, unlike Lévi-Strauss's conceptualization, this is not scientific or anthropological reportage, nor is it left to chance. Rather, *Dora Bruder* exhibits a carefully constructed form of bricolage which situates the narrator and his reactions at the heart of the novel. *Dora Bruder* becomes, in effect, a collection of lost objects and characters, drawn together by the narrator's mission to construct a new narrative from a late historical position.

The figure of the Jewish brocanteur, who appears twice in *Dora Bruder*—towards the opening of the novel and towards its close—acts as a personification of the narrative strategy. While, as Cooke observes, the brocanteur constitutes a symbolic point of connection for the novel's narrator thanks to their shared Jewish identity, as well as their mutual links with the area where both Dora and the narrator have lived and explored, this figure is also emblematic of the narrator's sense of lateness and of his subsequent attempt at redressing the neglected status of Jewish modernist literature. If, as Cooke notes, the reader is invited to make connections between the narrator and a brocanteur 'who puts the used and the forgotten to new use, and who deals in bits and pieces, [as] a symbol of Modiano's own approach in the recording of fragments of lives', then the connections between these figures draw further attention to the tensions inherent to the narrator's attempt to overcome his lateness while legitimizing his narrative.[49] While recalling his childhood at the beginning of the novel, the narrator recalls that 'un juif polonais vendait des valises [...] Des valises luxueuses, en cuir, en crocodile, d'autres en carton bouilli, des sacs de voyage, des malles-cabines portant des étiquettes de companies transatlantiques – toutes empilées les unes sur les autres' (*DB*, 11).[50] These many and various suitcases act as potent metaphors for the construction of a narrative of interlocking layers and distinct histories in *Dora Bruder*. The

---

[48] Lévi-Strauss, *La pensée sauvage*, 348. 'A multitude of images forms simultaneously, none exactly like any other, so that no single one furnishes more than a partial knowledge of the decoration and furniture but the group is characterized by invariant properties expressing a truth'. Lévi-Strauss, *The Savage Mind*, 263.

[49] Cooke, *Present Pasts*, 287.

[50] 'There was a Polish Jew who sold suitcases... Luxury suitcases, in leather, or crocodile-skin, cardboard suitcases, travelling bags, cabin trunks labelled with the names of transatlantic companies – all heaped one on top of the other'.

fact that they are sold on second hand complicates this metaphor, as does a later instances of the narrator himself taking and selling abandoned objects: recalling the palimpsestic literary provenance of *Dora Bruder* and the hidden lineage it conceals, this passing on suggests an underlying pre-occupation with questions of inheritance, legacy, and lateness.

Brocanterie in *Dora Bruder* is indicative not only of the narrator's pre-occupations with cultural lateness, however, but also with historical late-ness. Towards the end of the novel, the figure of the brocanteur reappears in one of the narrator's recollections of a time in his twenties when a girlfriend of his used to live in borrowed houses and flats. While staying with her, the narrator would take objects—including art books, antiques, clothes, and shoes—from these places in order to sell them on. The bro-canteur to whom he sold these goods is remarkably familiar, although the narrator seems not to notice, stating simply, 'Lui, il s'occupait d'un autre local du côté du marché aux Puces. D'ailleurs, il était né dans ce quartier [...] d'une famille de juifs polonais' (*DB*, 134).[51] It seems likely that these two figures are at least from the same community of Polish Jews, if not the same person, but the narrator does not pursue this similarity. Instead, he elects to bring up the topic of the Second World War and the Occupation during their conversation, revealing a preoccupation with the past and underscoring the difficulty—even impossibility—for him to reconcile the events of history with his present. His primary focus is on the continuation of his investigations of Dora and her family. The narrator's sense of histori-cal lateness is evoked by the empty houses and abandoned objects they contain. The fact that he steals these items and sells them on is not, how-ever, an indication of an ethically compromised narrator; rather, it reveals him as one who feels keenly the anxieties of the time and place he finds himself occupying. He steals out of necessity and poverty; his financial hardships and desperation are the legacies of preceding events, yet they pale in comparison with the horrors endured by Dora Bruder and her fam-ily. The narrator's actions, investigations, and perceptions are thus deter-mined by his sense of historical lateness and the melancholy understanding of history that this entails. He attempts to make something of these lost things, since they are all that he possesses. The earlier instance of the bro-canteur selling on these suitcases invites analeptic connections between the narrator's actions and his encounter with the suitcase seller, such that

---

[51] 'He himself had another shop, near the flea market [...]. It turned out that he came from a local family of Polish Jews.' (*DB*, 128).

the narrator's act of assembling a narrative in *Dora Bruder* becomes an act of *brocanterie* itself. The brocanteur passes on items that would encase the possessions of others, not the possessions themselves, whereas it is up to the narrator to find these abandoned objects and make something new of them. Becoming a brocanteur in his own right during the course of the narrative, the narrator metaphorically fills up the brocanteur's abandoned suitcases by creating his palimpsestic narrative, layering the abandoned objects of history over each other afresh.

If the narrator's casting of himself as a brocanteur emphasizes and thematizes concerns of lateness in the novel, then the exchanges between the narrator and the brocanteur figures further imbue the narrator's investigation with an epigonal desire for legitimacy through instances of symbolic investiture. For Eric Santner, symbolic investiture consists of 'rights and procedures [...] whereby an individual is endowed with a new social status, is filled with a symbolic mandate that henceforth informs his or her identity'.[52] The narrator's encounters with the figure of the brocanteur give his investigations and deductions just such a symbolic mandate. As a child, he is even offered a cigarette by the suitcase seller, then later the junk salesman suggests they go for a drink together, as if in reward or approval of his search for clues of Dora's life and fate (*DB*, 11 and 134). Their gestures of camaraderie towards the narrator indicate an acquiescence to, and even encouragement of, his excavation of history and, by extension, of the narrative he later constructs in *Dora Bruder*. Yet there is a lack of participation on the narrator's part. He does not say whether he takes the proffered cigarette, nor does he discuss much of what transpires when he has a drink with the brocanteur, just as he appears not to notice any similarities between the two figures themselves. Not only does this suggest his preoccupation with the events of the past, it also reveals his sense of coming late or after events, such that he is unable to feel fully present: when asked as an adult what he does for a living, he confesses, 'je ne savais pas très bien quoi lui répondre' (*DB*, 134).[53] Viewing himself as

[52] Eric L. Santner, *My Own Private Germany: Daniel Paul Schreber's Secret History of Modernity* (Princeton: Princeton University Press, 1996), xii. Prefiguring another resonance between the works of Modiano and Sebald, Katja Garloff investigates the narrator's quest for legitimacy in W. G. Sebald's novel *Austerltiz* along similar lines of symbolic investiture. See Katja Garloff, 'The Task of the Narrator: Moments of Symbolic Investiture in W. G. Sebald's *Austerlitz*', in *W. G. Sebald: History, Memory, Trauma*, ed. by Scott Denham and Mark McCulloh (Berlin: De Gruyter GmbH & Co., 2006), 157–170.

[53] 'I didn't quite know what to say' (*DB*, 128).

an epigonal latecomer, the narrator of *Dora Bruder* considers himself unworthy to be called a writer and thus has nothing to say, even as he still seeks validation of his undertaking. In the face if historical horrors, he is rendered mute.

The narrator's sense of epigonal lateness, his feelings of inadequacy, and his desire for validation and legitimacy via *Dora Bruder*'s bricolage are proleptic, foreshadowing later events recounted in the novel and, indeed, later discoveries made during his narrative investigation itself. His development and extension of instances of symbolic investiture over the course of *Dora Bruder* involve recalling earlier everyday activities and imbuing them with pathos. What might have been just the act of sharing a cigarette or going for a drink, for example, accumulates allegorical weight over the course of the narrative. For Walter Benjamin, it is in such instances of allegory, 'daß jene Requisiten des Bedeutens alle mit eben ihrem Weisen auf ein anderes eine Mächtigkeit gewinnen, die den profanen Dingen inkommensurabel sie erscheinen läßt und sie in eine höhere Ebene hebt'.[54] Crucially, the allegorical signifier appears insignificant and mundane, even as it gestures towards a significance beyond itself. 'Demnach wird die profane Welt in allegorischer Betrachtung sowohl im Rang erhoben wie entwertet', according to Benjamin, such that its mundane significance is hollowed out to provide space for new meanings, not unlike the 'marque en creux' left by the unknown experiences of the Bruder family.[55] The allegorical is thus for Benjamin a truly historical way of seeing, whereby history is perceived as a process of inexorable ending and decay, since 'Allegorien sind im Reiche der Gedanken was Ruinen im Reiche der Dinge'.[56] In rendering everyday objects allegorical in the narrative of *Dora Bruder*, therefore, the narrator renders them more significant than the quotidian, but in doing so, imbues them with a sense of lateness and of

[54] Walter Benjamin, 'Ursprung des deutschen Trauerspiels', in *Gesammelte Schriften I*, ed. by Rolf Tiedemann and Hermann Schweppenhäuser (Frankfurt am Main: Suhrkamp, 1980), 203–430 (351). 'That all of the things which are used to signify derive, from the very fact of their pointing to something else, a power which makes them appear no longer commensurable with profane things, which raises them onto a higher plane'. Benjamin *The Origin of German Tragic Drama*, 175.

[55] Benjamin, 'Ursprung des deutschen Trauerspiels', 351. 'Considered in allegorical terms, then, the profane world is both elevated and devalued'. Benjamin, *The Origin of German Tragic Drama*, 175.

[56] Benjamin, 'Ursprung des deutschen Trauerspiels', 354. 'Allegories are, in the realm of thoughts, what ruins are in the realm of things'. Benjamin, *The Origin of German Tragic Drama*, 178.

melancholy pathos. In Baudelaire's 'Le Cygne', the poet declares during his melancholy search for a vanished Paris that everything around him becomes allegorical:

> Paris change! mais rien dans ma mélancolie
> N'a bougé! palais neufs, échafaudages, blocs,
> Vieux faubourgs, tout pour moi devient allégorie
> Et mes chers souvenirs sont plus lourds que des rocs.[57]

Similarly, the world around the narrator of *Dora Bruder*, including the buildings that have survived the violence of the early twentieth century, as well as those erected later, along with the objects in them, cease to become mere physical objects. Under the aspect of the narrator's melancholy, Parisian edifices take on a higher significance, albeit one which is fragmentary and heavy to bear. As the narrator declares upon exploring the site of a former barracks:

> Derrière le mur s'étendait un no man's land, une zone de vide et de l'oubli. Les viex bâtimenrs des Tourelles n'avaient pas été détruits comme le pensionnat de la rue de Picpus, mais cela revenait au même. Et pourtant, sous cette couche épaisse d'amnésie, on sentait bien quelque chose, de temps en temps, un écho lointain, étouffé, mais on aurait été incapable de dire quoi, précisement. (*DB*, 131)[58]

They may as well be ruins, indeed: the melancholy husks of earlier structures. The narrator's inability or unwillingness to articulate fully the muted

---

[57] Charles Baudelaire, 'Le Cygne', *Œuvres complètes, tome 1*, ed. by Yves-Gérard le Dantec and Claude Pichois (Paris: Gallimard, 1966), 85. 'Paris may change, but in my melancholy mood / Nothing has budged! New palaces, blocks, scaffoldings, / Old neighbourhoods, are allegorical for me, / And my dear memories are heavier than stone'. Charles Baudelaire, 'The Swan', in *The Flowers of Evil*, trans. by James McGowan (Oxford: Oxford University Press, 2008), 173–177, 175. Benjamin was also fascinated by the figure of the Parisian chiffonier or rag-picker, exemplified in Baudelaire's 1853 poem 'Le Vin des chiffoniers', as an archetypal metaphor for the ravages of nineteenth-century capitalism, just as Paris itself was seen by many to be the capital of the nineteenth century. See also Antoine Compagnon, *Les Chiffoniers de Paris* (Paris: Gallimard, 2017).

[58] 'A no-man's-land lay beyond that wall, a zone of emptiness and oblivion. Unlike the convent in the Rue de Picpus, the twin blocks of Tourelles barracks had not been pulled down, but they may as well have been. And yet, from time to time, beneath this thick layer of amnesia, one can certainly sense something, an echo, distant, muted, but of what, precisely, it is impossible to say' (*DB*, 124–125).

echo of the past in the present re-expands the Barthesian dilatory area of his investigation while also reinforcing his late historical and aesthetic sensibility.

As this investigation of Dora's life and fate proceeds, the narrator continually develops and extends the first instance of symbolic investiture by emphasizing his suitability for the task of investigating the events of the past. He presents the first of many pieces of documentary evidence, from lists of addresses, to the forms he must complete to obtain information and the documents in response to his enquiries (*DB*, 14, 15, and 18–19). The narrator frames his presentation of this evidence by insisting not only on his aptitude in acquiring it, but also his own particular value, or even worthiness, in carrying out the task. He declares that in order to succeed in an endeavour such as this 'il suffit d'un peu de patience' (*DB*, 13),[59] before then emphasizing that he is just such a virtuously patient man: 'je peux attendre des heures sous la pluie' (*DB*, 14),[60] a pithy flourish typical of many of Modiano's narrators. There can be few images more melancholy than standing alone in the rain, yet this is also suggestive of a certain stubbornness on the part of the narrator. Much like the lost objects and the empty suitcases that litter the narrative of *Dora Bruder*, he appears here under an aspect of gloom and abandonment, while nonetheless building on instances of symbolic investiture across the novel to emphasize the suitability, even necessity, of his being the person who ought to investigate the past and construct the narrative of Dora's life and fate. These instances of symbolic investiture and self-belief, which on the surface are merely everyday activities, are given narrative weight, since the narrator bestows authority on himself by choosing to recall and include these encounters in his narrative.

Over the course of *Dora Bruder*, the narrator's investigations are legitimized, while his late historical position and epigonal status are reinforced. Although for Lévi-Strauss the concept of bricolage is founded on the notion of chance, the narrator's approach to the past in *Dora Bruder* transforms his bricolage into one which is consciously constructed and used as an attempt to legitimize his narrative, creating something new out of used and forgotten fragments. Recalling a key feature of Jewish modernist fiction and ensuring that the whole enterprise is framed as a late and epigonal undertaking, bricolage in *Dora Bruder*—as well as the

---

[59] 'All it takes is a little patience' (*DB*, 9).
[60] 'I can wait for hours in the rain' (*DB*, 10).

palimpsestic elements of the narrative's aesthetics—encapsulates the constitutive tensions of both the narrator's late historical position and his engagement with the past. As he attempts to suture the significance of Jewishness back onto the tradition of modern European literature, after which he situates himself, while simultaneously desiring to overcome the very epigonality that enables him to do just this, the sense of lateness in *Dora Bruder* is perpetuated and never overcome. The narrator is unable to bridge the gap between his present and the past, allowing Dora the chance of a *fugue*—a melancholy gulf between then and now that remains open—whose aesthetics likewise articulate and interrogate the constitutive tensions of the novel.

LIGHT AND SHADOW

In *Dora Bruder*, the narrator reflects at several points upon an image of a source of light guiding his and Dora's path as he retraces her footsteps through Paris. This solitary light metaphorically illuminates on the narrator's perceived obligation to investigate the past in a melancholy and self-conscious manner, while also implicitly recalling post-Enlightenment critiques of the notion of progress as the quintessential myth of modernity encapsulated, for example, by the Benjaminian Angel of History. Echoing the narrative's sense of lateness and the narrator's perceived duty to take on the burden of history, the image of a lone lamp bestows upon him a quasi-mystical feeling of being called to tell this story as he imagines himself as a beacon, a guiding light for how to engage with historical events in fiction. 'En écrivant ce livre', he declares, 'je lance des appels, comme des signaux de phare dont je doute malheureusement qu'ils puissent éclairer la nuit. Mais j'espère toujours' (*DB*, 42).[61] Casting his beams of light back into the past, he acknowledges that he does not possess the ability to reconcile his present with the catastrophic events that precede him, and yet he still endeavours to show them for what they are insofar as this is feasible. Due to his historical lateness and the view of history that this instils in him, he believes he has no choice. The image of a lighthouse bolsters his self-conscious engagement, yet also sets him at odds with Enlightenment meta-narratives of historical progress of the *Siècle des lumières*. The narrator perceives only one light shining towards the darkness of the past, and

---

[61] 'In writing this book, I am sending out signals, like a lighthouse beacon in whose power to illuminate the darkness I have, alas, no faith. But I live in hope' (*DB*, 37).

it is he. His words suggest both a self-consciousness awareness of his late and melancholy outlook, as well as a sense of doubt and humility, compounded at the last by traces of hope. In an image that recalls both the Angel of History and Nietzsche's formulation of epigonal modern poets as beings facing backwards, the narrator looks back towards the catastrophe of the century that came before him. While the signals sent out by his investigations in *Dora Bruder* may not directly or entirely illuminate the events of the past, his claim of indefinite hope nonetheless suggests a trace of optimism as opposed to an entirely hopeless melancholy aesthetic attitude. Nevertheless, the narrator's faint sense of hope is never realized in the novel, unless it is achieved *ex negativo* by the fact that he denies himself the chance to recount an imagined version of the events of Dora's *fugue*.

Photography—the art of drawing with light—also has a special resonance for the narrator of *Dora Bruder*. During the investigations he recounts in the novel, the narrator demonstrates a specific interest in photographs, which encapsulates his particular melancholy perspective and become crucial clues in the case of Dora Bruder. Photographs, indeed, constitute evidence of objects and are also evidentiary objects themselves, which assist in detection and deduction. The many abandoned and lost objects scattered throughout the narrative of *Dora Bruder* inculcate an aspect of decay and dereliction across the text, reflecting the late and melancholy mood of the novel itself. Through ekphrastic descriptions of the photographs that he uncovers, as well as an encounter with a photographer in Paris, the narrator's ruminations resonate with the work of both Benjamin and Barthes, thanks to a particular concentration on the viewer and their experiential perception of a photograph. The tension between the narrator as a viewer and his relaying of descriptions of photographs in the narrative suggests an inevitable unbridgeable distance between past and present via the narrator's intimacy to these photographs and the fact that he is nonetheless still historically removed from them as an observer.

While both Benjamin and Barthes express differing ideas on photography and its ontological significance, these overlap in their mutual fascination with the phenomenology of the photograph itself and with the need for the photograph to be beheld. Both Benjamin and Barthes emphasize the viewer's perceptual and imaginative participation in the singularity of any photographic image. Ascribing a certain dark agency to photography by identifying it as a symptom of modernity and tool for exposing it, Benjamin argues that a photograph's reproducibility has the potential to

undermine the uniqueness of the original image.[62] Barthes, writing later in
the century, turns to semiotic analysis in response to the rise of mass culture in the 1950s and 1960s.[63] For both thinkers, however, a focus on the
viewer of the photograph and the relations among the photograph and its
referent, the subject and the beholder, is key, as is an emphasis on the historical context in which the image was taken and beheld. The most precise
technology may imbue its products with a magical value, unlike that of a
painted picture, Benjamin observes;

> der Beschauer [fühlt] unwiderstehlich den Zwang, in solchem Bild das win-
> zige Fünkchen Zufall, Hier und Jetzt, zu suchen, mit dem die Wirklichkeit
> den Bildcharakter gleichsam durchgesengt hat, die unscheinbare Stelle zu
> finden, in welcher, im Sosein jener längstvergangenen Minute das Künftige
> noch heut und so beredt nistet, daß wir, rückblickend, es entdecken können.[64]

The viewer, for Benjamin, looks back at the image in a profoundly individual and personal way, which is refracted through their own experiences.
In *Dora Bruder*, crucially, the only beholder of the photographs is the
narrator. The reader, therefore, may only perceive the photographs of
Dora and her family that the narrator discovers via his mediating descriptions.[65] According to Barthes, the viewer's engagement with a photograph

[62] Walter Benjamin, 'Das Kunstwerk im Zeitalter seiner technischen Reproduzierbarkeit',
in *Gesammelte Schriften I.2*, ed. by Rolf Tiedemann und Hermann Schweppenhäuser
(Frankfurt am Main: Suhrkamp, 1974), 431–508. See also Walter Benjamin, 'The Work of
Art in the Age of Mechanical Reproduction', in *Illuminations*, ed. by Hannah Arendt, trans.
by Harry Zohn (New York: Schocken Books, 1968), 217–251.

[63] Roland Barthes, *La chambre claire: note sur la photographie* (Paris: Gallimard and Seuil,
1980). See also Roland Barthes, *Camera Lucida: Reflections on Photography*, trans. by
Richard Howard (New York: Hill & Wang, 1981).

[64] Walter Benjamin, 'Kleine Geschichte der Photographie', in *Gesammelte Schriften II.1*,
ed. by Rolf Tiedemann und Hermann Schweppenhäuser (Frankfurt am Main: Suhrkamp,
1977), 368–385 (371). 'The beholder feels an irresistible urge to search such a picture for
the tiny spark of contingency, of the here and now, with which reality has (so to speak) seared
the subject, to find the inconspicuous spot where in the immediacy of that long-forgotten
moment the future nests so eloquently that we, looking back, may rediscover it'. Walter
Benjamin, 'Little History of Photography', in *Selected Writings, Volume 2, Part 2, 1931–1934*,
trans. by Rodney Livingstone and Others ed. by Michael W. Jennings, Howard Eiland, and
Gary Smith (Cambridge, Massachusetts: The Belknap Press of Harvard University Press,
1999), 507–530 (510).

[65] For further discussion of the ekphrastic significance of the narrator's descriptions and
their relation to *Dora Bruder* as a work that is halfway between a memorial and an autobiog-

is likewise highly personal and existential: 'Dans l'image', he writes, citing Jean-Paul Sartre, 'l'objet se livre en bloc et la vue en est certaine'.[66] Nevertheless, Barthes understands a photograph fundamentally as an index, a tangible trace that its referent existed: 'dans la Photographie, je ne puis jamais nier que *la chose a été là*. Il y a double position conjointe: de réalité et de passé'.[67] He specifies photography's *noeme*, that is, the classification of its precise essence, as 'Ça-a-éte'.[68] For Barthes, however, 'the ontological and technological nature of the photographic image, on the one hand, and the reception, affect and interpretation of it, on the other, are always coexisting, although the relationship between them is highly variable', as Kathrin Yacavone summarizes.[69] While for Barthes, therefore, 'toute photographie est un certificat de présence', this constitutes a presence necessarily marked by death, such that every photograph reveals in its subject 'le retour du mort'.[70] In *Dora Bruder*, the photographs' mediation via the narrator ensures they are certificates of the Bruders' absence and of the presence in the narrative of the persistent gulf between the present and the past, a lingering absence from then until now.

Two principal instances in *Dora Bruder* when the narrator encounters photographs of Dora and her family demonstrate the Benjaminian and Barthesian inflections of his descriptions, embodying the tension between presence and absence that suggests a melancholy void between past and present.[71] The first set of photographs are from before the outbreak of the

raphy, see Annelies Schulte Nordholt, 'Photographie et image en prose dans *Dora Bruder* de Patrick Modiano', in *Neophilologus*, 96:4 (2012), 523–540.

[66] Barthes, *La chambre claire*, 165. 'In the image [...] the object yields itself wholly, and our vision of it is certain'. Barthes, *Camera Lucida*, 106.

[67] Barthes, *La chambre claire*, 120. Emphasis in original. 'Photography can never deny that *the thing has been there*. There is a superimposition here: of reality and of the past'. Barthes, *Camera Lucida*, 76.

[68] Barthes, *La chambre claire*, 120. 'That-has-been' Barthes, *Camera Lucida*, 77.

[69] Kathrin Yacavone, *Benjamin, Barthes and the Singularity of Photography* (London: Continuum, 2012), 122.

[70] Barthes, *La chambre claire*, 135 and 23. 'Every photograph is a certificate of presence'; 'the return of the dead'. Barthes, *Camera Lucida*, 87 and 9. A few years before Barthes's work was published, this connection between photography and death was also articulated by Susan Sontag, who declares that 'photographs state the innocence, the vulnerability of lives heading toward their own destruction' and that 'the contingency of photographs confirms that everything is perishable'. See Susan Sontag, *On Photography* (London: Penguin, 1977), 70 and 80.

[71] Regarding the ways in which photographs of Holocaust victims, while allowing false impressions and misreadings, have shaped private memories and collective histories over the

Second World War (*DB*, 31–33). They are, however, already tinged with the melancholy of the narrator's perspective as they are ominously prefaced by his observation that 'les années se sont écoulées [...] jusqu'à la guerre' (*DB*, 31).[72] These photographs of Dora's parents dressed in their best clothes, and of Dora after a school prizegiving ceremony, depict subjects unaware of what will eventually befall their family and others. From his late position, the narrator is able to project a melancholy air back onto this apparent innocence, armed as he is with the knowledge of what is to come. His presentation of the photographs highlights the unbreachable gulf between his present and the past, especially since the sentences that introduce them contain no verbs, implicitly suggesting an inability to act (*DB*, 26), which echoes the narrator's own self-conscious epigonality. Rather than bringing the narrator closer to the people in the photographs, the growing accumulation of unembellished factual details in his descriptions serves as a reminder that they are merely flat images. This recalls Mieke Bal's notion of photographic 'flatness' in her analysis of the relationship between text and image in Proust. For Bal, fiction is a verbal domain in which the visual can only be represented through subterfuge, which leads to the 'mirage of depth'.[73] If, therefore, a palimpsestic style in both Proust's and Modiano's work indicates the historical depth and aesthetic legacy of literary works and their provenance, then the narrator simultaneously bestows a sense of melancholy pathos upon the subjects of his narrative through the reminder of the photographs' physical and metaphorical flatness.

While his interaction with these photographs causes them to take on greater significance or singularity, his perception of their flatness and the absence they signify simultaneously reaffirms the centrality of the narrator and his fraught investigations, as well as the necessity of his perspective and his reactions to the Bruders' lives. The chronological progression through the photographs and his factual descriptions of them endows the narrator's historical perspective with a vertiginous sense of being overwhelmed by the past (*DB*, 32). At the same time, the more he engages

course of the twentieth century, exposing the gap between lived reality and a perceived ideal to witness contradictions that shape visual representations of victims, see Marianne Hirsch, *Family Frames: Photography, Narrative, and Postmemory* (Cambridge, Massachusetts: Harvard University Press, 1997).

[72] 'The years slipped by till the outbreak of war' (*DB*, 26).

[73] See Mieke Bal, *The Mottled Screen: Reading Proust Visually*, trans. by Anna-Lousie Milne (California: Stanford University Press, 1997), 1–14 (3).

with the photographs, the more distanced from them the narrator feels himself to be. In the last photograph he describes, Dora is younger than in the preceding one. This is partly suggestive of a sense of melancholy return in the past and a point beyond which the narrator cannot go: here, again, the gulf between him and Dora is emphasized through his perception of the photographs. The narrator's melancholy is further underscored by his contemplation of the colourlessness of the images. On the one hand, it is obvious to describe the photographs as black and white, since they were taken and developed before colour photography was widely available. On the other hand, the narrator's particular attention to the absence of colour in the items of clothing and the objects held by the people in the photographs reveal a further preoccupation. He focuses principally on the family members' clothes, all of which are monochromatically described. For the narrator, the fact that the items could be other dark or light colours does not figure in his account: colour or brightness do not matter here. He is interested only in the lack of colour or vibrancy in these photographs. Just as the Bruders are dressed up for the photographs to be taken, the narrator reveals himself to be similarly donning a costume of melancholy style cut from a cloth not dissimilar to Hamlet's trappings and suits of woe.[74] At the close of his description, even the seasons of the year are inflected by his melancholy, as the narrator remarks that 'ces ombres et ces taches de soleil sont celles d'un jour d'été' (*DB*, 33).[75] The bright and sunny weather is presented as fleeting or fragmented. No matter how bright and beautiful this summer's day is in the past, it is interpolated by approaching darkness. The stiff artificiality of the photographs inculcates a sense of fragile precarious existence captured in an instant.

Looking back from his late historical vantage point, the narrator reads his melancholy understanding of the past onto the photographs he describes, imbuing them with a sense of teleological inevitability. The narrator's second description of other photographs of Dora and her family later in the novel develops his melancholy perspective by drawing further attention to his role as both viewer and mediator of the images (*DB*, 90–91). The last photograph taken of Dora already comes laden with its own particular pathos, and the narrator remarks how it is in complete contrast to any other images he has obtained of her: 'son visage et son

---

[74] See Hamlet, I. ii. 85–86.
[75] 'These shadows and patches of sunlight are those of a summer's day' (*DB*, 28).

allure n'ont plus rien de l'enfance qui se reflétait dans toutes les photos précédentes' (*DB*, 90).[76] His plain factual descriptions communicate a sense of melancholy pathos as he perceives the serious facial expressions and sombre clothing of Dora, her mother, and her grandmother. His description ends in suppositions and further rhetorical questions about the photographer and his fate, evoking a growing sense of fatality, which is in opposition to the more innocent optimism of the earlier pre-war images. In a manner reminiscent of the centrality of the narrator and his reactions in Jewish modernist literature, the position of the photographer is vacated here, as the narrator writes himself into this role. Since the photographer is unknown, and the women in the picture face 'cet objectif anonyme' (*DB*, 91),[77] the narrator himself acts as the bridge between the photograph and the reader. He self-consciously mediates the past through his individual encounter with the images, endowing them with his melancholy and constraint. It would be possible to read this photograph of three generations of Bruder women as a synecdoche for all Jewish people who suffered and died during the Occupation: the family line ends with Dora's deportation and death.[78] That the photograph is of three women is significant for the narrator, since Jewish identity is traditionally matrilineal. Given that of his parents only the narrator's father is Jewish, his encounter with this photograph of the three Bruder women emphasizes his distance and melancholy separation from them all the more, since he has no immediate Jewish ancestors to connect him to their past.[79]

ABSENCE AND EMPTINESS

Above all, the thorny issue of presence and absence is most emphasized by the fact that the photographs described in *Dora Bruder*, which prove so crucial to the narrator's investigations, are not reproduced in the novel. The decision to describe his encounters with the photographs rather than to include these images in the narrative explicitly foregrounds the narrator's distance from Dora and the events of the past. He depicts subtle differences and distinctions in the photographs, confining himself

---

[76] 'Her face and her demeanour have none of the childlike qualities which shine out from the earlier photographs' (*DB*, 85).

[77] 'This anonymous lens' (*DB*, 86).

[78] For just such an analysis, see Nordholt, 'Photographie et image', 536–537.

[79] For further discussion of this see Ora Avni, 'Patrick Modiano: A French Jew?', *Yale French Studies*, 85 (1994), 227–247.

principally to factual description. Yet, as well as giving his narrative a more realistic documentary or biographical tone, his description also reinforces his own sense of melancholy pathos. As he ends his ruminations on the photographs, he finally begins to consider the potential colour of the images, but only to wonder, 'Dora porte-t-elle la jupe bleu marine indiquée sur l'avis de recherche?' (*DB*, 91), which returns him to his initial encounter with Dora Bruder and the start of his narrative.[80] The descriptions of the photographs in *Dora Bruder* are just as much a testament to their referents' absence as to their existence. Performing what the inclusion of the photographs themselves could not, this further contrasts the everyday mundanity of the staged photograph with the indescribable horrors shortly to befall the Bruder family captured in those images. Looking back for Benjamin's long-forgotten moment of contingent presentness in a photograph from the past, the narrator uncovers the tension between presence and absence in these images, as well as the melancholy contradictions involved in attempting to bridge the gap between Dora's past and his late position in the present. Recalling the techniques of Jewish modernist fiction, which Cohen claims centre the narrator's reactions in a text, these photographs likewise emphasize the narrator's view of the past and his self-conscious engagement with it through their Benjaminian and Barthesian concern with the viewer's individual encounter with an image.

It should be noted that in some later editions and translations of *Dora Bruder*, one or more of the photographs described by the narrator are, in fact, included as a paratextual frontispiece to the novel.[81] Rather than undermining the melancholy perspective of the narrator, however, their late inclusion may be understood as further—and, perhaps, inadvertent—reinforcement of his aesthetic attitude. On the one hand, the paratextual inclusion of the photographs alongside the descriptions by the narrator arguably lends the novel a sense of authenticity, simultaneously clarifying yet further blurring the novel's much-debated fictional or factual status.[82]

---

[80] 'Could it be that Dora is wearing the navy-blue skirt mentioned in the missing persons notice?'

[81] See, for instance, the German translation of the novel (Patrick Modiano, *Dora Bruder*, trans. by Elisabeth Edl (München: Hanser, 1998)) and the American edition of Joanna Kilmartin's English translation (Patrick Modiano, *Dora Bruder*, trans. by Joanna Kilmartin (Berkeley: University of California Press, 1999)). See also Dervila Cooke's analysis of the Japanese translation: Cooke, *Present Pasts*, 289.

[82] Unlike in W. G. Sebald's work, the inclusion of photographs in later editions of *Dora Bruder* is additive, as opposed to a fundamental element of the novel's aesthetics. Nonetheless,

In a Barthesian sense, then, the photographs testify to the existence of Dora and her family, included in translations as an act of commemoration and a testimony to their deaths. Yet these images further anchor the text in a specific time and place: the present of the narrator from which these photographic relics of an irretrievable past are invariably separated. They are present in their absence, while this absence determines the narrator's present. The inclusion of these images in translations of the novel results in further emphasis—however unintentional—of the temporal gulf between the narrator and the objects of his investigation when viewed alongside his descriptions. The melancholy irreconcilability of past and present returns, even as documentary photographs are included in an attempt to make the text appear less of a fictional construct and more an exercise in documentary autofictional reportage.[83]

In a similar manner to the figure of the brocanteur, the narrator's self-consciously melancholy mediation of the photographs in *Dora Bruder* is encapsulated in another figure he encounters. In this instance, however, the figure disappears over the course of the novel, leaving another space—another hollow imprint—for the narrator to occupy and overwrite. This figure is an unnamed photographer in Paris who positions himself 'dans le

---

the narrator's ekphrastic engagement with the photograph of the Bruder women recalls the concluding lines of Sebald's *Die Ausgewanderten* (1992), where the Sebaldian narrator describes a photograph of three women taken in the Łódź ghetto but refrains from reproducing the photographs in the text as he has previously done so throughout the narrative. Instead, he remarks, 'Wer die jungen Frauen sind, das weiß ich nicht. Wegen des Gegenlichts, das einfällt durch das Fenster im Hintergrund, kann ich ihre Augen nicht erkennen, aber ich spüre, daß sie alle drei herschauen zu mir [...] während die auf der rechten Seite so unverwandt und unerbittlich mich ansieht, daß ich es nicht lange auszuhalten vermag'. See W. G. Sebald, *Die Ausgewanderten: Vier lange Erzählungen* (Frankfurt am Main: Fischer, 1992), 350. Translation: 'Who the young women are, I do not know. The light falls on them from the window in the background, so I cannot make out their eyes clearly, but I sense all three of them are looking across at me [...] whilst the woman on the right is looking at me with so steady and relentless a gaze that I cannot meet it for long'. See W. G. Sebald, *The Emigrants*, trans. by Michael Hulse (London: Vintage, 1996), 237. For further discussion of Sebald's engagement with these photographs from the Łódź ghetto, see Lisa Bourla, 'Shaping and reshaping memory: the Łódź Ghetto photographs', in *Word & Image*, 31:1 (2015), 54–72, especially 62–64.

[83] For further discussion of the minutiae of alterations made between various French-language editions of *Dora Bruder*, see Alan Morris, '"Avec Klarsfeld, contre l'oubli": Patrick Modiano's *Dora Bruder*', in *Journal of European Studies*, 36:3 (2006), 269–293, and Jennifer Howell, 'In defiance of genre', 59–72.

flot des passants' (*DB*, 8).[84] While the narrator stands at a remove from those around him, attempting to engage with and capture fleeting, irretrievable moments of the past, he invites parallels between himself and this photographer. Although the photographer stands amid the crowd, people pass him by without paying him any attention. The narrator recounts how 'les passants ne semblaient pas vouloir se faire photographier. Il portait un vieux pardessus et l'une de ses chaussures était trouée' (*DB*, 8).[85] The fact that he remains ignored, alongside his shabby and dishevelled appearance, recalls how the narrative of *Dora Bruder* is related under an aspect of lateness, dereliction, and decay, as well as the narrator's sense of distance from events and the melancholy irreconcilability of the present with the past. Later, 'le flot des passants du dimanche […] avait dû emporter le gros photographe, mais je ne suis jamais allé vérifier' (*DB*, 8).[86] The photographer appears to have been swept away in his attempt to record events, echoing the narrator's concern with being submerged in the enormity of historical events that have gone before. This proleptically references instances of symbolic investiture whereby the narrator's unique suitability to the task is highlighted. The figure of the photographer has vanished, leaving the excavation of history in this novel and later mediation of the photographs of the Bruders to the narrator himself. This reaffirms his centrality—and that of his reactions—to the narrative of *Dora Bruder*, while emphasizing the constitutive tension of presence and absence in the novel's melancholy aesthetics. By focusing on the absent figure of the photographer, the narrator foregrounds his subsequent omnipresence in the narrative of *Dora Bruder*, filling the 'marque en creux' or hollow imprint left by the photographer, just as his narrative does with that left by the Bruder family. Yet he also gives himself licence and legitimacy to construct this narrative—to make his inky marks—as implied by the homophonic *double-sens* of 'marque en creux'.

The absence of photographers, as well as images of people, recurs towards the end of the novel in a final reinforcement of the narrator's centrality to the investigation of Dora's life and fate, as well as his late and melancholy perspective on the past. If, as Barthes suggests, 'non

---

[84] 'Amid the stream of passers-by' (*DB*, 4).

[85] 'People seemed not to wish to be photographed. His overcoat was shabby and he had a hole in one shoe' (*DB*, 4).

[86] 'The Sunday stream of passers-by […] must have swept away the fat photographer, though I never went back to check' (*DB*, 4).

seulement la Photo n'est jamais, en essence, un souvenir […] mais encore elle le bloque',[87] then this notion is actualized in the closing pages of *Dora Bruder* as, when visiting a military zone that prohibits photography or filming, the narrator remarks that everyone has forgotten the place and its significance: 'Je me suis dit que plus personne ne se souvenait de rien' (*DB*, 130).[88] In *Dora Bruder*, the ekphrastic descriptions of the photographs emphasize their referents' absence as much as their former existence, thereby further highlighting the unbridgeable gulf between the narrator's present and the past he investigates. From such irreconcilability emerges a narrative melancholy through which the narrator's act of remembering the Bruder family paradoxically limits how much they may be remembered and reinforces the brute fact of how few clues there are for the narrator to follow. The photographs ensure that both narrator and his objects of investigation remain fixed in their particular time and place. Although by the end of the novel the narrator has uncovered photographs of the area where the Bruders and the brocanteur lived (*DB*, 135–137), there are, crucially, no people in these photographs. On recalling a visit to the area during autumn, the narrator admits that 'de nouveau je ressentais un vide' (*DB*, 135).[89] The figure of the photographer, who might have constituted a conduit between the past and present, is gone, leaving only the narrator and his self-conscious investigation.

In their autobiographical writings on photography, Benjamin and Barthes both discuss what Katja Haustein refers to as 'the paradigm of the autobiographical self' by shifting the emphasis of the self onto the figure of the other.[90] In other words, the viewer sees themselves through the person whose image they encounter. In *Dora Bruder*, the narrator reveals just as much of himself as of those whom he investigates thanks to his focus on photography and his taking the place of the beholder while remaining distanced from the object of his observations.[91] This again

---

[87] Barthes, *La chambre claire*, 142. 'Not only is the Photograph never, in essence, a memory […], but it actually blocks memory'. Barthes, *Camera Lucida*, 91.

[88] 'I told myself that nobody remembered anything any more' (*DB*, 124).

[89] 'I had a sense of emptiness' (129).

[90] Katja Haustein, *Regarding Lost Time: Photography, Identity, and Affect in Proust, Benjamin, and Barthes* (London: Legenda, 2012), 5.

[91] For further discussion of how theorizations of such non-violent contemplation in the works of Helmuth Plessner, Theodor W. Adorno, and Roland Barthes may be conceived of in various ways as an ethics of indirectness, a suspicion towards certain forms of intimacy, as well as a preference for individual difference over communal identification, see also Katja

recalls Cohen's identification of the particular trait in Jewish modernist fiction of locating the narrative's centre in the narrator's reactions rather than in the text's nominal protagonist, while also highlighting the centrality of photography and the question of presence or absence to the constructions of melancholy in *Dora Bruder*. The narrator's echoes of Benjaminian and Barthesian views on photography are a further indication of self-conscious engagement with both a European and an often explicitly French cultural tradition, while also highlighting the narrator's centrality to the narrative, which reinforces the unbridgeable gulf between past and present in the novel.

A Dark Prison

In the final pages of the novel, the empty city of Paris comes to stand for Dora herself: 'la ville était déserte, comme pour marquer l'absence de Dora' (*DB*, 144). The immovable and unchangeable past is once more irrecoverably temporally distant from the narrator and the streets he wanders are more often than not entirely void of life. He experiences at various intervals 'cette même sensation de vide' (*DB*, 132) and 'l'impression de vide' (*DB*, 133), remarking also that 'il ne restait plus qu'un terrain vague' (*DB*, 133).[92] The streets' emptiness—clearly, for the narrator, a resonant metaphoric reminder of the Jewish absence in post-war European society—continues across the narrative: 'Je marche à travers les rues vides. Pour moi elles le restent, même le soir à l'heure des embouteillages, quand les gens se pressent vers les bouches du métro. Je ne peux pas m'empêcher de penser à elle et de sentir un écho de sa présence dans certains quartiers' (*DB*, 144).[93] Even when occasionally surrounded by people, the narrator senses the emptiness of the city; he is both within the crowd of passers-by and isolated from them. The allegorical gaze of the flâneur, as Benjamin notes, feeds on the melancholy that stems from being both within the

---

Haustein, 'How to Be Alone with Others: Plessner, Adorno, and Barthes on Tact', in *Modern Language Review*, 114:1 (2019), 1–21.

[92] 'The same sensation of emptiness'; 'the impression of emptiness'; 'nothing but a wasteland' (*DB*, 126–127).

[93] 'I walk through empty streets. For me, they are always empty, even at dusk, during the rush-hour, when the crowds are hurrying towards the mouth of the metro. I think of her in spite of myself, sensing an echo of her presence in this neighbourhood or that'.

crowd and an observer who is set apart from it.[94] Simultaneously detached from and connected to the masses in the arcades, the flâneur embodies the prevailing melancholy of modernity, much as the narrator of *Dora Bruder* embodies a sense of melancholy confinement in Paris. The emptiness of the Parisian cityscape where Dora lived is encapsulated in *Dora Bruder*'s abandoned and derelict aspect, while it also evoking a tension between absence and presence. Yet the narrator seems to wish to escape this emptiness as much as he desires to occupy it.

Over the course of the novel he draws at times closer to Dora, and at times further away, never quite reconciling his present with her past, all the while maintaining the narrative tension between presence and absence. While walking through Paris, he remarks that, 'sans savoir pourquoi, j'avais l'impression de marcher sur les traces de quelqu'un' (*DB*, 49).[95] Despite the sense of return in his wanderings, the closest he can come to reconciling Dora's past with his present is to stand where she may have once lived. In a concentrated moment of melancholy, he observes that

> le seul point commun avec la fugue de Dora, c'était le saison: l'hiver. Hiver paisible, hiver de routine, sans commune mesure avec celui d'il y avait dixhuit ans. Mais il me semble que ce qui vous pousse brusquement à la fugue, ce soit un jour de froid et de grisaille qui vous rend encore plus vive la solitude. (*DB*, 57)[96]

---

[94] 'Baudelaires Ingenium, das sich aus der Melancholie nährt, ist ein allegorisches. [...] Es ist der Blick des Flaneurs, dessen Lebensform die kommende trostlose des Großstadtmenschen noch mit einem versöhnenden Schimmer umspielt'. Walter Benjamin, 'Das Passagen-Werk: Erster Teil', in *Gesammelte Schriften V.1*, ed. by Rolf Tiedemann (Frankfurt am Main: Suhrkamp, 1982), 45–654 (54). 'Baudelaire's genius, which feeds on melancholy, is an allegorical genius. [...] The gaze which the allegorical genius turns on the city betrays, instead, a profound alienation. It is the gaze of the flâneur, whose way of life conceals behind a beneficent mirage the anxiety of the future inhabitants of our metropolises'. Walter Benjamin, *The Arcades Project*, trans. by Howard Eiland and Kevin McLaughlin (Cambridge, Massachusetts: The Belknap Press of Harvard University Press, 1999), 21.

[95] 'Without knowing why, I had the impression of walking in another's footsteps' (*DB*, 44).

[96] 'One point in common with Dora's, namely, the season: winter. A calm, ordinary winter, not to be compared with that eighteen years earlier. But it seems that the sudden urge to escape may be prompted by one of those cold, grey days which makes you more than ever aware of your solitude' (*DB*, 52).

Winter, the season of endings, reinforces his melancholy perceptions of Dora's past in his present. In contrast to winters in the past, this one is quite calm and ordinary, he claims. Yet it is this very fact that enables him to more clearly see how one might desire to escape one's current circumstances. This sense of apathy or disinterest with regard to his present recalls his epigonal feelings towards his writing and his investigations of Dora's life, suggesting that, in his melancholy, he would rather return to the winters of the past, although he knows this is impossible. All that remains to connect him with Dora is the bland ordinariness of this winter's day in Paris, which highlights more than ever his solitary lateness.

The narrator's particular use of the word *fugue* invites comparisons of the time in his youth when he ran away, and of his ride in a police van accompanied by his father, with Dora's flight from school and her ride in a police van to the Tourelles internment centre (*DB*, 60–65). This further suggests that it is only by engaging with Dora's life through his own experiences that can he attempt to bring the past and present together. Articulating once again the tension not only between absence and presence in *Dora Bruder*, but also between the narrator's centrality to a novel which purports to be an investigation of the life of another, this passage harks back to one of the hallmarks of Jewish modernist literature. In spite of this intergenerational link between traumatic experiences that are heightened by their Jewish connection, however, the narrator cannot fully connect with Dora's story in his present or his past. While the narrator is able to allow Dora her *fugue* by no longer investigating and writing elements of her story—the fact that he is the one who gets to decide this further underscores his centrality to the narrative—his melancholy solitude is emphasized by the fact that he seems unable to enact his own *fugue* from his unresolved abusive relationship with his father, a man who not unlike the brocanteur made a living from purloining various objects and materials. When recalling his traumatic trip with his father in the Black Maria following the arrest, the narrator admits that afterwards communication broke down between them. Within a matter of months they had ceased to see one another:

> Nous n'avons pas échangé un seul mot pendant tout le trajet ni dans l'escalier, avant de nous quitter. Je devais encore le revoir à deux ou trois reprises l'année suivante, un mois d'août au cours duquel il me déroba mes

papiers militaires pour tenter de me faire incorporer de force à la caserne de Reuilly. Ensuite, je ne l'ai plus jamais vu. (*DB*, 72)[97]

Still tormented by a father who seems determined to force his son to endure the experience of arrest and rounding-up that he had undergone in the 1940s, the narrator is never able to resolve this fraught relationship. The familial, for the narrator, becomes the historical. This sense of irresolution is prefigured earlier in the novel, as the narrator recalls a spontaneous attempt to visit his ill father in hospital, having not seen him since the aforementioned episode in his adolescence. Upon arriving at the hospital, however, the narrator is unable to find his father: 'j'ai arpenté les cours pavées jusqu'à ce que le soir tombe. Impossible de trouver mon père. Je ne l'ai plus jamais revu' (*DB*, 18).[98] In another subtle reference to the motif of the palimpsest, the narrator even recalls with reference to Abbé Prévost's *Manon Lescaut* (1731) that the building which is now the hospital had once been a prison for those waiting to be deported from France. Via a reference to imprisonment, the melancholy of the narrator's solitude and his unresolved relationship with his father is thus contrasted with Dora's pathos-filled *fugue* before her deportation and death. There is no sense of an equivalence between the two experiences being made by the narrator, only an overriding emphasis on the melancholy perspective resulting from an awareness of his inability to reconcile his present with Dora's past, which is compounded by his own frustrations with his family history. The geographical is imbued with the pathos of the historical. The contrast between the time serves to highlight the horror of the Occupation from the narrator's late perspective, while also solidifying his epigonal lateness. His reactions to what he uncovers of her life provide the means to reconstruct Dora's story and experiences from the inside out, as far as factual evidence goes, although the price is obsessive imprisonment within the confines of his own narrative.

Motifs of attempted escape and imprisonment encapsulate the tensions of the melancholy aesthetics of *Dora Bruder* that have been articulated and developed in this chapter so far. Indeed, the narrative of *Dora Bruder*

[97] 'On the way home, we didn't exchange a single word, not even when we parted on the staircase. I was to see him once or twice in August of the following year on an occasion when he hid my call-up papers as a ruse to have me carted off by force to the Reuilly army barracks. After that I never saw him again' (*DB*, 66).
[98] 'I tramped the cobblestoned courtyards till dusk. It was impossible to find my father. I never saw him again' (*DB*, 13).

is confined to a Parisian context to such an extent that the city itself is regularly described as a literal and metaphorical prison: 'une prison obscure' (*DB*, 56), in the words of the narrator.[99] This latecomer detective has constructed a prison for himself out of his investigations. Imprisonment motifs, as Cooke has observed, are a recurring theme across Modiano's œuvre:

> Whatever the forces that compel Modiano to write, a sense of the self arises through his compulsive repetition of the same themes, and his apparent inability to get to the heart of what he wants to say, endlessly producing narrators who cannot escape the pasts they wish to repress or who are somehow locked into repetition.[100]

In *Dora Bruder* the motifs of imprisonment reinforce the narrator's melancholy view of history, blurring the boundaries between city, text, and narrator. During the excavations retold in the novel, the city of Paris and the historical figures whose traces are sought become incorporated within a narrator figure. He thereby also encapsulates one of the central tensions of the novel via his attempts to escape, while remaining necessarily constricted by the means he chooses. Parisian locations connected to the Second World War and the Occupation recur across the narrative of *Dora Bruder* and particular reference is made to former prisons and military barracks. These nuance and complicate the narrator's self-consciously melancholy perspective on the past as he observes, for example, places connected to historical atrocities which occupy the same topographical space, such as the prison camp which 'occupait les locaux d'une ancienne caserne d'infanterie coloniale' (*DB*, 60).[101] The impossibility of reconciliation between his present and the past, along with a sense of trepidation about attempting it, is evoked in his anxious declaration that 'la perspective de vivre une vie de caserne […] me paraissait insurmontable' (*DB*, 96).[102] He claims that the notion of such imprisonment is something he is quite literally unable to overcome. This is later developed when he recalls that 'un haut mur entoure l'ancienne caserne […] et cache les bâtiments. J'ai longé

---

[99] 'A dark prison' (51). For further examples of this, see *DB*, 56, 60, 96, 130, and 138. Max Silverman also calls attention to this particular feature of the narrative of *Dora Bruder* in *Palimpsestic Memory*, 122.

[100] Cooke, *Present Pasts*, 44–45.

[101] 'Occupied a former colonial infantry barracks' (*DB*, 55).

[102] 'The prospect of barrack-life […] seemed to me unendurable' (*DB*, 90).

ce mur' (*DB*, 130).[103] A prison whose geographical location would connect him directly to the events of the Occupation is unreachable due to its
perimeter wall, which he follows. Cautious of making too many connections
between his life and that of Dora, he self-consciously traces where she
went but does not—or cannot—bring together his present and her past.
Unlike the literal imprisonment undergone by the narrator's literary fore-
bear Genet, it is through repeated references to imprisonment that the
narrator's investigations in the novel effectively become a prison for him.

Beyond the pervasive sense of repetition and uncertainty demonstrated
by the narrator's stream of rhetorical questions during his account of his
investigations, textual imprisonment is most explicitly shown through references to the city of Paris itself as a prison, not least because the narrative
of *Dora Bruder* is centred there. This Parisian imprisonment is also
reflected by the structure of the narrative: the novel does begin and end at
the flea market, but the narrator also returns at various intervals to places
where he and Dora lived at different times. Multiple references to trains
and railways made over the course of the narrative pre-empt Dora's eventual transportation to and incarceration in Auschwitz. There is a sense of
both repetition and irreconcilability in these references, which also highlight the narrator's perspective on history. He pursues his line of investigation in spite of understanding that he can never fully reconcile with the
past in the present, while images of Paris and of his narrative as prisons
exemplify and nuance his historically and geographically determined melancholy. As he attempts to enter the archives of the local Register Office
and the Palais de Justice to search for information on Dora's place and
date of birth, the narrator is shuttled from place to place by officials and
functionary advisors. Significantly, he describes the experiences as being
'comme à l'entrée d'une prison' (*DB*, 16–17).[104] He is required to submit
his belongings to a search or X-ray of some kind: 'Je n'avais sur moi qu'un
trousseau de clés. Je devais le poser sur une sorte de tapis roulant et le
récupérer de l'autre côté d'une vitre, mais sur le moment je n'ai rien com-
pris à cette manœuvre' (*DB*, 16).[105] This image of uncertainty and his
inability to act—he later does not dare to ask the way through the building

---

[103] 'The buildings of the former barracks are hidden behind a high perimeter wall. I followed it' (*DB*, 124).

[104] 'As at the gates of a prison' (*DB*, 12).

[105] 'I had nothing on me except a bunch of keys. This I was supposed to place on a sort of
conveyor belt for collection on the far side of a glass partition, but for a moment I couldn't
think what to do' (*DB*, 12).

(*DB*, 17)—is a manifestation of the historical distance between his present and Dora's past, as well as of the metaphorical distance between his narrative and Dora's experience. The conveyor belt is highly relevant: he previously held and could see the keys—symbolic of the means by which something may be unlocked—but he is subsequently unable to retrieve them from behind the glass. Significantly, here, the narrator may observe, but only from a clearly demarcated distance. The keys are placed on a conveyor belt, which turns in a repetitive cycle out of his reach. Just like this conveyor belt, the narrator remains trapped in a narrative investigation that at intervals comes closer and moves further away from reconciliation between the past and the present, while never quite achieving it. Although this image of the conveyor belt is merely a part of a simple bureaucratic process, the reference to imprisonment recalls the intensity of the narrator's melancholy perspective on the past. Ultimately, it suggests that, were the narrator to possess all possible information about Dora's life and fate—were he himself to have the key to discover everything about where she was and what she did—something of her would nonetheless still remain separated from him. Over the course of *Dora Bruder*, the narrative itself becomes a melancholy prison for its narrator, just like Paris, encapsulating one of the novel's central thematic tensions, namely, that between confinement and escape. The melancholy of the narrator's approach to the past is further exemplified in the proleptic structure of novel as a whole with its frequent moments of foreshadowing and return. Speculating about Dora's evening route home to the convent where she spent the summer of 1940, the narrator frames his imaginings within the context of his own later journeys along the same route, recalling that 'la station était déserte à cette heure-là et les rames ne venaient qu'à de longs intervals' (*DB*, 45).[106] This emphasizes the melancholy aspect of his reflections, since means of connection in the station are fewer and further between, before he imagines how Dora might have responded to going back to the convent: 'c'était comme de retourner en prison' (*DB*, 46).[107] His use of prison imagery as he wanders recalls how the past and the present remain unreconciled in the narrator's vision of the past. Between then and now

---

[106] 'At that hour the station was deserted, and there were long intervals between trains' (*DB*, 40).

[107] 'It was like going back to prison' (*DB*, 41).

there is still a dark gulf: 'il faisait déjà nuit' (*DB*, 46).[108] The image of early onset twilight here encapsulates the melancholy of the narrator's outlook.

In response to the narrator's sense of imprisonment through its evocation of departure from the city, imagery of rail travel recurs numerous times in the novel (*DB*, 29, 34, 45, 123, 143, for example). Through this recurrent imagery of trains and railways, potent symbols of modernity that inevitably recall Dora's ultimate fate in Auschwitz, the pathos of the unknown occurrences of Dora's *fugue* in *Dora Bruder*—as well as the overall melancholy aesthetic attitude of the novel and its constitutive tensions—is most explicitly articulated. Indeed, at one point the narrator observes that 'le mot "gare" évoque la fugue' (*DB*, 129).[109] Clearly foreshadowing Dora's eventual transportation to Auschwitz, these references also demonstrate both the narrator's and Dora's respective experiences of confinement and separation. She is confined to her fate, and he to his awareness of coming too late and facing the inevitable irreconcilability of his present and the past. Although the image of trains and stations might suggest a route out of his melancholy imprisonment, the narrator is always pulled back to Paris because of his awareness of the terrible fate that awaited Dora, which has already occurred. Here, the implications of his late historical position are once more apparent: even as the narrator might attempt to avoid the fact of Dora's demise, his inevitable return to it is staged alongside her—from the narrator's historically late perspective—inevitable death. All the while he remains unable to bridge the temporal distance between his present awareness of this and the moment of her *fugue* before she is captured. Although this reinforces the narrator's perspective on history and his self-consciousness in undertaking his investigations, it nevertheless also imposes limitations upon him, giving a further sense of pathos to the melancholy aesthetics of *Dora Bruder*. When at one point the narrator exits a metro station, this melancholy is exemplified particularly strongly, as he remarks that

> j'éprouvais une drôle sensation en longeant le mur de l'hôpital Lariboisière, puis en passant au-dessus des voies ferrées, comme si j'avais pénétré dans la zone la plus obscure de Paris. Mais c'était simplement le contraste entre les

---

[108] 'It was already dark' (*DB*, 41)
[109] 'The word "station" evokes escape'.

lumières trop vives du boulevard de Clichy et le mur noir, interminable, la pénombre sous les arches du métro.... (*DB*, 29)[110]

There is unbridgeable gap—an interminable wall, to use the narrator's phrasing—between his attempted excavations and the real story of the Bruder family. His realization that it was only the contrast of bright lights after a dark space that unsettled him appears to diffuse the gloom, but the endless wall of shadows under the repeating railway arches remains. This recalls his earlier image of a lone lighthouse casting tentative investigatory beams back into the past without ever managing to fully reconcile what he finds there with his present. Where the lighthouse image contains a trace of optimism, this moment near the Lariboisière hospital encapsulates the narrator's melancholy solitude in spite of the hopefulness his investigations might occasionally engender.

The narrator of *Dora Bruder* can escape neither the city that has become his dark prison nor his compulsion to investigate its past, yet the present and the past remain unreconciled in his narrative. Within the Barthesian 'dilatory area' that emerges between his investigations and Dora's *fugue*, the narrative of *Dora Bruder* is conditioned by the simultaneous possibility of resolution with the past and its sustained postponement. The constitutive tensions of the melancholy of history and of his narrative's aesthetics—the inevitable disconnect between then and now—reveal that escape is merely an illusion for the narrator of *Dora Bruder*. As an epigonal latecomer, he is condemned—indeed, through his melancholy aesthetics, he condemns himself—to inherit inadvertently another title of a novel mentioned earlier, this time by Jean Jausion, as he remains the man who wanders the dark streets of his Parisian prison: 'un homme [qui] marche dans la ville'. As with Simenon's commissaire Maigret, the object of his investigations spreads out before him, and as he takes these steps and continues walking through the cityscape of the past, there remains the potential, however latent, that some unknown truth at the end of expectation may yet be reached.

---

[110] 'Having a strange feeling as I followed the wall of Lariboisière Hospital, and again on crossing the railway tracks, as though I had penetrated the darkest part of Paris. But it was merely the contrast between the dazzling lights of the Boulevard de Clichy and the black, interminable wall, the penumbra beneath the metro arches' (*DB*, 24).

CHAPTER 3

Austerlitz by W. G. Sebald: A Late Fairy Tale

W. G. Sebald's *Austerlitz*, the last of his prose works to be published during his lifetime, is full of otherworldly dreams and spectral visions. As the protagonist Jacques Austerlitz remarks to the unnamed narrator, recalling a visit to the country home of his childhood friend Gerald Fitzpatrick, who later perished in an aviation accident, these impressions of allusively connected elsewheres 'g[e]ben einem das Gefühl, man sei jetzt in einer anderen Welt' (*A*, 122).[1] As with place, so with time: Sebald's final novel is a work that is not able to reconcile the past and the present, and moreover one that even resists doing so.[2] It is from the lack of consequence in the connections established in the narrative, from the absence of resolution, as well as its formal and stylistic aspects, and from its ever-diminishing returns, that *Austerlitz* derives its aesthetic force. The appearance of interconnection and mysterious similarity across place and time is intensified by the lingering sense that in the end something remains missing. Yet, even if *Austerlitz* is weighed down by the history and experience that precedes it, the denial of reconciliation, the lack of resolution, and any promise of future renewal articulated within the novel are merely deferred, neither fully actualized nor erased. Like the proximity and distance encapsulated by the galactic

---

[1] 'Give one the feeling one is now in another world'.
[2] See Timothy Bewes, 'Against Exemplarity: W. G. Sebald and the Problem of Connection', in *Contemporary Literature*, 55:1 (2014), 1–31.

© The Author(s), under exclusive license to Springer Nature   107
Switzerland AG 2022
I. Ellison, *Late Europeans and Melancholy Fiction at the Turn of the Millennium*, Palgrave Studies in Modern European Literature,
https://doi.org/10.1007/978-3-030-95447-5_3

namesake of Gerald's family home Andromeda Lodge, the one place where Austerlitz might have experienced some respite from the oppression of his foster family and the repression of his early life, *Austerlitz* invites imagining places and times beyond its own narrative, even as it embeds them deeper into the fabric of its narrative.[3] It contains constellatory connections and the vast spaces between them.

In his work on the concept of 'futurity'—which is to say, how the quest for uncovering and representing the past in contemporary literature is simultaneously both retrospective and prospective—Amir Eshel argues for the possibility for literature to 'affect our future condition' by looking beyond the text towards the potential futures it gestures towards.[4] Eshel argues that novels such as *Austerlitz* have enabled the emergence and evolution of a more democratic representational literary discourse, whereby Sebald is positioned not only as an author who seeks 'to move beyond exhausted language', but also as one who in doing so articulates an offer of beginning anew.[5] For Eshel, the 'significance of Sebald's prose fiction lies in its formal characteristics, not just in the scope of its thematic and semantic domains' and any Sebaldian sense of futurity is principally determined by his novel's engagement with time, which Eshel describes as its poetics of suspension. *Austerlitz* thus becomes, in essence, an exercise of an ever-deferred future-perfect. That is to say, the sense of time's passing and of the narrator's attempt to forestall his narration and stave off the moment when time will have passed 'suspends notions of chronology, succession, comprehension, and closure'.[6] For Eshel, 'Sebald's antiquarian manner, his uncompromised conscious slowness, halt the rapid pace of time and set limits to modernity's obliviousness, even if only in the realm of the text, even if only for the brief moment of reading'.[7] In *Austerlitz*, therefore, time is delayed and put off, such that a sense of futurity emerges, in 'the melancholic tone of Sebald's prose, by its insistence on keeping the tension between the historical event and its poetic figuration unresolved

---

[3] The Andromeda Galaxy is the closest to our own, yet remains at a distance of approximately two and a half million light-years.

[4] Amir Eshel, *Futurity: Contemporary Literature and the Quest for the Past* (Chicago: University of Chicago Press, 2013), 10.

[5] Eshel, *Futurity*, 37.

[6] Amir Eshel, 'Against the Power of Time: The Poetics of Suspension in W. G. Sebald's *Austerlitz*', in *New German Critique*, 88:1 (2003), 71–96 (74).

[7] Eshel, 'Against the Power of Time', 96.

and by its unique temporality'.[8] The novel both thematizes time and creates its own understanding of it, which has at its core a sense of slowing down and thereby resisting the accelerations of modernity.[9] This is indicative of key tensions within *Austerlitz*, not only between the past and the present, but also between the notions of *Spätlinge* and *Erstlinge*, between the condemned modern and the vestigially Romantic, as this chapter will show. The extent to which *Austerlitz*'s aesthetics of self-conscious lateness and melancholy are inflected by latent Romantic elements imbricated with the novel's thematic concerns reveals a constitutive tension between a national literary tradition and broader European literary context in the novel. It also suggests the possibility that, following Romantic cosmopolitan thinking, compromised literary forms and aesthetics might be salvaged from a past condemned by the Enlightenment and its legacy, such that a potential for cultural renewal is not yet exhausted.

In the opening pages of *Austerlitz*, the narrator recounts the story of the eponymous retired architectural historian's investigation of his unremembered childhood in Eastern Europe through a series of coincidental meetings that take place in a variety of places across Europe between 1967 and 1975. After their paths cross coincidentally once again in the saloon bar of the Great Eastern Hotel at Liverpool Street Station in 1996, the majority of the novel consists of the narrator's reporting of Austerlitz's continued investigations into his personal history, specifically his attempts to recover the memories of his early life, of which he has no recollection until a physical and mental breakdown many years later. Until his retirement after a long career as a lecturer in England, Austerlitz represses all memories of his past, of his transportation from Prague to Wales in the 1930s, and of his Jewish heritage. Having believed himself to be Dafydd Elias, having lived an alias life with a puritanical parson and his wife, he experiences a shocking moment of recollection as he returns to the site in

---

[8] Eshel, 'Against the Power of Time', 96.

[9] See Anne Fuchs, 'Temporal Ambivalence: Acceleration, Attention and Lateness in Modernist Discourse', in *Time in German Literature and Culture, 1900–2015: Between Acceleration and Slowness*, ed. by Anne Fuchs and J. J. Long (London: Palgrave Macmillan, 2016), 21–28. It should be noted that elsewhere Fuchs admonishes the Sebaldian narrator for his self-conceptualization as a melancholy collector who joins together the broken pieces of history into a study of destruction, which she reads as a self-interested or even self-indulgent performance, given his frequent turnings towards the metaphysical. See Anne Fuchs, *Die Schmerzenspuren der Geschichte: Zur Poetik der Erinnerung in W. G. Sebalds Prosa* (Cologne: Böhlau, 2004), especially 19–20.

Liverpool Street Station where he arrived as a *Kindertransport* evacuee. As
a result he sets out on a journey to Prague to meet his old nursemaid and
learn more of his mother, then travels to the Czech concentration camp
of Terezín (Theresienstadt), before finally heading to the Bibliothèque
Nationale in Paris on the search of more information about his father.
With every step and every uncovered clue, Austerlitz's sense of loss intensifies, his quest becoming more and more impossible to conclude. As the
narrator who mediates his story remarks, the sense of darkness 'verdichtet
sich bei dem Gedanken, wie wenig wir festhalten können, was alles und
wieviel ständig in Vergessenheit gerät, mit jedem ausgelöschten Leben,
wie die Welt sich sozusagen von selber ausleert' (*A*, 39).[10] As the novel
comes to a close, Austerlitz leaves his collection of photographs and his
writing to the unnamed narrator and heads off to attempt to discover more
of his father's life and fate. Perched by the moat of the Belgian fortress of
Breendonk, which he visits earlier in the novel on Austerlitz's recommendation, the unnamed narrator comes to the end of a chapter of the book
he is reading: *Heshel's Kingdom* by Dan Jacobson, a former colleague of
Austerlitz's. Significantly, however, he does not finish reading the book,
before he sets out on his way back to the nearby town of Mechelen, arriving 'als es Abend wurde' (*A*, 421).[11] Walking away into gathering darkness, the novel ends inauspiciously with a narrator haunted by the story he
has inherited and by his and Austerlitz's inability to reconcile their present
with the past. While Sebald himself did not care to use the term 'novel'
to describe his creative writing, preferring instead to refer to his works
as 'Prosa' or 'Fiktion', as opposed to 'Romane',[12] *Austerlitz* is generally
understood as his most novel-like work. Given that it lessens the confusion
between fiction and (auto)biographical memoir, which characterizes his
earlier prose works, *Austerlitz* is more like a 'real novel', as John Zilcosky
argues, than *Schwindel. Gefühle* (1990), *Die Ausgewanderten* (1992), or
Die Ringe des Saturn (1995).[13] Several posthumous reviews and accounts
of Sebald have attempted to ascribe a certain mystical quality to the author

[10] 'Becomes yet heavier as I think how little we can hold in our mind, how everything is
constantly lapsing into oblivion with every extinguished life, how the world is, as it were,
draining itself' (*A*, 31).
[11] 'As evening began to fall' (*A*, 415).
[12] See W. G. Sebald, 'Wildes Denken', in *Auf ungeheuer dünnem Eis: Gespräche 1971–2001*,
ed. by Torsten Hoffman (Frankfurt am Main: Fischer, 2011), 85.
[13] See John Zilcosky, 'Lost and Found: Disorientation, Nostalgia and Holocaust Melodrama
in Sebald's *Austerlitz*', in *Modern Language Notes*, 121 (2006), 679–698 (685–687).

and his work, variously alluding to his emergence onto the literary scene 'as if out of nowhere' as well as to his 'belonging, mysteriously, nowhere'.[14] If this is the case, at least in part, then this is certainly redolent of the mystical non-places and alternative fantastical realms of Romantic fairy tales, which ground *Austerlitz*, however subtly, in both a Germanic and a European literary context. Certainly many of its passages invoke an uneasy slippage between a dream world and reality: 'manchmal was es, als versuchte ich aus einem Traum heraus die Wirklichkeit zu erkennen' (*A*, 84), Austerlitz remarks when recalling his early years in Wales.[15]

Sebald's prose is so elusively allusive that almost every line can seem freighted with allegorical significance. New readers of his work, as well as those long acquainted with the Sebaldian, may struggle to shake the feeling similar to that expressed by the narrator himself during a fretful recollection of a trip to Marienbad 'daß ich wie ein Wahnsinniger dauernd dachte, überall um mich her seien Geheimnisse und Zeichen' (*A*, 312).[16] Connections are made and missed across a narrative that as it unfolds appears more and more to resemble Austerlitz's foster home, memories of which haunt him into later life: 'noch heute träumt es mir manchmal, daß eine der verschlossenen Türen sich auftut und ich über die Schwelle trete in eine freundlichere, weniger fremde Welt' (*A*, 69).[17] There is a lingering sense of something not quite fully grasped, lines of association drawn but not yet to their full extent. Even Austerlitz himself is unable at times to perceive all of the resonant echoes in his own narrative, as in his recollection near the novel's close of a performance by musicians in a travelling circus which he witnesses while convalescing in Paris. In their playing he hears many echoes of half-familiar music—Welsh hymns, a waltz, a funeral march—as well as strains of unknown melodies. The particular manner in which the music is played affects him unusually profoundly: 'Auf einen Wink hin, den sie einander gaben, hoben sie an zu spielen in einer verhalten und doch zugleich durchdringenden Weise, die mich, trotzdem oder vielleicht weil ich mein Leben lang so gut wie unberührt geblieben

[14] See Lynne Sharon Schwartz, ed., *The Emergence of Memory: Conversations with W. G. Sebald* (New York: Seven Stories Press, 2007), 18 and James Wood, 'W. G. Sebald: Reveries of a Solitary Walker', in *The Guardian*, 20 April 2013, respectively.
[15] 'Sometimes it was as if I were in a dream and trying to perceive reality' (*A*, 76).
[16] 'That I kept thinking, like a madman, that there were mysterious signs and portents all around me'.
[17] 'Even today I still sometimes dream that one of those locked doors opens and I step over the threshold, into a friendlier, more familiar world'.

bin von jeder Musik, von dem ersten Takt an zutiefst bewegte' (*A*, 388–389).[18] In drawing attention to the musicians themselves, Austerlitz seems to be moving towards recalling the only other musician mentioned earlier in his narrative, a girl playing a Bandoneon—an instrument that is also explicitly noted as being played by one of the circus troupe—who looked after him and his fellow refugee children as they travelled on the train through the dark countryside after crossing the North Sea: 'dieses Mädchen, von dem ich Jahre später noch, wie ich mich jetzt entsann, wiederholt träumte, daß es für mich in einer von einem bläulichen Nachtlicht erleuchteten Kammer ein lustiges Lied spielte auf einer Art Bandoneon' (*A*, 208–209).[19] Perhaps the different styles of playing are too disparate to allow Austerlitz to recall these two rare instances of his responding to music, but this unacknowledged echo—especially given the significance of this train ride to his own life—suggests that even the protagonist is not aware of all the resonances within his tale. It is also striking how frequently the narrative of *Austerlitz* is explicitly—and aptly—compared to a fantasy, or a dream, or even specifically one of the protagonist's nightmares, 'ein böser, nichtvollendenwollender Traum, dessen Haupthandlung vielfach unterbrochen war von anderen Episoden' (*A*, 204).[20] Take, for instance, that recollection of Austerlitz's flight on a train across Germany as a child, which is sparked by his spying from on board a train the Mäuseturm on the Bingen Loch in the Rhine Valley. As time folds back on itself, he is reminded of the straining tower on the Vyrnwy reservoir near his foster home, which he had long seemed uncanny to him. And yet, even as this association coalesces more clearly, closing a circle in the narrative, other matters remain unresolved and the world passing by outside the train window still appears unreal. The ruined castles atop the tree-covered mountains that rise out of the Rhine valley 'wirken auf den ersten Blick wie eine romantische Theaterkulisse' (*A*, 326).[21] In what follows, the Romantic staging of *Austerlitz* as a whole figures as a crucial element in the novel's pervasive mood of melancholy lateness. This chapter aims to peel back the

---

[18] 'At a signal between themselves they began playing in a restrained yet penetrating manner which, although or perhaps because I have been left almost untouched by any music all my life, affected me profoundly from the very first bar' (*A*, 382).

[19] 'Years later, as I now recalled again, I still had recurrent dreams of this girl playing to me a cheerful tune on a kind of Bandoneon, in a place lit by a bluish moonlight' (*A*, 201).

[20] 'A nightmarish, never-ending dream, with its main plot interrupted several times by other episodes' (*A*, 196).

[21] 'Resemble a romantic stage set' (*A*, 318).

'Theaterkulisse' of *Austerlitz*'s vestigial Romanticism to reveal its profound influence on the text and on its aesthetic attitude.

Although Sebald's millennial moment and his vertiginous perspective on the past are clearly relevant to his engagement with the legacy of the Holocaust as a second-generation post-war German writer, there is a relationship to be perceived between the promise of redemption in Sebald's aesthetics of resistance and the idealism of early German Romanticism. 'In Sebald's post-Holocaust inheritance of that cast of mind', as David Kleinberg-Levin claims, 'the tragic dimension of that dream – the scepticism and despair already felt by his illustrious predecessors, Hölderlin, Novalis, Schelling – has turned much darker'.[22] Romantic aesthetics in Sebald's work, that is to say, are inevitably cast under an aspect of epigonal gloom. Sebald's moral compulsion as a writer comprises for Kleinberg-Levin 'the particular guilty conscience of the latecomer' and is stimulated by the feeling of an intimate connection to events which neither Sebald nor his narrators directly experienced.[23] As Sebald notes in his lectures on *Luftkrieg und Literatur*: '[Es ist] mir bis heute, wenn ich Fotographien oder dokumentarische Filme aus dem Krieg sehe, als stammte ich, sozusagen, von ihm ab und als fiele von dorther, von diesen von mir gar nicht erlebten Schrecknissen, ein Schatten auf mich, unter dem ich nie ganz herauskommen werde'.[24] Sebald's œuvre is separated from yet unavoidably determined by earlier events in the twentieth century, which—as in the case of all three novels examined in this study—constitutes a fundamental component of their melancholy aesthetics. Sebald's writing is motivated by an attention to the potential for redemption in the work of remembrance, even as the hope and promise of the German Romantics have retreated into allegory, as Kleinberg-Levin suggests. Any promise of redemption in his work remains difficult to discern under the long shadow of melancholy that emerges in a narrative out of which colour and light appear to be continually, inexorably seeping, as when Gerald's great uncle Alphonso reminds him and Austerlitz in an image that recurs many times during the novel, 'daß von unseren Augen alles verblasse und daß die

[22] David Kleinberg-Levin, *Redeeming Words: Language and the Promise of Happiness in the Stories of Döblin and Sebald* (Albany, New York: State University of New York Press, 2013), 9.
[23] Kleinberg-Levin, *Redeeming Words*, 94.
[24] W. G. Sebald, *Luftkrieg und Literatur* (Frankfurt am Main: Fischer, 1999), 77. 'Yet to this day, when I see photographs or documentary films dating from the war, I feel as if I were its child, as if these horrors I did not experience cast a shadow over me'. W. G. Sebald, *On the Natural History of Destruction*, trans. by Anthea Bell (London: Vintage, 2011), 71.

schönsten Farben zum größten Teil schon verschwunden oder nur dort noch zu finden seien' (*A*, 134).[25] Nevertheless, by understanding *Austerlitz*'s many reworkings of German Romantic literary conventions as part of a self-consciously late and melancholy collection of literary works that collectively suggest an optimistic form of literary futurity in European literature, a potential for future aesthetic renewal remains discernible.

The previous chapter revealed a self-consciously late and melancholy narrator who comes to the fore to such an extent in *Dora Bruder* that the novel is just as much his story as that of the woman whose name it bears. In *Austerlitz*, the narrator figure is more reticent, revealing less of his personal life and circumstances. Yet the fluid complexity of his account of Austerlitz's words and of the fated, fairy tale improbability of their recurrent meetings—'die 'Unwahrscheinlichkeit unseres erneuten Zusammentreffens (*A*, 45)—ensures he and his structuring of the narrative never fully fade from the pages of the novel. His retreat during the narrative in order to allow the eponymous protagonist's voice to come to the fore suggests, even more so than in *Dora Bruder*, a case of narratorial epigonality with regard to telling the stories of others. However, in *Austerlitz* the narrator does not merely act as a frame for the novel's principal story. He conspicuously perceives himself as an historical and cultural latecomer, such that his concerns regarding creative and literary inadequacy, as well as his structuring hand in assembling the narrative, are evident at distinct moments in the novel. As he confesses following one of his meetings with Austerlitz, much of his free time after their conversation ends is spent hunched over a writing desk, 'um in Stichworten und unverbundenen Sätzen soviel als möglich aufzuschreiben von dem, was Austerlitz den Abend hindurch erzählt hatte'.[26] The final polished narrative is his later creation. Building on prior readings of Sebald's work as late modernist literature, this chapter shows how engagements with and enactments of lateness in *Austerlitz* also owe a significant debt to the German Romantic tradition: *Austerlitz*, that is to say, may be read as a late Romantic work as much as a late modernist one.[27] Delineating the lines of

[25] 'That everything was fading before our eyes, and that many of the loveliest colours had already disappeared' (*A*, 126).
[26] 'Writing down, in the form of notes and disconnected sentences, as much as possible of what Austerlitz had told me that evening' (*A*, 138).
[27] The term 'late Romantic' is understood here in the sense that the narrator is historically located after the German Romantic movement, rather than as anachronistically positioned towards the end of that period in the first decades of the 1800s. Nonetheless the late German

connection between the narrator's reworkings of the figure of the suffering Romantic artist and his sense of lateness, this chapter argues that his millennial melancholy has roots in various refashionings of the form of the Romantic literary fairy tale—the *Kunstmärchen*. If, as this study proposes, the narrator's self-conscious lateness and melancholy signifies *Austerlitz*'s inclusion in a literary mode of writing emerging in European fiction at the turn of the millennium, then this is complicated by what has traditionally been viewed as the avowedly nationalist legacy of German Romanticism. Drawing on readings of futurity in Sebald's work, this chapter shows that, while tensions between a German national literature and European literature are not brought to a resolution in *Austerlitz*, the possibility of their reconciliation is present yet deferred. By paying attention to the vestigially Romantic elements of Sebald's novel, these constitutive tensions are revealed. Recourse to the Romantic and to the *Kunstmärchen* form provides an enhanced understanding of the novel's aesthetic attitude.

GRANULAR NOVELTIES

Much of what the following chapter offers is a new reading of an author's work, the lines and shapes of which—not least its melancholy nature—have grown so familiar to scholars and readers in the decades since its initial publication that they have become almost synecdochic for the author and his œuvre. From this later perspective, looking back on Sebald's own literary lateness, what follows constitutes an attempt at hearing, acknowledging, and remembering the echoes of other voices in *Austerlitz*, paying particular attention to the constructed artistry of the text. Narratorial self-conscious awareness of the range of forms of lateness and melancholy in Sebald's novel, especially when read alongside the other works examined in this study, not only paints a clearer picture of the historical and geographical contingency of the novel's aesthetics, but also suggests how this may indicate a latent potential for artistic renewal in a German and a European cultural context. Romantic forms in Sebald's final novel are reworked and subverted, refusing or unable to offer an immediate sense of resolution, redemption, or restitution, yet not entirely erasing the

---

Romantics' concerns with the tenuous nature of cultural unity, as well as their emphasis on the tension between the world of the everyday and irrational, supernatural projections of otherworldliness by a creative artist loom large in the narrator's manner in *Austerlitz*, as this chapter will show.

possibility of their future instantiation.[28] Accordingly, this chapter examines these vestigial traces of the Romantic, proposing that they most clearly
articulate the tension in *Austerlitz* between the legacies of national literature and European literature.

Sebald and his œuvre may be—and, indeed, have been—construed in a
variety of ways as late. In both his prose fiction and his critical works,
Sebald consistently understands and critiques European modernity as a
late aftereffect of the Enlightenment notion of progress.[29] Stylistically,
moreover, his work may be regarded as an example of late modernism,
emerging historically at a late millennial moment, while also embodying a
sense of second-generation (and thus also late) post-war guilt.[30] Finally,
given his untimely demise at the age of fifty-seven in December 2001,
Sebald himself is late in a posthumous sense. Since his death, Sebald's literary estate has been held at the Deutsches Literaturarchiv in Marbach am
Neckar and materials made available from his personal library reveal a keen
awareness of and engagement with the entangled ideas of lateness and
melancholy and their potential for articulating a sense of European cultural futurity. By unpacking Sebald's library, to paraphrase Benjamin, and
by briefly examining the annotations and marginalia of the author's personal collection of books, a suggestive picture of the artist and intellectual
at work may be gleaned, alongside new insights into Sebaldian lateness
and the relevance of this study's approach and argument to Sebald's final
novel. It should go without saying—and thus ought to be said—that
archival discoveries such as these are not intended to establish vast generalities about the author and works to which they refer. Indeed, it is not
possible to be fully certain whether the markings or notations in these
volumes were made by Sebald himself or inscribed by another hand altogether. However, these discoveries do offer granular novelties regarding
the author's production of literary texts, alongside his engagement with
other fictional, theoretical, and philosophical works. It certainly suggests

[28] For a summary of the discourse around Sebald's writing as a form of restitution for lan-
guage with particular reference to Benjaminian philosophy, see Nikolas Jan Preuschoff,
'Schreiben als Restitution der Sprache', in *Mit Walter Benjamin. Melancholie, Geschichte und
Erzählen bei W. G. Sebald* (Heidelberg: Universitätsverlag Winter, 2015), 307–336.

[29] See, for example, J. J. Long, *W. G. Sebald: Image, Archive, Modernity* (Edinburgh:
Edinburgh University Press, 2007).

[30] See, for example, Richard Crownshaw, *The Afterlives of Holocaust Memory in
Contemporary Literature and Culture* (Basingstoke: Palgrave Macmillan, 2010), especially 41–116.

Sebald as a European writer engaging with European forms and perspectives, while simultaneously remaining deeply rooted in a German literary and philosophical tradition. Three volumes key to this study and its methodological approach that may be found in Sebald's *Nachlass* are Friedrich Nietzsche's *Unzeitgemässe Betrachtungen* (1874), Walter Benjamin's *Illuminationen* (1961), and Frank Kermode's *The Sense of an Ending: Studies in the Theory of Fiction* (1967). The copies of the three volumes owned by Sebald are to varying degrees highlighted and marked by notes made over the years, dating back to Sebald's early university days. Significantly, in his 1964 edition of the Nietzsche text, the corners of two of the most heavily annotated pages of Nietzsche's 'Vom Nutzen und Nachteil der Historie für das Leben' are folded down, indicating that Sebald may have returned to these extracts and engaged with their content repeatedly. One marked-up passage in particular deals with the overwhelming burden of history and lateness, which is highly relevant to Sebald's literary work and to this study:

> Jetzt regiert nicht mehr allein das Leben und bändigt das Wissen um die Vergangenheit: sondern alle Grenzpfähle sind umgerissen und alles was einmal war, stürzt auf den Menschen zu. So weit zurück es ein Werden gab, soweit zurück, ins Unendliche hinein sind auch alle Perspektiven verschoben. Ein solches unüberschaubares Schauspiel sah noch kein Geschlecht, wie es jetzt die Wissenschaft des universalen Werdens, die Historie, zeigt: freilich aber zeigt sie es mit der gefährlichen Kühnheit ihres Wahlspruches: fiat veritas pereat vita.[31]

Yet of even greater relevance to the interests of the present study are the three words written in the margin next to this particular highlighted passage: 'apokal. Historie. Angelus'. The abbreviation 'apokal.' in this annotation explicitly connects formulations of lateness from Kermode's work

---

[31] Friedrich Nietzsche, *Unzeitgemäße Betrachtungen* (Stuttgart: Alfred Kröner, 1964), 127. DLA Marbach: WGS:8 Geistes- und Kulturwissenschaften (einschließlich Geschichte, Psychologie, Philosophie etc.). 'Now the demands of life alone no longer reign and exercise constraint on knowledge of the past: now all the frontiers have been torn down and all that has ever been rushes upon mankind. All perspectives have been shifted back to the beginning of all becoming, back into infinity. Such an immense spectacle as the science of universal becoming, history, now displays has never before been seen by any generation; though it displays it, to be sure, with the perilous daring of its motto: fiat veritas, pereat vita' [let truth prevail though life perish]. Friedrich Nietzsche, *Untimely Meditations*, trans. by R. J. Hollingdale (Cambridge: Cambridge University Press, 1997), 77–78.

on modern modes of apocalyptic thought in his *The Sense of an Ending* with Nietzsche's theorizations of the overwhelming burden of prior literary works and Benjamin's melancholy *Angelus Novus*, recalling Nietzsche's suggestion that backward-looking epigonal latecomers might achieve future artistic renewal and innovation via self-consciousness.

Such discoveries in Sebald's annotations that suggestively connect with his novelistic praxis not only validate in part the methodological approach in this study; they also complicate the picture of what Lynn Wolff refers to as 'Sebalds Doppelperspektive als Beobachter der Literatur (Literaturwissenschaftler) [...] und als productiver Teilnehmer an der Literatur (Schriftsteller)'.[32] For Wolff, 'das Besondere an Sebalds Werken liegt darin, wie er solche meta-literarischen Fragen im literarischen Diskurs selbst (dar-)stellt'.[33] This chapter bears in mind such questions with respect to the kinds of lateness that are present in Sebald's final novel, while examining what forms of melancholy emerge from this and considering the (meta-)literary questions posed and embodied by the self-conscious narrator of *Austerlitz*. In its late re-enactment of conceptions of the Romantic suffering artist, the narrative of *Austerlitz* constitutes a reworking of various Romantic conventions that is inflected by nationalism on the one hand and a broader European cultural context on the other. The aesthetic attitude of *Austerlitz* thereby engages with the troubled legacies of both the Romantic and the modern, while suggesting a latent future possibility for renewal.

MODERN AND ROMANTIC LATENESS

Several volumes of German and European literary history published in the early decades of the twenty-first century have concluded with Sebald, chief among them Ben Hutchinson's work on *Lateness in Modern European Literature* (2016), which explicitly draws attention to this fact.[34] Especially

---

[32] 'Sebald's double perspective as observer of literature (literary scholar) [...] and as a productive participant in literature (author)'. Lynn Wolff, 'Zur Sebald-Forschung', in *W. G. Sebald – Handbuch: Leben, Werk, Wirkung*, ed. by Claudia Öhlschläger and Michael Niehaus (Stuttgart: Metzler, 2017), 312–318 (316).

[33] 'The particular thing about Sebald's work is how, within the literary discourse, he both poses and embodies such meta-literary questions'. Lynn Wolff, 'Zur Sebald-Forschung', 316.

[34] See, for example, Andreas Huyssen, 'Grey Zones of Remembrance', in *A New History of German Literature*, ed. by David E. Wellbery, Judith Ryan, Hans Ulrich Gumbrecht, Anton Kaes, Joseph Leo Koerner, and Dorothea E. von Mücke (Cambridge, Massachusetts:

given Sebald's international success, as Hutchinson remarks, he is regularly identified as 'something close to the *telos* of modern German – and,
indeed, giving his wide-ranging concerns – European literature' in the
twentieth century.[35] Michael Minden also argues, for example, that
Sebald's work stands as an attempt at the close of the twentieth century to
'redeem both the false meaningfulness that attaches to information in the
computer age and the false authenticity that attaches to the representations of the world mediated through technology'.[36] By looking back to
earlier times, Sebald's work offers, Minden argues, 'the possibility that the
Erlebnis of existing in the fallen world might indeed again become, if
treated with the appropriate aesthetic and cultural respect, the kind of
Erfahrung that makes survival in it valuable'.[37] *Erlebnis* here is understood
as the more immediate impact of external events upon the mind and memory in the creation of internal events, whereas *Erfahrung* signifies lessons
later learned, shared, and communicated, based on prior experience.[38]
Sebald's œuvre thus acknowledges the true nature of late modernity via its
aesthetic and thematic preoccupations, as well as its late historical perspective. Yet it also suggests a means of existing within it, living through it, and
perhaps even surviving beyond it. On a moral or ethical level, as Russell
Kilbourn argues, Sebald's literary work constitutes a form of restitution as

Harvard University Press, 2004), 970–976; Nicholas Boyle, *A Very Short Introduction to German Literature* (Oxford: Oxford University Press, 2008), 157–159; and Michael Minden, *Modern German Literature* (Cambridge: Polity, 2011), 231. Cited in Ben Hutchinson, *Lateness and Modern European Literature* (Oxford: Oxford University Press, 2016), 340, n. 23.

[35] Hutchinson, *Lateness*, 334.

[36] Minden, *Modern German Literature*, 231.

[37] Minden, *Modern German Literature*, 231.

[38] For further discussion of this distinction with particular reference to Benjaminian thought, see Minden, *Modern German Literature*, 183–189. Similarly to Hans-Georg Gadamer's later understanding in *Wahrheit und Methode* (1960) of experience as a dialectical process of learning over time, which synthesizes negative unpleasantness and positive affirmation to produce wisdom that may be transmitted through tradition across generations, Benjamin suggests that the immediate inner experience of *Erlebnis* was fragmented and iso-
lated, in contrast to the accretion of truth and transferrable wisdom that constitutes *Erfahrung*. Gadamer also credits Hegel with testifying to this distinction, since 'in ihm gewinnt das Moment der Geschichtlichkeit sein Recht. Er denkt die Erfahrung als den sich vollbringenden Skeptizismus'. Hans-Georg Gadamer, *Wahrheit und Methode* (Tübingen: J. C. B. Mohr, 1960). 'With him the element of historicity comes into its own. He conceives experience as scepticism in action'. Hans-Georg Gadamer, *Truth and Method* (London: Continuum, 2004), 348.

a secular alternative to notions of redemption, given its restoration of agency to the historically marginalized, while refusing to intervene in a manner that would compromise their otherness.[39] As far as literary aesthetics are concerned, this study contends that it may be possible to attain a literature of restitution that is complemented by the redemption of damaged literary forms, or at least gestures towards the possibility of this. When read in isolation *Austerlitz* articulates a quasi-apocalyptic, vertiginous sense of lateness, whereas a reading of the novel as part of a collective of resonant literary works opens up the more optimistic possibility of the kind of aesthetic redemption suggested by Minden.

Sebald's work appears suspended between this world and the next—historically located, yet simultaneously out of time and place. This results in a pervasive sense of historical rupture due to his late temporal position of hovering ambiguously over the ending of modernity, as Hutchinson describes it.[40] While Sebald himself did not have the chance to develop a particular late style in the works he produced towards the untimely end of his life and literary career, his œuvre in its entirety can in fact be understood as encapsulating the phenomenon of late style. That is to say, as Hutchinson observes, that the style of Sebald's work can be understood as one which is always late.[41] Just as for Edward Said, 'lateness is being at the end, fully conscious, full of memory, and very (even preternaturally) aware of the present', so a conscious awareness of the author's historical position—and by extension that of his ambiguously autobiographical narrators—is present across Sebald's œuvre.[42] This manifests itself principally as *Fortschrittskritik*, a critical position towards the Enlightenment notion of progress. From Sebald's millennial perspective, modernity is viewed as a poorly conceived and catastrophic excrescence of the Enlightenment;

---

[39] See Russell J. A. Kilbourn, 'The Question of Genre in W. G. Sebald's "Prose" (Towards a Post-Memorial Literature of Restitution)', *A Literature of Restitution: Critical Essays on W. G. Sebald*, ed. by Jeannette Baxter, Valerie Henitiuk, and Ben Hutchinson (Manchester: Manchester University Press, 2013), 247–264 (261).

[40] See Hutchinson, *Lateness*, 335.

[41] See Ben Hutchinson, *W. G. Sebald: Die dialektische Imagination*, 170: 'Damit sei nicht behauptet, dass Sebald einen Spätstil *hatte* – dass etwa eine klare Linie zwischen seinem Frühwerk und seinem Spätwerk zu ziehen wäre –, sondern dass seine Prosa gleichsam ein Spätstil *ist*.' [Emphasis in original]. 'That is not to claim that Sebald *had* a late style – that some clear line may be drawn between his early work and his late work – but rather that his prose *is* a late style, so to speak'.

[42] Edward Said, *On Late Style* (London: Bloomsbury, 2006), 14. Cited in Hutchinson, *Die dialektische Imagination*, 170.

historically speaking, the period of modernity itself is thus construed as late. If Sebald himself may furthermore be understood as a writer who is out-of-time, so to speak, in that he was producing work which is aesthetically modernist but located historically after modernism, then, as in the case of *Dora Bruder* and *Sefarad*, lateness is not only historically but also aesthetically inflected: 'engagement *with* lateness', as Hutchinson remarks, 'is also an enactment *of* lateness'.[43] Positioning Sebald as a millennial modernist both enables and requires reflection on the postmodern historical perspective afforded by the imminent close of the twentieth century and on the sustained *longue durée* of lateness in European literature. That Sebald's prose is not only about lateness, but is also an act of writing as lateness itself, is the chief cause of its characteristic sense of vertigo, Hutchinson argues. Sebald's texts are cut off from the past they thematize, while simultaneously being determined by it:

> The uncanny, vertiginous feeling afforded by Sebald's prose is predicated both on the narrator's distance from the events and individuals he describes and on the collapsing of this distance, where the past returns to haunt the present [...] Rendered dizzy and passive by the burden of modernity before him, the 'late modern' writer can only become busy and active though his own sleight of hand, through making his lateness the precondition – and thus in some sense also the subject – of his literature.[44]

The vertigo of Sebald's millennial moment, as well as the double sense of lateness through which he views modernity as late from a simultaneously late historical position, confers gravity and pathos on his œuvre. The pessimistic conclusion that may be drawn from this is, as Hutchinson observes, a reconceptualization of 'literature as condemned by its own machinery, by its own accumulated weight of experience. In short: literature itself, not just its exponent, emerges as always already late'.[45] If, however, as Hutchinson points out, 'literary modernity emerges in the wake of romanticism',[46] and if melancholy emerges from lateness, then to appreciate their Sebaldian forms in *Austerlitz* fully, attention must be paid not only to the narrator's late modernist tendencies, but also to his late reworkings of tropes and conventions of that great precursor to the modern, the

---

[43] See Hutchinson, *Lateness*, 336.
[44] Hutchinson, *Lateness*, 337–338.
[45] Hutchinson, *Lateness*, 338.
[46] Hutchinson, *Lateness*, 41.

Romantic. Examining *Austerlitz*'s Romantic inflections provides new insights into the ways in which forms of lateness and epigonality suggest a future of 'busy and active' literary production. If lateness is indeed the precondition for the narrator's literature in *Austerlitz*, then his aesthetic legerdemain is inflected by the Romantic just as much as it is by the modern.

Modernism in Western European literature emerges crucially after the German Romantics, such that, as Gordon McMullan contends, 'if German Romanticism was responsible for the invention of late style, then German modernism was in a sense responsible for its reinvention'.[47] There is an intimate, even fundamental, connection between constructions of lateness in the two periods and literary movements, which resonates back and forth across the centuries, in spite of the discrete categorizations of the Romantic and the modern. Modern lateness, this suggests, contains vestigial Romantic lateness. 'Twentieth century writers turn to Romanticism partly because', as Nicholas Saul remarks, 'they are self-consciously modernist writers, and the modernist's first move is creatively to experiment with received literary forms'.[48] As a self-consciously late modernist at the close of the twentieth century, then, Sebald looks back at what has come before him, enacting a form of late modernism in his writing. Yet, following McMullan and Saul, this begs the question of whether the sense of epigonal lateness in *Austerlitz* might not also have roots in a German Romantic tradition, with the narrator's—and, indeed, Sebald's—view of modernity finding its counterpart in the Romantics' dissatisfaction with the world of the everyday, as well as in their shared scepticism and repudiation of Enlightenment values.

Though far from unique to the German context, Romanticism nonetheless acquired a particular character within German literature, becoming a more politically charged and longer lasting movement than in other national cultural contexts. Its rise alongside the rapid expansion of a reading public within Europe coincided with a flourishing of Germanic literature in the second half of the eighteenth century. Occurring concomitantly with the modernization of the publishing industry, these events combined to demarcate the emergence of what Minden terms 'a self-consciously

---

[47] Gordon McMullan, *Shakespeare and the Idea of Late Writing* (Cambridge: Cambridge University Press, 2007), 277.

[48] Nicolas Saul, 'The Reception of German Romanticism in the Twentieth Century', in *The Literature of German Romanticism*, ed. by Dennis F. Mahoney (Rochester, New York: Camden House, 2009), 327–359 (334).

aspirational literary culture'.[49] Romanticism, however, is not only an historical period or literary movement, but also a literary typology. 'The Romantic is a disposition of mind that is not limited to an epoch', as Rüdiger Safranski declares. 'It found its most complete expression in the Romantic period, but it is not confined there: the Romantic is still with us today'.[50] While Friedrich Schlegel is generally credited with first using the term Romantic to broadly describe literature that depicted the emotional as an imaginative form,[51] Safranski draws in particular on Novalis's 1798 definition of the Romantic to ground his claims: 'Indem ich dem Gemeinen einen hohen Sinn, dem Gewöhnlichen ein geheimnissvolles Ansehn, dem Bekannten die Würde des Unbekannten, dem Endlichen einen Unendlichen Schein gebe, so romantisiere ich'.[52] Romanticism as an aesthetic practice continued well beyond the 1850s, informing the literary work of artists like Sebald centuries later, such that the dissatisfaction with reality expressed in Novalis's explication of Romanticism is not too dissimilar to Sebald's own view of modernity and its aftermath. Austerlitz himself seems many times during the novel to be alive to a sense of the world's fading. After having buried the manuscript he has been slaving over for months in the compost heap in his garden, he remarks how, 'erleichtert von der Last meines Lebens, merkte [ich] aber zugleich schon, wir die Schatten sich über mich legten. Vor allem in den Studen der Abenddämmerung, die mir sonst immer die liebsten gewesen waren, überkam mich eine zunächst diffuse, dann dichter und dichter werdende Angst, durch die sich das schöne Schauspiel der verblassenden Farben in eine böse, lichtlose Fahlheit verkehrte' (*A*, 184).[53] The soil and leaves of

---

[49] Minden, *Modern German Literature*, 5.

[50] Rüdiger Safranski, *Romanticism: A German Affair*, trans. by Robert E. Goodwin (Evanston, Illinois: Northwestern University Press, 2014), xiii.

[51] See Friedrich Schlegel, *Kritische Schriften*, ed. by Wolfdietrich Rasch (Munich: Carl Hanser, 1958), 37–38.

[52] Novalis, 'Vorarbeiten zu verschiedenen Fragmentsammlungen 1798', in *Novalis: Werke, Tagebücher und Briefe von Friedrich von Hardenberg Vol. 2.*, ed. by Hans-Joachim Mähl (Munich: Carl Hanser, 1987), 311–424 (334). 'By endowing the commonplace with a higher meaning, the ordinary with a mysterious respect, the known with the dignity of the unknown, the finite with the appearance of the infinite, I make it Romantic'.

[53] 'I felt some relief from the burden weighing down on my life, but I soon realized that the shadows were falling over me. Especially in the evening twilight, which had always been my favourite time of day, I was overcome by a sense of anxiety, diffuse at first then growing ever denser, through which the lovely spectacle of fading colours turned to a malevolent and lightless pallor' (*A*, 176).

the natural world, Austerlitz's intellectual and emotional life, as well as the sun setting on his world in both a physical and a metaphorical sense, combine here to join modern and romantic sensibilities. 'The Romantic crisis', as Saul later acknowledges, 'is merely the beginning of the still unsolved modern crisis'.[54] This suggests not only that repeated returns to the past by later writers are indicative of a profound affinity between the Romantic and the modern, but also that lateness in modernism—and, perhaps, *a fortiori* lateness in late modernism—has its origins, at least in part, in Romanticism. This would further imply resonances between Romanticism and the concerns of late modern writers, recalling their mutual distrust of and dissatisfaction with Enlightenment notions of progress in a benighted later age.

Suggesting a sense of cultural lateness with this idea of the twilight of art and reason, while further solidifying points of resonance between Romanticism and modernism at the turn of the millennium, Azade Seyhan notes that 'the trials of our modernity still carry the not so distant echoes of German Romanticism's anxiety for a world in which individuals, communities and nations struggle for freedom and agency, as they face the seemingly insurmountable challenges of consumerism, intolerance, lack of ethical vision, religious fanaticism and the twilight of creative reason and empowering art'.[55] Engagement with the Romantic, this suggests, acknowledges similarities and continuities between it and the modern, while also avoiding the trap of reading Romanticism as merely anti-modern or reactionary. Modernism emerges, after all, in Romanticism's wake, while both constitute in their own discrete ways responses to the Enlightenment.[56] Although modernism is ultimately founded on a utopian idea of universal

[54] Nicholas Saul, 'The Reception of German Romanticism', 358.

[55] Azade Seyhan, 'What is Romanticism, and where did it come from?', in *The Cambridge Companion to German Romanticism*, ed. by Nicholas Saul (Cambridge: Cambridge University Press, 2009), 1–20 (19). For further discussion of these ideas, see also Azade Seyhan, *Representation and its Discontents: The Critical Legacy of German Romanticism* (Berkeley: University of California Press, 1992).

[56] It must be acknowledged that much of the bogus grandeur of the National Socialist movement derived its significance and sense of legitimacy from the German Romantic tradition via its folkloric focus and insistence on a mystical, almost spiritual connection between the German people and the land as an organic nation state. Recent scholarship, however, emphatically situates German Romanticism as a contributing factor in modern European life and culture. 'German Romanticism was a modern movement engaged in a modern critique of modernity', as Margarete Kohlenbach emphatically affirms. See Margarete Kohlenbach, 'Transformations of German Romanticism, 1830–2000', in *The Cambridge Companion to*

truths, one of the basic tenets of the Romantic is what Minden describes as 'a notion of ineffable truth touched by feeling but not accessible to reason or even words in any direct sense'.[57] This fundamental unknowability of universal truths is often expressed in Romantic literature through a fascination with the emotional and the irrational, not unlike Austerlitz's recollection of a summer trip to Barmouth Bay as a child, where the landscape begins once more to dissolve into a mirage-like haze and its clear features are blurred: 'in einem perlgrauen Dunst lösten sämtliche Formen und Farben sich auf; es gabe keine Kontraste, keine Abstufung mehr, nur noch fließende vom Licht durchpulste Übergänge, ein einziges Verschwimmen, aus dem nur die allerflüchtigsten Erscheinungen noch auftauchten' (*A*, 143).[58] In a post-Romantic world lying in the wake of the cataclysm of European modernity, and in particular the Holocaust, this sense of unknowability persists in Sebald's work and in the *Fortschrittskritik* evinced within it. The Romantic search for expression of the self through symbols in landscape and the aestheticization of nature, as well as the Romantic prestige of grief and death, are at once preserved, repurposed, and subverted in Sebald's prose. In the imagery that emerges across his œuvre of cut-down trees and bleak bodies of water, desolate towns and derelict industry, washed-up sea life and drowned towns, it is clear that the natural world for Sebald belongs to history. The Sebaldian Romantic, just as much as the modern, is thus located 'after nature', with landscape and nature serving as inspiration and metaphorical interlocutor in Sebald's attempt to create a literature of restitution.[59]

One of Sebald's English translators, Anthea Bell, has explicitly noted the author's great debt to the poetry and style of the Romantics, who themselves sought to evoke the art and beauty of a pre-Enlightenment age.[60] In its suggestion of the imitation of those artists who already saw

German Romanticism, ed. by Nicholas Saul (Cambridge: Cambridge University Press, 2009), 257–280 (260).

[57] Minden, *Modern German Literature*, 33.

[58] 'All forms and colours were dissolved in a pearl-grey haze; there were no contrasts, no shading any more, only flowing transitions with the light throbbing through them, a single blur from which only the most fleeting visions emerged' (*A*, 135).

[59] The phrase 'after nature' is lifted directly from Sebald's first notable publication, the extended poem 'Nach der Natur', which clearly expresses his understanding of modernity as a catastrophic result of Enlightenment progress. See W. G. Sebald, *Nach der Natur* (Frankfurt am Main: Fischer, 1989).

[60] See Anthea Bell, 'On Translating W. G. Sebald', in *The Anatomist of Melancholy: Essays in Memory of W. G. Sebald*, ed. by Rüdiger Görner (Munich: Iudicium, 2003), 11–18 (12).

themselves as imitators and latecomers, Bell's observation anticipates one aspect of the narrator's epigonal sense of coming late in *Austerlitz*.[61] Several scholars have also noted Romantic tendencies in Sebald's work, although none has yet explicitly connected this to an engagement with literary lateness in European literature. Drawing on analyses of Sebald's *Fortschittskritik*, for example, Gabriele Eckart affirms that 'Sebald's literary work, with its efforts to dissolve binary oppositions and its attack on instrumental reason, must be read in the tradition of literature that attempted to break down the enlightenment discourse of instrumental rationality. Therefore, Sebald's aesthetic is [...] Romantic'.[62] Such a reading is indicative of how the Romantic may be understood as an intrinsic component of Sebald's lateness, while also highlighting the connections between Sebald's late modernist critique of the Enlightenment and that of the German Romantics. His intimate aesthetic affiliations with conventions of German Romanticism—the figure of the solitary wanderer, the tragic dignity of metaphysical angst, the appreciation of (often deliberately unfinished) literary fragments as a conscious creative endeavour—are further evidence of this.[63] Aesthetic connections are often evoked between Sebald's work and the Romantic tradition, which is exemplified by the proliferation in most of the secondary literature on Sebald of 'terms such as *eerie, sublime, ghostly, spectral,* and above all *haunting*', as James

[61] As Heinrich Heine observed in 1833, 'Was war aber die romantische Schule in Deutschland? Sie war nichts anders als die Wiedererweckung der Poesie des Mittelalters'. See Heinrich Heine, *Die romantische Schule*, ed. by Karl-Maria Guth (Berlin: Hofenberg, 2017), 8. 'But what was the Romantic School in Germany? It was nothing else but the Reawakening of the Middle Ages'.

[62] Gabriele Eckart, 'Against "Cartesian Rigidity" in W. G. Sebald's Reception of Borges', in *W. G. Sebald: Schreiben Ex Patria / Expatriate Writing*, ed. by Gerhard Fischer (Amsterdam: Rodopi, 2009), 509–521 (519). Eckart adds the caveat that such an understanding of Sebald's aesthetics entails a need to 'define Romanticism not as the desire for a restorative utopia identified with the Middle Ages, but in the sense of the early Romantic poets as a "program that allows the members of society to free themselves at least momentarily from the repressive alienating intellectual pressures of modernity"'. Eckart quotes here from Jochen Schulte-Sasse, 'The Concept of Literary Criticism in German Romanticism' in *A History of German Literary Criticism: 1730–1980*, ed. by Peter Uwe Hohendahl (Lincoln, Nebraska: University of Nebraska Press, 1988), 99–178 (114).

[63] For further discussion of these particular constitutive aspects of Romanticism, see *Romantic Prose Fiction*, ed. by Gerald Gillespie, Manfred Engel, and Bernard Dieterle (Amsterdam: John Benjamins, 2008), pp. 41–52, 122–138, and 452–475.

Chandler notes.[64] Sebald's work and reception are indeed haunted by many ghosts, some of which are Romantic. 'Much of Sebald's fictional prose', as Manfred Jurgensen notes, 'does retain overtones of Romantic folktales and traditional stories associated with home, school, childhood and adolescence', while also acknowledging that on a deeper level 'much of his fictional and critical writing is strongly reminiscent of German Romanticism'.[65] Karin Bauer also suggests aesthetic connections between the Romantic and the modern in *Austerlitz*, noting that 'the novel's rich texture derives from the myriad allusions to literature and cultural history, and, more concretely, from the multifarious references to Baroque, Romantic, and modern literary tropes, traditions, and figures', thereby reaffirming a sense of literary works as existing in a fluid and resonant literary continuum, instead of in separate and strictly delineated epochs.[66] Such is the extent to which this Romantic influence is articulated in Sebald's œuvre, that, as Peter Morgan suggests, 'Sebald takes the melancholic self-stylization of his Romantic forebears to an extreme; his pessimism [...] repeats established German cultural patterns of frustrated destructiveness and espousal of myth', while his texts also 'evince an *Endzeitstimmung* and a pervasive imagery of apocalypse which situates them clearly in a particular German literary cultural continuum'.[67] Through such established cultural patterns and images, Sebald's literary works encapsulate a highly literary malaise that emerges out of his affiliation with German culture, rather than through a form of retrospective identification with Holocaust victims. On both a linguistic and a thematic level, this gestures towards a clear connection between Sebald's reworkings

---

[64] See James Chandler, 'About Loss: W.G. Sebald's Romantic Art of Memory', in *The South Atlantic Quarterly*, 102:1 (2003), 235–262 (243). Emphasis in original.

[65] Manfred Jurgensen, 'Creative Reflection: W. G. Sebald's Critical Essays and Literary Fiction', in *W. G. Sebald: Schreiben Ex Patria / Expatriate Writing*, ed. by Gerhard Fischer (Amsterdam: Rodopi, 2009), 413–446 (418 and 419).

[66] Karin Bauer, 'The Dystopian Entwinements of Histories and Identities in W. G. Sebald's Austerlitz', in *W. G. Sebald: History, Memory, Trauma*, ed. by Scott Denham and Mark McCulloh (Berlin: de Gruyter, 2006), 233–250 (234).

[67] Peter Morgan, 'Literature and National redemption in W. G. Sebald's On the Natural History of Destruction', in *W. G. Sebald: Schreiben Ex Patria / Expatriate Writing*, ed. by Gerhard Fischer (Amsterdam: Rodopi, 2009), 213–229 (217). See also, Peter Morgan, 'The Sign of Saturn: Melancholy, Homelessness and Apocalypse in W.G. Sebald's Prose Narratives', in *German Life and Letters*, 58:1 (2005), 75–92, in which Morgan also significantly identifies Sebald as the latest in a long line of 'Romantic nihilists' who exhibited a 'cultural pessimism in which everything is interpreted under the sign of destruction and disorder' (86–87).

of the Romantic and the sense of ending—the *Endzeitstimmung* noted by Morgan—articulated in his work through his vertiginous millennial lateness. Sebald not only positions himself in a German literary and cultural continuum, but also self-consciously positions himself at what is perceived to be this tradition's *Endzeit*, given his late historical position at the end of the twentieth century. Sebald's engagement with the Romantic—in particular through resonances in his work with the figure of the suffering Romantic artist—thus intensifies the sense of lateness and melancholy loss in his works.

ARTISTS AND RUINS

Given the fragmented subjectivity prevalent in an historically postmodern age, Sebald's refashioning of the Romantic from a late modern perspective appears not only appropriate but inevitable, especially since the narrator of *Austerlitz* draws on the figure of the Romantic artist, out of whose reliance on and emphasis of metaphorical representations of the natural world, ageing, and decay, the notion of late style itself originally grew.[68] Sebald's prose works frequently feature artists or scholars, such as Max Aurach in *Die Ausgewanderten* and Austerlitz himself, who fulfil the role of the narrator or are occasionally the subject of the narration. These Sebaldian narrator figures frequently mirror a Romantic model of an artist who values displacement or wandering, as well as suffering, as Austerlitz does, in the production of their creative works. Several scholars have also noted how the narrator figures in Sebald's work establish themselves as Romantic artists.[69] As Mary Cosgrove observes, Sebald draws on a strain of Romantic melancholy in constructing his narrators as 'a man of sensibility or *Weltschmerzler* who is able to negotiate his affective existence between introversion, sentimentalism, and a more worldly perspective that enables, through imaginative projection, humanitarian empathy with the

---

[68] See Hutchinson, *Lateness*, 6.

[69] See, for example, Richard Sheppard, 'Dexter-Sinister: Some observations on Decrypting the Mors Code in the work of W. G. Sebald', in *Journal of European Studies*, 35:4 (2005), 419–463; Lynn Wolff, 'W. G. Sebald: A "Grenzgänger" of the 20th/21st Century', in *Eurostudia – Revue Transatlantique de Recherche sur L'Europe*, 7:1–2 (2011), 191–198; and Fridolin Schley, *Kataloge der Wahrheit: Zur Inszenierung von Autorschaft bei W. G. Sebald* (Göttingen: Wallstein, 2012).

sufferings of others'.[70] These narrators and characters draw on the Romantic notion that suffering or even madness are instrumental in the blossoming of creativity and imagination, as well as recalling the wanderings and journeys recounted in the earlier German Romantic works of writers such as Ludwig Tieck and Novalis, in which a journey's destination is deemed to be of less significance than the road travelled and experiences made along the way. A foundational Romantic text, Novalis's unfinished fragment novel *Heinrich von Ofterdingen* (1800), itself tinged with lateness given its posthumous publication as 'ein nachgelassener Roman' is a fitting example of such journeying.[71] The eponymous protagonist, a young medieval poet, dreams of a blue flower calling him and embarks upon a search for this symbol of striving for the unreachable, during which he is instructed in the poetic arts and falls in love.[72] For Peter Fritzsche, the suffering and itinerancy of the artist in Romantic literature constitutes a response to a perceived historical rupture, which recalls Sebald's late historical position, from which his narrators look to the past, remaining separated from it and yet beholden to it. Sebald's reconfiguration of the German Romantic artist who wanders and suffers in *Austerlitz*, and his subsequent melancholy regarding an irrecoverably distant past, emerge out of just such an appreciation of historical lateness. Indeed, as Fritzsche argues, the qualities exhibited by the suffering itinerant Romantic manifest themselves in 'a deepening sense of melancholy, a feeling of disconnection with the past, a growing sense of dread of the future, and uncertainty over the capacity to act'.[73] While redemptive visions or sensations of optimism are suggested only in the most oblique fashion in Sebald's work, and while the Romantic artist is envisioned as one who must suffer and remain condemned to endless displacement, itinerancy,

---

[70] Mary Cosgrove, *Born under Auschwitz: Melancholy Traditions in Postwar German Literature* (Rochester: Camden House, 2014), 153.

[71] See Novalis, *Heinrich von Ofterdingen* (Stuttgart: Reclam, 1987). 'A left-behind novel'.

[72] In further testament to the melancholy afterlife of the romantic in the modern era, Walter Benjamin writes in the opening line of his fragmentary essay 'Traumkitsch' that 'Es träumt sich nicht mehr recht von der blauen Blume. Wer heut als Heinrich von Ofterdingen erwacht, muß verschlafen haben' ('No one really dreams any longer of the Blue Flower. Whoever awakes as Heinrich von Ofterdingen today must have overslept'). See Walter Benjamin, *Gesammelte Schriften II.2*, ed. by Rolf Tiedemann and Hermann Schweppenhäuser (Frankfurt am Main: Suhrkamp, 1980), 620–622.

[73] Peter Fritzsche, 'Spectres of History: On Nostalgia, Exile, and Modernity', in *The American Historical Review*, 106:5 (2001), 1587–1618 (1592).

and exile, late reworkings of Romantic conventions nevertheless constitute a key that may unlock *Austerlitz*'s latent potential for futurity and renewal.

The Romantic notion of redemption or return through wandering and suffering are taken up and nuanced in *Austerlitz* through the construction of the novel's protagonist, as well as its narrator, as figures reminiscent of the Romantic artist. The narrator's remediation of Austerlitz's account of his incomplete investigation into his family's past mirrors Austerlitz's own interminable research on architectural history, his tragic never-to-be-completed project.[74] The narrator's status as a wandering and suffering Romantic artist is prefigured towards the beginning of the novel and then most clearly implied towards its close, as if he has inherited the mantle of Romanticism from Austerlitz as, following the protagonist's departure, the narrator begins to write the narrative that will become *Austerlitz*. In the novel's opening sentence, the narrator frames the journeys he makes across Europe in the narrative that follows in a distinctly mysterious Romantic manner, claiming that he travels 'teilweise zu Studienzwecken, teilweise aus anderen, mir selber nicht recht erfindlichen Gründen' (*A*, 1).[75] Following their initial encounter in Antwerp and a period of twenty years where the two men fall out of touch, Austerlitz and the narrator unexpectedly cross paths once more in the saloon bar of the Great Eastern Hotel in London. The purpose of the narrator's visit to London in the first place, however, is to consult an ophthalmologist following the temporary loss of sight in his right eye. Though perturbed by his loss of sight, he

---

[74] It is worth noting here that, aside from observing the much-fêted elusively autobiographical narration in his novels, it is necessary to clarify the nature of the narrator's remediation of Austerlitz's story and confront the question of the appropriation of Jewish victims' stories in Sebald's work. There is a potential tendency towards an identification of the German with the figure of the Jewish other that emerges over the course of *Austerlitz* in particular. However, as Anne Fuchs has noted, the self-conscious and self-reflexive style of Sebald's narrative prevents this identification between the German narrator and the Jewish victim from occurring. See, Fuchs, *Die Schmerzenspuren der Geschichte*, 28–32. Specifically, for further discussion of German–Jewish relations in *Austerlitz*, see Stuart Taberner, 'German Nostalgia? Remembering German-Jewish Life in W.G. Sebald's *Die Ausgewanderten* and *Austerlitz*', in *Germanic Review*, 79 (2004), 181–202; Brad Prager, 'The Good German as Narrator', in *New German Critique*, 96 (2005), 75–102; and Mary Cosgrove, 'The Anxiety of German Influence: Affiliation, Rejection, and Jewish Identity in W. G. Sebald's Work', in *German Memory Contests: The Quest for Identity in Literature, Film, and Discourse since 1990*, ed. by Anne Fuchs, Mary Cosgrove, and Georg Grote (Rochester, New York: Camden House, 2006), 229–252.

[75] 'Partly for study purposes, partly for other reasons which were never entirely clear to me' (*A*, 9).

nonetheless also imagines a 'Vision der Erlösung, in der ich mich, befreit von dem ewigen Schreiben- und Lesenmüssen, in einem Korbsessel in einem Garten sitzen sah, umgeben von einer konturlosen, nur an ihren schwachen Farben noch zu erkennenden Welt' (*A*, 56).[76] Evoking the image of an operatic diva given a tincture of belladonna to make her eyes shine on stage, but which renders her unable to see, the narrator compares himself to an artist suffering for their art, while also suggesting a sense of imminent ending and artistic inadequacy in his own work through '[die] Falschheit des schönen Scheins und [die] Gefahr des vorzeitigen Erlöschens' (*A*, 56).[77] With a sense of relief, he imagines the satisfying conclusion he will arrive at following the end of his creative toils: a comfortable chair in a garden, surrounded by nature in all its blurred glory, the faded echoes of Romantic wildness, which he is unable to properly experience. If suffering may lead to a sense of fulfilment or reconciliation for the narrator, then it is only in a vague and domesticated natural setting. This is suggestive of a self-conception as an epigonal latecomer unable to attain the ecstatic heights reached—or at least striven for—by earlier Romantics. For the narrator, nature represents freedom from work, from the artistry to which he is bound, but its wildness is lost and any sense of freedom remains faded and unachieved. Though the Romantic is gestured towards here, sublime respite or reconciliation is muted and unattained. The eye specialist the narrator later visits diagnoses him, not with a degenerative eye condition as he first feared, but with a temporary disability caused by a bubble of clear liquid formed on the macula of his eye. All the doctor is able to tell him of this apparently mysterious ailment is 'daß sie fast ausschließlich auftrete bei Männern mittleren Alters, die zuviel mit Schreiben und Lesen beschäftigt seien' (*A*, 59).[78] It is difficult to discern whether this suffering may lead to any transcendent understandings on the narrator's part, but as a reader and a writer, he is certainly constructed here in a Romantic vein as one who suffers for his work and his creative pursuits. This, moreover, inadvertently brings him back into contact with Austerlitz.

It is not only the unnamed narrator of the novel, but also Austerlitz himself, who is constructed as a figure who echoes the suffering and

---

[76] 'Vision of release in which I saw myself, free of the constant compulsion to read and write, sitting in a wicker chair in a garden, surrounded by a world of indistinct shapes' (*A*, 48).

[77] 'The falseness of beautiful appearance and the danger of its premature extinction'.

[78] 'That it occurred almost exclusively in middle-aged men who spent too much time reading and writing' (*A*, 51–2).

wandering Romantic artist, distinctly expressing a sense of lateness and epigonality in the narrator's account of events. From their initial encounter in the waiting room of the central station in Antwerp, Austerlitz with his rucksack and boots, and later his insomnia, his recollections of meandering around Europe, and his inhospitable house on Alderney Street in London, is marked out as an uprooted figure. The pathos of Austerlitz's perception of creativity as a painful process endows him with traits redolent of the figure of a Romantic wanderer and a suffering artist. Upon encountering difficulties with his research and writing—occupations which he had previously enjoyed—Austerlitz announces the physical and mental suffering and anguish he experienced in response to the work he produces as an architectural historian:

> je größer die Mühe, die ich über Monate hinweg an dieses Vorhaben wandte, desto kläglicher dünkten mich die Ergebnisse [...] als drängte eine seit langem in mir bereits fortwirkende Krankheit zum Ausbruch [...] Wäre damals einer gekommen, mich wegzuführen auf eine Hinrichtungsstätte, ich hätte alles ruhig mit mir geschehen lassen, ohne ein Wort zu sagen. (*A*, 179, 182)[79]

Labouring away at his unfinished project, Austerlitz is almost suicidal, presented as only being driven on by a desire for truth and knowledge, inspired by a life and history that he has been so far able to grasp only tangentially. He is constructed by the narrator as a *Dichter* figure, not unlike a wandering poet with tragic symptoms that mark him out as a *Sonderling* whose physical suffering metaphorically evoked through his nomadic lifestyle, which hints that traumatic exile and dislocation have been the primary causes of his unhappiness for the majority of his life.[80]

Having returned to London following his discoveries concerning his and his parents' pasts in Prague, Austerlitz experiences physical suffering as the immensity of his anguish overwhelms him, eventually causing him to experience both emotional and physical collapse. While walking with him through the Tower Hamlets cemetery in London at twilight, the narrator recalls how Austerlitz has been obsessively visiting the graves of the

---

[79] 'The more I laboured on this project over several months, the more pitiful did the results seem [...] as if an illness that had been latent in me for a long time were now threatening to erupt [...] If someone had come then to lead me away to a place of execution I would have gone meekly, without a word' (*A*, 171, 173–174).

[80] For further discussion of these terms in relation to *Austerlitz*, see Taberner, 'German Nostalgia?', 194–195.

dead who lie buried there: 'er habe [...] die Namen und die Geburts- und Todesdaten der Verstorbenen auswendig gelernt, habe Kieselsteine und Efeublätter nach Hause getragen, auch eine Steinrose einmal und eine abgeschlagene Engelshand' (*A*, 330).[81] The text here is interspersed with photographs of the overgrown graveyard, showing broken and crumbling gravestones strewn with dead leaves and unkempt foliage. Austerlitz, the narrator indicates, is familiar with the place and has spent much time there, returning frequently enough to know the inscriptions of the graves and even to have taken away with him pieces of the ruins along with leaves and stones. His engagement and affiliation with decay and dereliction in nature in this scene firmly imbues the narrative with a Romantic sense of coming late or lingering too long after what is acceptable. Such contemplation of ruins in particular calls to mind a significant aesthetic trait of German Romanticism through its symbolic associations that acknowledge the passing of time and the cycle of life and death, as in many works, such as August Wilhelm Schlegel's 1805 elegy 'Rom', to take just one notable example.[82] Even outside the realm of literature, landscape paintings by German Romantic artists like Caspar David Friedrich such as *Abtei im Eichenwald* (1809/10), *Klosterruine Eldena bei Greifswald* (1824/25), or *Ruine Elden am Riesengebirge* (1830/34) feature the contemplation of ruins as a means of meditating of personal subjectivity and human transience.[83] For the German Romantics, as Theodore Ziolkowski notes, ruined buildings specifically encapsulated 'the struggles of the German historical past, rather than a general cultural tradition, together with a growing sense of national pride as Germans dreamed of the unification of

---

[81] 'He had learned by heart the names and dates of birth and death of those buried here, he had taken home pebbles and ivy leaves and on one occasion a stone rose, and the stone hand broken off one of the statues'. (*A*, 322).

[82] 'Zwar es umlächelt die Erde von Latium heiterer Himmel, / Rein am entwölkten Azur bildet sich Roms Horizont, / Wie es die Ebne beherrscht mit den siebengehügelten Zinnen / Bis zu dem Meer jenseits, dort vom Sabinergebirg / Aber den Wanderer leitet ein Geist tiefsinniger Schwermuth / Mit oft weilendem Gang durch des Ruins Labyrinth'. See August Wilhelm Schlegel, *Poetische Werke 2* (Heidelberg: Mohr und Zimmer, 1811), 41–66.

[83] For further discussion of the significance of ruins and nature for Romanticism, see Catherine Wilkins, 'Revolutionary Romantic Landscapes', in *Landscape, Imagery, Politics, and Identity in a Divided Germany: 1968–1989* (London: Routledge, 2013), 31–50. For a broader expanded history of the artistic appreciation of architectural decay, see Rose Macaulay, *Pleasure of Ruins* (New York: Walker, 1953).

their independent states and duchies'.[84] Given *Austerlitz*'s historical position after the wreckage of twentieth-century modernity and its lingering
aftereffects, however, the ruins contemplated in Sebald's final novel are
not only implicitly anti-nationalist; they are also no longer able to be
turned to an aesthetically beautiful or comforting advantage.[85] As Austerlitz
himself remarks, when contrasting the semblance of comfort promised by
smaller than average domestic buildings with the way one might gaze in
wonder then dawning horror at the bewildering grandiosity of vast modern edifices, 'irgendwo wüßten wir natürich, daß die ins Überdimensionale
hinausgewachsenen Bauwerke schon den Schatten ihrer Zurstörung
vorauswerfen und konzipiert sind von Anfang an im Hinblick auf ihr
nachmaliges Dasein als Ruinen' (*A*, 32).[86] This implies a muted and
regretful characterization of Austerlitz and the narrator as epigonal latecomers who are no longer able to exult optimistically in the beauty of the
ruins and contemplate the graveyard to the same higher ends as their
Romantic literary forebears once may have done.

An awareness of the cycle of life and death is intensified by Austerlitz's
attachment to the fallen leaves surrounding him in the cemetery, which
echoes the Romantic desire to find expression for the self in the natural
world. However, this induces a further sense of his appreciation of such
things as being a form of epigonal imitation. While his emotional and

---

[84] Theodore Ziolkowski, 'Ruminations on Ruins: Classical versus Romantic', in *The German Quarterly*, 89:3 (2016), 265–281 (278). For a consideration of the centrality of ruins to Western art and literature, especially in the works of Goethe, Piranesi, Blake, and Wordsworth, see Susan Stewart, *The Ruins Lesson: Meaning and Material in Western Culture* (Chicago: University of Chicago Press, 2019).

[85] This also recalls Sebald's commentary on the ruin of the Herz-Schloss in the ruined town of Sonthofen in *Luftkrieg und Literatur* (1999). As Anne Fuchs observes, 'in this image of the romantically wild yet still eerie war ruin, the sentimental, nostalgic, and critical discourse on *Heimat* is brought together'. While the ruin gestures towards the utopian possibility that humanity might leave behind its destructive history for a more ethical relation-
ship with the natural world, as Fuchs claims, Sebald is unclear as to whether he necessarily advocates this. In any case *Luftkrieg und Literatur* certainly suggests that 'the idea of human autonomy and the attendant separation of human history from nature have had disastrous consequences'. See Anne Fuchs, 'A *Heimat* in Ruins and the Ruins as *Heimat*: W. G. Sebald's *Luftkrieg und Literatur*', in *German Memory Contests: The Quest for Identity in Literature, Film, and Discourse Since 1990*, ed. by Anne Fuchs, Mary Cosgrove, and Georg Grote (Rochester, New York: Camden House, 2006), 287–302 (299).

[86] 'Somehow we know by instinct that outsize buildings cast the shadow of their own destruction before them, and are designed from the first with an eye to their later existence as ruins' (*A*, 24).

intellectual breakdown recalls the figure of the Romantic suffering artist, Austerlitz's experience does not lead to any sense of transcendent understanding or artistic fulfilment. Instead, the desire to find meaningfulness and self-expression in nature only leads to further despair as his interaction with the ruined graveyard and its wild flora acts as the catalyst for his recollection of his subsequent collapse and illness:

> Die Vernunft kam nicht an gegen das seit jeher von mir unterdrückte und jetzt gewaltsam aus mir hervorbrechende Gefühl des Verstoßen- und Ausgelöschtseins [...] In kürzester Frist trocknete die Zunge und der Gaumen mir aus, so als läge ich seit Tagen schon in der Wüste, mußte ich schneller und schneller um Atem ringen, begann mein Herz zu flattern und zu klopfen bis unter den Hals, brach mir der kalte Schweiß aus am ganzen Leib, sogar auf dem Rücken meiner zitternden Hand, und war alles, was ich anblickte, verschleiert von einer schwarzen Schraffur. (*A*, 330–331)[87]

Unable to move and unable to speak, Austerlitz's crisis ends in his physical and mental collapse that 'sämtliche Denkvorgänge und Gefühlsregungen lahmgelegt hatte' (*A*, 332).[88] Austerlitz's reason—that bastion of Enlightenment understanding—gives way to feeling and emotion when prompted to self-reflection stimulated by the contemplation of ruins and nature. Yet, rather than physical suffering acting as a path to transcendence, as the Romantic view would have it, the ordeal provides no such satisfying conclusion for Austerlitz. When he awakens three later weeks later in hospital, his Romantic activity has assumed a diminished and epigonal cast: '[Ich spazierte] die ganze Winterszeit in den Gängen herum, blickte stundenlang durch eines der trüben Fenster in den Friedhof, in welchem wir jetzt stehen, hinab und spürte in meinem Kopf nichts als die vier ausgebrannten Wände meines Gehirns. [...] Nur an mich selber, an meine eigene Geschichte und jetzige Verfassung war es mir unmöglich zu denken' (*A*, 332–333).[89] Following the crisis of his breakdown, Austerlitz

---

[87] 'Reason was powerless against the sense of rejection and annihilation which I had always suppressed, and which was now breaking through the walls of its confinement. [...] All of a sudden my tongue and palate would be as dry as if I had been lying in the desert for days, I had to fight harder and harder for breath, my heart began to flutter and palpitate in my throat, cold sweat broke out over my body, even on the back of my trembling hand, and everything I looked at was veiled by a black mist'. (*A*, pp. 322–323).

[88] 'Paralysed all thought processes and emotions' (*A*, 323).

[89] 'I wandered, all through that winter, up and down the long corridors, staring out for hours through one of the dirty windows at the cemetery below, where we are standing now,

is separated from the cemetery where he was able to indulge his Romantic appetites, and is only able to wander the sterile corridors of the facility, viewing the cemetery from a distance. Even returning to it with the narrator later on, Austerlitz is emotionally and physically drained. His similarities here to the notion of the Romantic as a suffering artist heighten the sense of epigonal lateness in the narrative, and Austerlitz is soon drawn back into uncovering the past via H. G. Adler's writing on the Theresienstadt ghetto. Before that, however, he achieves a temporary reprieve from this while working as an assistant gardener in Romford. While this episode might suggest that Austerlitz's Romantic disposition is salved somewhat, the only landscape he engages with there is tamed and artificial (*A*, 334–335). In his echoing of Romantic traits, Austerlitz faces either a route to overwhelming confrontation with his situation, or a briefly therapeutic stint in a garden centre that eventually leads him to return to his investigations, neither of which offers the expected transcendence or fulfilment promised by Romanticism in spite of his enactment of Romantic traits. Recourse to Romanticism here constitutes a double bind: either Austerlitz no longer undertakes his investigations and his recuperative activities are epigonal imitations of his Romantic exploits; or, alternatively, he elects to undertake his investigations and his Romantic reactions to his historical separation from the past and its secrets lead him to further suffering. In both cases, reworkings of the figure of the Romantic suffering artist serve to bolster narrative constructions of epigonal latecoming.

FORTRESSES AND FALSE WORLDS

Following Austerlitz's final departure towards the end of the novel in order to continue searching for further information regarding his father's life and fate, the narrator returns alone to the fortress of Breendonk, a former Nazi prisoner camp near Mechelen in Belgium, which he first visits earlier in the narrative, prompted by his initial conversation with Austerlitz. At the novel's conclusion, it is as if he has now assumed Austerlitz's self-conception as a late Romantic wandering artist, since the narrator is soon to begin writing the novel of *Austerlitz* after the narrative ends. As the narrator arrives at the fortress on foot, carrying a rucksack much like Austerlitz's signature tote, further suggestions of Romantic connections

feeling nothing inside my head but the four burnt-out walls of my brain. [...] But I found it impossible to think of myself, my own history, or my present state of mind' (*A*, 324–325).

between the two figures emerge. The narrator's observations are centred on the natural features surrounding the fortress as well as the building itself: 'Wie vor dreißig Jahren war es ungewöhnlich heiß geworden [...] Die Festung lag unverändert auf der blaugrünen Insel' (*A*, 417–418).[90] The weather at Breendonk is in fact so unseasonably hot that 'das Dach und die Wände knisterten in der Hitze, und der Gedanke streifte mich, das Haar auf meinem Kopf könnte Feuer fangen wie es des heiligen Julian auf dem Weg durch die Wüste' (*A*, 418).[91] Nature is thus perceived as unbearable, and upon observing this the narrator makes comparisons between himself and St Julian, another suffering wanderer, who achieved redemption in the desert.[92] For the narrator, however, there is no sense of resolution to be found, further echoing the sense of unfulfilment and anticlimactic epigonality experienced in his Romantic wanderings. Observing the sculpted, landscaped natural features surrounding the fortress—itself a late edifice, existing after modernity and after nature—the narrator watches a bird, which encapsulates the Romantic echoes of his narrative: 'Auf dem dunklen Wasser ruderte eine graue Gans, einmal ein Stück in die eine Richtung, dann in die andre wieder zurück' (*A*, 418).[93] Sitting alone, the narrator stops reading *Heshel's Kingdom*, leaving the book unfinished and setting out to return to the nearby town of Mechelen 'als es Abend wurde' (*A*, 421).[94] The novel ends inauspiciously with a narrator haunted by an inability to reconcile with the past, with his work left incomplete and his narrative unresolved. That *Austerlitz* concludes with the image of a setting sun not only evokes the notion of the *Abendland*, of Europe as a 'land of the evening'. It also further suggests a sense of epochal lateness and of incompleteness, since the sun is still setting but has not yet entirely set. The figure of the suffering Romantic wanderer thus offers neither a compensatory response nor a redemptive reprieve from the burden of the past

---

[90] 'It had turned unusually hot, just as it was thirty years ago [...] The fortifications lay unchanged on the blue-green island' (*A*, 411).

[91] 'The roof and the walls creaked in the heat, and the thought passed through my mind that the hair on my head might catch fire, as St Julian's did on his way through the desert' (*A*, 412).

[92] This is a reference one of Gustave Flaubert's *Trois contes*, 'Légende de Saint Julien l'Hospitalier', first published in 1877 and also partly an inspiration for Herman Hesse's later novel *Siddhartha* (1922).

[93] 'A grey goose was swimming on the dark water, going a little way in one direction and then a little way back in the other' (*A*, 412).

[94] 'As evening began to fall' (*A*, 415).

in *Austerlitz*. Instead, the narrator's Romanticism serves to reinforce and complicate the narrative's intense sense of lateness.

Austerlitz ends by presenting a quintessentially epigonal chain of literary inheritance: the passing on of the book from Jacobson to Austerlitz to the narrator encapsulates both an indefinite continuity and a sense of diminished returns, especially given the narrator's solidary return to Breendonk at the novel's conclusion. This time, however, the narrator does not enter the fortress, as he does on his first visit, choosing instead to wait outside and eventually walk away into the sunset. Rather than any triumphant process of return or repetition, the conclusion of *Austerlitz* is more suggestive of never quite coming full circle and not quite being able to measure up to what came before. This is sustained by a passing on of narratives as a means of attempting, but not quite managing, to bridge the gulf between the past and the present, which Jacobson refers to as 'der Abgrund, in den kein Lichtstrahl hinabreicht, [...] die untergegange Vorzeit' (*A*, 420).[95] In referencing such a chasm, the narrator once more recalls the Romantic trait of drawing on natural metaphors in order to question subjective experiences of the world. By reworking and subverting traits such as this, as well as the figure of the Romantic artist, his wandering, and his contemplation of ruins, the narrator of *Austerlitz* constructs a novel that is steeped in a distinctly Romantic sense of epigonal lateness. The melancholy understanding of history that emerges out of this, which acknowledges and engages with the irreconcilable gulf between the present and the past, is bound up with further Romantic traits in *Austerlitz*, particularly the act or idea of crossing back and forth into a *Märchen*-like realm, much like Austerlitz's aforementioned unrealized dream that he might 'über die Schwelle trete[n] in eine freundlichere, weniger fremde Welt' (*A*, 69).[96] So intrinsic is this to the novel that it occurs many times, both in Austerlitz's account of his investigations and in the narrator's construction of the narrative as a whole.

It has become something of a commonplace to talk of Sebald's melancholy and, indeed, this study is not the first to claim so.[97] Drawing on the sensation of melancholy that arises from a feeling of helplessness when confronting the past, Sebald fashions what he terms, following Peter

---

[95] 'The chasm into which no ray of light could penetrate [...] the vanished past' (*A*, 414).

[96] 'Step over the threshold into a friendlier, more familiar world'.

[97] See, for example, Kaisa Kaakinen, *Comparative Literature and the Historical Imaginary: Reading Conrad, Weiss, Sebald* (London: Palgrave Macmillan, 2017), 214.

Weiss, his own 'aesthetics of resistance'.[98] Discussions of melancholy in Sebald's work have generally taken place, as Kaisa Kaakinen affirms, 'either in relation to his position as a postwar German author or in relation to discussions on ethics of alterity'.[99] This simultaneously historicizes Sebald's works and situates them in an historically removed conceptualization of ethical encounter. Eric Santner notes the overwhelming gloom of Sebaldian melancholy, remarking that his work 'generates not so much profane illuminations as apocalyptic darkenings, moments where the last traces of light are, as it were, sucked back into black holes of despair and pain'.[100] In the most lucid and comprehensive account of melancholy in Sebald's œuvre, Mary Cosgrove delineates how it may be interpreted as an ethical, albeit ambivalent, vessel for memory of the Holocaust by questioning Sebald's own assertion in his critical work that melancholy constitutes a form of resistance.[101] Drawing on Dominick LaCapra's theories of trauma, Cosgrove argues that an understanding of the Holocaust as an historical caesura, which divides those who came after from those who came before, resulting in what J. J. Long calls the 'marooning [of] the survivors and those born after in a futureless vacuum of the present'.[102] This understanding of history looms large in Sebald's work and encapsulates both his sense of historical lateness and the vertiginous separation of the past and present from which the melancholy aesthetic attitude of his prose fiction stems. For Cosgrove, Sebald's mobilization of melancholy's performative potential entails a 'response to the impossible path of Western history both during and preceding the twentieth century'.[103] This 'special brand of sadness' emerges over the course of Sebald's literary works as 'insightful, mnemonic, and ethically driven mourning work, cross-dressed

---

[98] See W. G. Sebald, 'Die Zerknirschung des Herzens. Über Erinnerung und Grausamkeit im Werk von Peter Weiss', in *Orbis litterarum*, 41 (1986), 265–278. Reprinted in W. G. Sebald, *Campo Santo*, ed. by Sven Meyer (Munich: Carl Hanser, 2003), 128–148. See also Peter Weiß, *Die Ästhetik des Widerstands* (Frankfurt am Main: Suhrkamp, 1975, 1978, 1981).

[99] Kaakinen, *Comparative Literature and the Historical Imaginary*, 215.

[100] Eric Santner, *On Creaturely Life: Rilke, Benjamin, Sebald* (Chicago: University of Chicago Press, 2006), 61.

[101] See W. G. Sebald, *Die Beschreibung des Unglücks: Zur österreichischen Literatur von Stifter bis Handke* (Salzburg: Residenz, 1985), 12.

[102] See J. J. Long, 'W. G. Sebald: A Biographical Essay on Current Research', in Anne Fuchs and J. J. Long, eds., *W. G. Sebald and the Writing of History* (Würzburg: Königshausen & Neumann, 2007), 11–29 (21).

[103] Cosgrove, *Born under Auschwitz*, 147.

in traditional melancholy apparel'.[104] According to Cosgrove, these trappings of melancholy draw on sources of inspiration as varied as Renaissance
iconography, eighteenth-century conceptualizations of *Empfindsamkeit*
(sentimentality), and even psychoanalytical theories on the condition of
sadness. Such psychoanalytical conceptualizations largely entail, as
Cosgrove observes, a reductive narrowing of the definition of melancholy
to a pathological condition which causes the disintegration of an individual's conscious experience and leads to an inability to engage with and
accept the legacy of preceding events. In earlier literary criticism, such an
interpretation resulted in long-entrenched Manichean conceptualizations
of good and bad melancholia, the former providing the literary artist with
the opportunity to transcend sadness, while the latter relegates them to
inertia. Following Cosgrove, Sebaldian melancholy is understood to exist
beyond such a binary: it is both performative discourse and narrative tool,
through which the conventionalized expression of subjectivity enables
ethical engagement with the past. If a form of *Vergangenheitsbewältigung*
in Sebald's work thus occurs, then according to Cosgrove it is through a
process of 'melancholy self-fashioning'.[105] This recalls a Romantic emphasis on subjectivity, which finds expression in *Austerlitz* via conventions and
tropes reminiscent of the Romantic literary fairy tale, an aspect of Sebald's
melancholy aesthetic that has heretofore remained underdiscussed.

The remainder of this chapter accordingly makes the case for reading
Sebald's final novel as a late iteration of the Germanic literary fairy tale. In
Kunstmärchen, unlike in traditional folk tales or *Volksmärchen*, places and
objects are described in detail, given names and background contextualization. Characters tend to exhibit more individuality and psychological
depth, but they can also be read as allegorical personifications. Fantastic,
irrational, or coincidental elements are experienced as problematic and
alarming, and often there is no clear moral and no 'happy end' to the
story. Reworkings of *Kunstmärchen* tropes such as these in *Austerlitz* contribute towards the novel's refusal of any conventional reconciliation or
satisfying conclusion, leading to a sustained melancholy perspective centred around the perceived irreconcilability between the past and the present. The novel's *Kunstmärchen* echoes thus constitute an essential
component of its aesthetics. Reading the novel as a late and melancholy
Kunstmärchen for the end of the twentieth century also suggests that

---

[104] Cosgrove, *Born under Auschwitz*, 151.
[105] Cosgrove, *Born under Auschwitz*, 24.

3 AUSTERLITZ BY W. G. SEBALD: A LATE FAIRY TALE   141

Austerlitz's particular forms of late Romanticism complicate the notion of false worlds in the novel. This much discussed category of a 'falsche Welt' in *Austerlitz* might thus be read not only as a moral or ethical category, but also as an aesthetic one. As the falsity of Austerlitz's world is revealed during his investigations of his past and of his parents' fates, so the narrator constructs an alternative reality—a false world—in his narrative. By reworking Romantic *Kunstmärchen* tropes of crossing thresholds into other realities and encounters with the unfamiliar or the fantastic, he both facilitates and produces a melancholy perspective on the past, grounded in a lateness that is not only modern but also vestigially Romantic. A reading of *Kunstmärchen* features in the novel enhances prior understandings of Sebaldian melancholy in *Austerlitz*, while also drawing lines of connection from the novel's lateness and melancholy to ideas of European cultural renewal.

While it may seem initially surprising, even counter-intuitive, to suggest parallels between Sebald's deeply serious literary work and the form of the Romantic fairy tale, there are many lines of connection to be drawn between the two. One immediately striking link to Romantic *Kunstmärchen* in *Austerlitz* can be inferred from the protagonist's discovery that his mother performed the role of Olympia in a production of *Tales of Hoffmann* (*A*, 234) by the French Romantic composer Jacques Offenbach, to whom Austerlitz owes his first name.[106] In E. T. A. Hoffmann's original tale, *Der Sandmann* (1806), Olympia, the apparent daughter of the protagonist Nathaniel's professor, is revealed to be an automaton, hastening Nathaniel's descent into madness, which resonates with Austerlitz's breakdown.[107] In his literary criticism, Sebald also draws on the tales of Jacob (1785–1863) and Wilhelm Grimm (1786–1859), and specifically on the figure of Rumpelstiltzchen, for his analysis of memory and cruelty in the work of Peter Weiss.[108] Moreover, in what constitutes the clearest utterance of Sebald's novelistic praxis in his literary works, expressed via words given to the character of Max Aurach in *Die Ausgewanderten*, connections between the Sebaldian and

---

[106] This is suggested in Ann Pearson, '"Remembrance … Is Nothing Other than a Quotation": The Intertextual Fictions of W. G. Sebald', in *Comparative Literature*, 60:3 (2008), 261–278 (269).

[107] See E. T. A Hoffmann, *Der Sandmann* (Stuttgart, Reclam, 1996). For further discussions of the implications of this for the Oedipal drama of *Austerlitz*, see Helen Finch, *Sebald's Bachelors: Queer Resistance and the Unconforming Life* (London: Legenda, 2012), 127–128.

[108] See W. G. Sebald, 'Die Zerknirschung des Herzens', 265–278.

the fairy tale are explicitly articulated.[109] For Aurach, his investigations of his mother's memoirs, as well as his engagement with memory of the past more generally, are akin to 'eines jener bösen deutschen Märchen, in denen man, einmal in den Bann geschlagen, mit einer angefangenen Arbeit, in diesem Fall also mit dem Erinnern, dem Schreiben und dem Lesen, fortfahren muß'.[110] The fairy tale here is presented not only as a distinctly German form, but also as one which is evil. Yet, despite the introduction of this moral complication, it is also a revelatory form for Aurach, which insinuates itself into all aspects of the ongoing creative process. It is all-pervasive; its magic spell makes possible further artistry, and this sense of enchantment finds its later echo in Austerlitz's own admission of being 'noch im Bann [...] dieser für mich [...] tatsächlich mythologischen Landschaft' (A, 326),[111] as he stares out of the window of his train carriage at the sun setting across the Rhine valley. At the conclusion of *Austerlitz* Sebald's narrator also recounts Austerlitz's experience of entering a hidden Jewish cemetery in London by using the form of the fairy tale as a reference point: 'In dem hellen Frühlingslicht, das die frisch ausgeschlagenen Lindenblätter durchstrahlte, hätte man meinen können, sagte Austerlitz zu mir, man sei eingetreten in eine Märchenerzählung, die, genau wie das Leben selber, älter geworden ist mit der verflossenen Zeit' (A, 415).[112] This sentence, with its exemplification of the author's famed hypotaxis and his narrator's mediated narrative of another's story, is quintessentially Sebaldian, recalling the clearly self-conscious mode of narration in the novel. Here, the narrator suggests a heightened sense of Romantic optimism of being in nature as he recounts Austerlitz's walk under the newly opening leaves of the trees on a bright spring day, before immediately connecting this with the idea of

[109] The character of Max Aurach was renamed Max Ferber in the English translation of *Die Ausgewanderten*, after the painter Frank Auerbach, upon whom the character of Aurach was partly based, expressed reservations about being closely identified with the book. See Jaggi, 'Recovered Memories'.

[110] W. G. Sebald, *Die Ausgewanderten: Vier lange Erzählungen* (Frankfurt am Main: Fischer, 1992), 285. 'One of those evil German fairy tales in which, once you are under the spell, you have to carry on [...] with whatever work you have begun, in this case, the remembering, writing, and reading'. W. G. Sebald, *The Emigrants*, trans. by Michael Hulse (London: Vintage, 1996), 193.

[111] 'Still under the spell of this, to me, truly mythological landscape'.

[112] 'In the bright spring light shining through the newly opened leaves of the lime trees you might have thought, Austerlitz told me, that you had entered a fairy tale which, like life itself, had grown older with the passing of time' (A, 409).

3 AUSTERLITZ BY W. G. SEBALD: A LATE FAIRY TALE   143
crossing over a threshold and entering into the world of a fairy tale. This fairy tale is not simply a fixed form, however: it is suffused with melancholy at the inexorable passing of time. This dissolves the Romantic optimism suggested a few lines earlier, while simultaneously gesturing towards a sense of ageing and ending that recalls the particular vertiginous historical and literary lateness of Sebald and his works. Here in this single sentence, then, is a microcosmic summary of Sebaldian melancholy as it emerges in *Austerlitz*.

The over-determination of individual identity by history is a distinctly Romantic notion. Endless wakefulness, as well as the desire to give life to the voices of the dead, also constitute compensatory Romantic responses to a reality held to be insufficient. To return to Novalis, the idea that 'die Welt muß romantisiert werden'—that the world must be made Romantic—expresses clear dissatisfaction with reality, which provides the impetus to create new fictive worlds.[113] The narrative of *Austerlitz* makes multiple references to the notion of a 'falsche Welt' or a 'falsches Leben'—a false world or a false life (see, e.g., *A*, 11 and 199). Such utterances are well documented as references to Adorno's maxim that 'es gibt kein richtiges Leben im falschen', which is reflected in Austerlitz's growing sense of unease over the course of his investigations at the moral and ethical falsity of his own life.[114] In this aphorism, Adorno suggests that, following the moral catastrophe of the Holocaust as the apogee of modernity, literature and even life exist beyond what is acceptable and thus may be construed as late.[115] Yet what if false worlds in *Austerlitz* not only articulate a Sebaldian

---

[113] Novalis, *Novalis Werke*, ed. by Gerhard Schultz (Munich: C. H. Beck, 1969), 384. 'The world must be made romantic'.

[114] Theodor W. Adorno, *Gesammelte Schriften 4. Minima Moralia: Reflexionen aus dem beschädigten Leben* (Frankfurt am Main: Suhrkamp, 1980), 43. 'A wrong life cannot be lived rightly', or, more literally, 'there is no right life in a wrong one. See Theodor Adorno, *Minima Moralia: Reflections from Damaged Life*, trans. by E. F. N. Jephcott (London: Verso, 2005), 39. See also Helmut Schmitz, *On Their Own Terms: The Legacy of National Socialism in Post-1990 German Fiction* (Birmingham: University of Birmingham Press, 2004), 296–299.

[115] While encapsulating Sebald's view of modernity in its entirety as late, his reliance on Adorno here is also evidence of his sustained engagement throughout his life with the work of the Frankfurt School, particularly that of Adorno, Max Horkheimer, and Herbert Marcuse, which had a great influence on Sebald's prose, especially on the development of his idiosyncratically dialectical syntax, his critique of Enlightenment progress, and his predilection for modernist works. See Graham Jackman, '"Gebranntes Kind"? W. G. Sebald's "Metaphysik Der Geschichte"', in *German Life and Letters*, 57:4 (2004), 456–471; Ben Hutchinson,

form of lateness alongside the difficulties of representing and thereby attempting to come to terms with the past in literature? The false world in *Austerlitz* may also reflect a constructed fictional reality grounded in artificiality, exhibiting allegorical narrator and protagonist figures, as well as problematic or uncanny coincidences and quest narratives, with no clear ending, moral, happy, or otherwise. In short, Austerlitz's false world may indicate latent echoes of *Kunstmärchen* conventions.

Dissatisfaction with reality and Romantic antipathy towards modernity underlie the fairy tale constructions in *Austerlitz*. *Kunstmärchen* such as E. T. A. Hoffman's *Der goldne Topf* (1814/19), for example, often contrast the reality of the everyday with fantastical episodes of an alternative reality.[116] There are two principle evocations of figurations, motifs, and tropes from the *Kunstmärchen* in *Austerlitz*: firstly, the key moment of self-discovery in Austerlitz's story when he crosses the threshold of the Liverpool Street Station, undergoing a physical and metaphorical journey into an underworld to recall for the first time in his life his arrival in London as a four-year-old refugee. Secondly, the narrator's initial visit to the fortress at Breendonk and his subsequent return to it at the conclusion of the novel. There are discrete instances of *Kunstmärchen* tropes during the narrative of *Austerlitz*, as well as in the overarching structure of the novel as a whole, which also mirrors the conventional narrative patterning of the *Kunstmärchen*. In keeping with these Romantic conventions, resolution and conclusion are denied both the narrator and the eponymous protagonist of the novel. Providing the structural underpinning for many German Romantic texts, the *Kunstmärchen* is at its heart an expression of dissatisfaction with the real world of the everyday, a yearning for a new world as a form of aesthetic compensation. Novalis, for example, conceived of this as a 'Traumbild [...] ein *Ensemble* wunderbarer Dinge und Begebenheiten'.[117] For Tieck, meanwhile, the episodes that made up such an ensemble comprised everything that had 'eine Wirkung ohne eine

'The Shadow of Resistance: W. G. Sebald and the Frankfurt School', in *Journal of European Studies*, 41: 3–4 (2011), 267–284; and James R. Martin, 'On Misunderstanding W. G. Sebald', in *Cambridge Literary Review*, 4:7 (2013), 123–138.

[116] See E. T. A. Hoffmann, *Der goldne Topf* (Stuttgart: Reclam, 1986).

[117] Novalis, *Novalis: Werke, Tagebücher und Briefe*, 696. 'A dream vision [...] an *ensemble* of wonderful things and occurrences'. Emphasis in original.

Ursache'.[118] The Sebaldian reconfiguration of *Kunstmärchen* conventions and traits in *Austerlitz*, however, draws on these conceptualizations of the Romantic form but makes the novel's historical position an intrinsic part of its aesthetics, such that *Austerlitz* may be read as a late and melancholy *Kunstmärchen* for the close of the twentieth century. Resisting Enlightenment rationalism and reason, while drawing on earlier literary forms and conventions, both heightens the pathos of the novel's historical lateness and solidifies its melancholy aesthetic attitude.

Before examining the ways in which they emerge in *Austerlitz*, however, it will be helpful to briefly outline some key aspects of the original *Kunstmärchen* form, which itself adapts many metaphors from folk tales, while also adopting similar elements, styles, and themes to give them a particularly fairy tale quality (*das Märchenhafte*).[119] That said, *Kunstmärchen* tend to be neither so one-dimensional in their narrative form as folk tales, nor so reliant on the stereotypical abstraction of place, time, and character. They frequently provide contextualization regarding persons or events, and characters, as well as their problems, are often psychologized so that inner alterations may be perceived to have taken place alongside external changes of fortune such as typically occur in folk tales. Characters' morality, furthermore, is often composed of shades of grey as opposed to folk tales' binary black-and-white categorization of the forces of Good and Evil. Indeed, the world of the *Kunstmärchen* is far from a cheerful place where Good always triumphs. These tales frequently devote themselves to exploring darker aspects of human nature, revelling in melancholy, delusion, and a sense of longing for death. The plot of many a *Kunstmärchen*

---

[118] Ludwig Tieck, *Kritische Schriften* (Berlin: de Gruyter, 1974), 65. Tieck: 'An effect without cause'.

[119] The following summary of the German *Kunstmärchen* is synthesized from various works, which discuss the elements, styles, and themes of the *Kunstmärchen*, both in the context of the German literary tradition and in a broader European historical context. These include Friedmar Apel, *Die Zaubergärten der Phantasie: Zur Theorie und Geschichte des Kunstmärchens* (Heidelberg: Carl Winter, 1987); Volker Klotz, *Das europäische Kunstmärchen: Fünfundzwanzig Kapitel seiner Geschichte von der Renaissance bis zur Moderne* (Munich: Deutscher Taschenbuchverlag, 1987); Mathias Mayer and Jens Tismar, eds., *Kunstmärchen* (Stuttgart: Metzler, 2003); Paul W. Wührl, *Das deutsche Kunstmärchen: Geschichte, Botschaft und Erzählstrukturen* (Baltmannsweiler: Schneider, 2012), as well as Jack Zipes, *Breaking the Magic Spell: Radical Theories of Folk and Fairy Tales* (Austin: Texas University Press, 1979), 62–75.

is driven by its protagonist's inner conflict, which results from a discrepancy between the everyday world and unfulfilled yearning or desire. Though heterogenous in form and style, most *Kunstmärchen* narratives generally offer more than one perspective on events, while stressing a gap between the self and the rest of the world that is unable to be bridged. The protagonist, who is typically male and often associated with artistic or creative pursuits, is displaced and does not belong to a particular community. Isolated and lonely, his goal is to transcend his current existence and to find—or even bring into being—a new and better world. At the beginning of a *Kunstmärchen*, the protagonist is usually in a distressed or disoriented state, unsure of how to proceed; either they may be physically lost somewhere or in an anxious state of existential uncertainty. Following this, a mentor figure is introduced to accompany the protagonist and guide them through a journey of self-discovery. At this point, the protagonist will typically cross a threshold into another world (*Schwellenüberschreitung*) where the natural laws of space and time are suspended (*Zeitaufhebung*) and, indeed, where cause and effect may no longer be entirely logical or even predictable. Following some initial shock or confusion in this new alternative world (*Gegenwelt*), as well as confrontations with fantastical characters or mythical figures, the protagonist undergoes a form of trial or challenge to test them. After this, they will typically return to their world, but not before a final farewell meeting between the protagonist and their mentor at the tale's conclusion. There is rarely a happy end to the *Kunstmärchen* and, should there be one, it typically takes place in an alternative world, heightening the protagonist's separation from his place of origin. Such aesthetic, stylistic, and narratorial elements of the traditional *Kunstmärchen* have their late echoes in *Austerlitz*. Through these refashionings the novel's melancholy aesthetic attitude is emphasized and compounded by divisions between the self and the world, the creation of false worlds, and journeys into new subterranean realms, both real and metaphorical. Occurring on both the micro level of individual episodes in Austerlitz's life story and the macro level of the narrative in its entirety, these reworkings of *Kunstmärchen* conventions are fundamentally connected to and, indeed, exert great influence on, the melancholy perception of the fundamental gulf between the present and the past articulated in *Austerlitz*.

The overall structure of the novel itself echoes these fairy tale descents. The narrator's journey over the course of the novel mirrors Austerlitz's own, particularly in his aforementioned sense of being driven to travel 'aus [...] mir selber nicht recht erfindlichen Gründen' (*A*, 1), which foreshadows the similar way that Austerlitz finds himself drawn on in Liverpool Street Station by forces he cannot identify. This is reminiscent of the wandering protagonists of many *Kunstmärchen*, who feel drawn on by unknown forces, such as Christian, the protagonist of Tieck's *Der Runenberg* (1804), who leaves his hometown 'um eine fremde Umgebung zu suchen, um sich aus dem Kreise der wiederkehrenden Gewöhnlichkeit zu erfernen' and is later driven up the Runenberg itself by 'irre Vorstellungen und unverständliche Wünsche'.[120] Like Austerlitz, the narrator experiences a life-changing meeting in a station, namely, his initial encounter with the novel's protagonist. Later, after a visit to the Breendonk fortress, the narrator feels unwell, just as Austerlitz does upon leaving Liverpool Street Station, which echoes the sense of confusion or upset experienced by protagonists in the *Kunstmärchen* upon entering an alternative world. In *Austerlitz*, this metaphorical crossing of thresholds from one world to another occurs as a transition from one episode of the novel to the next, or from one character's story to another, all the while encompassed by an overarching narrative that follows a similar structure. Austerlitz has guides to help him navigate his way through his false world or deeper into the depths of the underworld of the past: there is the archivist Teresa Ambrosová, for example, or the antiquarian bookseller Penelope Peaceful, or Marie de Verneuil, a friend from his youth with whom he has an intimate yet fraught relationship. The narrator, however, has only Austerlitz, who is absent when not recounting his investigations of his family history. The structure of the novel as a whole thus mirrors the *Kunstmärchen* episodes in Austerlitz's life story, albeit with a melancholy inflection that yields diminishing returns, as the narrator is left without a guide. He returns to his world, having been submerged in Austerlitz's story, whereas Austerlitz himself departs without a final meeting, leaving any sense of resolution unfulfilled. In this way, the conclusion of *Austerlitz* both draws on and reworks traits and conventions of the *Kunstmärchen* in order to reinforce the novel's melancholy aesthetics.

Returning to the episode at Breendonk at the beginning of the novel will shed further light on instances of *das Märchenhafte* in *Austerlitz* and how the novel as a whole is structured following the form of the *Kunstmärchen*. On Austerlitz's recommendation, the narrator journeys to

---

[120] Ludwig Tieck, *Der blonde Eckbert/Der Runenberg* (Reclam XL: 2018), 27 and 35. 'To search for foreign surroundings, to remove himself from the circle of recurring normality'; 'astounding ideas and incomprehensible desires'.

148   I. ELLISON

Breendonk, the military fortification that was originally built for the
Belgian army at the start of the twentieth century. Initially intended as a
place of refuge, the *Festung* was used as a Nazi prison camp during the
German occupation of Belgium and has since become a national memorial
and public museum. Surveying the structure, the narrator declares it to be
'eine einzige monolithische Ausgeburt der Häßlichkeit und der blinden
Gewalt' (*A*, 35).[121] He views the building as emblematic of modern
European society, while also being indicative of the final destination of the
rationalist procedures of Enlightenment thinking and progress. As the
narrator later summarizes when recalling a discussion with Austerlitz in
the latter's office in Bloomsbury about the form of 'Ordnungszwang' (*A*,
52)[122] prevalent in twentieth-century Europe, and particularly expressed,
according to Austerlitz, in its architecture, this leads to a 'Zug ins
Monumentale, der sich manifestierte in Gerichtshöfen und Strafanstalten,
in Bahnhofs- und Börsengebäuden, in Opern- und Irrenhäusern und den
nach rechtwinkligen Rastern angelegten Siedlungen für die Arbeiterschaft'
(*A*, 52).[123] The unspoken end-point of this chain of modern edifices is the
concentration camp—or perhaps, subsequently, the tourist attraction—
where the narrator and, previously, Austerlitz stand in Breendonk.

As any visitor to the site knows, or indeed as any glance at a map of the
Willebroek area will show, the fortress is hardly in a remote location. Yet
the narrator of *Austerlitz* paints a picture of the ruined fortification as
being far removed from civilization. The narrator's description of the fortress—'umgeben von einem Erdwall, einem Stacheldrahtzaun und einem
breiten Wassergraben [...] fast wie eine Insel im Meer' (*A*, 33)[124]—is
replete with references to its being shut off from the everyday reality the
narrator usually occupies, as if the structure were located in an alternative
world. Not only does the narrator perceive the building as monstrous,
resulting from violence and ideas of progress, he also struggles to comprehend its form as he draws closer: 'was ich jetzt vor mir hatte, das war eine

[121] 'A monolithic, monstrous incarnation of ugliness and blind violence' (*A*, 26).
[122] 'Compulsive sense of order' (*A*, 44).
[123] 'Tendency towards monumentalism evident in lawcourts and penal institutions, railway
stations and stock exchanges, opera houses and lunatic asylums, and dwellings built to rect-
angular grid patterns for the labour force (*A*, 44).
[124] 'Rather like an island in the sea and surrounded by an embankment, a barbed-wire fence
and a wide moat' (*A*, 25).

niedrige, an den Außenflanken überall abgerundete, auf eine grauenvolle Weise bucklig und verbacken wirkende Masse Beton, der breite Rücken, so dachte ich mir, eines Ungetüms, das sich hier wie ein Walfisch aus den Wellen, herausgehoben hatte aus dem flandrischen Boden' (*A*, 33).[125] The structure is monstrous and misshapen and does not conform to the orderly image of a star-shaped bastion that the narrator has imagined following an earlier conversation with Austerlitz. It seems unworldly to him, incomprehensible, as if it had emerged from some subterranean other place. Having drawn on *Kunstmärchen* traits in order to refuse resolution and emphasize the melancholy perspective in the narrative, while responding to the legacy of twentieth-century modernity, the narrator reveals again the vestigially Romantic within the modern. Yet the conventions of the *Kunstmärchen* are inverted here: rather than returning to his previous reality a changed man, having been submerged in Austerlitz's story, he emerges from the imagined reality of Austerlitz's account to find the actual fortress itself altered from his expectations.

Breendonk is continually presented as an unnatural place that does not belong in the world, not only because of its history as a concentration camp, but also because, as the narrator later admits, the place is so far beyond his understanding, 'daß ich sie zuletzt mit keiner mir bekannten Ausformung der menschlichen Zivilization, nicht einmal mit den stummen Relikten unserer Vor- und Frühgeschichte in irgendeinen Zusammenhang bringen konnte' (*A*, 34).[126] The edifice is temporally as well as physically disconnected. This sensation of being in an unnatural or distorted world continues to grow: 'je länger ich meinen Blick auf sie gerichtet hielt und je öfter sie mich, wie ich spürte, zwang, ihn vor ihr zu senken, desto unbegreiflicher wurde sie mir' (*A*, 34).[127] The creeping sense of otherworldliness at Breendonk is not only confined to the narrator's perception of the building itself; it is also intensified by the weather

---

[125] 'What I now saw before me was a low-built concrete mass, rounded at all its outer edges and giving the impression of something hunched and misshapen: the broad back of a monster, I thought, risen up from this Flemish soil like a whale from the deep' (*A*, 25).

[126] 'That in the end I found myself unable to connect it with anything shaped by human civilization, or even with the silent relics of our prehistory and early history' (*A*, 26).

[127] 'The longer I looked at it, the more often it forced me, as I felt, to lower my eyes, the less comprehensible it seemed to become' (*A*, 26).

which is 'ungewöhnlich heiß' (*A*, 33).[128] The narrator is furthermore perturbed by 'das unnatürlich tiefgrüne, fast blaufarbene Gras, das auf der
Insel wuchs' (*A*, 33).[129] Its location on an island further emphasizes the
separation of the fortress from the realm of the everyday and, surrounded
by what he perceives as the otherworldly strangeness of the local landscape, the narrator confesses that 'ich scheute mich, durch das schwarze
Tor in die Festung selber zu treten' (*A*, 33).[130] Unlike in traditional
Kunstmärchen, the narrator of *Austerlitz* is without a guide or mentor
figure to lead him across the threshold to a state of enlightenment or resolution as he moves into this otherworldly fortress. As he walks through the
corridors of Breendonk, the narrator makes connections to the lives of
prisoners, before ending this episode with the recollection of the letter 'A'
drawn repeatedly by Gastone Novelli upon his return to his home country
after being interned in the concentration camp at Dachau (*A*, 40–44).
The narrator likens this to 'ein lang anhaltender Schrei' (*A*, 44),[131] pre-
empting Austerlitz's inability to make a sound during the physical and
mental collapse he later recounts. In an enactment of the gulf between
past and present, the narration subsequently jumps to the narrator's next
meeting with Austerlitz, leaving his account of his excursion in Breendonk
unfinished, in much the same way as Austerlitz later remarks, following his
epiphany in the Ladies Waiting Room of Liverpool Street Station: 'Ich
habe keinerlei Begriff davon, wie lange ich in dem Wartesaal gestanden
bin, [...] noch weiß ich, auf welche Weise ich wieder nach draußen
gelangte' (*A*, 203).[132] For Austerlitz and for the narrator, these excursions
into alternative realities are reworked instantiations of the traditional
Kunstmärchen features, which lack resolution. The instance of threshold
crossing at Breendonk at the opening of the novel has, moreover, a double
significance: it is both a moment of discovery for the narrator and a mark
of the beginning of his own journey as he crosses over into the alternative
world of Austerlitz's investigation into his past.

The narrator in *Austerlitz* is distanced from his reality, from the world
of the everyday, and this is also inflected by what he perceives as his late
historical position. His descent into the dungeon chambers of the fortress

---

[128] 'Unusually hot' (*A*, 25).

[129] 'The unnaturally deep-green, almost blue-tinged grass growing on the island' (*A*, 25).

[130] 'I felt reluctant to pass through the black gateway into the fortress itself' (*A*, 25).

[131] 'A long drawn-out scream' (*A*, 36).

[132] 'I have no idea how long I stood in the waiting room [...], nor how I got out again'
(*A*, 195).

are likened to crossing a threshold into a separate world, and his perspective on these events, as he recounts them from a future date, emphasizes this separation. Once inside the fortress, 'zwischen Portal und Ausgang' (*A*, 38),[133] it becomes even clearer that the narrator feels as if he has crossed from one world into another:

> Die Erinnerung [...] hat sich in mir verdunkelt im Laufe der Zeit, oder vielmehr verdunkelte sie sich, wenn man so sagen kann, schon an dem Tag, an welchem ich in der Festung war, sei es, weil ich nicht wirklich sehen wollte, was man dort sah, sei es, weil in dieser nur vom schwachen Schein weniger Lampen erhellten und für immer vom Licht der Natur getrennten Welt die Konturen der Dinge zu zerfließen schienen. (*A*, 38)[134]

There is a sense of dread evoked at the unknown horrors that await him in this new place in which he finds himself and, indeed, the darkness below ground acts as a metaphor for the inhumane events that occurred in the fortress in the past. The hypotaxis of the narrator's sentences, his accumulation of clauses, and his use of the subjunctive mood all contribute towards the growing sense of distance and separation, of entering a different reality or an unnatural world which, as the narrator declares, is cut off from the light and where the clear outlines of the everyday world are blurred and unclear. It is an interior prefiguration of Austerlitz's later recollection of his and Gerald's evening flight in an aeroplane over the Suffolk coast, 'als die Schatten aus der Tiefe des Meeres emporwuchsen und sich nach und nach über uns neigten, bis der letzte Glanz an den Rändern der westlichen Welt erlosch' (*A*, 170).[135] Even when the narrator returns to Breendonk thirty years later at the end of the novel, there is a sense of irresolution encapsulated by the narrator's unfinished book, Austerlitz's unfinished history, and the inauspicious sense that, given their distanced and late historical positions, the narrator and Austerlitz are condemned to walk towards a setting sun that keeps sinking but never quite sets. In

---

[133] 'Between portal and exit'.

[134] 'My memory [...] has clouded over in the course of time, or perhaps I could say it was clouding over even on the day when I was in the fort, whether because I did not really want to see what it had to show or because all the outlines seemed to merge in a world illuminated only by a few dim electric bulbs, and cut off forever from the light of nature' (*A*, 29–30).

[135] 'When the shadows emerged from the depths of the sea, gradually rising and inclining towards us, until the last gleam of light was extinguished on the horizons of the western world' (*A*, 162).

contradistinction to the 'strahlende[r] Frühsommertag' (*A*, 9) on which
Austerlitz begins, the novel's close is decidedly crepuscular.[136] However,
the various journeys undertaken over the course of *Austerlitz*, as well as
the narrative's structure as a descent into the underworld of Austerlitz's
story of his past, are prefigured on the very first page of the novel with the
narrator's remark that 'als der Zug [...] in die dunkle Bahnhofshalle hin-
einrollte, war ich ergriffen worden von einem Gefühl des Unwohlseins'
(*A*, 9).[137] The melancholy of the novel's lack of resolution and the sustained gulf between present and past are thus fully inflected by Romantic
elements from the outset.

UNDERWORLDS AND THRESHOLDS

In enacting an historically late form of Romanticism, *Austerlitz* brings
German national literature into a modern consciousness through a cooperation of both the natural and artificial, the naïve and the self-conscious,
thereby highlighting the deliberately constructed nature of the novel itself.
For Minden, the specifically Romantic form of the *Kunstmärchen* exists
uniquely as a form that 'blurred the boundary between philological exac-
titude and modern Romantic creativity'.[138] Such a modern affirmation of
self-consciousness is for Romantic literature a guarantee of authenticity,
which all the while draws on the notion of Romantic irony. Said irony
involves a perpetual awareness of artificiality understood as a natural property of the human mind. As a result, any literary authenticity in a Romantic
sense is guaranteed since self-conscious awareness of literary artifice and
invention precludes any naïve sense of closure. Sebald's final novel is one
which continually resists closure: conjecture replaces certainty, and playful
Romantic irony becomes weighed down by the burden of the past and an
elegiac melancholy. Historical difference and contingency thus emerge as
essential components of *Austerlitz*'s reworked Romantic elements, re-
enforcing the novel's particular forms of lateness and the melancholy view
of history it espouses. Both the narrator's and the protagonist's metaphorical *Schwellenüberschreitungen* into other worlds demonstrate how
the sense of melancholy disconnection in the novel between the narrator's
millennial present and the past stems from a sense of historical and literary

---

[136] 'Glorious summer's day' (*A*, 1).
[137] 'As the train rolled into the dark station concourse, I had begun to feel unwell' (*A*, 1).
[138] Minden, *Modern German Literature*, 38–39.

lateness. Through this emerges an outlook on the traumatic and complex events of twentieth-century European history that is fundamentally immersed in a Romantic sensibility. Via its self-reflective transformations and reconfigurations throughout German literary history, the *Kunstmärchen* form offers moral and political critiques of society. The German obsession with the fairy tale over the centuries is at its core 'vital and dynamic', as Jack Zipes has observed, offering writers and readers 'a means to participate in a dialogue and discourse about specific social conditions', which 'express a German proclivity to seek resolutions of social conflicts within art'.[139] *Austerlitz*, with its protagonist's quest to uncover the past and its narrator's respectful mediation of Austerlitz's story, is a late echo of such artistic forms. Indeed, the assemblage of stories and information in *Austerlitz* has artistic and methodological parallels with the purported approach of the Brothers Grimm towards gathering folk tales: 'not only did they edit and prepare the "found" materials they collected for publication', as Minden summarizes, 'but these materials themselves were by definition examples of spontaneous artifice'.[140] While the narrator's meticulous artifice in *Austerlitz* can hardly be called spontaneous, exhibiting as it does something rather more akin to an artificial spontaneity in its staged coincidental encounters, a closer examination of the *Kunstmärchen* form and of its echoes in the novel reveals how Austerlitz's growing awareness of living in a false reality is compounded and nuanced by reworkings of *das Märchenhafte*.

In spite of this growing awareness, however, narratorial ambiguity and confusion still remain essential elements in the traditional Romantic *Kunstmärchen*. It may never become clear, for example, whether their protagonists are to be trusted, since they may be either in some way *verirrt* or under the influence of a form of enchantment. In *Austerlitz*, meanwhile, metaphorical crossings from one world to another offer less a sense of a complete loss of reality and heightened delusion than another way of perceiving the reality occupied by the narrator and the protagonist as tinged with lateness and melancholy. In a key episode of Austerlitz's story in the centre of the novel, aspects of the *Kunstmärchen* are reconfigured in the establishment of an alternative world or 'falsches Universum' (*A*, 199) where time and space are altered or undone, in order to attempt a

[139] Jack Zipes, *The Brothers Grimm: From Enchanted Forest to the Modern World* (Basingstoke: Palgrave Macmillan, 2002), 85.
[140] Minden, *Modern German Literature*, 39.

reconciliation with history. Plagued by insomnia and distanced from society, Austerlitz has fallen into the habit of wandering London during the night and claims to be irresistibly drawn back to Liverpool Street Station. Later, he recalls for the first time in his life his arrival at this station with a *Kindertransport* from Europe, waiting for his new foster parents. This catalytic revelation gives him the impulse to travel to the city of Prague where he was born and hunt for further clues as to his family's lives and fates. In a direct echo of a Proustian moment of involuntary recollection, the specific sensation of walking across uneven cobblestones unlocks a dawning familiarity in Austerlitz:

> wie ich, Schritt für Schritt, bergan steigend, die unebenen Pflastersteine der Šporkova unter meinen Füßen spürte, war es mir, als sei ich auf diesen Wegen schon einmal gegangen, als eröffnete sich mir nicht durch die Anstrengung des Nachdenkens, sondern durch meine so lange betäubt gewesenen und jetzt wiedererwachenden Sinne, die Erinnerung. (*A*, 220)[141]

Instead of resolution, however, this leads only to his physical collapse and further melancholy separation from the events of the past.

Entering the Liverpool Street Station underground, Austerlitz describes it as 'einer der finstersten und unheimlichsten Orte von London, eine Art Eingang zur Unterwelt' (*A*, 188).[142] Crossing the threshold into this station leads to a strange other world and in his recollection of this hellish place, Austerlitz draws particularly on the convention of katabasis, a journey down into an underworld. Although this convention has its origins in Antiquity, it also finds itself reworked in literary fairy tales, such as in Christian's disappearance into a mountain in *Der Runenberg*.[143] Alan Itkin argues that Sebald repurposes katabasis not just as a classical trope for engaging with the relationship between

---

[141] 'When I felt the uneven paving of the Šporkova underfoot as step by step I climbed uphill, it was as if I had already been this way before and memories were revealing themselves to me not by means of any mental effort but through my senses, so long numbed and now coming back to life' (*A*, 212–213).

[142] 'One of the darkest and most sinister places in London, a kind of entrance to the underworld' (*A*, 180).

[143] For further discussion of the notion of katabasis in literature, particularly in terms of a descent into an underworld, see John J. Collins and Michael Fishbanel, eds., *Death, Ecstasy, and Other Worldly Journeys* (Albany, New York: State University of New York Press, 1995); Radcliffe G. Edmonds III, *Myths of the Underworld Journey: Plato, Aristophanes, and the 'Orphic' Gold Tablets* (Cambridge: Cambridge University Press, 2004); and Rachael Falconer,

the past and the present, but also as a means of conceptualizing history as destiny.[144] Austerlitz's katabatic entry into the alternative world in Liverpool Street Station resonates not only with Adorno's aforementioned theorization of a false world, but also with the Germanic tradition of the *Kunstmärchen*. Such a reading of a Romantic threshold crossing is borne out by the way the laws of time and space appear altered in *Austerlitz*. Distortions of space, and of Austerlitz's own perspective, suggest a transition into an alternative world as the moment of katabasis occurs in the novel. Consistent with the form of the *Kunstmärchen*, the protagonist undertakes this journey into what appears to be another realm, following his unconscious desire, which will lead to a transformative confrontation with the fantastical. In the case of *Austerlitz*, this is the protagonist's shocking and epiphanic moment of self-knowledge through the sudden recollection of himself as a young boy with his foster parents that he later experiences upon coming back to the Ladies' Waiting Room which is no longer in use (*A*, 200–203). Having entered the underworld of the station, Austerlitz's katabasis has already begun, but this sense of otherworldliness intensifies as he draws closer to the Ladies' Waiting Room where his as yet unremembered past awaits him. Having followed the enigmatic figure of a station cleaner (*A*, 196), who appears almost to lead him on, he stands before the door and remarks, 'Ich zögerte, an die Schwingtür heranzutreten, aber kaum hatte ich meine Hand auf den Messinggriff gelegt, da trat ich schon, durch einen im Inneren gegen die Zugluft aufgehängten Filzvorgang, in den offenbar vor Jahren bereits außer Gebrauch geratenen Saal' (*A*, 197).[145] Drawing on the convention of *Schwellenüberschreitung* to articulate his exploration of the past, Austerlitz not only evokes the idea of crossing into another world, but also reinforces the late aesthetics of his tale, since the room beyond the curtain has fallen into disuse. Time, indeed, in this waiting room seems to no longer function as in the everyday world, as

---

Hell in Contemporary Literature: Western Descent Narratives Since 1945 (Edinburgh: Edinburgh University Press, 2005).

[144] Alan Itkin, '"Eine Art Eingang zur Unterwelt": *Katabasis* in Austerlitz', in *The Undiscover'd Country: W. G. Sebald's Poetics of Travel*, ed. by Markus Zisselsberger (2010), 161–185. See also Alan Itkin, *Underworlds of Memory: W. G. Sebald's Epic Journeys through the Past* (Evanston, Illinois: Northwestern University Press, 2017), especially 23–76.

[145] 'I hesitated to approach the swing doors, but as soon as I had taken hold of the brass handle I stepped past a heavy curtain hung on the inside to keep out draughts, and entered the large room, which had obviously been disused for years' (*A*, 189).

Austerlitz observes: 'es mögen Minuten oder Stunden vergangen sein, während derer ich, ohne mich von der Stelle rühren zu können, in dem, wie es mir schien, ungeheuer weit hinaufgehenden Saal gestanden bin' (*A*, 197).[146] The vertiginous height of the ceiling further emphasizes the sense of lateness of the narrative here, since it metaphorically recalls the distant historical position from which the novel is written at the end of the twentieth century. Not only is the ceiling dizzyingly high, it is 'ungeheuer'—monstrously so—as if of another world. The space he has entered appears disorienting for Austerlitz, and it appears to him as if the reality in which he has now found himself is becoming increasingly unreal. He recalls 'das eisgraue, mondscheinartige Licht, das durch einen unter der Deckenwölbung verlaufenden Gaden drag und einem Netz oder einem schütteren, stellenweise ausgefransten Gewebe gleich über mir hing' (*A*, 197–198),[147] which adds to the mystical otherworldly atmosphere of the waiting room. When Austerlitz's moment of epiphany finally arrives, he seems to stand not only outside of everyday reality, but also outside of history:

> Tatsächlich hatte ich das Gefühl, sagte Austerlitz, als enthalte der Wartesaal, in dessen Mitte ich wie ein Geblendeter stand, alle Stunden meiner Vergangenheit, all meine von jeher unterdrückten, ausgelöschten Ängste und Wünsche, als sei das schwarzweiße Rautenmuster der Steinplatten zu meinen Füßen das Feld für das Endspiel meines Lebens, als erstreckte es sich über die gesamte Ebene der Zeit. (*A*, 200–201)[148]

In the narrator's account, Austerlitz, dazzled by his otherworldly environs, imagines himself in a form of endgame, the last confrontation of his life. This is to be played out in the station waiting room, the site of his shocking epiphanic realization, which he continues to perceive in unworldly terms.

---

[146] 'Minutes or even hours may have passed while I stood in that empty space beneath a ceiling which seemed to float at a vertiginous height, unable to move from the spot' (*A*, 189).

[147] 'The grey icy light, like moonshine, which came through the windows in a gallery beneath the vaulted roof, and hung above me like a tight-meshed net or a piece of thin, fraying fabric' (*A*, 189–190).

[148] 'In fact I felt, said Austerlitz, that the waiting room where I stood as if dazzled contained all the hours of my past life, all the suppressed and extinguished fears and wishes I had ever entertained, as if the black and white diamond pattern of the stone slabs beneath my feet were the board on which the endgame would be played, and it covered the entire plane of time' (*A*, 192–193).

In this episode of Austerlitz's story, the reworking of the *Kunstmärchen* trope of crossing from one world and into another embellishes the novel's sense of melancholy not only via the protagonist's entry into a perceived alternative reality, along with his growing understanding of the falsity of his own. His interactions with the fantastical denizens of the underground *Gegenwelt* in which he finds himself add to the melancholy and the pathos of his katabatic journey. Crossings from one world into another occur not only in one direction in Liverpool Street Station, however. As Austerlitz is drawn into the underworld of the station concourse, the passengers milling around him are imagined as ghosts of the dead from the past rising up towards him. He describes how 'in dieser ewigen Düsternis, die erfüllt war von einem erstickten Stimmengewirr, einem leise Gescharre und Getrappel, bewegten sich die [...] ungezählten Menschen in Strömen' (*A*, 189).[149] Connecting these milling crowds of passers-by with a feeling of being unreconciled with the passing of time, he remarks how he felt 'dieses andauernde Ziehen in mir, eine Art Herzweh, das, wie ich zu ahnen begann, verursacht wurde von dem Sog der verflossenen Zeit' (*A*, 190).[150] These crowds of people are brought together as one anonymous mass, gathering at the entrance to this other world as Austerlitz enters, ascending as he descends, attempting to acquire some secret knowledge just as he is. It is not just the protagonist of this *Kunstmärchen* who is seeking resolution, however. This becomes clearer as Austerlitz progresses on his journey, observing 'Stege und Zugbrücken, die die tiefsten Abgründe überquerten und auf denen winzige Figuren sich drängten, Gefangene, so dachte ich mir, sagte Austerlitz, die einen Ausweg suchten aus diesem Verlies' (*A*, 198).[151] Yet there is no escape for these ghosts of the past, and no reconciliation with his own story for Austerlitz, only the shock discovery of the buried memory of his arrival in London and his resultant collapse. It is not possible, Austerlitz comes to realize, for him or for the ghosts of the dead to bridge the gulf of time and be reconciled with one another. Although threshold crossing is attempted in both directions here, the *Kunstmärchen* form is reworked and no resolution is reached for either party.

[149] 'In this eternal dusk, which was full of a muffled babble of voices, a quiet scraping and tramping of feet, innumerable passed in great tides' (*A*, 181).

[150] 'That constant wrenching inside me, a kind of heartache which, as I was beginning to sense, was caused by the vortex of past time' (*A*, 182).

[151] 'Jetties and drawbridges crossing the deepest chasms that thronged with tiny figures who looked to me, said Austerlitz, like prisoners in search of some way of escape from their dungeon'.

Kunstmärchen are highly structured with clear moments of anagnorisis for their protagonists, as when in Hoffmann's *Der Sandmann* (1816) Nathaniel sees the automaton Olimpia's eyes on the ground, which pushes him over the edge into madness, or when in Tieck's *Der blonde Eckbert* (1797) the character Walther lets slip the name of the protagonist's wife's dog, even though it had not been mentioned previously, thus leading him to suspect deceptions being worked against him. The moment of anagnorisis in the Ladies Waiting Room of Liverpool Street station is a key turning point in Austerlitz's life, a critical discovery at the centre of the novel which acts as confirmation of his growing awareness of living in a false world. Indeed, as he states earlier, he feels, upon entering the station, 'wie ein Schauspieler [...], der auf die Bühne hinaustritt und im Augenblick des Hinaustretens das von ihm auswendig Gelernte mitsamt der Rolle, die er so oft gespielt hat, unwiderruflich und restloß vergißt' (*A*, 197).[152] It is only by crossing the threshold into the alternative reality—or false world— of the waiting room that he is able to realize that his everyday life is one in which he simply plays a role. As he steps on to the metaphorical stage within the *Gegenwelt* in Liverpool Street Station, he recognizes a sense of artificiality in his wanderings. The new revelations and perspectives he has on his life occur, he now realizes, 'wie das nur in einem derartigen falschen Universum möglich war' (*A*, 199).[153] Crucially, it is through reconfigurations of the *Kunstmärchen* in the narrative and in particular the convention of crossing out of the everyday world into an alternative reality that Austerlitz's own sense of coming to consciousness about the falseness of his reality develops. Encountering or perceiving the dead only leads Austerlitz towards melancholy, dispossession, and lack of reconciliation with the past as opposed to any reconciliation with or ownership of the ghosts of history. Although his journey brings him some insights into the circumstances of his flight from Europe as a child, along with a sense of commonality with the ghosts of the dead, he and the narrator are nevertheless adrift in melancholy incompleteness. Both worlds, in their distinct ways, seems as false as each other.

---

[152] 'Like an actor who, upon making his entrance, has completely and irrevocably forgotten not only the lines he knew by heart but the very part he has so often played' (*A*, 189).

[153] 'In such a way that was only possible in such a wrong universe'.

BEARABLE SURVIVAL

It is no coincidence that the station building in which this metaphorical crossing into another world takes place is itself a monument to Enlightenment progress, a relic of the era of European colonialism and imperialism. The industrialization required to construct what Austerlitz perceives as a hellish underworld of modernity entailed massive destruction of human habitation, the remains of whose victims lie beneath the station's foundations, as Austerlitz recounts (*A*, 192–195). The skeletons of the corpses of Bedlam patients that have been unearthed in the course of an archaeological dig in the station undermine the myth of historical progress represented by the station, signifying those left behind by the project of modernity. Furthermore, this instance of anagnorisis in the station proves not to be the endgame for Austerlitz, since he continues to exist beyond it, which quietly intensifies his sense of melancholy lateness. The station's archaeological strata reveal the ravages of modernity, encapsulating the negative dialectic of the Enlightenment, which holds that the notion of progress already contains within it the seeds of destruction and devastation, just as the modern encapsulates the vestigially Romantic.[154] And, indeed, in response to this imagined endgame, the narrative nonetheless reflects certain Romantic sensibilities.

The narrator's account of his and Austerlitz's experiences is saturated with Romantic echoes—not only the contemplation of ruins, but also the situating of himself within a *Kunstmärchen* false world in order to recount and attempt to work through his personal reality. Arriving in Prague later in the novel, Austerlitz's perception of living in a false world has grown, and the crossing of borders between worlds appears to occur everywhere he goes, 'als gäbe es überhaupt keine Zeit, sondern nur verschiedene, nach einer höheren Stereometrie ineinander verschachtelte Räume, zwischen denen die Lebendigen und die Toten, je nachdem es ihnen zumute ist, hin und her gehen können' (*A*, 269).[155] Even when, after further investigation,

---

[154] This is a very brief and rather crude rehearsal of Adorno and Horkheimer's argument in their work on the dialectic of Enlightenment. For the original argument, see Theodor W. Adorno and Max Horkheimer, 'Dialektik der Aufklärung: Philosophische Fragmente', in Max Horkheimer, *Gesammelte Schriften 5. 'Dialektik der Aufklärung' und Schriften 1940–1950*, ed. by Alfred Schmidt and Gunzelin Schmidt Noerr (Frankfurt am Main: Fischer, 1987).

[155] 'As if time did not exist at all, only various spaces interlocking according to the rules of a higher form of stereometry, between which the living and the dead can move back and forth as they like' (*A*, 261).

he discovers the identity of his parents, their ultimate fates remain unknown. Narrative melancholy is never resolved, only extended, with the past and the present remaining separated and reworkings of elements of the Romantic *Kunstmärchen* playing a crucial role in the denial of closure or reconciliation in the novel: these are 'ineinander verschachtelt' just as much as the spaces of the living and the dead that Austerlitz images. The novel thus emerges as a late and melancholy iteration of the *Kunstmärchen* for the end of the twentieth century and the turn of the twenty-first, which has, moreover, to plagiarize Austerlitz's aforementioned description of the hidden Jewish cemetery, become older with the passing of time. There remains, however, a subtle suggestion of the latent possibility if not of redemption or restitution for Austerlitz, then perhaps a form of cultural re-enchantment for the historical and artistic forms with which he engages.

Fairy tales as a form are both plastic and resilient. 'At their best', as Zipes proclaims, 'fairy tales constitute the most profound articulation of the human struggle to form and maintain a civilizing process'.[156] For Marina Warner, the fairy tale has a long and fluid history of crossing national and linguistic borders, and the recurrence of their thematic and structural features in contemporary fiction across the ages acts as 'connective tissue between a mythological past and the present realities'.[157] In the German literary tradition, and perhaps most particularly after the works of the Grimms were published, the fairy tale became a national institution.[158] The Grimms perceived their work to be a social intervention towards the fostering of a sense of national pride in a German folk tradition, even while Germany was yet to emerge as a united nation. Through the collection and dissemination of folk tales from across the German *Staatenkonglomerat* of the eighteenth century, the Grimms aimed to provide the nascent national bourgeoisie—who responded positively given the household setting of many tales, as well as their democratic ideals and their protestant ethics—with what Zipes calls 'a German cultural spirit [as] part of an effort

---

[156] Jack Zipes, *The Enchanted Screen: The Unknown History of Fairy-tale Films* (London: Routledge, 2011), 1. See also, Jack Zipes, 'The Cultural Evolution of Storytelling and Fairy Tales: Human Communication and Mimetics', in *The Irresistible Fairy Tale: The Cultural and Social History of a Genre* (Princeton: Princeton University Press, 2012), 1–20.

[157] Marina Warner, *Once Upon a Time: A Short History of Fairy Tales* (Oxford: Oxford University Press, 2014), xvi.

[158] See Jack Zipes, 'Chapter 5: The German Obsession with Fairy Tales', in *The Brothers Grimm: From Enchanted Forest to the Modern World*, 75–95.

to contribute to a united German front against the French'.[159] Despite 'an intense seriousness bordering on the religious, and nationalist overtones [that] have often smothered the philosophical and humanitarian essence of the tales', Zipes observes that Germans have 'repeatedly used fairy tales to explain the world to themselves'.[160] In German literary history since the eighteenth century, the fairy tale has been 'Germany's most democratic literary institution',[161] taken seriously by cultural critics and creative writers alike, who have used it as a reference point to consider German society. Take Walter Benjamin, for example, who remarks in 'Der Erzähler' (1936) that 'der erste wahre Erzähler ist und bleibt der von Märchen. Wo guter Rat teuer war, wußte das Märchen ihn, und wo die Not am höchsten war, da war seine Hilfe am nächsten'.[162] Understanding the German literary fairy tale as such an institution, however, does not render it static. On the contrary, it enables a view of literature as it transforms itself historically, as well as taking into account the contingent historical and cultural forces at work outside of literature that affect its production. It should not be forgotten, however, that the Grimms's tales were 'much more permeated with literary French influence than the Romantic brothers wished', as Warner indicates.[163] While the Germanic folk tale and later literary fairy tales like the *Kunstmächen* may originally have been conceived as nationalist, albeit with more positive connotations than those the term carries today, they nonetheless remain inconspicuously transnational. The publication of the Grimms's tales marked, as Minden notes, a key moment when 'modern German letters seemed naturally to settle into the vanguard of European literature'.[164] If *Austerlitz* is therefore read as a self-consciously late and melancholy *Kunstmärchen* emerging at the turn of the

---

[159] Jack Zipes, *The Brothers Grimm*, 78.

[160] Jack Zipes, *The Brothers Grimm*, 75.

[161] Jack Zipes, *The Brothers Grimm*, 79.

[162] Walter Benjamin, 'Der Erzähler: Betrachtungen zum Werk Nikolai Lesskows', in Walter Benjamin, *Gesammelte Schriften II.2*, ed. by Rolf Tiedemann and Hermann Schweppenhäuser (Frankfurt am Main: Suhrkamp, 1980), 438–465 (456). 'The first true storyteller is, and will continue to be, the teller of fairy tales. Whenever good counsel was at a premium, the fairy tale had it, and where the need was greatest, its aid was nearest'. Walter Benjamin, 'The Storyteller', in *Illuminations*, ed. by Hannah Arendt, trans. by Harry Zohn (New York: Schocken Books, 1968), 83–109 (102).

[163] See Marina Warner, *From the Beast to the Blonde: Of Fairy Tales and their Tellers* (London: Vintage, 1995), 193.

[164] Minden, *Modern German Literature*, 39.

millennium, then its Romantic inflections encapsulate a fluidity between a German and a broader European context.

In contrast to the effusively cosmopolitan attitudes displayed by key figures of the earlier period of German Classicism, such as Herder and Kant, the Romantic movement in Germany is often characterized as essentially nationalist, in part because of its later appropriation and corruption by the National Socialist regime, but also due to the Romantics' critique of the Enlightenment and its emphasis on reason, universalism, and abstract principles.[165] Nevertheless, many Romantics, while admittedly motivated on patriotic grounds, remained wedded to internationalist ideals propagated by their classicist antecedents, such that any nationalist tendencies evinced by German Romanticism necessarily encompass residual traces of more cosmopolitan attitudes.[166] Rather than being antithetical to more cosmopolitan attitudes, German Romanticism exhibits its own distinct cosmopolitan nature, as Pauline Kleingeld has argued, in that it centres on ideas of connections felt and experienced between individuals and communities through a common capacity in part for aesthetic creativity.[167]

Since the fairy tale itself may be considered to constitute a supranational form, existing as it does across and beyond the borders of national literatures, *Austerlitz*'s aesthetic attitude, inflected by Romantic lateness and melancholy, points beyond itself, suggesting that a latent possibility of future cultural renewal may be salvaged through reworkings of damaged or compromised literary forms. When understood solely as a late modernist novel, *Austerlitz* may indeed exemplify a form of European literature condemned by its own machinery. Yet an appreciation of the reworkings of Romantic literary conventions in *Austerlitz* may indicate a potential for the future restitution and renewal of modern European literature, the

[165] See, for example, Hans Kohn, 'Romanticism and the Rise of German Nationalism', in *Review of Politics*, 12:4 (1950), 443–472, and Carl Niekerk, 'Romanticism and Other Cultures', in *The Cambridge Companion to German Romanticism*, ed. by Nicholas Saul (Cambridge: Cambridge University Press, 2009), 158–177.

[166] See Friedrich Schlegel, 'Versuch über den Begriff des Republikanismus (1796)', *Kritische Friedrich Schlegel Ausgabe*, Vol. 7, ed. by Ernst Behler, Jean-Jacques Anstett, and Hans Eichner (Paderborn: Schönigh, 1958), 11–25. See also Wolfdietrich Rasch, 'Zum Verhältnis der Romantik zur Aufklärung', in *Romantik: Ein literaturwissenschaftliches Studienbuch*, ed. by Ernst Ribbat (Königstein: Athenäum, 1979), 7–21.

[167] See Pauline Kleingeld, 'Romantic Cosmopolitanism: Novalis's "Christianity or Europe"', in *Journal of the History of Philosophy*, 46: 2 (2008), 269–284 (283), and *Kant and Cosmopolitanism: The Philosophical Ideal of World Citizenship* (Cambridge: Cambridge University Press, 2012), especially 151–154.

seeds of which are already contained within its condemned form at the turn of the millennium. This potentiality reveals itself all the more clearly when the novel is read as an example of a turn-of-the-millennium collective of self-consciously late Europeans and their melancholy fiction. In its aesthetic enactment of future cultural renewal and re-enchantment, the narrative of *Austerlitz* resonates keenly with the sense of futurity suggested by Nietzsche's theorization of *Spätlinge* and *Erstlinge*. A kernel of futurity is embedded in backwards-facing late and melancholy aesthetics, however fleeting their Romantic echoes may be in the novel; as Austerlitz himself remarks, 'seltsamerweise, daran erinnere ich mich genau, ist es gerade die Flüchtigkeit dieser Erscheinungen gewesen, die mir damals so etwas wie ein Gefühl für die Ewigkeit gab' (*A*, 143).[168] To recall Minden's characterization of Sebald's œuvre, it is through Sebald's looking back to earlier times in *Austerlitz*—and, by extension, looking back to earlier literary forms—that 'the possibility that the *Erlebnis* of existing in the fallen world might indeed again become, if treated with the appropriate aesthetic and cultural respect, the kind of *Erfahrung* that makes survival in it valuable'.[169] The means of existing within late modernity, of living through it, and even of existing beyond it are gestured towards in the Romantic inflections of *Austerlitz*'s self-consciously late and melancholy aesthetics. Ultimately, to paraphrase Minden, the *Erlebnis* of Romantic lateness and melancholy in *Austerlitz* may promise the *Erfahrung* of future cultural renewal.

---

[168] 'Strangely – I remember this well – it was the very evanescence of those visions that gave me, at the time, something like a sense of eternity' (*A*, 135).

[169] Minden, *Modern German Literature*, 231.

CHAPTER 4

Exiled Lateness in *Sefarad* by Antonio Muñoz Molina

Chance encounters between individuals and books recur throughout Antonio Muñoz Molina's *Sefarad*, his eleventh novel but only the second of his works to be translated into English. The evocation in its early pages of how 'en un viaje se escucha una historia o se encuentra por azar un libro que acaba abriendo una onda concéntrica en la emoción de los descubrimientos sucesivos' (*S*, 227) could stand as a guiding motif for this sprawling, cacophonic novel.[1] In one of its few recollections of a journey with positive associations, which accompanies this pronouncement, the final volume of Marcel Proust's *A la recherche du temps perdu* (1913–1927) emerges not unfittingly as just such a book that will trigger associative discoveries: 'en un tren que me alejaba de Granada, recién terminado el curso en la facultad, a principios del verano de 1976, yo iba leyendo el relato del viaje a Venecia que hace Proust en *El tiempo recobrado*' (*S*, 224–225).[2] In a conversation with a colleague in the United States by the

---

[1] 'On a journey a story is heard or by chance a book is found which sends out ripples of concentric rings that affect succeeding discoveries'.

[2] 'At the beginning of the summer of 1976, after wrapping up my courses, I took a train from Granada and during the trip read Proust's account of a journey to Venice in *Le temps retrouvé*. In just one instance of numerous errors and omissions, the published English translation of *Sefarad* refers to the incorrect volume of Marcel Proust's *A la recherche du temps perdu* and to the city of Vienna, not Venice. There is, therefore, less consistent recourse

© The Author(s), under exclusive license to Springer Nature   165
Switzerland AG 2022
I. Ellison, *Late Europeans and Melancholy Fiction at the Turn of the
Millennium*, Palgrave Studies in Modern European Literature,
https://doi.org/10.1007/978-3-030-95447-5_4

name of Francisco Ayala, it transpires that 'él también la asociaba con la felicidad simultánea de un viaje' (*S*, 225),[3] so much so that

> llevaba siempre consigo un volumen de Proust, y le parecía que la relectura era aún más sabrosa porque al apartar los ojos del libro veía unos paisajes como del otro extremo del mundo, transitaba en un instante de las calles de París en 1900 y de las playas nubladas de Normandía a las inmensidades deshabitadas de América (*S*, 225).[4]

Despite the apparently engrossing experience of reading—and, indeed, of pausing to read—that it recalls, this brief episode of exile in the Americas is tinged with a nostalgic desire to return to somewhere other than an imagined Paris. Yet this nostalgia is implicitly transmuted into a melancholy sense of displacement and irresolution, not least because 'aquel libro [...] era su único lazo con su vida anterior, con la España perdida a la que tal vez no podría volver y la Europa que aún no había emergido de los cataclismos de la guerra' (*S*, 225).[5] Proust's novel thus constitutes both a reminder of a home and a culture left behind, of the realized impossibility of return, and of the uncertainty of the future. From the perspective of exile, with the geographical and historical distance this entails, Spain and Europe are associatively brought together, yet also set apart. Having explored in the previous two chapters examples of late European novels from French and German literature, this study now turns its attention to the Spanish literary tradition. This final chapter serves not only to introduce a Peninsular perspective but also to verify the European paradigm of the study as a whole. Within Europe, Spain's perceived later development, as well as the question of its relative cultural and economic (in)dependence, offer a distinct background against which to test the flexibility and viability of this study's ideas, while exploring further instantiations of the late European novel in a different yet related cultural milieu so often

to that translation in this chapter's footnotes than there has been to the generally more accurate English translations of *Dora Bruder* and *Austerlitz* referenced in the preceding chapters.

[3] 'He, too, connected it with the simultaneous pleasure of a journey'.

[4] 'He always took a volume of Proust with him, and it seemed to him that re-reading it was even more delicious, because when he raised his eyes from the book, he saw landscapes from the other ends of the earth, he was whisked away in an instant from the streets of Paris in 1900 and from the cloudy beaches of Normandy to the immense uninhabited spaces of South America'.

[5] 'That book was his only tie with his previous life, with a lost Spain to which he may not be able to return and to a Europe which still had not emerged from the cataclysm of war'.

understood historically and contemporaneously as an appendix to Europe. Spain's participation in the European constellation of exclusion and persecution is treated in the novel, with Muñoz Molina seeming to insinuate that at a time when the nation considers itself positively integrated into the destinies of the European continent, this should also trigger a review of how the worst chapters of their respective histories have overlapped and brutally fed into each other, hence the diversity of *Sefarad*'s characters and histories. This novel is not simply a multicultural polyphonic collage, however; it is a striking challenge to understanding the enmeshment of the Hispanic and the European at the millennial moment.

The narrator of *Sefarad* sets out to construct a pan-European narrative by bringing together various histories of twentieth-century exile, persecution, and suffering over the course of the novel to suggest a commonality of experience. As he remarks directly to the reader, 'no eres una sola persona y no tienes una sola historia' (*S*, 596).[6] In attempting to write the novel into a broader European literary context from which Spanish literature has long been excluded, the narrator of *Sefarad* effectively stages an encounter between European and Hispanic literary and cultural traditions.[7] On the one hand, *Sefarad* confronts the misconceived yet long established European construction of Spain as an outsider—an anachronistic relic—in Western culture and history. On the other hand, the narrator's sense of himself as a epigonal latecomer nonetheless results in a reverential focus on predominantly non-Spanish European culture within the narrative. The late and melancholy aesthetics of *Sefarad* thereby emerge in a curious double-bind, which replicates the European conception of Spain as un(der)developed, even as the narrator simultaneously tries to address this by writing his Spanish novel into a European literary tradition. Particularly during the Franco regime, Spain experienced a process of retraditionalization, which stymied in many ways the social, political, and cultural progress made in earlier decades in the twentieth century. With this transformation, the image of the Spanish nation became one

---

[6] 'You are not an isolated person and do not have an isolated story' (*S*, 288).

[7] The title of special issue of the German-language journal *Literaturmagazin*, 'Auch Spanien ist Europa' ('Spain is also Europe'), which was published in the late 1980s, encapsulates this historical exclusion. Interestingly, a German translation of an early short story by Muñoz Molina ('Un amor imposible') is also included in this issue. See Antonio Muñoz Molina, 'Eine unmögliche Liebe', trans. by Maralde Meyer-Minnemann, in *Literaturmagazin 23: Auch Spanien ist Europa*, ed. by Martin Lüdke, Delf Schmidt, and Hans-Jürgen Schmitt (Rowohlt: Reinbek bei Hamburg, 1989), 66–70.

which existed in when compared to the European context, existed for many in 'otra realidad: la de una España que, con arreglo a Europa, vive en otra época y conforme a un ritmo distinto – dicho con el eufemismo púdico que consiste en describirla como diferente'.[8] The narrator's sense of lateness in *Sefarad* thus articulates a sense of Spanish alterity within—or, indeed, exclusion from—the category of the European, although the narrative purportedly attempts to overcome these divisions. This is complicated, moreover, by a narrator seemingly suffused with a nostalgic desire to return to the past and to a lost homeland. This apparent nostalgia for lost places and earlier moments in time is, however, revealed over the course of the novel to be more a case of exile-induced melancholy, which implicitly acknowledges that the past cannot be recaptured, nor can historical and geographical ruptures be fully resolved. Just as Spain's purportedly non-modern sense of difference may, in fact, lead to its inclusion within the broader paradigm of European modernity, as this chapter will discuss, so *Sefarad*'s literary and cultural distinctions may yet suggest it as an exemplum of a mode of writing emergent in European literature around the turn of the millennium. The novel's distinct forms of self-consciously late and melancholy aesthetics, this chapter contends, encapsulate long-standing constructed tensions between Hispanic and European literature, drawing in particular on the legacy of the Spanish Golden Age, while also indicating a potential possibility of future cultural longevity and rejuvenation amid these tensions and out of *Sefarad*'s seemingly contradictory narrative impulses.

Sepharad is the Anglicized form of the name that may derive from the Aramaic *sephar* meaning a far shore or distant boundary which has been given by Spanish Jews to the Iberian peninsula. While the term appears but once in the Hebrew Bible and may not even directly refer to that specific area, its invocation in the title of Muñoz Molina's novel has resonant geographical and historical significance, not least because it is a moniker employed by citizens ostracized from that very region. The marriage in 1469 between the Catholic monarchs Isabella of Castile and Ferdinand of Aragon resulted in the foundation of a Spanish kingdom. With the conquest of the last Iberian Muslim kingdom of Granada in 1492, religious

---

[8] Edmond Cros, *El sujeto cultural: sociocrítica y psicoanálisis* (Montpellier: CERS 2002), 243. 'Another reality: that of a Spain which, according to Europe, lives in another era and according to a distinct rhythm – said with the modest euphemism that consists in describing it as different'.

unity—for want of a better term—was subsequently established with the official expulsion of all Jewish citizens who refused to convert to Catholicism. Castilian was imposed as the language of Spain, thus ensuring linguistic homogenization both in peninsular territories and abroad in Spanish imperial colonies. The name Sepharad thus bears connotations with the founding of a Catholic Spanish nation and empire that subsequently went hand in hand with Jewish exile from and displacement within Hispanic territories. In Muñoz Molina's novel, then, the lost Sephardic homeland functions analogically in relation to twentieth-century as well as fifteenth- or sixteenth-century forms of cultural and historical lateness. The Sephardic homeland thereby alludes to people, places, and histories beyond the confines of the Iberian peninsular and even the bounds of the novel itself. Not limited to the Jewish diaspora following the 1492 expulsion, traces of which mark the pages of the novel, even if they are rarely addressed, *Sefarad* stands as a synecdochic novelistic arena in which the conflicts arising from leaving behind one's customs and home when expelled by malignant forces—be it totalitarian politics, or exclusionary communities, or illness, or death—are confronted.

Sefarad is a novel constructed of fragments, a cycle of seventeen chapters, which share stylistic and thematic features, as well as recurring characters and settings. Shifting across many locations and drawing on various epochs and events including the Spanish Civil War, the Second World War, and the Sephardic diaspora of the fifteenth century, the novel explores ideas of guilt and shame, wandering and alienation, and exile and homeland in European history. Over the course of its discrete yet interrelated chapters, *Sefarad* refers to and reproduces the stories of the lives of figures such as Jean Améry, Walter Benjamin, Margarete Buber-Neumann, Victor Klemperer, Milena Jesenskà, Franz Kafka, and Primo Levi, among many others. The novel explores various geographical locations and historical periods in order to elaborate a history of European exile and totalitarian suffering, all of which is presented via the empathetic imaginings of a reserved and reticent narrator who acts as both a mediator and a transmitter for all these stories. Yet, despite initial appearances, the novel's seventeen chapters are not seventeen separate stories narrated by seventeen separate figures.[9] Through what Nicola Gilmour terms 'empathetic identification', the narrator figure of *Sefarad* 'serves as a filter or mediator for all these other stories, but he is also their creator in that he transforms them as he transmits them to the reader'.[10] The narrator is thus able to reconstruct accounts of others' lives and experiences while remaining at a remove, even almost entirely unnoticed at points. The novel's long paragraphs and hypotactic sentences prove disorienting, especially given the narrator's tendency suddenly to switch the tense he is writing in, while also alternating between the first, second, and third persons of the verb, as well as the singular and the plural. Through their swirling grammar and syntax, Sefarad's chapters bring together a cacophony of various historical instances of trauma and persecution, exile and displacement, restlessly shifting the narratorial perspective from the past to the present, all the while demonstrating a distance on the part of the narrator from the past and from the literary works on which he draws. This certainly recalls the periscopic—to use Sebald's terminology—forms of narration common to the novels examined in this study's previous chapters, whereby the events they recount are mediated in various ways through multiple narrative layers, such that distance is maintained between their narrators and their subjects, while the self-conscious and constructed nature of the novel's narration is highlighted. In Sefarad, however, while nonetheless present, this form of narration is less immediately conspicuous. The principal narrator figure composes the seventeen-chaptered text in its entirety, but only occupies the foreground of the novel in the first and the final chapter, although he periodically resurfaces in other chapters explicitly to comment on the writing and construction of the text itself, as well as to give his

[9] The names of the seventeen chapters in *Sefarad* are as follows: 'Sacristán' ('sacristan'); 'Copenhague' ('copenhagen'); 'Quien espera' ('those who wait'); 'Tan callando' ('silencing everything'); 'Valdemún' ('Valdemún'); 'Oh tú que lo sabías' ('oh you, who knew so well'); 'Münzenberg' ('münzenberg'); 'Olympia' ('olympia'); 'Berghof' ('berghof'); 'Cerbère' ('cerbère'); 'Doquiera que el hombre va' ('wherever the man goes'); 'Sherezade' ('sheherazade'); 'América' ('america'); 'Eres' ('you are…'); 'Narva' ('narva'); 'Dime tu nombre' ('tell me your name'); and, lastly, 'Sefarad' ('Sepharad'). These English titles are taken from the 2003 translation by Margaret Seyers Peden, which renders them entirely in lowercase letters as here. Throughout this chapter these chapters will be referenced in Spanish in the main body of text.

[10] Nicola Gilmour, 'The Afterlife of Traumatic Memories: The Workings and Uses of Empathy in Antonio Muñoz Molina's *Sefarad*', in *Bulletin of Spanish Studies*, 88: 6 (2011), 839–862 (840 and 842).

reflections on empathetically imagining the experiences undergone by those characters who are the focus of the chapters he writes.

In the chapter 'Münzenberg' (*S*, 355–400), for example, the narrator interrupts the tale he is telling and refocuses his narrative on himself in the act of writing. Abandoning his reconstruction of the life of the German communist activist Willi Münzenberg and the story of a doctor tending to a man suddenly taken ill, who turns out to have been a supporter of the Third Reich, the narrator reflects on the process of constructing his narrative. As his eyes close during his reading, he remarks that 'el libro casi se me desliza entre las manos, mientras Willi Münzenberg camina perdido entre la multidud' (*S*, 356),[11] before later observing that 'en noches en las que he aguardado vanamente el sueño en la oscuridad he imaginado los insomnios de ese hombre, Willi Münzenberg' (*S*, 362).[12] Not only does his imagined physical proximity to Münzenberg suggest a certain intimacy of experience, but the narrator also asserts that his own insomnia from trying to write his narrative is similar to that experienced by Münzenberg in the days leading up to his murder. The narrator's anxiety about his writing are likened in the narrative to Münzenberg's fears of his impending demise, and, by extension, to the other tales of persecution and exile included in *Sefarad*. Nevertheless, the narrator's inability to sleep suggests that he is disturbed not only by his research into Münzenberg's life and fate, but also—self-consciously—by how he ought to tell this story. When it comes to recounting Münzenberg's death by hanging at the hands of persons unknown in a forest after his escape from prison, the narrator further distances himself from the event. As when the narrator of *Dora Bruder* maintains a respectful distance from Dora's *fugue* and from her ultimate fate, and when the narrator of *Austerlitz* is kept up at night carefully transcribing Austerlitz's account of his life, the narrator of *Sefarad* remarks that 'hay una parte final de la historia [...] que no puede contar nadie' (*S*, 399).[13] Having mediated the past in such a way that suggests an awareness of the necessity for such a periscopic mode of narration, the narrator allows himself distance from his empathetic imaginings, ensuring that his late and melancholy narrative's engagement with the past remains

---

[11] 'The book nearly slips from my hands, as Münzenberg walks on among the throngs' (*S*, 124).

[12] 'During nights when I lay in the darkness, waiting in vain to fall asleep, I have imagined the sleepless hours of Willi Münzenberg' (*S*, 128).

[13] 'There is a final part of the story [...] that no one can ever tell' (*S*, 151).

self-consciously constructed. Indeed, the narrator explicitly acknowledges at numerous points during the novel the process of planning, drafting, and assembling the narrative of *Sefarad*, perhaps mostly notably in this very chapter: 'He intuido, a lo largo de dos o tres años, la tentación y la posibi-lidad de una novela, he imaginado situaciones y lugares', he writes:

> cada uno cobraba una valiosa cualidad de misterio, se yuxtaponía sin orden a los otros, se iluminaban entre sí en conexiones plurales e instantáneas, que yo podía deshacer o modificar a mi antojo, y en las que ninguna imagen anulaba a las otras o alcanzaba una primacía segura sobre ellas, o perdía en beneficio del conjunto su singularidad irreductible (*S*, 383).[14]

Not only does such disordered juxtaposition allow for 'the empathetic relationship between the writer and his subjects and the transmission of this empathy to the reader', as Samuel O'Donoghue suggests.[15] It is through this mutually illuminating constellation of Hispanic and European places and histories that the novel's preoccupation with forms of lateness emerges.

Much scholarship on *Sefarad* since its first publication has read the novel as an example of trauma fiction or Holocaust fiction.[16] 'It is widely accepted', as O'Donoghue observes, 'that the novel achieves its power through the multiplicity of the voices of the dead, a chorus that reiterates the need to remember the victims of totalitarian repression'.[17] Even the cover images of both the Spanish and English language editions of *Sefarad* gesture towards this, having variously depicted a Jewish man wearing a

[14] 'For two or three years I have toyed with the idea of writing a novel, imagined situations and places [...]. Each of these accrued a useful sense of mystery, juxtaposed alongside each other without order, they illuminated the multiple, instantaneous connections among them-selves, which I could break or modify at my whim, and in which no single image nullified the others or gained certain precedence over the others, or lost its irreducible singularity while benefiting from their coming together'.

[15] Samuel O'Donoghue, 'Errancy and alterity: Antonio Muñoz Molina's search for lost time', in *Journal of Iberian and Latin American Studies*, 19: 3 (2013), 211–232, 211.

[16] See, for example, David K. Herzberger, 'Representing the Holocaust: Story and Experience in Antonio Muñoz Molina's *Sefarad*', in *Romance Quarterly*, 51: 2 (2004), 85–96; Gabriele Eckart, 'The Rereading of Willy Münzenberg's and Margarete Buber-Neumann's Lives in Antonio Muñoz Molina's Novel *Sefarad* (2001)', in *Romance Notes*, 48:1 (2007), 59–66; Nicola Gilmour, 'The Afterlife of Traumatic Memories'; and Marije Hristova, *Reimagining Spain: Transnational Entanglements and Remembrance of the Spanish Civil War since 1989* (Maastricht: Universitaire pers Maastricht, 2016), 213–225.

[17] O'Donoghue, 'Errancy and alterity', 211.

yellow star, shadowy figures on a train platform and—most starkly in the latest Spanish critical edition—a black and white image of the railway tracks leading to the gates of Auschwitz-Birkenau.[18] *Sefarad*, this suggests, is a Spanish Holocaust novel *par excellence*. Nevertheless, a third of the novel's chapters in fact contain no reference to the Holocaust or to the broader Jewish diaspora alluded to by the novel's title.[19] While not invalid, then, such exclusively trauma- or Holocaust-focused readings are none-theless apt to miss other nuances and complexities of the novel's narrator and the aesthetics of the narrative he constructs. *Sefarad* does indeed bring together various reconstructions of historical memories and experi-ences of trauma, persecution, and exile from both a Peninsular and a broader European context. Nevertheless, it does not follow that a reading of the novel should only focus on extracts that directly deal with events and experiences such as train journeys to concentration camps during the Holocaust ('Copenhague'), imprisonment by the Gulag ('Quien espera'), post-war Jewish exile in Tangier ('Oh tú que lo sabías'), Russian emigrants in Spain ('Sherezade'), and destitute outcasts in Madrid ('Doquiera que el hombre va'). As Adolfo Campoy Cubillo intimates, to concentrate solely on the aspects of *Sefarad* that fall within the realm of so-called Holocaust literature necessitates ignoring significant extracts that escape or exceed the events of twentieth-century European totalitarianism.[20]

Sefarad's aesthetic workings reveal themselves not only in the narra-tor's empathetic imaginings of these events, but also in his moments of self-conscious introspection and reflection during the writing of the text. What follows in this chapter therefore attempts to take into account the construction of *Sefarad*'s narrative in its entirety alongside its engagement with the horrors of the twentieth century. The novel's original subtitle of 'una novela de novelas' invites such a reading, not least because this phrase might be understood to mean both 'a novel of novels' and 'a novel about novels'. While gesturing towards *Sefarad*'s fragmented state, as well as to its structural, grammatical, and syntactical ambiguities, this subtitle also

---

[18] See the various editions and translations of the novel, including Antonio Muñoz Molina, *Sefarad* (Madrid: Alfagura, 2001); *Sefarad* (Madrid: Suma de Letras, 2002); *Sefarad*, ed. by Pablo Valdivia (Madrid: Cátedra, 2013); *Sefarad* (Barcelona: Seix Barral, 2014); and *Sepharad* trans. by Margaret Sayers Peden (London: Harcourt Press, 2003).

[19] These chapters include 'Sacristán' (159–197), 'Valdemún' (282–309), 'Olympia' (401–436), 'Doquiera que el hombre vaya' (500–523), and 'América' (551–595).

[20] See Adolfo Campoy Cubillo, *Memories of the Maghreb: Transnational Identities in Spanish Cultural Production* (Basingstoke: Palgrave Macmillan, 2012), 103–4.

helpfully recalls the fictional status of the novel itself. Several readings of *Sefarad* confuse and conflate the figure of the narrator with the author himself, drawing reductive lines of comparison between Muñoz Molina's hometown of Úbeda and the hometown described by the narrator in *Sefarad*, to give just one example. Rather than debating whether extracts or aspects of the text are based on actual events and persons, or whether the narrator is identical to the author himself, this study understands Muñoz Molina's novel as a highly constructed work of fiction, as is the case with the other works examined over the course of this study.

Thanks to the novel's empathetic imaginings of experiences of persecution and exile beyond national boundaries, Lasse-Emil Paulsen, among many others, describes *Sefarad*'s narrative as a 'paradigmatic example of a transnational memory discourse', in spite of the fact that Holocaust (Shoah) memory in Spain has long been a fraught discourse.[21] Not only has there been a significant absence of Spanish memory of the Holocaust until fairly recently given the country's isolation from the rest of Europe under Franco, along with its limited role in the Second World War. There is also in Spain a relative lack of historical and cultural memory—the so-called pacto de olvido, or 'pact of forgetting'—in relation to the nation's own traumatic dictatorial history in the twentieth century.[22] To take just one literary example, with whose work the narrator of *Sefarad* demonstrates a keen familiarity, while the Spanish author and politician Jorge Semprún (1923–2011) has written extensively about his experiences in concentration camps, he has done so in French and is better known as a

---

[21] See Lasse-Emil Paulsen, '"The great night of Europe is shot through with long, sinister trains": Transnational memory and European identity in Antonio Muñoz Molina's *Sepharad*', in *Forum*, 1: 4 (2015), 1–12 (1), as well as Alexis Grohmann, 'Errant Text: *Sefarad*, by Antonio Muñoz Molina', in *Journal of Iberian and Latin American Studies*, 12: 2–3 (2006), 233–246; Dagmar Vanderbosch, 'Transnational Memories in Antonio Muñoz Molina's *Sepharad*', in *European Review*, 22: 4 (2014), 613–622; and Janneke Adma and Marije Hristova, 'The Exile Condition: Space – Time Dissociation in Historical Experience – A Reading of *Sefarad*', in *Krisis: Journal for contemporary philosophy*, 1 (2010), 62–76.

[22] See Jo Labanyi, 'The languages of silence: historical memory, generational transmission and witnessing in contemporary Spain', in *Journal of Romance Studies*, 9 (2009), 23–35; Alejandro Baer, 'The Voices of Sepharad: The Memory of the Holocaust in Spain', in *Journal of Spanish Cultural Studies*, 12 (2011), 95–120; and Salvador Orti Camallonga, 'A "European memory of Jewish Extermination"? Spain as a Methodological Challenge', in *European Review*, 20 (2012), 475–91.

literary figure in France than in Spain.[23] Negotiating a Spanish memory discourse surrounding the often problematically equated catastrophes of the Civil War and the Holocaust is not infrequently complicated by an latent conception of Spanish culture as not entirely European.[24] This has influenced the development of a literary discourse, which propagates a Spanish culture of victimhood via an obsession with interconnected traumatic pasts and a concurrent lack of engagement with the political fallout of the events of the twentieth century. The desire of Spanish writers at the turn of the millennium to prove their democratic affiliations and sensibilities by returning to the past articulates a particular cultural need, given the relative absence of democracy in Spanish political and cultural discourse until recently, and in particular 'Muñoz Molina has taken seriously the ethical duty to remember', as Jo Labanyi observes.[25] If, moreover, as O'Donoghue's suggests, *Sefarad* has been 'instrumental in breaking down the national borders that appear to have isolated Spain from the wider narratives of twentieth century history',[26] then contained within this is the potential for exclusionary narratives regarding Spain's position in Europe to be—however inadvertently—perpetuated via the adoption of European literary conventions and aesthetics, which presuppose and uphold a longer history of perceived Spanish cultural lateness in Europe. One of the principal aims of this chapter is to interrogate the implications of this.

Addressing the legacies of post-Enlightenment Europe and post-modernity Spain from a perspective at the turn of the millennium, *Sefarad* is a late modern Spanish novel, which draws on and aims to write itself into canonical European literature. However, it transpires that the novel's

[23] See, for example, Jorge Semprún, *Le grand voyage* (Paris: Gallimard, 1963), *L'écriture ou la vie* (Paris: Gallimard, 1994), and *Le mort qu'il faut* (Paris: Gallimard, 2001). For further discussion of representations of the Holocaust in Semprún's work with particular reference to that of Muñoz Molina, see Samuel O'Donoghue, 'Negotiating Space in Literary Representations of Holocaust Trauma: Jorge Semprún's *Le grand voyage* and Antonio Muñoz Molina's *Sefarad*', in *Bulletin of Hispanic Studies*, 93: 1 (2016), 45–61 and 'The "Truth" of the Past: Fiction as an Alternative to History in Contemporary Spanish Narratives of the Civil War and the Holocaust', in *Hispanic Research Journal*, 17:4 (2016), 322–338.

[24] See, for example, Antonio Gómez López-Quiñones and Susanne Zepp, eds., *The Holocaust in Spanish Memory: Historical perceptions and Cultural Discourses* (Berlin: Leipziger Universitätsverlag, 2010) and Paul Preston, *The Spanish Holocaust: Inquisition and Extermination in Twentieth-Century Spain* (London: Harper, 2012).

[25] See Jo Labanyi, *A Very Short Introduction to Spanish Literature* (Oxford: Oxford University Press, 2010), 73.

[26] O'Donoghue, 'The "Truth" of the Past', 324.

particular strain of historical and cultural lateness ensures this European scope and focus is achieved partly at the expense of the prestige of Spanish literature, history, and culture. As Richard Sperber observes, reflecting on how Muñoz Molina aims to address, recuperate, and revise the post-Enlightenment project of European modernity in his work, 'terms like late, post, or supermodernity indicate the contemporary distance from an Enlightenment concept of modernity anchored in scientific, technological, social, political, and moral progress. Muñoz Molina's texts express this distance in terms of their return to older literary forms', drawing on Spanish and European works from the past.[27] With the approach of the millennium, several authors and works attempted to reimagine Spain's past, present, and future in a new iteration of Spanish literary lateness. In a reaction to an externally imposed, and later internally reinforced, sense of inferiority within Spanish literature, an initial rejection of Spain's historical and cultural exceptionalism, and even of the notion of a Spanish national literature itself, emerged. Spain, as Teresa Vilarós observes, 'disposed of its national history as a form of repudiation of the grand metanarratives. At the end of history, [...] the Spanish novel beyond modernity performed as a spectacular site for such reimagining'.[28] Rejecting the notion of a national narrative of literary development constituted an attempt to write Spanish literature out of its past restrictions and into a broader modern European literary context. With the end of Francoism, 'for the first time in modern history, the country ha[d] undertaken a successful process of overcoming its perennial international cultural deficit', as Gonzalo Navajas notes.[29] By writing literary works into a European context, Spanish literature was thus able to consider itself 'fully integrated in the global discourse through the double path of a consolidated Europe and the vast and increasingly influential Hispanic world'.[30] In spite of this desired end to Spanish and European difference, however, the long history of Spanish literary lateness is neither halted nor erased with the arrival

---

[27] See Richard Sperber, *The Discourse of Flanerie in Antonio Muñoz Molina's Texts* (Lewisburg, Pennsylvania: Bucknell University Press, 2015), 26.

[28] Teresa M. Vilarós, 'The Novel Beyond Modernity', in *The Cambridge Companion to the Spanish Novel: From 1600 to the Present*, ed. by Harriet Turner and Adelaida López de Martínez (Cambridge: Cambridge University Press, 2003), 251–262 (262).

[29] Gonzalo Navajas, 'The Curse of the Nation: Institutionalized History and Literature in Global Spain', in *New Spain, New Literatures*, ed. by Luis Martín-Estudillo and Nicholas Spadaccini (Nashville, Tennessee: Vanderbilt University Press, 2010), 165–182 (169).

[30] Navajas, 'The Curse of the Nation', 179.

of the second millennium. In reimagining Spanish literature's historiography from a millennial vantage point, new novels of this period—including *Sefarad*—exhibit a certain liminality. Situated on a threshold, neither entirely one thing nor another, such liminal fiction is fundamentally imbricated with Spanish literary lateness, just as Spanish cultural lateness emerges as an intrinsic driver of European understandings of modernity. A European perspective reinforces the construction of Spanish literature as inferior to European 'high' culture, even as novels like *Sefarad* attempt to articulate a rapprochement. Ultimately, the narrator's 'melancolía de un largo destierro' (*S*, 746) in *Sefarad* has just as much to do with Spanish exile from a European cultural context as it does with the experiences of the subjects of the narrator's imaginings.[31] The melancholy of a long exile is thus not only a key thematic element of Muñoz Molina's novel, but also deeply embedded in its aesthetics, as well as in its historical and geographical contexts.

ENDINGS AND EPIGRAPHS

Perhaps not inappropriately, it will be helpful to begin by examining forms of lateness in *Sefarad* that emerge at the end of the novel, particularly in the *nota de lecturas* that concludes the text. The misleading translation in the English-language edition of the *nota de lecturas* as an 'Author's note' (instead of a 'note on reading') does not acknowledge that this note is a key part of the narrative. The *nota de lecturas* establishes key perspectives on narrative constructions of historical and cultural lateness in the novel, as well as the narrator's sense of epigonality in relation to writers who precede him. It encapsulates *Sefarad*'s late perspective as a whole and also highlights the narrator's reliance on canonical European modernist authors.[32] Moreover, it mirrors the European perspective on Spanish

---

[31] 'The melancholy of a long exile' (*S*, 381).

[32] It should be noted that there is a distinction to be made between modernism (and all of its various guises and incarnations) and the distinctly Spanish movement of *el modernismo*. Towards the end of the nineteenth and the beginning of the twentieth centuries, *modernismo* emerged predominantly in Spanish poetry and (somewhat crudely summarized) comprised a blending together of key elements of Romanticism and Symbolism. See Cathy L. Jrade, *Modernismo, Modernity, and the Development of Spanish American Literature* (Austin: University of Texas Press, 1991) and Richard A. Cardwell, 'The Poetry of *Modernismo* in Spain', in *The Cambridge History of Spanish Literature*, ed. by David T. Gies (Cambridge: Cambridge University Press, 2004), 500–512.

culture which the narrator embraces, hoping to bring the Spanish literary tradition into the fold. The *nota* outlines the many literary and cultural figures whose work the narrator has drawn on to complete *Sefarad*, including Franz Kafka, Margarete Buber-Neumann, Eugenia Ginzburg, Tzvetan Todorov, Victor Klemperer, Jean Améry, and Primo Levi (see *S*, 749–753). As a means of narrative mediation of the past, this list of sources adds a partly testimonial dimension to the text, while imbuing the narrative with a sense of historical coherence and a trajectory towards a European literary context.[33] It also reinforces the narrator's own historical position and his epigonal narrative perspective. Coming at the close of the twentieth century, he looks back not only to those who came before him and suffered under twentieth-century European totalitarianism, but also to those writers without whose work his own could not exist, since he draws on theirs so explicitly. These are writers, he remarks, 'sin los cuales es muy probable que ni este libro se me hubiera ocurrido ni habría encontrado el estado de espíritu necesario para escribirlo' (*S*, 751).[34] Concluding the novel with the *nota de lecturas* provides a final late perspective on the narrative in its entirety. This constitutes an intriguing point of departure for further examination of constructions of lateness and epigonality in *Sefarad*. The narrator casts himself as an historical latecomer in his attempt to write a European account of twentieth-century persecution and exile in which Spain is included. *Sefarad*'s narrative replicates a hierarchy of literary significance through what O'Donoghue refers to as its 'search for a common European identity steeped in the comprehension of the suffering of others'.[35] That the novel embraces a broader normative teleology of European modernity, history, and culture, wherein Spain is perceived as having been left by the wayside, reflects the narrator's conception of his own epigonal lateness and his awareness of the fraught history stretching between the Hispanic and the European. More broadly, however, *Sefarad* encapsulates a particular moment in Spanish letters at the end of the twentieth century, which was inflected by a long-established preoccupation with literary, cultural, and historical lateness.

With the end of the Renaissance and the Spanish Golden Age, that period of flourishing in Spanish arts and literature between the end of the

[33] See Herzberger, 'Representing the Holocaust', 95.

[34] 'Without whom it is likely that this book would not have occurred to me, nor would I have reached the state of mind necessary to write it'.

[35] Samuel O'Donoghue, 'Negotiating Space', 56.

1400s and the mid-1600s, a tendency to romanticize Spain became common in other European nations, such as France, Germany, and Great Britain. This coincided with collapse of the Spanish imperial project in the mid-seventeenth century. Having replaced Spain as a dominant political and cultural entity in Western Europe, the populations of Britain, France, and Germany considered the Spanish nation to be wild, backward, and rural, a primitive, folkloric, and tragic land, which could not be considered fully European.[36] Such a perception of Spain came about and was sustained beyond and within the nation's borders due to the very historical events which demarcate this change in attitude.[37] With the loss of its colonies, and thereby its status as an imperial power, Spain fell off the map of modernity described by other ascendant European nations, despite having previously occupied its centre during the fifteenth and sixteenth centuries.[38] Most Western European literary activities in the eighteenth and nineteenth centuries were linked to the ascendance of the nation state and nation-building practices, such as the emergence of German nationalism under the threat of Napoleon and the increased prevalence of a national literature in the early 1800s.[39] However, the uncertainty of Spain's status as a nation due to an earlier lack of political and linguistic unity was a further contributing factor to the later emergence of its national literature in

[36] See, for example, Diego Saglia, *Poetic Castles in Spain: British Romanticism and Figurations of Iberia* (Amsterdam: Rodopi, 2000) and Barbara Fuchs, *Exotic Nation: Maurophilia and the Construction of Early Modern Spain* (Philadelphia: University of Pennsylvania Press, 2009). The widening gap between Spain and the ascendant colonial powers of Europe and the United States in the sixteenth and seventeenth centuries is, moreover, perhaps best encapsulated in the racist and peripheralizing aphorism often falsely attributed to Alexandre Dumas that 'Africa begins at the Pyrenees'.

[37] See, for example, Barbara Fuchs, *The Poetics of Piracy: Emulating Spain in English Literature* (Philadelphia: University of Pennsylvania Press, 2013), in which Fuchs understands Spain as both political rival to the English nation, as well as a literary resource for English writers of the Early Modern period. Fuchs argues that appropriations from Spain were reimagined as heroic looting, which complicated contemporaneous Spanish texts by turning them to anti-Spanish purposes amid European imperial competition.

[38] See Walter Cohen, *A History of European Literature: From Antiquity to the Present* (Oxford: Oxford University Press, 2017), 239–308, as well as Labanyi, *Spanish Literature*, 2–9 and 42–74. For further discussion of what is termed the problem of Spain and the cultural map of Europe, particularly in regard to modernist literary history, see Gayle Roberts, *Modernism and the New Spain: Britain, Cosmopolitan Europe, and Literary History* (Oxford: Oxford University Press, 2012), especially 3–12.

[39] See Itamar Even-Zohar, 'The Role of Literature in the Making of the Nations of Europe: A Socio-Semiotic Study', in *Applied Semiotics/Sémiotique appliquée*, 1:1 (1996), 39–59.

the nineteenth century. Material and historical difficulties in Spain delayed the emergence of a conception of Spanish literature, such that during the period of European modernity, an incipient Spanish national literature appears likewise fraught with a sense of lateness and inadequacy in comparison to other European nations. 'When we look back at Spanish modern literary historiography', Vilarós argues, 'it soon becomes evident that Spain's literary corpus as a whole was often and overly conceptualized as "different" in relation to the Western European canon'.[40] Both Spanish lateness and cultural difference emerge as concomitant results of uneven modernization, which is itself due to earlier historical upheaval, including the legacy and loss of imperial power within Europe. Having established large-scale state rule across the European continent and having laid the foundations of transatlantic commerce, 'it was as if', as Andrew Ginger pithily puts it, 'the Spanish domains had opened the door to the modern world only to be shut outside'.[41] The Hispanic, in other words, is both European and non-European; the European is partly founded by, then excludes, the Hispanic.

Matters late and epigonal in *Sefarad* are bound up with questions of difference and being construed as an outsider. Historically, as in the novel's aesthetics, other European nations that came to fill the vacuum left by the collapse of Spanish imperialism play a significant role in determining the perception of Spanish literature within Europe during modernity, and since. 'The first practical foundational myths of Spanish literary history', as Wadda C. Ríos-Font remarks, 'are those imagined by foreigners during a period of considerable instability. Predictably, all of them point to fragmentation and unfeasibility as main features of a precarious, and decidedly un-modern, Spanish nation'.[42] Over subsequent decades, a European construction of Spain as late remained intrinsic to the development of a Spanish literary tradition from the Renaissance to modernity. In comparison with other European nations, such as France and Germany, then, the concept of a national literature in Spain may be understood as a late arrival. 'Although the notion that a nation's literature is the expression of its peo-

---

[40] Vilarós, 'The Novel Beyond Modernity', 251.

[41] Andrew Ginger, *Instead of Modernity: The Western Canon and the Incorporation of the Hispanic (c. 1850–75)* (Manchester: University of Manchester Press, 2020), 5

[42] Wadda C. Ríos-Font, 'National Literature in the Protean Nation: The Question of Nineteenth-Century Spanish Literary History', in *Spain Beyond Spain: Modernity, Literary History, and National Identity*, ed. by Brad Epps and Luis Fernández Cifuentes (Lewisburg, Pennsylvania: Bucknell University Press, 2005), 127–147 (131–132).

ple (the *Volk*) dates back to the Romantic period', as Labanyi remarks, 'it is [only] from the late nineteenth century that one can talk of "Spanish literature" as an established corpus'.[43] For Spanish literature both within Spain and Europe at large, this has lasting consequences, such that, to quote Labanyi, 'the northern European construction of Spain as "unmodern" has produced an anxiety about "belatedness", which dogs the whole history of Spanish literary criticism'.[44] It is to just such sustained Spanish literary lateness that *Sefarad* responds at the turn of the millennium.

The epigraph of *Sefarad*, as well as the editorial choices behind it, draw on the perceived Spanish exclusion from a European cultural and literary context, clearly demonstrating how the novel brings together Spanish and European literatures, even while a European perspective towards the Spanish literary tradition appears to dominate. First published in 2013, the annotated critical edition of *Sefarad* reveals that the original epigraph for the novel was not the quotation in the final published version. In the context of Spanish literary lateness and difference within Europe, however, this fact acquires a far greater significance than simply an editorial change. The epigraph in the published novel is from Kafka's *Der Process* (1925) and hints at solidarity among those unjustly accused of crimes: '"Si", dijo el ujier, "son acusados, todos los que ve aquí son acusados." "¿De veras?" dijo K. "Entonces son compañeros míos"' (*S*, 157).[45] This reinforces a desire to elaborate a pan-European account of suffering and persecution in the novel via reference to a wide range of literary touchstones. Yet, intriguingly, as the critical edition reveals, the novel's original epigraph was to have been a quotation from Benito Pérez Gáldos's novel *Fortunata y Jacinta* (1886–87): 'porque doquiera que el hombre va lleva consigo su novela'.[46] This phrase from Galdós does in fact appear several times in *Sefarad* almost like a mantra in order to explain and emphasize the narrator's act of empathetically imagining others' experiences, with a fragment of it even appearing in the name of one of the novel's chapters (see *S*, 242 and 500, for example). Its removal as the novel's epigraph at

---

[43] Labanyi, *Spanish Literature*, 27.

[44] Labanyi, *Spanish Literature*, 44.

[45] '"Yes", said the usher, "they are accused, everyone you see here is accused." "Really?" asked K. "Then they are my comrades"' (*S*, xi). The German original reads as follows: '"Ja", sagte der Gerichtsdiener, "es sind Angeklagte, all die Sie hier sehn, sind Angeklagte". "Wirklich?" sagte K. "Dann sind es ja meine Kollegen"'. See Franz Kafka, *Der Process* (Stuttgart: Reclam, 2017), 66.

[46] 'Wherever a man may go he carries his novel with him'.

the final editorial stages suggests, however, an implicit rejection of wanting to carry the burden, so to speak, of a Spanish novel. While it may appear to be a minor editorial matter, this substitution of a quotation from a classic work of nineteenth-century Spanish realism for a quotation from a key figure of twentieth-century European modernism lays the foundations at the outset of the narrative's construction for bringing together these two literary contexts and animating the tensions between them.

Galdós is an author who has long been downgraded within the canon of European literature or, indeed, entirely left out of it. As Fredric Jameson thunders, 'the absence of Galdós from the conventional nineteenth-century list of the "great realists" – even one limited to Europe – is more than a crime, it is an error which seriously limits and deforms our picture of this discourse and its possibilities'.[47] George J. Becker's influential 1963 anthology of literary realism encapsulates this, hailing Galdós as 'the leading Spanish realist, though he left no work to rank with the major achievements of the movement or to become part of the broad body of European literature'.[48] This is a clear indication of the long-established European construction of Spanish literature as late and unworthy of inclusion within the canon of European literature. The removal of the Galdós quotation as the epigraph of *Sefarad*, and its replacement with an extract from the work of a canonical European modernist, thus demonstrates even on a paratextual level the ways in which the novel perpetuates the construction of Spanish literature as late in spite of its attempts to write it into a broader European context. Given this removal, it is also ironic that Jameson remarks how Galdós himself profited aesthetically and stylistically from his late historical location, 'not only arriving at the moment when everything remained to be said about the belatedly bourgeois world of nineteenth-century Spain and of Madrid as the last great European metropolis; he also inherited fully developed all those novelistic innovations and instruments of representation which, since Balzac, a century of novelists had worked to perfection'.[49] If this is mirrored in Muñoz Molina's novel by the narrator's

[47] Fredric Jameson, 'Perez Galdós, or, the Waning of Protagonicity', in *The Antinomies of Realism* (London: Verso, 2013), 95–113 (95).

[48] George J. Becker, ed., *Documents of Modern Literary Realism* (Princeton: Princeton University Press, 1963). Cited in James Mandrell, 'Realism in Spain: Galdós, Pardo Bazán, Clarín and the European Context', in *Spanish Literature from 1700 to the Present*, ed. by David William Foster, Daniel Altamiranda, and Carmen Urioste-Azcorra (London: Garland, 2001), 99–128.

[49] Jameson, 'Perez Galdós', 95.

self-conception as a latecomer, then his outlook is decidedly less trium-phant than that ascribed to Galdós by Jameson.[50] For the narrator of *Sefarad*, his coming late, both historically and culturally, is unavoidably tied to feelings of epigonality, which further underscores the construction of Spanish literary lateness in the novel.

As the novel opens, the narrator himself is, in fact, already presented as being distanced from its action. The novel begins with the return of the narrator as an adult to his childhood hometown where an old shoemaker does not recall him, even when prompted by the nickname he gave to the narrator as a boy, which gives this first chapter its title: 'Sacristán' (*S*, 196–197).[51] Complicated by further allusions and direct references to canonical European modernist literature, subsequent constructions of the narrator's lateness and epigonality further highlight Spanish and European literary difference and separation in the text. *Sefarad*'s opening paragraph recalls the beginning of Proust's *Recherche*, for example, as O'Donoghue notes, claiming that such echoes and inflections in *Sefarad*'s narrative allow the narrator's vocal errancy to explore questions of otherness and alterity as he imagines others' pasts and experiences.[52] Yet, for this study's purposes, the most significant alterity articulated here is that between Spanish and canonical European works of literature. The use of rapturous allusions to food from the narrator's infancy as a catalyst for memory— 'disfrutamos de los alimentos y de las recetas de nuestra tierra' (*S*, 161)[53]— recalls the famous madeleine episode from the opening of Proust's *Recherche*, while the narrator's shifting tenses and hypotactic sentence structure suggest further Proustian resonances. The entire narrative proj-ect of *Sefarad* therefore achieves its impetus from a thematic nod to a canonical work of European modernism. Yet while the focus here is on the community to which the narrator once belonged, the aesthetic focus is on

---

[50] For further discussion of the ways in which Galdós's particular variety of the nineteenth-century novel may be read not as a late form of realist fiction, but rather as a newer form that erases the generic frontier between the real and the fictional, see Stephen Gilman, *Galdós and the Art of the European Novel: 1867–1887* (Princeton: Princeton University Press, 1981).

[51] This nickname itself carries (albeit slightly heavy-handed) symbolic and metaphorical significance: a sacristan is a member of the church charged with the care of the sacristy where valuables and important records are kept, much like the narrator envisions his novel will prove to be. Even when unrecalled by other characters, this nickname thus nevertheless endows the narrator with a form of symbolic investiture in telling the stories he recounts in *Sefarad* similar to the narrators of *Dora Bruder* and *Austerlitz*.

[52] See Samuel O'Donoghue, 'Errancy and alterity', 214.

[53] 'We enjoy the food and recipes of our homeland' (*S*, p. 1).

the narrator's obsolescence and lateness, since crucially he has been forgotten. At the beginning of *Sefarad*, a narrator who has left the rural
Spanish region of his childhood (*S*, 159) employs references to Proust's
magnum opus and thereby establishes an historically late narrative perspective of looking back on the past, while he himself remains unremembered
in his hometown. Despite his bringing Spanish literature into close contact with a broader European literary tradition in his narrative, he nevertheless situates himself as an epigonal latecomer from the outset. The
narrator's perspective in this text is so late that even in the first chapter he
is already figuratively erased from the narrative. He appears so long after
these events that he no longer has a place in them and is also relegated to
the background of the subsequent stories included in *Sefarad* as an assem-
bler and custodian of the narrative. Lending more pathos to the narrator's
subsequent remark that 'se me hacía muy tarde para una cita que ya quizás
estaba fracasada de antemano' (*S*, 196),[54] this reading of epigonal lateness
reinforces his self-perception as a latecomer, whose efforts are futile and
who cannot measure up to the literary works of those writers who came
before him. As the chapter closes, the narrator pulls away from the shoemaker, who remains motionless (*S*, 197). This again indicates not only the
narrator's distance from the people and events he recounts, but also
underscores his sense of lateness in regard to them. Firstly, it hints at a
sense of futility in constructing this narrative, which will return towards
the end of the novel; secondly, it reinforces the narrator's epigonality,
which will be later more fully articulated in the *nota de lecturas* at the
novel's close, but which is prefigured here in the novel's opening pages
and grows over the course of the narrative.

Later chapters, which take the form of the narrator's empathetic imag-
inings of others' experiences, crystallize both the narrator's self-
conceptualization as an epigonal latecomer and his preoccupation with the
European construction of Spanish literature as late. In the fourth chapter
'Tan callando', which is told from the imagined perspective of a former
Spanish soldier in the *División Azul*, this preoccupation is articulated
through an imagined sequence of dreaming and awakening. This 'Blue
Division' was the unit of Spanish volunteers who served in the German
army on the Eastern Front between 1941 and 1944, and in this chapter,
the narrator imagines a soldier dreaming about an occasion when he hid
from Russian soldiers during the Second World War. Upon waking, he

---

[54] 'I was very late for an appointment that was probably futile in the first place' (*S*, 20).

finds himself at home and much older at the end of the twentieth century. The imagined former soldier then declares himself to be experiencing 'pánico [...] a encontrarse extraviado en la memoria insegura y en el desorden del tiempo, pánico y sobre todo vértigo, porque en un solo instante su conciencia salta a una distancia de más de medio siglo, de un continento entero' (*S*, 279–280).[55] Recalling the vertiginous late perspective on the events of the twentieth century of the other late European novels examined in this study, this sentence encapsulates the narrative strategy and perspective of *Sefarad*'s narrator. Distanced from the past he investigates, yet over-determined by it, the narrator is self-consciously situated after the events he describes. This is reflected and reinforced by his empathetic imagination of the Blue Division soldier who 'no llegó a tiempo' (*S*, 280).[56] The former soldier's geographical confusion and sense of temporal distortion upon waking recall the challenges of Spain's cultural difference and exclusion suggested by the narrator's particular position and perspective. Wishing to 'adormilarse y que durante unos minutos o segundos ahora se convierta de nuevo en entonces' (*S*, 281),[57] the narrator's imagining of the former soldier is unable to do so, which only further emphasizes his historical sense of coming after.

The sense of lateness evoked in 'Tan callando' is not only historically inflected, however; it is also literary. The title of this chapter is lifted from the first stanza of a forty-stanza poem by the fifteenth-century Castillian poet Jorge Manrique entitled *Coplas a la muerte de su padre* and composed in 1476. The entire chapter of 'Tan callando' is thus—ironically, given its title—in dialogue with this masterpiece of medieval Spanish poetry, with the narrator suggesting himself not only as historically but also as culturally late, further casting himself in an epigonal light. The first of Manrique's *coplas* reads

> Recuerde el alma dormida,
> avive el seso e despierte
> contemplando
> cómo se passa la vida,
> cómo se viene la muerte

---

[55] 'Panic, lost somewhere in the tangle of unreliable memories and the chaos of time, and vertigo, because in a single instant his mind has leaped more than half a century and an entire continent' (*S*, 69).

[56] 'Did not arrive in time'.

[57] 'Fall asleep and for a few minutes or seconds have now again become then'.

186   I. ELLISON

tan callando;
cuán presto se va el plazer
cómo, después de acordado,
da dolor;
cómo a nuestro parescer,
cualquier tiempo passado
fue mejor.[58]

The poem's musings on the silent approach of death and the poet's resigned acceptance of this intensify the looming sense of ending in this chapter. Yet this allusive embellishment of *Sefarad*'s narrative is also complicated by the fact that Manrique's *coplas* from the early years of the Golden Age of Spanish literature recall a time prior to Spain's loss of empire and its subsequent ostracization from European letters by other imperial powers.[59] While itself drawing on earlier classic works of medieval peninsular literature, Manrique's poem also contains allusions to recent contemporary history of the formation of the Spanish nation, recalling the deaths of key political figures, such as the King of Aragón in the sixteenth stanza.[60] As the narrator of *Sefarad* brings classic works of Spanish literature into contact with his attempted construction of a pan-European narrative, therefore, the distinctions and divisions between the two contexts are brought into sharper relief. Yet, crucially, this later echo of Manrique's poem in *Sefarad* remains unacknowledged: Spanish literature and its Golden Age are relegated in favour of later European cultural contexts. Through explicit referential marking of non-Spanish sources elsewhere in the novel, such as the writers and works acknowledged in the *nota de lecturas*, the narrator appears to accord them greater prominence than Spanish literary works. Since he is so keen to stress and even to mention by name the authors whose lives and works he draws on, it is notable that

[58] 'Let the dozing soul remember, / let the mind awake and revive / by contemplating / how our life goes by so swiftly / and how our death comes near / so silently; / how quickly pleasure fades, / and how when it is recalled / it gives us pain, / how we always seem to think / that times past must have been better / than today'. See *The Golden Age: Poems of the Spanish Renaissance*, trans. by Edith Grossman (New York: Norton, 2006), 37.
[59] For further discussion of the significance and legacy of Manrique's poem, see Frank A. Domínguez, *Love and Remembrance: The Poetry of Jorge Manrique* (Lexington: The University Press of Kentucky, 1989) and Nancy Marino, *Jorge Manrique's* Coplas por la muerte de su padre: *A History of the Poem and Its Reception* (Woodbridge: Tamesis, 2011).
[60] '¿Qué se hizo el rey don Joan? / Los infants d'Aragón / ¿qué se hizieron?'. 'Where is the King, Don Juan? / Each royal prince and noble heir of Aragon?'.

he neglects to do so for this significant literary figure of the Spanish Golden Age. Less suggestive of a lack of esteem for the *coplas* on the part of the narrator, given his reliance on the poem itself, but instead revealing something rather more akin to his own feelings of inadequacy towards earlier Spanish literary figures, to whose prowess and significance he is unable to measure up, this deliberate omission is indicative of a key double-movement of lateness in *Sefarad*. The narrator, conceiving of himself as historically and culturally late, also casts Spanish culture itself as late; its Golden Age is over.

ARTEFACTS OF LATENESS

Throughout the establishment of the Spanish nation state in the late 1800s, and even until the end of the twentieth century, Spain was 'apparently doomed to be the permanently sick nation of Europe', as Navajas observes.[61] So late a developer was the Spanish nation considered to be that many regarded it as 'a cultural and political "anomaly", a grotesque and absurd version of the conventional paradigm of Western culture'.[62] Such normative perspectives are echoed in *Sefarad* by the narrative's sense of lateness, which is reinforced in the fifth chapter 'Valdemún' (*S*, 282–309). Named after his wife's childhood village, where a dying aunt of hers still lives, this chapter comprises the main narrator's recollection of a visit to the aunt's home, where he feels himself to be an outsider.[63] The narrative's sense of lateness is enhanced and even given a futile, hopeless air in this chapter, such that the narrator feels separate and distanced from his surroundings. His engagement with the abandoned objects he sees around him in the house of his wife's aunt, such as the dusty old furniture and faded pictures in long-empty rooms, reflects *Sefarad*'s mounting sense of lateness and preoccupation with Spanish exclusion in a European cultural context. During this visit the village and objects in the house—'las

---

[61] Navajas, 'The Curse of the Nation', 179.

[62] Navajas, 'The Curse of the Nation', 166.

[63] According to the latest annotated Spanish critical edition of *Sefarad*, the chapter was originally entitled 'Ademuz', which is a real village in Valencia. In order to avoid reductive readings of the novel as an autobiographical or semi-autobiographical account, the author uses a fictional name for the village described in this chapter. This is further evidence that, as discussed earlier, reading *Sefarad* as an entirely fictional work is more revealing and illuminating than simply comparing and contrasting the events in the narrative with Muñoz Molina's own life (See *S*, 282).

cosas que ella no volvió a ver, las últimas' (S, 282)[64]—are presented under an aspect of ending or dying. These places are not portrayed as beautiful, but instead decaying and lifeless: 'todo es muy viejo, no antiguo, despojado de pronto de la belleza embustera con que lo bruñía el recuerdo' (S, 299).[65] This is intensified by the fact that there are many uninhabited houses in this village and the narrator implies that all the objects and people connected to the past are simply waiting to expire: 'Hay un aire insomne y fatigado de espera en la casa, la espera de la llegada lenta de la muerte' (S, 300).[66] He, however, keeps himself apart and is haunted by an inability to sleep, which recalls the Blue Division soldier he imagined in the previous chapter: 'quién podrá dormir esa noche' (305).[67] Mirroring European perspectives on Spanish cultural and historical lateness, the narrator's own sense of coming late is bound up with a notion of being distanced and construed—or even to the extent of construing himself—as an outsider.

So prevalent is this in the narrator's account of his and his wife's visit to Valdemún that he sees himself as distinct from the rest of the inhabitants of the house and the village, explicitly emphasizing how his perspective is different to theirs. Indeed, he remarks to his wife that 'soy conciente de que no veo lo mismo que tú' (S, 297) and later goes so far as to refer to himself as her shadow (S, 299).[68] He sets himself apart, casting himself as an outsider and an enlightened European cosmopolite, who feels out of place in what he perceives to be a backwater village in rural Spain. In viewing himself as a pale shade in comparison to his wife and her family, the narrator implicitly reinforces stereotypes of the Spanish nation, most especially of its rural areas, as wild and passionate, thereby perpetuating long-held and suspect European constructions of Spain. As a shadow in the house, the narrator and his account of events are presented under a distinct aspect of degeneration and decay, while he remains passive, observing from an historically late and distant vantage point. Unable to sleep in 'la habitación que huele ligeramente a humedad y a cerrado' (305),[69] only

---

[64] 'The things she never saw again, the last things' (S, 71).

[65] 'Everything is simply old, stripped of the beauty with which memory endows things from the past' (S, 84).

[66] 'There is an air of weary insomnia in the house, of waiting for the ponderous arrival of death' (S, 84).

[67] 'Who can sleep this night' (S, 88).

[68] 'I know I'm not seeing what you're seeing' (S, 82).

[69] 'The room that smells of mildew and gloom' (S, 88).

able to watch and wait, he is surrounded by these unremembered and decaying objects, which are 'ya rosada por la melancolía, por la intuición gradual de una pérdida irremediable' (*S*, 307).[70] In setting himself apart from that which he recounts in this chapter, the narrator effectively casts himself as a ghostly presence in his own narrative, haunting the remains of an historically and culturally outdated and decayed Spanish nation in a literary work that he desires to write into a broader European context. Constructed from a European perspective, then subsequently adopted by Spanish writers and artists themselves, the legacy of Spanish lateness is evoked in *Sefarad* by the narrator's constructions of his return to rural Spain. The gradual inkling of inevitable loss, that rising sense of melancholy which he experiences, will, moreover, resurface in later characters' desire to return to lost homelands.

While the events of the twentieth century, after which the narrator positions himself, include the Spanish dictatorship, it is nonetheless striking that this period hardly features in *Sefarad*, in spite of its significant influence on the European conceptions of Spanish lateness with whose legacy the novel engages. Spanish lateness in Europe remained a defining feature of Spanish literature and culture during the twentieth century and may be seen—albeit somewhat reductively—as a contributing factor to the rise of Francoism. That this historical period is conspicuous by its absence from the narrative of *Sefarad* further suggests a narratorial preference for an extra-Hispanic focus. In the face of Spain's loss of empire, the Spanish Civil War arguably encapsulates a debate between those who thought that Europe was either the answer to or the cause of Spain's problems.[71] One consequence of Spain's apparent exclusion from European modernity was what Vilarós diagnoses as 'a period when the perceived non-modern Spanish difference became the mold in which to shape a set of essentialist values'.[72] Emerging in the context of an inward turn in Spanish culture and drawing on Imperial Spanish rhetoric, as well as the iconography of essentialist Spanish heroism, the Franco military regime (1939–1975)

---

[70] 'Already brushed by melancholy and the inkling of inevitable loss' (*S*, 90).

[71] See, for instance, the work of the philosopher and essayist José Ortega y Gasset (1883–1955), which reflects a great deal of these issues such as his *Meditación de Europa* (1960). Originally given as a lecture in Berlin with the title *De Europa meditatio quaedam* in 1949, this was later published in a collected volume of his writing. See José Ortega y Gasset, *Obras de Ortega y Gasset, Vol. 26: Europa y la idea de nación*, ed. by Paulino Garagorri (Madrid: Alianza, 2003).

[72] Vilarós, 'The Novel Beyond Modernity', 250.

ensured Spanish isolation from Europe for many decades.[73] Drawing lines
of connection from the outcome of the European perspective on Spanish
culture to the rise of Francoism, Vilarós observes that 'after the period of
exploration and expansion typical of the imperial enterprise, the country
[Spain] became increasingly self-centred and it retreated into itself, identifying with the defence of institutions and values that were disconnected
from the more advanced trends of European culture'.[74] Already isolated
from European literature by the beginning of the twentieth century,
Spanish literary practitioners and artists themselves thus adopted Europe's
conceptualization of their country and its culture as late.[75] External constructions of Spain thereby became internalized.

    This self-understanding as an anachronistic and backward country par-
ticularly during the years of the dictatorship was principally due to censor-
ship, suppression of cultural activities, and the ensuing mass exile of
pro-Republican artists and writers. With the end of Francoism, however,
and with the establishment of democracy in Spain during the second half
of the twentieth century, new Spanish writers simultaneously looked to
the past and sought to distance themselves from everything that had come
before them. 'Spain's cultural and political trajectory', Navajas notes, 'has
been characterized by an apparently insurmountable conflict between the
need to permanently cast away the traditional parameters of national history and the imperative to critically study that history in order to defini-
tively overcome its limitations'.[76] In the early 1970s, writers such as Juan
Benet, Juan Goytisolo, and Carmen Martín Gaite, and later Javier Marías
and Pere Grimferrer, sought to change Spanish literature anew in the final
decades of the twentieth century. Literary works by these and other writers are unavoidably linked to the literature that preceded them, however.
In order to demarcate themselves as something new, after all, authors must

[73] See Stanley G. Payne, *The Franco Regime, 1936–1975* (Madison: University of Wisconsin
Press, 1987), 119. See also Duncan Wheeler, *Following Franco: Spanish culture and politics
in transition* (Manchester: Manchester University Press, 2020).

[74] Navajas, 'The Curse of the Nation', 169.

[75] In spite of or, perhaps better, because of this, some significant Spanish writers would
later draw on and rework contemporaneous canonical works of European literature, such as
Proust's *Recherche*, in order to galvanize their creative impetus, shape their imaginative acts,
and guide their stance against Francoism. See Samuel O'Donoghue, *Rewriting Franco's
Spain: Marcel Proust and the Dissident Novelists of Memory* (Lewisburg, Pennsylvania:
Bucknell University Press, 2018).

[76] Navajas, 'The Curse of the Nation', 165–166.

define their own works *ex negativo* in terms of what came before. Towards the end of the twentieth century in Spanish literature, then, as Navajas remarks, 'great cultural referents of the past are used to mitigate the insufficiencies of the present'.[77] Prior literary works thereby act as catalytic touchstones for new Spanish writing, even when this is defined in stark contrast to them. Constructions of lateness and epigonality thus remain fundamental to Spanish literature as the twentieth century comes to a close.

The last chapter of *Sefarad* provides a culmination of the narrator's self-configuration as an epigonal latecomer in comparison to a European literary context, as well as of his sustained reinforcement of conceptions of Spanish literature itself as late. Drawing together the novel's principal themes of exile and displacement, this chapter not insignificantly bears the same title as the novel itself. It deals in part with a literal displacement of the idea of Spain and Spanish culture in the twentieth century, while revisiting and recapitulating characters and locations encountered in previous chapters from the perspective of the main narrator. Drawing once more on Spanish literary figures from the Golden Age and on European modernist thinkers, the narrator seems to adopt a preferentially European stance towards this division. This is indicated by his encounter with relics of Spanish literature and culture outside of Europe in a museum in New York, as well as by a meeting with a woman working there, who personifies the Spanish literary canon. As a result the division between the Spanish and the European is perpetuated and, as the narrative of *Sefarad* comes to an end, Spanish literary artefacts are presented as physically displaced from Europe, kept isolated, and left to decay in an infrequently visited museum. The narrator evokes the sustained tension between Spanish and European by recalling the museum of the Hispanic Society of America and the objects it houses (*S*, 729), consigning Spanish literature to lateness and obsolescence, while simultaneously positioning himself as an epigonal latecomer in relation to European culture. America is thus cast as a land of cultural refuge while at the same time the history of Hispanic imperial oppression is invoked. This free museum and library was founded by Archer Huntington (1870–1955) in 1904, crucially a mere six years after Spain relinquished its final colonies to the United States of America, the nation's ultimate loss of imperial power, which coincided with—and

---

[77] Navajas, 'The Curse of the Nation', 167.

arguably prompted—its loss of prestige on the European literary stage.[78] The narrator's descriptions of the museum and its holdings are inflected with a sense of ending and dereliction. Removed from a Spanish or European context, these objects and characters continue to exist but are presented as slowly expiring. The narrator suggests there is no desire to return the museum's holdings to their place of origin; he, moreover, will return home as a cultural latecomer left with only the imitative ekphrastic accounts of them that he can produce in his writing. Spanish culture and literature have quite literally been removed from Europe here but have also been abandoned in the so-called New World and left to decay slowly and unobserved. The museum in New York is flanked by statues of El Cid and Don Quixote, twin pillars of the Golden Age of Spanish literature, yet the building itself is tucked away in a corner of the city that is difficult to reach (S, 730–731). Upon entering, the narrator and his wife realize 'que a este lugar no viene casi nadie, y que todo en él sufre un desgaste uni-forme, el de las cosas que no se renuevan, que siguen durando cuando ya están gasatadas y se han quedado obsoletas, aunque todavía puedan usarse' (S, 730).[79] The objects of cultural, historical, and literary significance held here with their yellowing paper labels are either obsolete or unwanted (S, 734). Even though they are preserved in a museum, they are presented in the narrative of Sefarad as abandoned cultural artefacts, depleted of any significance.

The descriptions of the extensive collection that Huntington acquired and shipped to America as he followed the route of El Cid through Spain—effectively also casting himself as a kind of literary latecomer or imitator—are inflected by the narrator of Sefarad with a sustained sense of obsolescence and ending. The woman who works in the museum is like-wise characterized as one who has come late or is clinging to the past. She has 'los ojos vivos y fieros de una mujer mucho más joven' (S, 730).[80] Her

---

[78] For further discussion of the life of Archer Huntington, see Patricia Fernández Lorenzo, *Archer M. Huntington: El fundador del Hispanic Society of America en España* (Madrid: Marcial Pons, 2018). See also Mitchell Codding, 'Archer Milton Huntington, Champion of Spain in the United States', in *Spain in America: The Origins of Hispanism in the United States*, ed. by Richard L. Kagan (Champaign, Illinois: University of Illinois Press, 2002), 142–170.

[79] 'That hardly anybody comes to this place, and that everything in it suffers from a com-plete state of decay, that of things which are not renewed, which continue to last when they are already worn-out and which have stayed obsolete when they could still be used.'

[80] 'The lively and fiery eyes of a much younger woman'.

office is 'desordenado, con un olor a papel rancio, con muebles de oficina de los años veinte' (*S*, 736).[81] Not only has this woman taken on the decaying sense of lateness exuded by the museum and its holdings, and surrounded herself with objects from the past, she further claims that after years of working in the museum and its library that she has memorized all of her favourite works of literature. This is a not inconsiderable feat, given that, according to the narrator, the museum has

> toda la literatura española y todos los saberes e indignaciones posibles reunidos en esa gran biblioteca a la que apenas va nadie. Pero a ella no le hacía falta abrir los volúmenes de poesía de la colección de Clásicos Castellanos porque en la época de sus clases con Professor García Lorca había adquirido, animada por él, nos dijo, el hábito de aprenderse de memoria los poemas que más le gustaban (*S*, 739–740).[82]

Having memorized many canonical works of Spanish literature, the unnamed woman in the museum then enumerates them for the narrator and his wife (*S*, 740–741), casting herself as both an inheritor of and a repository for the canon of Spanish literature. Since she studied under the brother of the playwright and poet Federico García Lorca at the University of Columbia, she claims a closer affinity with a Spanish literary tradition than that of the narrator. Earlier in his stay in New York, he had visited the grave of García Lorca's father. However, since his poet son's burial site is unknown as his body was never found after his assassination by nationalist forces in 1936, the narrator can only stop and reflect upon the impossibility of achieving a more intimate familiarity with this canonical literary figure (*S*, 719–721). The woman in the museum no longer has need of the books held in the library and is fulfilled in her reading; for her, literature is literally obsolete. The narrator, meanwhile, is dependent on the texts of others, as he reveals in the *nota de lecturas*. He remains, moreover, dissatisfied with the writing he produces that is inspired by them. Next to the woman in the museum he can only reflect on his own lateness and epigonality. In a further ironic twist, it is later implied that she is a character

---

[81] 'Cluttered, and smelled of old paper, and had office furniture from the 1920s'.

[82] 'All of Spanish literature and all possible knowledge and research concerning Spain gathered in this one great library that almost no one visits. But she doesn't need to open the volumes of poetry of the Clásicos Castellanos collection to recite, because while she was studying under Professor García Lorca, she told us, she had acquired, at his urging, the habit of memorizing the poems she liked best' (*S*, 377).

from an earlier chapter in the novel, a former nun who flees rural Spain for a new life in America (S, 551–595). Within his own narrative, then, the narrator's fictional characters have more access to the literary tradition that is closed off to him. He constructs himself as an epigonal latecomer not only in relation to European literature and Spanish literature, but also even in relation to whose stories he recounts in his own narrative.

The narrator's sense of epigonal inadequacy that emerges towards the end of *Sefarad* during his time in New York draws in particular on an earlier memory that he relates of when he was invited to give a talk in Germany years before, and this is subsequently echoed in the museum episode. He recalls being extremely dissatisfied with his own writing while on this trip to Germany, remarking that 'me desalentaba pensar en todas las páginas que me quedaban por delante y me aburría e irritaba lo que yo mismo había escrito' (S, 704).[83] Later, in contrast to this, the woman in the museum reverentially takes pleasure in the canon of Spanish literature that she has internalized, including works by Garcilaso de la Vega (1498–1536), Fray Luís de León (1528–1591). San Juan de la Cruz (1542–1591), Luis de Góngora y Argote (1561–1627), Lope de Vega (1562–1635), Francisco de Quevado y Villegas (1580–1645), and Pedro Calderón (1600–1681). Notably, these are all writers from the Golden Age of Spanish letters, who were active before Spain's loss of empire and the emergence of a European conceptualization of Spanish literature as a backward outlier in Europe. The narrator of *Sefarad*, meanwhile, is plagued by a sense of his own literary inadequacy. He later claims to be physically and intellectually tired, crumpled, and worn-out (S, 709–710).

In the final chapter of *Sefarad*, then, the rift between Spanish and European literary traditions evoked by the narrator's lateness appears to be insurmountable. Spanish literature seems unable to be written into a tradition of European 'high' culture without losing something of—or even much—itself. Some critics have indeed condemned this particular aspect of Muñoz Molina's novel, claiming that through its reinforcing of a European perspective Spanish culture is kept in its place, so to speak, and the conception of it as underdeveloped is sustained. Despite—or, perhaps better, because of—his attempt to work through this long history of Spanish and European separation in the novel, the narrator's late perspective ensures that he relies upon and reproduces the division he attempts to

---

[83] 'I became depressed thinking of all the pages I had to go, and was disgusted and irritated by my own words' (S, 355).

overcome in order to engage with the histories and experiences his narrative chronicles. Marije Hristova, in her work on memory of the Spanish Civil War, likewise remarks that *Sefarad* is one of several Spanish novels written around the end of the twentieth century which are 'marked by hegemonic frameworks that set the possibilities and limits for approximating the Holocaust and that establish clear boundaries for a European identity'. She argues that these novels 'produce a new set of very clear boundaries for transnational memory, because they ultimately fail to engage with the exclusions they have generated themselves'.[84] In its reconciliatory attempt to write Spanish literature into a European literary tradition, *Sefarad* does not resolve the European conception of Spanish literature as late. Instead, the novel suggests that this conceptualization will always be part of Spanish literature. Cubillo also remarks that 'despite his interest in the European project and his willingness to transcend what he perceives as provincial nationalities, Muñoz Molina's narrative in *Sefarad* continues to resort to the same notion of a Spanish non-European exceptionalism that he was supposedly critiquing'.[85] The challenge, in short, by *Sefarad*'s narrator to Spanish literary lateness and alterity in Europe appears to end up perpetuating it.

At the end of *Sefarad*, however, the narrator explicitly casts himself as one who is so late that the canon of Spanish literature is inaccessible to him. Leaving America, where he has encountered material remnants of Spanish literature and culture outside of Spain, as well as a woman whom he views as an embodiment of the canon of the Spanish Golden Age, he envisages himself and his wife as 'dos fantasmas en este lugar, los anteriores ocupantes desconocidos e invisibles' (*S*, 722).[86] Recalling their earlier trip to Valdemún, the narrator emphasizes the ghostliness of their presence in a place described in terms of decay and disintegration. Whereas earlier the narrator assumed the role of the elite cosmopolitan in a backward village, now the tables are turned. Here, it is as if he and his wife are erased by leaving America and returning to Europe, which entails their separation from physical manifestations of a canonical Hispanic literary heritage. Since the narrator's attempt to bring together Spanish and European literary traditions presupposes a divide between the two, and since his preference for a European perspective sustains this, he is left bereft, cast adrift in

---

[84] See Hristova, *Reimagining Spain*, 25 and 185–232.
[85] Cubillo, *Memories of the Maghreb*, 111.
[86] 'Two ghosts in this place, the former occupants, unknown and invisible'.

his own narrative, while styling himself as the ultimate epigonal latecomer as *Sefarad* approaches its conclusion. He and his narrative are imbued with a sense of lateness, such that this is prolonged indefinitely. Yet this in fact suggests a further possibility, however latent and late, for a more harmonious coming together of Spanish or European literary traditions.

LATENESS AND LIMINALITY

Uneven modernization in Europe may have resulted in Spanish culture being overdetermined by external conceptualizations which sought to cast it as late, underdeveloped, and unworthy of inclusion within the literature of Europe. Yet Spanish literary lateness may not, in fact, indicate Spain's complete exclusion from a modern European literary context. If, as Vilarós argues, 'Spain's non-modern literary difference should be understood as akin to a political, cultural and economic configuration deeply and unavoidably linked to the realities of Western economic modernization and to its corollary of hegemonic and political dominance',[87] then, essentially, the exclusion caused by Spain's perceived difference and lateness in terms of modern Western European cultural development must, in fact, be considered constitutive of Spain's particular form of modernity. It is, in short, the very thing that ensures its inclusion within the European cultural landscape. Drawing on Fredric Jameson's work on the postmodern cultural turn, Vilarós elaborates how 'the much-mocked anti-modern Spanish literary difference in fact falls within the logic of modernity', since 'difference is in fact a wholly modernist construct'.[88] Setting aside the admittedly weighty political and historical baggage of empire, its legacy, and its losses, it is possible—particularly from the perspective of exile so frequently invoked in *Sefarad*—to conceive of nineteenth- and twentieth-century Spain as a site of an alternative modernity, through the very sense of cultural and historical lateness that signalled its exclusion. As Ginger observes, while considering the cultural supernova of European modernity after the Spanish Golden Age alongside the concomitant peripheralization of Hispanic culture, 'the tracing of similarities between the mid-century "Hispanic" world and more canonical art and literature affords nineteenth-century "Hispanic" cultures a visibility that they were habitually denied historically. The point is to write the history of culture

[87] Vilarós, 'The Novel Beyond Modernity', 251.
[88] Vilarós, 'The Novel Beyond Modernity', 252.

differently, so as retrospectively to reactivate their resonances and possibilities'.[89] As then, so later: there is not simply one template for modernity, as the hegemonic Western European perspective on Spain from outside might suggest. 'The complex interaction of cultural, social, and political alternatives which competed in the past,' Labanyi and Helen Graham note, reveal 'not a "single," homogenous "modernity" but many potentials'.[90] The complex valences of lateness in the Spanish literary tradition constitute one such potential. While *Sefarad*'s narrator seems to revere canonical European culture over a Spanish literary tradition, he is unable to set aside the burden of history until confronted with the catalogue of lateness and his own epigonality in the Hispanic Society of America museum. If *Sefarad* thus reinforces, promotes, and ultimately sustains the separation of Spanish letters from a canon of European culture, then this is deeply inflected by the narrator's historical position at the turn of the millennium. In response to the resultant anxiety caused by the European perspective, namely, a Spanish quest for legitimacy, *Sefarad* partly perpetuates a European construction of Spain as late. Yet, in doing so, it also calls into question the very legitimacy of such an outlook, offering a reminder that these traditions are as discordant as they are harmonious, as intimately connected as they are dynamically diverse.

Uncertainty inflected with a sense of lateness and Spanish exceptionalism is, after all, distinctly characteristic of what Chris Perriam, Michael Thompson, Susan Frenk, and Vanessa Knights call 'New Spanish Writing' at the end of the twentieth century, a category in which Muñoz Molina's work is frequently located. With the arrival of the millennium, Spanish literature begins 'shaping new Spains whose fragments connect and disconnect as we turn the kaleidoscope' via new literary movements and new discourses, as Perriam et al. observe.[91] Spanish literature is understood at the millennial caesura as fluid, always changing and different, never static, and able to incorporate multiple identities, including the Spanish and the broader European, the old and the new. Novels by writers such as Muñoz Molina demonstrate what Navajas considers to be a prime characteristic of Spanish literature at the end of the twentieth century, which 'make[s]

---

[89] Ginger, *Instead of Modernity*, 16.
[90] Helen Graham and Jo Labanyi, eds., *Spanish Cultural Studies. An Introduction: The Struggle for Modernity* (Oxford: Oxford University Press, 1995), 18.
[91] See Chris Perriam, Michael Thompson, Susan Frenk, and Vanessa Knights, *A New History of Spanish Writing: From 1939 to the 1990s* (Oxford: Oxford University Press, 2000), 220–221.

apparent the power of the aesthetic medium to broaden and renovate the narrow national culture and integrate it into diversified international currents'.[92] If *Sefarad*'s narrator attempts to construct a narrative within both the broader contexts of European memory and European literature, then, as Dagmar Vanderbosch remarks, this narrative's attempt to create 'a European space of totalitarian repression and persecution' is nevertheless 'conditioned by the strong relation with the Spanish context of enunciation'.[93] *Sefarad* is a Spanish novel complicated by a European scope and focus tinged with historical and cultural lateness; it is a European novel complicated by its Hispanic heritage. Muñoz Molina's works are, as Perriam et al. indicate, considered to be characterized by such eclectic, allusive forms that they have variously been described as 'neo-neo-realism' and as 'postmodern', terms which both already evoke a sense of coming after.[94] In attempting to articulate an end to Spanish exceptionalism and isolationism through an act of writing into Europe, therefore, Spanish literature at the end of the century ensures that lateness and difference are two of its essential components. Yet the attempt to end Spanish exclusion from the canon of European literature presupposes that Spain is late in being incorporated into it. Lateness, then, returns as a long-exemplified feature of Spanish literature in various guises. Jessica Folkart draws lines of connection from pre-dictatorship Spain in its crisis of lateness during European modernity at the start of the twentieth century to the post-dictatorship identity crisis at the end of the twentieth century. She observes that a sense of liminality is 'essential to the vision of Spanish national identity at the brink of the Civil War and, decades later, at the end of the millennium'.[95] The Spanish nation and its literature, she argues, is and always has been in 'perpetual transition between old and new'.[96] At the turn of the twenty-first century, liminality may therefore be understood as the most recent iteration of Spanish literature's sense of coming after, the newest instantiation of its European lateness. Liminality, however, is a symptom of Spanish literary lateness not a cause. Folkart observes that Spanish literary identity 'defies stasis and sameness', since novels engaging

[92] Navajas, 'The Curse of the Nation', 170.

[93] Vanderbosch, 'Transnational Memories', 614.

[94] See Perriam, Thompson, Frenk, and Knights, *A New History of Spanish Writing*, 146, 172, and 208 respectively.

[95] Jessica A. Folkart, *Liminal Fiction at the Edge of the Millennium: The Ends of Spanish Identity* (Lewisburg, Pennsylvania: Bucknell University Press, 2014), 2.

[96] Folkart, *Liminal Fiction*, 207.

with liminality at the turn of the twenty-first century 'in their exploration of the development of identity in Spain at the millennium's edge, [...] enact and embody the liminal not simply as a transitional and transient mode but as the structuring principle of identity in Spain'.[97] Spanish literature, this would suggest, is constructed as late, even when attempting not to be. From a European perspective on modernity and literary history, Spain is still perceived as an outsider: a latecomer in perpetual transition towards the potential of renewal.

In *Sefarad* this sense of liminality is expressed most clearly first through the novel's status as a late work by a narrator who likewise considers himself to be an epigonal latecomer and secondly through the encounter between Spanish and European cultural traditions he stages in the narrative. The final scene of *Sefarad* underscores these two fundamental aspects of the novel. Themes of lateness and exclusion are rearticulated and reemphasized through the narrator's reflections concerning the objects in the museum and the objects he himself has on his desk. These include a shell from a beach mentioned earlier in the chapter 'Berghof' (*S*, 439) and a postcard he bought at the museum in New York. In his final reflections, the narrator offers an extensive list of the paintings adorning the walls of that museum and what they portray, which includes scenes from many different regions of Spain (*S*, 745). These paintings have been taken out of the context of their country of origin, however, and arranged in a museum, which he describes as exemplifying a 'desorden de las láminas de una enciclopedia [...] y también la minuciosidad abrumadora de un catálogo o de un reglamento' (*S*, 744–745).[98] The tone of this description is unfavourable, even dismissive, towards the attempt to taxonomize Spanish cultural and literary history. As in parts of *Dora Bruder* and *Austerlitz*, there is an implied critique of Western European Enlightenment thinking here, which almost defensively reinforces Spanish exceptionalism, given the nation's conceptualization as late and separate within the European grand narrative of progress and modernity. Removing the artefacts of Spanish literature and culture out of Europe and displaying them in a museum maintains their exceptionalism, which is reinforced by the narrator's description of this as a clumsy and mechanical process. These artefacts' exiled lateness encapsulates, however, the fraught tensions not

---

[97] Folkart, *Liminal Fiction*, 6.
[98] 'A jumble of encyclopaedia illustrations [...] and also the grinding meticulousness of a catalogue or rule book'.

only of the liminality of the Hispanic in relation to the European, but also of the complex histories of oppressive expansion and suggested by the Spanish presence in the Americas.

In the novel's final paragraph, the narrator's focus moves from the catalogued objects in the museum to the abandoned artefacts on his desk, which he has collected over the course of recounting the stories included in *Sefarad*. As he contemplates them, he remarks how 'el tiempo se nos deshacía entre los dedos con una inconsistencia de papel quemado, de hojas de ceniza, minutos y horas sin sosiego' (*S*, 745).[99] The end of his narrative is inflected not only by a sense of ending but also by a literal counting down of time passing, recalling once more Walter Benjamin's figure of the Angel of History who views preceding events as one great catastrophic accumulation. Surrounded by the objects left behind after the stories he has recounted, coming after the Spanish cultural figures that he is unable to access, as well as the European canonical figures on whom he draws in the construction of his narrative, the narrator casts himself as a being facing backwards in the Nietzschean sense. He reinforces his own epigonality in comparison to others, imbuing his narrative with a sense of futility and inadequacy. In a final moment of quasi-Proustian introspection after his attempt to produce a narrative bringing together empathetically imagined accounts of exile, suffering and persecution from both within and beyond Spain, he reminds himself, 'puedo tener la sensación de que nada de lo que invento o recuerdo está fuera de mí, de este espacio cerrado' (*S*, 745).[100] He is self-consciously aware that, in the act of writing, this is just an illusion. Arriving historically late, as well as being unable directly to synthesize Spanish and European traditions through the machinations of his own narrative, he concludes *Sefarad* by conceiving of himself as the epitome of epigonal latecoming in the narrative so far. His narrative, he acknowledges, stands as an illusory testament to the perpetuation of the unresolved tension between the Spanish and the European that also brings these together in liminal uncertainty. All that is left to him are these abandoned objects, as well as the realization that he himself is superfluous to the narrative, a ghostly presence exiled from his attempt to write Spanish literature into a European literary context. At the close of

---

[99] 'Time was disintegrating in our hands with the flimsiness of burned paper, pages of ash, anxious minutes and hours' (*S*, 380).

[100] 'I can entertain the illusion that nothing I invent or remember exists outside of me, beyond this reduced space' (*S*, 380).

the novel, then, the narrator appears to obviate any resolution of the encounter he has staged between Spanish and European literature by separating himself from these cultural artefacts, thereby reinforcing the lateness and Spanish exceptionalism that have been present throughout the narrative. Yet in his very self-consciousness of this, the potential for renewal to emerge out of an awareness of lateness—for the liminality of the Hispanic in relation to the European to defy stasis—still remains.

In a final crystallization of its narrative epigonal lateness, *Sefarad* concludes with a reproduction of a Diego Velásquez portrait from around 1640 (*S*, 747). While this image is curiously absent from the English translation of *Sefarad*, its inclusion in the original Spanish novel pre-empts the narrator's admission of epigonality in the subsequent *nota de lecturas*, focalizing his gaze as one looking back to the Golden Age of Spanish culture before the loss of its empire and concomitant cultural prestige in Europe. Gazing at the portrait, the narrator is acutely aware that 'la niña que me mira desde la pálida reproducción de una postal mira y sonríe levemente en un lienzo verdadero y tangible, […] colgado en un gran salón medio en penumbra de un museo que visita muy poca gente' (*S*, 746).[101] His musings on the reproduced nature of the postcard and the fact that it lacks something that only the original possesses recall Benjamin's observation that 'Noch bei der höchstvollendeten Reproduktion fällt *eines* aus: das Hier und Jetzt des Kunstwerks – sein einmaliges Dasein an dem Orte, an dem es sich befindet'.[102] By concluding his narrative with a mere reproduction of a work of art from the Spanish Golden Age that has been left hanging in a gloomy and infrequently visited room, the narrator recalls his preoccupation with Spanish cultural and historical lateness, while also emphasizing his concerns with his own epigonality in relation to both Spanish and European culture. The original painting has been removed from Spain and from Europe, and all that is left for the narrator is a

---

[101] 'The girl who watches me from the pale reproduction of a postcard is showing the hint of a smile on a real and tangible canvas, […] hung in semidarkness in a large room of a museum that few people visit' (*S*, 381).

[102] Walter Benjamin, 'Das Kunstwerk im Zeitalter seiner technischen Reproduzierbarkeit', in *Gesammelte Schriften I.2*, ed. by Rolf Tiedemann und Hermann Schweppenhäuser (Frankfurt am Main: Suhrkamp, 1974), 431–508 (437). 'Even the most perfect reproduction of a work of art is lacking in one element: its presence in time and space, its unique existence at the place where it happens to be'. Walter Benjamin, 'The Work of Art in the Age of Mechanical Reproduction', in *Illuminations*, ed. by Hannah Arendt, trans. by Harry Zohn (New York: Schocken Books, 1968), 217–251 (220).

mass-produced copy. The final chapter of *Sefarad* thus concludes with his musings on recognizing 'la melancolía de un largo destierro' in the eyes of the girl in the portrait (*S*, 746).[103] Unable to resolve the tensions between Spanish and European literary traditions in *Sefarad* thanks to his own constructions of epigonal lateness, the narrator, exiled from his narrative, chooses instead to adopt a decidedly melancholy outlook on the past as unavoidably unreachable and unalterable. Even though he attempts to overcome the long history of literary division between Spain and Europe in his narrative, *Sefarad* ultimately restages this separation, as the narrator self-consciously dwells on Spanish literary lateness and on his own sense of epigonality. The aesthetic preoccupations of the novel echo the misguided European conception of the Hispanic as late, yet allow that this Hispanic lateness may not only signify incorporation into European culture, but also offer the possibility that a future overcoming of this lateness—through narratorial self-consciousness and through Spanish literature's liminal refusal of stasis—may occur.

THE FANTASY OF NOSTALGIA

The narrator's attempt at a rapprochement between Spanish and European literature ensures that his melancholy of long exile not only may be understood to concern the thematics of the novel and its characters, but also emerges as fundamentally imbricated with *Sefarad*'s aesthetic and literary historical circumstances. Emanating from epigonal lateness, *Sefarad*'s constructions of melancholy are nonetheless crucially determined by forms of nostalgia. In seemingly sentimental and artificial—or even violent—ways, this complicates and nuances the construction of a melancholy outlook on the past that the narrator strives to establish over the course of the novel. It is therefore not only *Sefarad*'s sense of narrative lateness that emerges as 'conditioned by a strong relation to the Spanish context of enunciation', to use Vanderbosch's formulation.[104] The narrator's express desire to produce a melancholy aesthetic and outlook on history is conditioned by nostalgic undertones for a Spanish childhood, lost moments in time, and the idea of a lost homeland, which evoke not only the irreconcilability of tensions between past and present, but also between the Spanish and the non-Spanish. Apparent instances of nostalgia

---

[103] 'The melancholy of a long exile' (*S*, 381)
[104] See Vanderbosch, 'Transnational Memories', 614.

in the novel produce a lingering sense of melancholy irresolution out of which—seemingly paradoxically—commonality emerges.

The very title of Muñoz Molina's novel is burdened with the potential for nostalgia in the most literal sense of the word—a longing for a homeland.[105] The narrator of *Sefarad* draws at various intervals in the novel on nostalgia for the Sephardic homeland and persistently lapses into nostalgic longing of his own. This becomes the foundation for his personal reflections and his empathetic imaginings of others' lives and experiences. Through the many nostalgic reflections and meditative moments in *Sefarad*, the narrator is at pains to stress the melancholy nature of the novel's aesthetics. Unlike the narrators of *Austerlitz* or *Dora Bruder*, the narrator of *Sefarad* explicitly uses the word 'melancholy' many times over the course of the novel.[106] In a conscious attempt to imbue the narrative with a melancholy aesthetic attitude, even the novel's concluding line, as discussed above, reflects on the narrator's sense of 'la melancolía de un largo destierro' (*S*, 746).[107] The frequency of thematized moments of nostalgic longing alongside the heavy emphasis on melancholy in the narrative inevitably draws attention to this tension. Forms of apparent nostalgia are thereby continually tempered by melancholy realization.

This melancholy perspective on history partly results from the ways in which *Sefarad*'s lateness is compromised by being rooted in both geographical and temporal forms of nostalgia, which embody the potential for violence against the past. This can be seen both in nostalgia for the notion of a lost homeland evoked and then undermined over the course of the novel and secondly in nostalgia for lost moments in time carries a potential for violence and historical erasure. This, then, constitutes both the cause and the object of reflection in the narrator's constructed melancholy state, recapitulating and complicating the tensions between a European cultural and historical ideal and a Hispanic contextual specificity. Critics such as Cubillo have argued that if such a 'tension between the respect for cultural

---

[105] The word nostalgia is derived from the Greek words 'nóstos', meaning 'homecoming', and 'álgos', meaning 'pain' or 'ache'. It was first coined in 1688 in a dissertation by the medical scholar Johannes Hofer (1669–1752) at the University of Basel to describe the condition of Swiss mercenaries fighting away from their homeland. See www.etymonline.com/word/nostalgia

[106] The word 'melancholy' appears once in *Dora Bruder* (52) and twice in *Austerlitz* (243 and 385), whereas in *Sefarad* it is explicitly stated over twenty times (such as 165, 225, 236, 254, 285, and 309, for example).

[107] 'The melancholy of a long exile' (*S*, 381).

and ideological diversity and the hegemonic drive' needs to be overcome in order to achieve a European literary identity, then *Sefarad* goes so far as to stage this tension, but does not resolve it.[108] However, rather than precluding the possibility of commonality with European literature, the narrator's melancholy in *Sefarad* emerges out of nostalgia and ultimately establishes—in its exiled form—an aesthetic double-bind, whereby the apparent tensions and limitations of his attempts empathetically to construct a pan-European narrative in a melancholy aesthetic mode suggest a common sense of distance and isolation from the past and from aesthetic forebears. This ensures that the complex similarities and key distinctions of this work of European literature and others are preserved. In commonality there is difference; in difference there is commonality.

One of this study's principle points of departure echoes Walter Moser's understanding that nostalgia expresses a desire to return to the past, whereas melancholy stems from the realization that a reconciliation of the past and the present is impossible.[109] More clearly, perhaps, than *Dora Bruder* or *Austerlitz*, *Sefarad* both encapsulates and complicates this distinction between melancholy and nostalgia. Nostalgia is mobilized by the narrator in *Sefarad* in the creation of his self-consciously melancholy narration. *Sefarad*'s melancholy narrative mode is thus inflected by seemingly reactionary nostalgia for earlier moments in time evoked in various chapters in *Sefarad*. This ensures that a potentially violent sense of reconfiguration of the past, and even of its erasure, metaphorically occupies the space left in the narrative by nostalgia for a lost homeland, which is periodically rejected or invalidated during the novel. The cumulative effect of empty nostalgia for a lost homeland, combined with personal nostalgia for an earlier time, as well as its implications of erasing and reconfiguring of the past, complicates the narrator's vision of a melancholy aesthetic mode in the narrative of *Sefarad*. Certainly, as Tabia Linhard remarks in her analysis of *Sefarad* and its representation of Jewish memory in the Mediterranean, 'the desire to return to a lost and consequently mythical homeland necessarily leads to fragmented and open-ended narratives'.[110] Yet the intrinsic contradictions and compromises that arise from the nostalgic roots of *Sefarad*'s

---

[108] See Cubillo, *Memories of the Maghreb*, 114.

[109] See Walter Moser, 'Mélancholie et nostalgie: Affects de la *Spätzeit*', *Etudes littéraires*, 32 (1999), 83–103.

[110] Tabia Linhard, *Jewish Spain: A Mediterranean Memory* (Stanford: Stanford University Press, 2014), 64.

aesthetic attitude not only result in the separation of the past from the present, but also, in their fractured and unresolved state, provide the conditions of possibility for *Sefarad*'s inclusion within a European community of late and melancholy novels.

Nostalgia is a complex and polyvalent concept, which has generated a wealth of scholarship. Indeed, as Svetlana Boym warns, 'the moment we try to force it into a single image it breaks the frame'.[111] From Homer's *Odyssey*—the original European narrative of longed-for homecoming—and beyond, nostalgia has been a staple feature of European literature and one which persists until today.[112] 'The longing to return to a lost homeland', John J. Su observes 'becomes a central feature of the Western literary tradition long before the term "nostalgia" was coined to describe it'.[113] Yet nostalgia does not only belong to literature of classical Antiquity: as Su later acknowledges, 'the economic, social, and political forces associated with late modernity have evoked widespread nostalgia' in more contemporary literary fiction.[114] For Boym, too, nostalgia is an affliction that is particularly prevalent in the modern age due to new understandings of time and space, such as an increased awareness of the unrepeatability and irreversibility of passing time.[115] In spite of her caveat regarding its conceptual slipperiness, Boym suggests two principal forms of nostalgia: first, 'restorative nostalgia', which represents the somewhat aggressive impulse that motivates attempts to recapture and reanimate an imagined past in the present, and secondly, 'reflective nostalgia', which is more escapist and optimistic in nature, and is characterized by wistful longing for what is lost to time and tends to be experienced in particular for eras perceived (however misguidedly) to be historically uneventful, devoid of momentous social or political events, and thus characterized by a sense of simplicity and stability.[116] If *Sefarad*'s nostalgia tends to be of the more reflective strain, then it emerges over the course of the narrative as being equally bound up with melancholy. Much scholarship has denigrated nostalgia as

---

[111] Svetlana Boym, *The Future of Nostalgia* (New York: Basic Books, 2001), 1.

[112] See Kathleen Riley, *Imagining Ithaca: Nostos and Nostalgia Since the Great War* (Oxford: Oxford University Press, 2021).

[113] John J. Su, *Ethics and Nostalgia in the Contemporary Novel* (Cambridge: Cambridge University Press, 2005), 1.

[114] Su, *Ethics and Nostalgia*, 3.

[115] Boym, *The Future of Nostalgia*, xiv.

[116] See Boym, *The Future of Nostalgia*, xviii.

a 'social disease', as in Susan Stewart's famous formulation.[117] This classification further highlights nostalgia's distinction from melancholy, which,
when discussed in nostalgia studies, is usually understood as an individual
depressive malaise. Boym, for example, understands nostalgia 'not merely
an individual sickness but a symptom of our age, a historical emotion'.[118]
Boym is thus able to distinguish the two concepts of nostalgia and melancholy, devoting her analysis to the former as a broadly conceptualized
Zeitgeist of the twentieth century. If, as in this study, melancholy is conceptualized as an aesthetic mode influenced by the looming end of the
twentieth century, which acknowledges the impossibility of reconciliation
between the past and the present, then in *Sefarad* this mode is heralded by
a vestigial desire to return to earlier times and places. So, if Spain at the
end of the twentieth century was a culturally 'sick nation' in Europe, to
use Navajas's terms, then the manifestations of this sickness in *Sefarad*
emerge from nostalgia but ultimately arrive in melancholy.

Within the context of Spanish literature, instances of nostalgia capture
in particular the contradictory nature of modernity hinted at by Boym and
Su. 'While born out of a modern world, and hence modern in its character', Sarah Bracke asserts, '[nostalgia's] sentimentalized yearning for a
place or past long (or perhaps not so long) gone became systematically
attributed to modernity's "others", i.e. to those groups inside and outside
of Europe, that were considered "incompletely modernized", and were to
"cling" to an older world as it was destroyed by a newer one'.[119] Resonating
clearly with the long history of Spanish literary lateness, this feeds into the
complexities of nostalgia and melancholy in Muñoz Molina's novel, inter-
twining Hispanic exclusion from Europe and Jewish exclusion from Spain.
Even if, following Jameson, Spain's apparent non-modernity may, in fact,
constitute its inclusion within a broader logic of European modernities,
then the normative European perspective seemingly perpetuated in the
narrative of *Sefarad* acts as a trigger for nostalgic sentiment, out of which
a melancholy sense of irresolution coalesces. According to Vilarós, the
aforementioned perception of non-modern Spanish literary exceptionalism was mobilized during Spanish modernity in order to shape symbolic
values that nostalgically represented a vanished heroic Spanish national

---

[117] See Susan Stewart, *On Longing: Narratives of the Miniature, the Gigantic, the Souvenir, the Collection* (Durham, North Carolina: Duke University Press, 1992), ix.

[118] Boym, *The Future of Nostalgia*, xv.

[119] Sarah Bracke, 'Nostalgia's Violence', in *Forum* 15 (2012), 1–6 (6 n. 4).

character.[120] These essentialist notions of heroic Spanishness were hall-marks of an obsolete imperial state, from which Francoism with its enthusiastic embracing of imperial iconography and heroic traditions emerged in the early twentieth century. After the end of the Franco dictatorship in 1975, contradictory nostalgic traits persisted in Spanish culture. As Brad Epps argues: 'in post-Francoist Spain nostalgia was most succinctly expressed in two apparently contradictory, but actually quite complementary, phrases: "with Franco we lived better" and "against Franco we lived better"'.[121] Writers at this time, he suggests, simultaneously refused to fall prey to nostalgia and nonetheless expressed it in their work. Such post-dictatorship nostalgia, expressed variously by supporters and dissidents alike, is suggestive of a longing for the cer-tainties afforded by the moral positions of yesteryear.[122] These brief examples gesture towards a long-standing nostalgia in Spanish litera-ture, as well as the ambiguous and contradictory nature of its promises and potentialities.

It is on similarly ambiguous ground that the narrator attempts to estab-lish such a melancholy aesthetic attitude in *Sefarad*. Nostalgia may well be considered as a common feature of the novel's seventeen chapters. *Pace* Linhard, however, who argues that 'it is not the sadness of melancholy but rather the promise of nostalgia that ends up unifying the different texts', a melancholy view of history emerges out of nostalgia as the narrator fash-ions his narrative of long exile and its promise is one of potential revivifica-tion rather than nostalgic longing.[123] If, as Linhard suggests, 'the idea of a return to a lost home is not only meandering and often misleading, it is never to be realised', then this is certainly indicative of the melancholy separation of past and present in the novel, but crucially one which is com-plicated but not overwhelmed by nostalgic tendencies.[124] This has signifi-cant implications for a novel that encapsulates tensions between the Hispanic and the European, as well as between nostalgia and melancholy, and whose multiple narratorial strands coalesce around the idea of exile.

[120] See Vilarós, 'The Novel Beyond Modernity', 251.

[121] Brad Epps, 'Spanish Prose, 1975–2002', in *The Cambridge History of Spanish Literature*, ed. by David T. Gies (Cambridge: Cambridge University Press, 2004), 705–723 (708).

[122] For further discussion of this, especially in relation to the Spanish transition to democ-racy, see Teresa M. Vilarós, *El mono del desencanto: una crítica cultural de la transición española (1973–1993)* (Madrid: Siglo XXI, 1998).

[123] See Linhard, *Jewish Spain*, 64.

[124] See Linhard, *Jewish Spain*, 64.

By placing these elements side by side and revealing the constitutive frictions between them, yet removing them geographically and historically from their points of origin, *Sefarad* implies a new, albeit latent, possibility for their reconfiguration cast from their late and melancholy state. Writing from his position of historical and cultural lateness, the narrator is torn between forms of nostalgia and a desire to create a melancholy aesthetic attitude in his narrative. Towards the end of the novel, he recognizes the tensions inherent to his narrative, suggesting that in attempting to chart the melancholy of long exile he is unable to marshal the past to his present aesthetic wishes. Reflecting at the novel's close when he is alone in his study, the narrator observes that 'al inventar uno tiene la vana creencia de que se apodera de los lugares y las cosas, de la gente acerca de la que escribe' (*S*, 745).[125] He is conscious here of the impossibility of his narrative to move beyond the contradictions and divisions it communicates, thereby recalling Spanish exceptionalism and European cultural hegemony in the course of the novel, even as it ostensibly attempts to move beyond such distinctions. Only by escaping the specific geographical and historical location of these, however, can the narrative of *Sefarad* point beyond itself to the potential for Spanish and European *Erstlinge* to arise from the melancholy of the novel's long exile. Melancholy is thus ultimately an unexpectedly enabling, inclusive, forward-looking aesthetic mode, as opposed to being a debilitating and limiting condition condemned by the past, which is suggestive once more of the inherent dynamism of Spanish liminal lateness. A similar conundrum emerges in the narrator's attempt to create a melancholy narrative inflected by nostalgic yearnings.

Homelands and Erasure

The two principal forms of nostalgia in *Sefarad* are evoked, first, in the title of the novel itself and, later, in various reminiscences of idealized times before instances of persecution that enact a potentially violent erasure of the past, sometimes masked by a sense of mourning or pity, within the narrative. *Sefarad*'s title, as discussed above, echoes the name of a lost Sephardic Jewish homeland. This is immediately suggestive of Su's and Boym's more contemporary sense of nostalgia for a lost homeland as a response or reaction to the ravages of twentieth-century modernity. In

---

[125] 'When you invent, you have the vain belief that you are controlling places, things, the people you write about' (*S*, 380).

spite of its eponymous status, however, the place Sepharad itself is barely addressed in the course of the novel, only surfacing by name in the chapters 'Oh tú que lo sabías' (*S*, 310–354)—one of the narrator's empathetic imaginings of the life of a Hungarian Jewish exile—and the narrator's final reflections on the text he has assembled in the last chapter, also entitled 'Sefarad'. Both occasions establish a sense of nostalgia, which is then emptied out or rejected during the narrative, leaving a space into which a compromised form of melancholy aesthetics may enter. Disorientingly, the narrator's empathetic imaginings of others' experiences are entwined with his own personal nostalgia, as well as an implied nostalgia for the Sephardic Jewish homeland, even as his narrative predominantly stays rooted in the twentieth century. If, as Su remarks, writers may make use of 'nostalgia's tendency to interweave imagination, longing, and memory in their efforts to envision resolutions to the social dilemmas of fragmentation and displacement described in their novels',[126] then the narrative of *Sefarad* concerns itself with the dilemma of fragmentation that results from the creation of a network of common experience among victims of totalitarian oppression across Europe and beyond, as well as from the concurrent intention of resolving divisions between Spanish and European cultural traditions. The narrative of *Sefarad* exhibits such fragmentation and displacement not only in the range of experiences it recounts, but also in its unresolved tensions between Spanishness and Europeanness, as well as the question of locating the legacy of the Sephardic Jewish homeland among these concerns. The melancholy aesthetic attitude established by the narrator is thus variously complicated and nuanced by its constitutive nostalgic tendencies. His attempt to create a pan European novel of memory and melancholy relies on nostalgic stories that perpetuate the divisions and differences within the novel, even while the narrator seeks to move beyond them.

The most explicit reference to the Sephardic Jewish homeland occurs during the narrator's empathetic imagining of Isaac Salama, an elderly Sephardic Jewish exile born in Hungary and now living in the Moroccan port of Tangier in the chapter 'Oh tú que lo sabías'. The narrator imagines Isaac's recollections of his family's being rounded up in Budapest in 1944, and a visit later in life to the concentration camp where his mother and sisters died, as well as his father's perpetual state of mourning following their murder. Isaac and his father remain exiled from the mythical homeland of

---

[126] Su, *Ethics and Nostalgia*, 3.

210   I. ELLISON

Sepharad, living on the margins of the Jewish community in Tangier. Isaac recalls how his father would reminisce about the idea of a Sephardic homeland, the house his family had owned, and the keys to the homes that were left behind centuries earlier. His phrasing is such that it is as if he had experienced all of these occurrences personally:

> Sefarad era el nombre de nuestra patria verdadera aunque nos hubieran expulsado de ella hacía más de cuatro siglos. Me contaba que nuestra familia había guardado durante generaciones la llave de la casa que había sido nuestra en Toledo, y todos los viajes que habían hecho desde que salieron de España, como si me contara una sola vida que hubiera durado casi quinientos años (*S*, 337).[127]

For Isaac's father, Sepharad is the lost homeland in the past to which he can nostalgically cling in exile to such an extent that he even remarks during the decolonization of Tangier during the 1950s, 'sólo espero que nos echen con mejores modales que los húngaros, o que los españoles en 1492' (*S*, 340).[128] He does not see himself as Spanish, choosing instead to align himself with a lost homeland, even though, as his son indicates earlier in the narrative, 'un decreto de 1924 nos devolvió a los sefardíes la nacionalidad española' (*S*, 338).[129] Isaac's father draws on the history of a Spanish nation being founded in opposition to the Jewish homeland of Sepharad. During this chapter, Isaac himself also makes reference to the Sephardic Jewish homeland. In a reversal of his father's behaviour, however, he does so in order to distance himself from his Jewishness. By mentioning Sepharad, Isaac implies nostalgic sentiments. Yet, in fact, he is afraid of returning to Spain with his father, whom he describes as having become a 'pinta de judío viejo de caricatura' (*S*, 332),[130] whom others back in Spain would look down upon. Isaac establishes further negative connotations with the idea of return to the Sephardic homeland when recalling the accident that paralysed him at the age of twenty-two while he

[127] 'Sepharad was the name of our true homeland, although we'd been expelled from it more than four centuries ago. My father told me that for generations our family had kept the key of the house that had been ours in Toledo, and he detailed every journey they'd made since they left Spain, as if he were telling me about a single life that had lasted nearly five hundred years' (*S*, 110).

[128] 'I hope they throw us out with better manners than the Hungarians, or the Spanish in 1492' (*S*, 112).

[129] 'A 1924 decree restored Spanish nationality to the Sephardim'.

[130] 'Caricature of an old Jew' (*S*, 107)

had returned to Spain for a time to study. From Isaac's perspective, his return to the Sephardic homeland led to this 'castigo de su propia soberbia, de la culpable desmesura que le había empujado a avergonzarse de su padre' (*S*, 340),[131] such that the fulfilment of his father's notion of nostalgic return to their homeland only leads to disaster and emptiness. This realization contributes towards the construction of the melancholy aesthetic of *Sefarad*'s narrative founded on nostalgic complications. Nostalgia for the lost homeland of Sepharad moves from being an imagined memory of Isaac's father to a broken notion for Isaac, before finally becoming a blank slate on which the narrator may inscribe a melancholy mode of narration, as any nostalgic potential of solace in Sepharad seen as a false promise by Isaac.

Isaac's father's nostalgic reveries become emptied of their prior significance and overwritten with the impressions of others, such that the lost homeland of Sepharad and its potential for nostalgia are overwritten by the narrator's inscribing the stories he wishes to tell in his self-consciously constructed melancholy mode. Isolated from the Jewish community in Tangier, Isaac himself and the Ateneo Español museum where he works have become seldom-frequented fixtures in the city, which visiting writers and academics recall via Sephardic and more generally Jewish stereotypes: 'Aquel sitio, que estaba cayéndose. Entranable, el judío, y muy servicial, ¿no es verdad? [...] Parece que era de una familia de dinero, en Checoslovaquia o por ahí, y que tuvieron pagar un dineral para que los nazis los dejaron salir' (*S*, 348).[132] Isaac once more lessens the nostalgic potential of the notion of a Sephardic homeland, describing it as 'un sitio casi inexistente de tan remoto, un país inaccesible, desconocido, ingrato, llamado Sepharad, añorado con una melancolía sin fundamento' (*S*, 339–340),[133] in spite of his geographical proximity to the Iberian peninsular when living in Tangier. In contrast to Isaac's assertions, however, the melancholy of *Sefarad*'s narrative does, in fact, have a basis and it lies in precisely this nostalgic longing for a Sephardic homeland. Isaac stresses, albeit regretfully, that when he was younger 'lo que yo quería no era que

---

[131] 'Punishment of his own pride, for the self-indulgence that had pushed him to be ashamed of his father' (*S*, 112)

[132] 'The place was falling apart, you know. Very accommodating that Jew was, [...] didn't you think? [...] It seems he came from a moneyed family, from Czechoslovakia or somewhere like that, and they had to pay an enormous sum to the Nazis to get out' (*S*, 117).

[133] 'So remote that it is nearly nonexistent, an inaccessible, unknown, thankless country they call Sepharad, longing for it with a melancholy without basis' (*S*, 111).

los judíos nos salváramos de los Nazis. [...] lo que yo quería era de no ser judío' (*S*, 342–343).[134] He wished to sever all ties and nostalgic links to a Jewish homeland and its people. While the name Sepharad holds the potential for nostalgia for a lost homeland, this becomes hollowed out and rejected during the narrator's empathetic imagining of Isaac Salama's reflections on his life. In its place the narrator constructs a melancholy aesthetic attitude towards history, which remains nonetheless rooted in and complicated by sentiments of nostalgic longing. Although the notion of the Sephardic Jewish homeland is barely mentioned let alone interrogated in *Sefarad*, it is aptly employed as the title of the novel, even if its absence in the narrative is ultimately of greater significance than its presence.

The empathetic imaginings in *Sefarad*, which form the majority of the novel's chapters, are recounted by a narrator figure who is himself also nostalgic on occasion. Sequences in the novel such as the chapter recounting Isaac Salama's life are thus rooted not only in the nostalgic potential of Sepharad as Jewish homeland before the establishment of a Spanish nation, but also in the narrator's personal nostalgia, which intersects with and complicates the aesthetic attitude of his empathetic imaginings. During *Sefarad*'s Proustian opening, in which the narrator reflects on the food he used to eat in his hometown, he confesses in his very first sentence that 'nos gusta cultivar su nostalgia' (*S*, p.159), before reflecting on 'la misma [...] melancolía que nos quedaba' (*S*, 165).[135] By drawing attention to his own nostalgia here, the narrator clearly indicates its connections to—and its knotty relationship with—the melancholy mode of narration that will emerge over the subsequent pages, ensuring that the tense symbiosis between these two aesthetic sensibilities is established at the outset of the novel. The narrator's own nostalgia thereby becomes another catalyst in the creation of a melancholy aesthetic mode that is both personal and collective, in that it subsumes the stories and experiences of others, thereby ensuring that the violent potential of nostalgia for the past to revise or erase earlier events and experiences is also folded into and addressed by the aesthetic attitude of *Sefarad* as a whole. Such violence is endemic to nostalgic sentiment, as scholars such as Sarah Bracke, Paul Gilroy, and Renato

---

[134] 'What I wanted was not for us Jews to be saved from the Nazis. [...] what I wanted was to not be a Jew' (*S*, 114).

[135] 'We like to nurture our nostalgia' (*S*, 1). And 'The same [...] melancholy that awaited us'.

Rosaldo have argued, although nostalgia's very nature ensures that its violent potential is not always immediately perceptible. For Rosaldo, the violence of colonial nostalgia in particular, for example, takes the form of a contradictory commitment of imperial violence and subsequent mourning of its victims by the colonizers.[136] Originating from a modernized perspective, this constitutes a longing in Western European civilization for premodern societies to be a stable and static reference point. The uneven conditions of modernity and imperialist destruction thus lead to nostalgic longings. 'While such longing emerges from violence and destruction', as Bracke argues, 'a disavowal of violence occurs at the heart of nostalgia, notably through its characteristic mode of innocence'.[137] Nostalgia thereby enables an erasure of colonialism's crimes by locating the agent of change within time passing rather than within those exhibiting nostalgia. As Nauman Naqvi observes, 'the authority of nostalgia relies on a remarkably violent set of epistemological and institutional histories'.[138] These obscure nostalgia's violence and power, while attempting to uphold Western cultural privilege and legitimize the erasure of other perspectives. And, in the Hispanic case, nostalgia for a cultural Golden Age is further complicated by the fact that such prior cultural efflorescence occurred concomitantly with Spanish imperial prowess. Nostalgia is predicated on cultural and historical privilege, which also recalls the misguided European former construction of Spain as a late cultural outsider.

Nostalgia for another time and place arises when one has opportunity, as well as the requisite power and the privilege, to be nostalgic. The narrator of *Sefarad* draws on such a position as this, since he is not only able to be nostalgic in his empathetic imaginings, but also able to transform said nostalgia into a melancholy aesthetic mode of reflection on the past. In *Sefarad*, the passing of time—and, by extension, the gulf between past and present—that is essential to a melancholy perspective on history thus conceals the potential violence in the narrator's nostalgic tendencies. Whereas for Paul Gilroy, power and privilege lead to what he calls 'postimperial melancholia', which is to say, for instance, the inability to acknowledge the painful changes wrought by the end of the British Empire and the

---

[136] See Renato Rosaldo, 'Imperialist Nostalgia', in *Representations*, 26 (1989), 107–122 (108).

[137] Bracke, 'Nostalgia's Violence', 4.

[138] Nauman Naqvi, *The Nostalgic Subject: A Genealogy of the "Critique of Nostalgia"* (Università di Messina: CIRSDIG, working paper 23, 2007), 3. Cited in Bracke, 'Nostalgia's Violence', 3.

unwillingness of certain beneficiaries of imperial power or its afterlife to mourn its crimes, for the narrator of *Sefarad*, any form of melancholy or nostalgia that is postimperial is intrinsically bound up with the bygone Golden Age of Spanish literature and its implications.[139] Gilroy's transference of a Freudian reading of melancholia from an individual's behaviour to the behaviour of a society at large entails a conflation of the terms melancholia and nostalgia, as Bracke and Alistair Bonnet have noted.[140] Nevertheless, when melancholy is understood—as it is in the present study—as a late literary mode that engages with the past from a perspective of acknowledging its irreconcilability with the present, then it constitutes a step beyond nostalgia. In *Sefarad*, however, these vestigial nostalgic elements still linger to trouble the narrative's melancholy.

Although the nostalgia in *Sefarad* is not directly bound up with the colonial history of Western European modernity *per se*, it nevertheless contains an inherent potential for metaphorical violence towards past events, given the enmeshed histories of persecution, expulsion, and exile alluded to across the entire novel. Intimately connected with Enlightenment understandings of progress, the destructiveness of modernity is inherited by—and thus constitutive of—subsequent nostalgia. The contradictions of modernity, along with the ambivalences of human nature and experience, are thematized in *Sefarad*'s narrative, such that the violence of nostalgia is imported into the narrator's construction of the novel's explicitly melancholy aesthetics. For Cubillo, this leaves the impression that the narrator 'seems to have a hard time imagining a world in which cultural difference does not become an alienating factor', despite the narrator's desire to establish a pan-European melancholy narrative.[141] The sudden estrangement of Jewish citizens and political dissidents, for example, are presented alongside stories of cultural differences between lovers ('Valdemún'), childhood reminiscences ('Sacristán'), and other experiences outside of twentieth-century European totalitarianism, exile, or diaspora. Cubillo's reading suggests that in trying to bring together these discrete experiences, the narrator ends up reiterating the divisions that prevented their being drawn together initially. Yet, rather than either establishing the

[139] Paul Gilroy, *After Empire: Multiculture or Postcolonial Melancholia* (London: Routledge, 2004).

[140] See Bracke, 'Nostalgia's Violence', 4 and Alistair Bonnet, *Left in the Past: Radicalism and the Politics of Nostalgia* (New York: Continuum, 2010), 125.

[141] See Cubillo, *Memories of the Maghreb*, 115.

perpetuation—and implied condemnation—of such differences or suggesting a troubling equivalence among the lives and fates of those whose
tales he tells, the narrator of *Sefarad* walks a finer line from nostalgia
towards a distinct form of melancholy. Remaining deeply sensible of the
unchangeability of the past from which he is separated, he also maintains
a keen awareness both of the dangers and of the importance of difference,
as well as the tensions between individuals and communities and among
Spanish, Jewish, and European cultural identities. The narrator of *Sefarad*
resorts to a form of melancholy that grows out of his personal nostalgia, as
well as out of his attempt to corral the experiences and histories of others.
Not only does this evince a tendency towards suggesting a commonality
among others' experiences that might be mistaken for universalization, it
also gestures towards a euphemistic longing for a pre-difference time.
That is to say, a temporal nostalgia for a time when those who have been
persecuted were unaware of the forthcoming dangers visited on them
because of what makes them different, in most cases their Jewishness. The
resultant melancholy of long exile described in these stories (*S*, 746) ultimately emerges as a narrative aesthetic compromised by a euphemistic
form of temporal nostalgia.

When carried over into his empathetic imaginings of others' lives, there
is a vestigial threat of replicating of nostalgia's potential for violent erasure, which, in turn, feeds back into the narrator's own recollections. By
inheriting nostalgia's violent potential, however, the narrator's melancholy
aesthetic attitude in *Sefarad* is revealed to be profoundly sensible of these
tensions. In 'Sefarad', the novel's final chapter, for example, the narrator's
voice surfaces again as he echoes Isaac Salama's story and the nostalgia of
Isaac's father for the lost Jewish homeland. When describing the Jewish
quarter of his Spanish hometown located near the Alcázar (a Moorish cita-
del or palace), the narrator muses how 'Quizás la llave que se correspondía
con el gran ojo de la cerradura se la llevaron los expulsados y la fueron
legando de padres a hijos en las generaciones sucesivas del destierro igual
que la legua y los sonorous nombres castellanos' (*S*, 694).[142] Recalling the
narrator's earlier imagining of Isaac Salama's recollection of his father's
nostalgia, this reinforces the notion of passing on or inheriting nostalgia
through analeptic structures in the novel, while also implicitly echoing

---

[142] 'Maybe the people who have gone carried with them the key that fit this large keyhole,
maybe they handed it down from father to son through generations of exile, just as the language and sonorous Spanish names were perpetuated' (*S*, 349).

forms of narrative epigonality and literary inheritance in *Sefarad*. In another explicit evocation of the Jewish expulsion from Sepharad outside of Isaac Salama's chapter, the narrator recalls being told by a school teacher that the Jewish expulsion was a moment 'de mayor gloria en la Historia de España [...] cuando se reconquistó Granada, y se descubrió América, y nuestra patria recién unificada empezó a ser un imperio' (*S*, 695).[143] This reaffirms the complexity of the entanglements and the divisions between Spanish imperial cultural history and a lost Jewish homeland. The nostalgic potential of Sepharad's name is recalled through the image of a house key passed on through generations of exiles. Yet, as in Isaac's story, nostalgia for the past is overwritten and transformed. Sepharad is no longer seen here by the teacher as the lost Jewish homeland, but rather as a conquered part of a new Spain, indeed a new Spanish empire. It is only the Spanish language and Spanish names, furthermore, that are passed on down the generations in the teacher's account. The narrator's desire to construct a pan-European narrative of exile, displacement, and oppression that acknowledges the separation of past and present wrestles with his reliance on instances of nostalgia for earlier moments in time, alternative histories, and lost places, which suggests a potential to redress not only the historical gulf between past and present, but also the separation of Spanishness and Europeanness.

The threat of erasure and entrenchment are further intensified by the narrator's subsequent account of meeting Emile Roman, a Romanian writer of Sephardic Jewish origin, whom he describes as speaking an antiquated form of Spanish 'que debía de parecerse al que hablaban en 1492 los habitants de aquella casa del barrio de Alcázar' (*S*, 696).[144] The narrator's remark draws a direct line of connection between this exiled writer—also a latecomer, out of time and place—in his present and the Sephardic Jews as representatives of nostalgic sentiment towards the lost Jewish homeland, while also recalling the genesis of the Spanish nation and its imperial project whose later collapse would inculcate Spanish cultural and literary epigonal lateness within Europe. Nevertheless, the nostalgic potential of the idea of Sepharad is emptied out as Roman declares of his family, 'pero nosotros no nos llamábamos sefardíes, [...] nosotros éramos

---

[143] 'Of the greatest glory in the history of Spain [...] when Granada was reconquered and America discovered, and when our newly unified country became an empire' (*S*, 350).

[144] 'Which must have been very similar to the Spanish spoken in 1492 by the people who lived in that house in the Alcázar barrio' (*S*, 351).

españoles' (*S*, 696).[145] Here, again, the idea of a lost Jewish homeland is reconfigured in terms of the Spanish nation. As before, on the few occasions that Sepharad is mentioned in the novel that bears its name as its title, the nostalgia connected with the lost homeland is evoked and then removed. In this instance, the narrator presents himself as an outside observer, who, given his own lack of identification with the former inhabitants of this neighbourhood, may be presumed to not be Jewish. At a certain remove, then, he attempts to reconcile the notion of a lost Sephardic Jewish homeland with the Spanish nation in his narrative reconstruction of events. Thematizing these cultural distinctions, setting them beside one another yet erasing neither, leads to the narrator's melancholy sensibility of the irreconcilability of the past and the present. Aware of their coincidence and contingency, and positioned at a remove from the conflicts he stages, the narrator is able to bend them to his will in fashioning a nostalgia-inflected melancholy narrative that desires to resolve them, yet holds them in tension. In the final chapter of the novel, the narrator recalls 'los romances y los cantos de niños que los hebreos de Salónica y Rodas llevarían consigo en el largo viaje infernal hacia Auschwitz' (*S*, 694).[146] Here an explicit link is forged between the fifteenth-century expulsion of the Jews from Sepharad and the Holocaust, which, as Linhard suggests, are brought together here via a literary cultural connection, not necessarily an historical one. Nevertheless, it is once again a connection that is profoundly suggestive of temporal nostalgia, of the desire to return to the past and for history to take another course. The narrator, exiled from these moments, can only gaze back towards history, such that the novel's nostalgic moments emerge ultimately as freighted with melancholy.

Both the narrator's empathetic imagining of Isaac Salama's life and his account of his own nostalgia indicate how longing for a return to the past paves the way towards *Sefarad*'s constructed melancholy aesthetic attitude. In both cases, the expulsion of the Sephardic Jews from their homeland is connected to twentieth-century history through the explicit invocation of the name of Sepharad. Yet Isaac Salama not only suggests a direct temporal and historical connection between these events, but also a literary and cultural affiliation.[147] In the narrator's empathetic imagining,

---

[145] 'We didn't call ourselves Sephardim, […] We were Spanish' (*S*, 351).
[146] 'The poems and children's songs that the Jews of Salonica and Rhodes would carry with them on the long, hellish journey to Auschwitz' (*S*, 350).
[147] See Linhard, *Jewish Spain*, 63.

Isaac repeatedly quotes from Baudelaire's poem 'A une passante' ('To a Woman Passing By'), first published in *Les fleurs du mal* (1857), one of the most significant cornerstones of modern European literature. Isaac's moments of Baudelairean allusion invite parallels between the poem's nostalgic account of fleeting encounter with a woman in the street and the missed opportunities that have passed Isaac by during his life of exile, including his loss of mobility after a car crash with an oncoming truck left him paralysed, and his encounter with a Spanish woman on a train with whom he experiences an instantaneous mutual attraction, but whom he never contacts again (*S*, 350–54). As Isaac's story comes to a close, he recites the poem's final lines, which give this chapter its title, while simultaneously echoing the thoughts of his nostalgic father:

> Oh tú a quien yo hubiera amado, recitó el señor Isaac Salama aquella tarde en su dispacho del Ateneo Español, con la misma grave persadumbre conque habría dicho los versículos del kaddish en memoria de su padre, mientras llegaba por la ventana abierta el sonido de la sirena de un barco y la salmodia de un muecín, oh tú que lo sabías (*S*, 354).[148]

By quoting from Baudelaire's poem, the narrator's empathetic imagining of Isaac invokes an earlier work of modern European literature, echoes of which are complicated by a sense of nostalgia for the Sephardic Jewish homeland. Yet, in a further example of abandoning nostalgia even as it is invoked, Isaac imagines that his father—the embodiment of Sephardic nostalgia earlier in the novel—has now passed away. In this passage, questions of Spanishness, Europeanness, and Jewishness are brought together as Isaac cites Baudelaire and simultaneously imagines chanting the Kaddish in mourning of his father, while in his office in a Spanish cultural museum in Tangier. Spanish culture here is exiled and cordoned off in a museum,

---

[148] '*Oh you, whom I would have loved*, he recited that evening in his office at the Ateneo Español, moved as deeply as if he were chanting the Kaddish in his father's memory, the sound of a ship's horn and the music of a muezzin's call came through the open window. *Oh you, who knew so well*' [Italics in translation] (*S*, 122). The final stanza of the original French poem reads 'Ailleurs, bien loin d'ici! trop tard! *jamais* peut-être! / Car j'ignore où tu fuis, tu ne sais où je vais, / Ô toi que j'eusse aimée, ô toi qui le savais!'. See Charles Baudelaire, *Œuvres complètes, tome 1*, ed. by Yves-Gérard le Dantec and Claude Pichois (Paris: Gallimard, 1966), 88. The most recent English translation reads, 'Far from this place! too late! *never* perhaps! / Neither one knowing where the other goes, / O you I might have loved, as well you know!'. See Charles Baudelaire, 'To a Woman Passing By', in *The Flowers of Evil*, trans. by James McGowan (Oxford: Oxford University Press, 2008), 189.

while his father and the idea of a lost Jewish homeland have also passed away. Isaac is left to chant lines from Baudelaire, transforming the poem's nostalgia into a melancholy reflection on these losses. Once again, the conflicts and contradictions of these multiple cultural traditions are evoked but not reconciled, troublingly thematized but not erased, from the narrator's perspective of historical and geographical exile. His imagining of the exiled Isaac's poetic allusions thus enhances the pathos of melancholy of *Sefarad*, while ensuring it remains partly determined by nostalgic inflections.

Boym's own analysis of Baudelaire's poem, which Salama implicitly recalls in this passage as an example of his own nostalgia, asserts that 'the chance of happiness is revealed in a flash and the rest of the poem is a nostalgia for what could have been; it is not a nostalgia for an ideal past, but for the present perfect and its lost potential'.[149] Imagining that which might have been thereby enacts a violent rewriting of that which was. Isaac's father's nostalgia for a lost homeland and his son's nostalgia for a lost moment in time are brought together here, but ultimately their nostalgic potential is extinguished. Isaac's encounter with the woman on a train in 'Oh tú que lo sabías' mirrors that which is described in Baudelaire's poem and gestures towards a heightened fictionality in the narrative, as well as its overtly and overly constructed melancholy nature. It serves once more to recall the staged conflict between a European and a distinctly Spanish cultural tradition in *Sefarad*. These examples of irrecoverable losses transform the nostalgia in *Sefarad*'s narrative into a partially compromised form of melancholy. The irreconcilability of present with the past for the narrator, and for those whose lives he empathetically imagines, is articulated from a nostalgic point of departure, which develops into a melancholy outlook on history and awareness of the gap that cannot be bridged, the tensions that appear to be insoluble, and the absence that cannot be filled. The nostalgia for a time before, however, brings with it a potentially violent desire to reconfigure or even erase the events of the past, while re-emphasising the conflicts and divisions that the narrator struggles to overcome in the writing of *Sefarad*.

The narrator's melancholy perspective in the novel, which views the events of the past as unbridgeably distant from the present, is not only rooted in forms of nostalgia for the Sephardic homeland, but also inflected by a nostalgia for specific moments in the past like Isaac Salama's encounter on the train. These cannot be altered. This nostalgia, then, is a

---

[149] Boym, *The Future of Nostalgia*, 21.

nostalgia for another time, not just another place, as well as the desire to undo or remake those moments, to return to a particular temporal juncture, and to wish that history might proceed along another path. Nostalgia is not only reworked in the creation of *Sefarad*'s melancholy aesthetic attitude, but the violent potential for temporal nostalgia to erase or rewrite the past remains embedded within this melancholy, which further complicates it and constitutes a key element of its sense of irresolution. Throughout *Sefarad*, the narrator regularly imagines instances where characters' differences—be they ethnic, religious, social, or political—suddenly endanger them. Potentially violent nostalgia for a time before these moments when differences became a liability, for the possibility that things might have turned out differently, and for characters not to have lost a relatively stable identity, is explicitly suggested in the chapter 'Eres'. Such temporal nostalgia is also articulated by Isaac Salama in the chapter 'Oh tú que lo sabías', drawing further connections between his nostalgia for an earlier time and his father's nostalgia for Sepharad as he echoes his father's nostalgic speech patterns:

> Se da cuenta de que está repitiendo las mismas palabras que le escuchó a su padre tantas veces, el mismo afán de corregir el pasado tano solo en unos minutos, en segundos: [...] la vida entera quebrada para siempre en una fracción imperceptible de tiempo, en una eternidad de remordimiento. (*S*, 341)[150]

Crucially, however, the structuring narrator of the entire novel is consistently revealed to as a self-conscious melancholy latecomer in both an historical and a cultural sense. Cubillo argues that in attempting to tell one paradigmatic story of exile and persecution in twentieth-century Europe, Muñoz Molina ends up transforming potential hybridity into a monolingual identity: 'Rather than developing a polyphonic discourse, [he] longs for a time when those who would later be persecuted were still not aware of how their difference could be used to separate them from the rest'.[151] Each of *Sefarad*'s chapters is structured around particular moments where, in Cubillo's words, people 'woke up one day to find out that they were no longer members of the community at large, and suddenly realized their

---

[150] '[He] realizes he is reprising the words he heard his father speak so many times, the same desire to go back and correct a few minutes, a few seconds – [...] an entire life shattered forever in one fraction of a moment, an eternity of remorse' (*S*, 113).

[151] Cubillo, *Memories of the Maghreb*, 115.

cultural or political diversity had turned them into a liability'.[152] By paying attention to the narrator's late historical perspective and the melancholy attitude that emerges from nostalgia, however, it becomes clear that *Sefarad* articulates a more nuanced realization of the impossibility of changing the past rather than simply wishing it had been different. This self-conscious melancholy emerges as ultimately more complex and more sophisticated than blunt nostalgic longing. In thematizing forms of nostalgia from his late perspective, the narrator of *Sefarad* allows the desire to return to times and places in the past to transform into the melancholy acknowledgement that this cannot occur.

The chapter 'Eres', where the narrator predominantly speaks in the second person in an effort to communicate empathy for the historical figures with whose plight he engages, closes with a summary of the moments when the narrator's imaginings of, among others, Walter Benjamin, Jean Améry, Primo Levi, Margarete Buber-Neumann, and Eugenia Ginzburg realize the precarity of their situations in places that no longer belong to them: 'Caminas por la ciudad que ya no es la tuya' (*S*, 616), the narrator ominously declares.[153] He then explicitly quotes the opening line from Kafka's *Die Verwandlung* (1912). Returning as a mantra-like literary touchstone in this chapter, the quotation builds on earlier references to the lives of Kafka and his lover Milena Jesenskà in other chapters: 'Una mañana, al despertarse, Gregor Samsa se encontró convertido en un enorme insecto' (*S*, 615).[154] Once again, the narrator cites a canonical European modernist text as a means of expressing the moments of sudden, perilous difference experienced by the historical figures he includes in *Sefarad*. With this direct citation he once more recalls the conflict between European and Spanish literary traditions staged in the novel. The narrator's words here revivify the tensions between European literary and cultural reference points as the narrator attempts to express a commonality of experience among those lives and histories he mentions. Yet here, it is the differences and distinctions which stand out, as nostalgic desire to return to the past, to change it, and even to erase and rewrite it, becomes transformed into the melancholy resignation of the impossibility of this.

---

[152] Cubillo, *Memories of the Maghreb*, 115.

[153] 'You walk through the city that is no longer yours' (*S*, 299).

[154] 'One morning, Gregor Samsa awoke and found himself transformed into an enormous insect' (*S*, 298). See also Daniela Omlor, 'Death and Desire: Memories of Milena Jesenská in Jorge Semprún and Antonio Muñoz Molina', *Modern Language Review*, 116:3 (2021), 387–407.

His narrative thus appears to be unable to reconcile its more specific contexts, namely, distinct but connected national and cultural traditions, with
the broader picture of common experience of geographical and temporal
exile which it seeks to paint.

DIFFERENCE AND COMPROMISE

If there is one image above all others in *Sefarad* that encapsulates the act
of setting these diverse elements alongside one another, it occurs in the
chapter 'Berghof', when the narrator remarks how, while sat working at
his desk,

> Otro lugar surge cuando la penumbra empieza a volverse oscuridad y fos-
> forecen en ella la luz de la pantalla del ordenador y la de la lámpara [...] La
> mano que posa sobre el ratón deja de ser la mía. [...] De la oscuridad [...]
> surge sin premeditación mía una figura, una presencia que no es del todo
> invención ni tampoco recuerdo (*S*, 439).[155]

As he begins to imagine the character whose story he is imagining and
retelling, he experiences a sense of disorientation. Nevertheless, he is still
able to distinguish himself from those whom he imagines in his narrative.
This gestures towards a distinct self-consciousness with regard to constructing his narrative and an awareness that what is emerging is uncertain or
inchoate. He acknowledges that it is neither memory nor invention, allowing himself some distance from his attempted mapping of interconnected
lives and fates. As he goes on to describe a memory of walking home from
the beach one day, he observes that other people's 'pisadas [...] se con-
vierten en las delicadas oquedades de sombra' (*S*, 439), before returning to
the image of him working in the dark at his desk.[156] Redolent of *Dora
Bruder*'s 'marque en creux'—the hollow imprints left by historical figures
that are to be filled by the narrator's words over the course of that novel—
these traces in the sand constitute metaphorical receptacles for the narrator's lateness and melancholy. That this scene takes place at the narrator's
desk surrounded by his collected objects also prefigures the novel's epigonal

[155] 'Another place rises before as shadows begin to turn to darkness lighted only by the
phosphorescence of the computer screen and the lamp [...] The hand resting beside the
mouse isn't mine any longer. [...] From the darkness [...] without any premeditation on my
part, a figure emerges, a presence that is not entirely invention, or memory either' (*S*, 177).
[156] 'Footprints [...] become delicate hollows of shadows' (*S*, 177).

and melancholy conclusion. He offers an image which implies, on the one hand, an awareness of the contradictory elements and constitutive tensions of the self-consciously late and melancholy aesthetics in the narrative of *Sefarad*, while on the other hand, observing a commitment to the construction of the narrative in spite of this. 'Unas cosas traen otras', remarks the narrator, 'como unidas entre sí por un hilo tenue de azares triviales. Las conchas en la orilla del mar [...], los trozos curvados de ánforas rotas. Hay que ir dejándoles llegar, o que tirar poco a poco de ellas [...] sin que el hilo se quiebre' (*S*, 441).[157] The narrator evokes a sense that discovery or understanding is just out of reach, as well as articulating through the image of the delicate thread the precarity of the narrative of interwoven empathetic imaginings that he has created. This is subtly reminiscent of the Benjaminian Angel of History and its melancholy perception of connected events proceeding it as one great piled up catastrophe, an image which is itself not dissimilar to the fragments of pottery in the grains of sand on the shore in *Sefarad*. A few pages later, the narrator recounts how, when he returned to the beach,

> Tomaba un puñado de arena en la mano y luego la abría para que la arena fuse cayendo poco a poco, en un hilo tenue, en la fugacidad de unos segundos. Primero era algo sólido en el interior del puño apretado, cerrado como las valvas de un molusco para los dedos pequeños de mi hijo, que intentaba abrirlo y no podia, si acaso lograba desprender un dedo respirando muy fuerte, pero el dedo volvía a su lugar y el puño continuaba cerrado. Se abre luego despacio, y la arena tan compacta se disuelve en nada, no quedan más que unos granos mínimos en la ancha palma abierta, puntas minerales heridas por la luz (*S*, 449).[158]

Combining his two earlier images, this recollection shows a narrator who is aware of the instability and possible futility of his narrative enterprise, who may break the threads in attempting to weave a web of

---

[157] 'Some images evoke others, as if joined by the slim thread of coincidence: shells on the seashore [...], curved bits of a broken amphora. One must let the thread roll off the spool, or pull lightly lest it break'.

[158] 'I took a handful of sand then opened my fingers to let it trickle away in a thin thread. First it was something solid inside my closed fist, closed like the valves of a mollusk to the small fingers of my son, who tried to pry it open but couldn't; if he managed to pull up one finger, breathing hard, the finger would lock back into place. Then the hand would open, slowly, and the sand that had been so compact would dissolve, leaving nothing but a few tiny grains on my broad, open palm, mineral dots sun glinting in the sun' (*S*, 182–183).

interconnections or who may allow fragments to fall from his grasp like an unspooling thread as he tries to cling to them. Nevertheless, his intent remains to retain at least some glinting particles of this, suggesting that, beyond the tensions and contradictions of *Sefarad*'s narrative, something might yet remain to be salvaged from its fragments. The rewards of trying to prise open the connective tissues between the intermingled tragedies of exile and expulsion in *Sefarad* may be residual, but there is—this image would suggest—something worthwhile to be achieved in the attempt.

Unlike the figures whose lives and fates he empathetically imagines, the narrator of *Sefarad* was not a victim of totalitarian persecution during the twentieth century. From his historically and culturally late perspective, the melancholy aesthetic attitude in *Sefarad* that expresses not only the fundamental irreconcilability of the past and the present, but also the nuanced differences of culture, context, and experience, stems from nostalgic impulses. Their mobilization in the service of constructing of a self-consciously melancholy mode of narration does not erase the potential contained within the narrator's nostalgia for the further erasure of those who were not so fortunate to arrive as late as he. Nevertheless, this violent potential is transformed precisely through his self-conscious awareness of this lateness into a form of aesthetic melancholy. Such rewriting moves beyond what Boym identifies as the negative outcomes of solely 'reflective nostalgia', which is to say, an 'abdication of personal responsibility, a guilt-free homecoming, an ethical and aesthetic failure'.[159] The narrator of *Sefarad* chooses instead to channel his nostalgic personal longings into a broader melancholy outlook on the past and on cultural, historical, and experiential difference. His acknowledgement of the gulf between the past and the present may not repair the violence of the nostalgia that initiates it, yet it cannot but gesture towards an awareness of such potential. If the recognition that nothing can be done about the past includes his nostalgic longings for another place and another time, then the replication of those feelings are, for better or for worse, a constitutive part of the melancholy in *Sefarad*. In writing a nostalgia-inflected, yet ultimately melancholy pan-European saga of suffering and persecution, the narrator fashions an outlook on the past that embodies the potential violence of nostalgia's capability to erase others' stories, yet remains sensible of its shortcomings. As Su observes, 'even the most ideologically compromised forms of

---

[159] Boym, *The Future of Nostalgia*, xiv.

longing express in attenuated fashion a genuine human need'.[160] *Sefarad* accordingly takes pains to employ the tools of nostalgia to point beyond itself. In its late and melancholy aesthetic state, Muñoz Molina's novel offers less a perpetuated distinction between the Hispanic and the European, but something more akin to the potential for permeability.

Returning to the narrator's self-conscious reflection on the process of writing the novel that might one day become *Sefarad*, his suggestion that the situations and places which he considered including in his narrative mysteriously came together without assuming precedence over each other now takes on a new importance. He observes how they illuminated each other, remarking that 'podía deshacer o modificar a mi antojo, y en las que ninguna imagen anulaba a las otras o alcanzaba una primacía segura sobre ellas, o perdía en beneficio del conjunto su singularidad irreductible' (*S*, 383–384).[161] Given the historically and culturally late position the narrator establishes in *Sefarad*, the creation of melancholy out of nostalgia, as compromised as this could be, proves itself to be generative in that it draws on and highlights extant tensions between Hispanic and European literary and cultural contexts, undoing—and perhaps 'unravelling towards sameness', as Ginger might term it—the ambiguous relations between them.[162] Rather than consigning it to the background, leaving its legacy ostracized or relegated to obscurity, *Sefarad* suggests a possibility for Spanish literature to exist as a dynamic, native cultural agent alongside— or even within—European culture. This is not, however, an act of normalization or subsummation, but a mutually enriching process of illumination; neither homogenization nor conflation, but a search for commonality in complexity and uncertainty, and—by extension—futurity. Just as for Jameson, non-modern Spanish literary difference is ultimately indicative of Spanish literature's worthy inclusion within the broader paradigms of European modernity and modernism, so *Sefarad*'s lateness and nostalgia-inflected melancholy constitute another distinct iteration of the late European novel. An iteration, moreover, which perhaps more than any other novel in this study, evokes fundamental constitutive tensions between the national and the European.

---

[160] Su, *Ethics and Nostalgia*, 3.

[161] 'I could break or modify at my whim, and in which no single image nullified the others or gained certain precedence over the others, or lost its irreducible singularity while benefiting from their coming together'.

[162] Ginger, *Instead of Modernity*, 6.

CHAPTER 5

The Event Horizon of European Fiction

When a glass falls and shatters, the pieces do not spring back together and reform a vessel. When a building falls into ruins, its stones will not stack themselves on top of one another and reconstitute the edifice that once stood. If you were to tear out all of the pages of this book, they would not reassemble themselves without assistance into *Late Europeans and Melancholy Fiction at the Turn of the Millennium*. Atomically speaking, there is no actual reason why this should be the case. Yet the universe moves from an ordered to a diffused state: once dispersed, matter cannot be retrieved. This entropy, which governs reality, tends towards disorder. On a subatomic level, any change is reversible; on this plane of existence, however, things age and decay, defining a strict direction of travel in time, a universal entropic lateness. The amount of disorder always increases. The above scenarios can never occur as the requisite suspension of entropy needed to reconstruct broken glassware, a crumbling ruin, or a vandalized tome is, if not impossible, then just highly unlikely. And, in a way, it is in this entropic shadowland that the present study, as well as the collection of late and melancholy novels it has examined, situate themselves. And it matters where one stands to observe them.

In answer to the question of what literature is good for—'à quoi bon la littérature?'—W. G. Sebald once remarked, 'einzig vielleicht dazu, daß wir

© The Author(s), under exclusive license to Springer Nature
Switzerland AG 2022
I. Ellison, *Late Europeans and Melancholy Fiction at the Turn of the
Millennium*, Palgrave Studies in Modern European Literature,
https://doi.org/10.1007/978-3-030-95447-5_5

uns erinnern und daß wir begreifen lernen, daß es sonderbare, von keiner Kausallogik zu ergründende Zusammenhänge gibt'.[1] One key aim of this study, however, was to investigate the apparent coincidence of the mutual articulation of shared thematic concerns, as well as aesthetic and stylistic similarities, in several novels from different national linguistic and literary contexts around a particular moment in time, while also shedding light on these works' significant literary influences and aesthetic interlocutors. This book has sought to consider the imaginative affinities and the productive differences among the three novels it takes as its objects of investigation and to think about what these say about the individual works and about European literature more broadly. If the preceding chapters have reflected the legacies of various literary traditions, along with what Cohen terms the 'conditions of possibility' for the emergence of the literary works they examine, then these novels' late and melancholy aesthetics constitute the dark back of the mirror which makes reflections visible.[2]

This study began by asking what makes European literature European. In order to shed some light on this complex issue, the close readings of *Dora Bruder*, *Austerlitz*, and *Sefarad* in the preceding chapters have attempted to provide an account of their self-conscious narrators, of their late and melancholy aesthetics, as well as of the implications of understanding these novels as a collective expression of a latent potential for the re-enchantment of European literature and culture. Aesthetic attitudes of melancholy lateness, this study suggests, are a constitutive element of European novels written and published at the end of the twentieth century and the beginning of the twenty-first. In order to ascertain whether such a thing as European cultural renewal emerges in the wake of the novels that have been examined in this study's preceding chapters and, indeed, other novels, further observation and analysis will be required from a future perspective. This will be a task for later reading.

---

[1] W. G. Sebald, *Campo Santo*, ed. by Sven Meyer (Munich: Carl Hanser, 2003), 247. 'Perhaps only to help us to remember, and teach us to understand that some strange coincidences cannot be explained by causal logic'. The translation is taken from *Campo Santo*, trans. by Anthea Bell (London: Penguin, 2005), 213–214.

[2] See Walter Cohen, *A History of European Literature: From Antiquity to the Present* (Oxford: Oxford University Press, 2017), 7 and 501.

Whither 'European' Fiction?

Lateness, in this study, is understood not merely accident or happenstance, but as its first principle, a deliberately sought after and repeatedly implemented motif in the novels examined in the preceding pages, as well as a key structural and aesthetic element in these works. *Dora Bruder*, *Austerlitz*, and *Sefarad* respond in different ways to a sense of cultural exhaustion and senescence in Europe, such that the narrators understand themselves as epigonal figures coming after canonical writers and works of modern European literature, as well as to a sense of historical lateness, since they are writing at the close of the twentieth century. Folding such cultural and historical lateness into an aesthetics of lateness contributes towards the establishment and enhancement of the melancholy perspective on history exhibited in these novels: the past is always irrecoverably separated from their narrators' present. This allows for, this study has attempted to suggest, both the culmination of and potential departure from their late and melancholy state.

The variously mediated—or, to recall Sebald's Bernhard-inspired term, 'periscopic'—narratives of these novels indicates a self-consciousness of their lateness and melancholy. By holding on to Nietzsche's notion that latecomers (*Spätlinge*) have the potential to become firstcomers (*Erstlinge*) through their self-consciousness of their lateness—and, by extension, their melancholy outlook—this study has attempted to show that in the novels it examines, each narrator's self-conscious mode of writing contains the latent potential to overcome their lateness and melancholy, since it implies in various ways a sense of possible futurity and renewal. Such self-consciously styled lateness and melancholy, moreover, may be read as a distinctly—albeit not uniquely—European stance that might further imply a sense of futurity due to its parallels with Nietzsche's figure of the 'good European': an intentionally assumed pose. The mode of writing among this group of novels might indeed be considered a kind of Andersonian 'imagined community' of works that exists across national contexts in European culture, while still having national literary traditions at heart. The sustained tension between the nation and a broader European context, not its resolution, is key to these late and melancholy novels. Ultimately, this study has brought together a group of novels with common thematic, aesthetic, and stylistic concerns across national borders, each of which at the same time exhibits its own specificities that are determined by its national context. What has emerged, then, over the course of

Late Europeans and Melancholy Fiction at the Turn of the Millennium is a sense that among these novels, there throbs a tension between the contexts of the national and the European—a tension, moreover, which is a foundational element of their aesthetic practice and which can be most clearly observed and analysed by reading these novels alongside one another.

Tensions among the national and the European thus emerge in various ways in all of the novels examined in this study as constitutive elements of their aesthetics. It is this most of all, this study submits, that marks them out, both as distinctly European works of fiction and as distinct works of European fiction. Inevitably, perhaps, in such comparative work, there exists the danger of overlap and repetition. Comparative work on Modiano and Sebald has remained heretofore principally limited to thematic and formal concerns, often focusing upon areas of commonality, generally regarding the presentation and articulation of memory in the novels. Indeed, Modiano's novel shares many thematic resonances with the work of W. G. Sebald in particular, of which this book has chosen to steer well clear for fear of duplication and staleness. The present volume is not, however, the first time that *Dora Bruder* and *Austerlitz* have appeared alongside one another in literary criticism. The two authors are practically contemporaries, after all: both belong to the same post-war generation of writers, who grew up in the shadow of the Second World War and the collective silence of their parents' generation with regard to it. Both Sebald's and Modiano's subsequent œuvres might be summarized as forms of enquiry, yet while Sebald invents a plausible fiction out of historical fact, Modiano attempts to reconstruct a single historical existence out of documentary evidence and hypothesis. Sebald puts forward an infinitely detailed and labyrinthine meditation on the crisis of European culture, while Modiano returns to question identity, family, and flight during the Occupation. Where Sebald's novel broadens its scope, in other words, Modiano's tightens its focus. It is also worth noting that, unlike Sebald's looping hypotaxis, Modiano's prose is characteristically straightforward, employing for the most part a relatively unchallenging vocabulary. Moreover, whereas in *Austerlitz* the narrator is submerged in extended periods of the protagonist's recollections and layers of history, the narrative of *Dora Bruder* is much more disordered. The narrator's recollections of his investigations into the lives of the Bruder family and others are presented unchronologically in short sections resembling unmarked chapters, most of which are between two and eight pages in length with the longest running to fourteen. These sections are composed of relatively short paragraphs, again unlike Sebald's largely unparagraphed style. This suggests that, while conscious of his historical and literary lateness, like the narrator of *Austerlitz*, the narrator of *Dora Bruder* is animated with a sense of urgency in completing his task, as opposed to a more resigned weariness in undertaking it.

Modiano's Dora, who appears in photographs that remain unseen by readers of the novel, once existed; Jacques Austerlitz did not, despite his seeming to appear in photographs in the novel. How is it possible, then, to distinguish between the archival historical identity and the fabricated once, particularly given the Nazi regime's predilection for annihilating traces of annihilation? Both novels confront their readers on a very everyday level of association with visual or textual reproductions of images, cuttings from newspapers, tickets, and letters. Yet there is also a subtextual attempt to comprehend it all. The narrators of *Dora Bruder* and *Austerlitz*, as well as the narrator of *Sefarad* to a certain extent, are not certain of being able to make sense of everything they come across except in the effort of recording it. And whatever sense there is, it is primarily aesthetic: creating in prose a decent pattern out of what happens to come their way becomes a preoccupation free from higher ambitions other than, for a brief moment in time, to salvage something out of the stream of history that keeps rushing past.

If *Austerlitz*'s scope is widened as the narrative drives into the dark heart of a European cultural ideal, then *Sefarad*'s expands out from this into exile. The narrator of Muñoz Molina's novel realizes his own ghostly superfluity and his sense of aesthetic inadequacy. Constructed from an external perspective, his lateness is symptomatic of this, a sign that epigonality is recognized and thus diagnosed in the text as it inhabits the ruins of European modernity, remembering the ostracized of Sepharad and the Hispanic in Europe. *Sefarad*, along with *Austerlitz* and *Dora Bruder*, infers that any evocation of an endangered European spirit emerges under its own aspect of historical lateness, now that the survivors of the totalitarian persecutions of the twentieth century, those who still carry some direct cultural memory of the Jewish diaspora in Europe, are passing away. One of the earliest principal justifications for undertaking the comparative readings in the preceding pages was the fact that lateness and epigonality are haunted by—though not always to be explained by—knowledge of the Shoah. In one form or another, the Shoah is unavoidably present in the political unconscious of all three texts. Considering ideas of Europe alongside Jewishness throws up ambiguities about the relationship of Europe to its discontents, to what is or is enforced as extra-European: legacies of cultural difference; the tensions between assimilation and the persistent history of antisemitism; and, of course, the spectre of twentieth-century genocide and how Jewish European modernist literature addressed this cultural history and the attempt to erase it.

None of the writers examined in the chapters of this book has as their ultimate objective the repudiation of European culture and identity. Rather, they seize upon the moral ambiguity of a cultural identity and heritage whose relatively recent antecedents took questions of nationality and belonging to catastrophic extremes. The European ideal, to the extent that one is postulated in—and, indeed, among—these novels, is revealed as a cultural milieu bound by the sutures of the railway lines along which countless citizens travelled towards refuge or were compelled towards their deaths. Travel stands out as a foundational experience of the European imaginary and is, too, an ambivalent element in these novels. This is a characteristic paradox of the Europe, a place marked by highly historical density that contributes to consolidating the identities of the communities that comprise it through the mass experience of wandering, either sought or imposed, which can thus be understood respectively as an experience of both emancipation and exclusion.

The three standout literary works that have been examined in the present study endure as cardinal reflections of imagining and critiquing continental cultural integration alongside the identity politics associated with the European. Each displays symbolic treatment of the past that reaches beyond the intimate archaeology of extensive testimonial material from survivors of the twentieth-century European cataclysm. Published around the crossing of the threshold out of the catastrophic twentieth century, these novels delve into the fraught idea of identity forged out of the experience of the subjects of the political regimes that marked the early decades of the century. All three authors' work starts from the evocation of apparently real yet fictionalized episodes that are narrated through a suggestive and thorough comprehension of the events that marked recent continental history. These novels' explorations of the twentieth-century European tragedy that underlies the present dynamics of immigration are oriented from temporal and geographical peripheries, the edges of cities, communities, continents, and epochs, suggesting, perhaps, that later European society and culture still remains unable fully to address the origins and consequences of the horror it engendered and out of which it emerged. Sebald and Muñoz Molina weave their narratives by addressing the testimonies that recreate an awareness of the fragile vitality and vital fragility of the European. Whereas Modiano and Sebald plunge into the past through exhaustive exploration of an historical and a fictional individual, respectively, Muñoz Molina recreates expansive fictionalizations of multiple individuals. Ultimately, all three novelists reorient themselves towards Jewish exclusion and extermination as an epitome of a dispossessed European identity.

Late Europeans and Melancholy Fiction at the Turn of the Millennium has not only offered new readings of the individual novels that are the focus of its chapters, but also attempted to establish a sensibility for a particular mode of writing in European fiction at the turn of the millennium. In divining connections among the discourses of lateness and melancholy, and thereby arguing for their potential progressive causality as exemplified by literary works at a particular moment in history, this study has suggested the possibility that such a collective of literary works may optimistically—if unexpectedly, given its late and melancholy provenance—be considered as an expression of possible futurity in European literature. Delineating this mode of writing constitutes a heuristic manoeuvre that enables acknowledgement of the presence of aesthetic and stylistic formulations of cultural and historical lateness, as well as a melancholy view of history, in European fiction. It also highlights the sense of future-oriented potential that emerges when self-consciously late and melancholy novels are read alongside one another, while also emphasizing their constitutive tensions.

These persist. If late European novels and their melancholy aesthetics derive their significance from their narrators' self-understanding as latecomers at the end of an era, then how might this linear, teleological view of history be reconciled with their melancholy sense of an unbridgeable gulf between their present and the past? If, as Ben Hutchinson has argued, modern literature is 'dialectically dependent on the lateness from which it attempts to demarcate itself', then late European novels are dialectically dependent on their internal tensions.[3] They are an embodiment of the idea of a perceived end point—both *finis* and *telos*—at the conclusion of the twentieth century which coincides with the perceived obsolescence of European literature. At the same time, when understood as a community of novels facing backwards, the possible synthesis of their lateness and melancholy into the bringing into existence of something new—the suggestion of their future-oriented potential—is implied when they are read

---

[3] Ben Hutchinson, *Lateness and Modern European Literature* (Oxford: Oxford University Press, 2016), 6.

alongside one another, yet this remains ever deferred within the novels themselves. Ending thus appears to suggest continuity. While any form of critique always implies an alternative futurity, a new realm of possibility where things may be other than they are, an examination of the aesthetics of lateness and their concomitant melancholy in these novels is a hermeneutic mode heavily invested in the potential of its own overcoming. Such finality, however, is likewise always deferred. Nevertheless, at the turn of the millennium, the constitutive tensions in European literature are not incongruous discrepancies, but rather integral elements holding the concept together. Melancholy late European novels thus recall a form of dialectic somewhat more Adornian than Hegelian, which encapsulates the tensions at their heart. Whereas, for Hegel, in the process of *Aufhebung* (not only 'sublation' or 'lifting up', but also 'cancellation' or 'abolition') distinct elements are both preserved and changed, then resolved into a new, greater form through dialectical interaction, any ultimate synthesis is deferred in late European novels. The optimism of future renewal is therefore neither cancelled outright nor fully achieved, but postponed. Yet, insofar as it is postponed, its potential remains. *Aufgeschoben*, as the German adage goes, *ist nicht aufgehoben*.[4]

CONSOLATION AND DEFIANCE

While this study does not claim lateness or melancholy—or, indeed, futurity—as aesthetic elements exclusive to European works of literature, it has attempted to draw on them in order to generate a hermeneutic model for exploring the aesthetic attitudes of significant European novels written and published around the turn of the millennium. Yet, to the extent that this study crosses borders, it subsequently comes up against others: the inclusion of particular authors, works, languages, cultures, and literary traditions necessitates the exclusion of others. In the end, this is the inevitable nature of the comparative enterprise, since decisions must be made, lines drawn, and limitations demarcated. Particularly in comparative literary study, tensions between national contexts and traditions are

---

[4] It is not easy to translate this phrase succinctly into English in such a way that preserves its multiple meanings and ambiguities, but it might be somewhat clumsily rendered as follows: 'to be deferred or postponed is neither to be cancelled nor to be resolved'. The more idiomatic renderings of 'a pleasure deferred' or 'forbearance is not acquittance' may be less maladroit, but they lack the Hegelian *double-sens* implied by the word *aufgehoben*.

predominantly seen as obstacles to be overcome, not least because nation states and national literatures have long defined the discipline in a European context. However, this study has attempted to show how the interplay between the national and the European can be understood not as a problem to be solved, but as a key constitutive element of what makes European novels European at the end of the twentieth century and the turn of the twenty-first. Although a reading of late European novels unavoidably erects its own borders, in spite of the implicit goal of suggesting commonality, such a reading is also necessary in order to examine the particularities of individual literary works. In the three novels examined in this study, which variously engage with the troubled legacies of European modernity and of European literature, there still remains a residual potential for renewal within their sustained 'sense of ending' and their melancholy perspective on the past. Lateness and melancholy acknowledge the aesthetic system they occupy: the reality that makes the idea of a shared European cultural milieu feel like an impossible idea. Yet they also maintain the possibility of exactly this by registering reality and continuing their imaginative work in spite of this. In unexpected defiance of the millennial moment's sense of historical and cultural exhaustion and obsolescence in European culture, these novels collectively constitute a defence of literary fiction's power to not only react to the world and history, but also suggest the possibility that it could be recast. This might only be perceived in the novels examined in this study, however, if the act of reading them crosses borders and languages, while remaining true to each work's specificities and resisting totalizing impulses.

But is this perhaps all too optimistic? What is really to be gained by such a reading of late European novels and their melancholy aesthetics? Is meditation on such potential for a revitalization of European literature not itself untimely, to echo Nietzsche, in a way that may all too well exemplify the very sense of obsolescence it purports to repudiate? Reading to seek the alleviation of the burden of history and of the reversal of European obsolescence—or even the possibility of its instantiation—might to some sound irresponsible, disingenuous, or even unacceptable. Certainly, Herbert Marcuse would think so. In his work on what he terms the 'affirmative character of culture', Marcuse condemns the idea of searching for consolation in aesthetics.[5] Drawing on the example of Shakespearean

---

[5] For further discussion not only of Marcuse, but also more broadly of consolation in contemporary Anglophone fiction, see David James, *Discrepant Solace: Contemporary Literature*

verse, Marcuse warns against subordination and acquiescence to the reality of the present, suggesting that 'In Versen sprechen die Personen über alle gesellschaftlichen Isolierungen und Distanzierungen hinweg von den ersten und letzten Dingen. Sie überwinden die faktische Einsamkeit in der Glut der grossen und schönen Worte'.[6] However unwittingly or indulgently, such a reader, in Marcuse's view, seeks in aesthetic experience and appreciation of the beautiful words of literary works—crucially, for the purposes of this study, from the earliest to the latest—a form of blinkered sanctuary from the world as it is. 'Die Einheit, welche die Kunst darstellt, die reine Menschlichkeit ihrer Personen ist unwirklich', Marcuse admonishes. 'sie ist das Gegenbild dessen, was in der gesellschaftlichen Wirklichkeit geschieht'.[7] Is, therefore, a tacitly optimistic reading of late European novels, as attempted in the present study, guilty of falsely offering 'der Trost des schönen Augenblicks in der nicht enden-wollenden Kette von Unglück'?[8] In concluding this study, it would not be incorrect to suggest that the novels collectively assembled for examination here stand as a refutation of Marcuse's picture of passive readers' ignorant acquiescence to the *status quo*. The method, approach, and arguments of *Late Europeans and Melancholy Fiction at the Turn of the Millennium*, moreover, share this repudiation not only by identifying a mode of late and melancholy European fiction writing emergent around the turn of the millennium, but also by actively imagining its more optimistic future potentiality. This is not a form of sentimental consolation, but rather an act of imaginative defiance, grounded in the late and melancholy reality of the texts themselves, as well as in the traditions on which they draw.

and the Work of Consolation (Oxford: Oxford University Press, 2019), especially 44–45 and 213–226.

[6] Herbert Marcuse, 'Über den affirmative Charakter der Kultur', in *Zeitschrift für Sozialforschung*, ed. by Max Horkheimer (Paris: Librairie Félix Alcan, 1937), 54–94 (66). 'In poetry men can transcend all social isolation and distance and speak of the first and last things. They overcome the factual loneliness in the glow of great and beautiful words'. Herbert Marcuse, 'The Affirmative Character of Culture', in *Art and Liberation: Collected Papers of Herbert Marcuse, Volume Four*, ed. by Douglas Kellner, trans. by Jeremy J. Shapiro (London: Routledge, 2007), 82–112 (92).

[7] Marcuse, 'Über den affirmative Charakter der Kultur', 66. 'The unity represented by art and the pure humanity of its persons are unreal; they are the counterimage of what occurs in social reality'. Marcuse, 'The Affirmative Character of Culture', 92.

[8] Marcuse, 'Über den affirmative Charakter der Kultur', 79. 'The consolation of a beautiful moment in an interminable chain of misfortune'. Marcuse, 'The Affirmative Character of Culture', 103.

To read a latent consolatory form of defiance into works that are inherently melancholy—even traumatic—alters critical and creative parameters in useful and interesting ways by observing and imagining the potential for aesthetic and cultural renewal in works of fiction that revolve around calamity and catastrophe. *Dora Bruder*, *Austerlitz*, and *Sefarad* are novels less to do with representing hopeful instances of consolation and more to do with investigating and giving expression to the seemingly indescribable legacy of devastation and destruction wreaked by modernity. Yet witnessing not only the full force of these works, but also connecting their late and melancholy sensibilities, allows for a way of rethinking connections to literary works and the traditions out of which they emerge. In this way, a counterintuitive—even paradoxical—defiance of obsolescence that embraces the possibility of cultural renewal comes into view. By providing their readers with resonant accounts of twentieth-century history and the 'meta-problem' of European modernity, as well as their late and melancholy aesthetic responses to it, novelists like Modiano, Sebald, and Muñoz Molina embrace the paradox of re-enchantment through melancholy lateness. For some critics and scholars, such a view may well sound unpalatable. Valuing literary works as a means of thinking through cultural revivification and the defiance of European obsolescence is hardly par for the course in the current intellectual climate. Yet enchantment with disenchantment, such as is prevalent in much current literary criticism, risks obscuring a fundamental reason for why literary works matter. To prosecute literature's insufficiencies, as opposed to imagining its potentialities, entails precluding the possibility of considering literary works to be anything more than mimetic representations of reality.

Obsolescence and renewal cohabit in literary culture in significant ways that demand close attention. As this study has attempted to show, lateness and melancholy display the same mutability and variety as newness and youth. The implications of evoking lateness and melancholy in literature, especially around the turn of the millennium, as Modiano, Sebald, and Muñoz Molina do, in ways that scrutinize the facility of aesthetic representation in several languages are far from minimal or incidental. Collectively they appreciate the significance of representing in 'beautiful words' ideas of loss, lateness, tiredness, obsolescence, exhaustion, and inadequacy, without suggesting that this should be intolerable, all-consuming, or all that literary works may amount to. Their novels assess the stakes of taking on aesthetic and stylistic modes that may themselves seem overwhelmingly unbearable or pessimistic, collectively transmuting them into something more affirmative. They—and the present study—collectively risk articulating the potential that re-enchantment of European literary culture may impart to lateness at the moment of its depiction by refusing individually to offer immediate consolation or resolution. In this way, they continue to expand the possibilities of literature and of the novel. For the history of the novel form itself reveals that perceived moments of crisis that put life at odds with its humanized form in literature rarely spell the death of the novel but rather emerge as the very condition of its possibility. Throughout its history, critics and readers of the novel—as well as novelist themselves—have expressed an intuitive sense there is something deathly or unfitting about the novel as a form, which makes it always precarious, always moribund. It is as if, despite its dominance as a means of giving life or narrative shape, the novel always touches on a form of death, continually pushing against its own expressive limits. Yet this makes possible certain kinds of imaginative thought and knowledge, which are in part historical: the novel stands as an intimate archive of the changing ways in which life has been shaped throughout the history of modernity. Even as it preserves its own history, the novel has always been a future-oriented form, a form that offers new ways of conceiving of life and the world.

This study has only begun to scratch the surface of late European novels and their implications. Future avenues of research could broaden the scope of European fiction at the end of the twentieth century to include other writers whose work also engages with the legacy of European modernity. Javier Marías's *magnum opus*, the three-volume *Tu rostro mañana* (2002–2007), for instance, regularly embarks upon digressive disquisitions on the horrors of Europe's past which haunt the narrative's present.[9] Further afield, melancholy aesthetics manifest themselves in the works of writers such as Orhan Pamuk, whose oeuvre may be conceived of as an enactment of the Turkish concept of *hüzün*, a term signifying a form of collective melancholy, which, as Pamuk himself explains, 'is meant to convey a feeling of deep spiritual loss'.[10] Consideration might also be given to literary

---

[9] See Javier Marías, *Todas las almas* (Barcelona: Anagrama, 1989), *Negra espalda del tiempo* (Madrid: Alfaguara, 1998), and *Tu rostro mañana I: Fiebre y lanza* (Madrid: Alfaguara, 2002), *Tu rostro mañana II: Baile y sueño* (Madrid: Alfaguara, 2004), and *Tu rostro mañana III: Veneno y sombra y adiós* (Madrid: Alfaguara, 2007).

[10] Orhan Pamuk, *Istanbul: Memories and the City* (London: Faber & Faber, 2005), 111. For further discussion of the term *hüzün*, see Emily Apter, *Against World Literature: On the Politics of Untranslatability* (London: Verso, 2013), 149–150.

forms beyond the novel, such as the poetry of Michael Hamburger and Alice Oswald. Each of these writers and many others—not least, for example, the two most recent winners of the Nobel Prize for Literature Peter Handke and Olga Tokarczuk, as well as other authors such as Joanna Bator, Rachel Cusk, Jenny Erpenbeck, Elena Ferrante, Felicitas Hoppe, Karl Ove Knausgård, Imre Kertész, Lázló Krasznahorkai, Péter Nádas, or Dušan Šarotar, perhaps—in a variety of ways achieve a distinctly melancholy tenor in their prose. No doubt there are many more.[11]

Potential re-enchantment or revivification of the idea of European literature—that *Spätlinge* might become *Erstlinge*—is never fully actualized in the individual works examined in this study. It is suggested, yet continually put off. The futurity collectively alluded to by melancholy late European novels is *aufgeschoben* without being *aufgehoben*—deferred, but neither cancelled outright, nor fully brought into reality. The lack of resolution here emerges as a key constitutive element of these works' aesthetics, just as a lack of resolution between the categories of the national and the European marks them out as works of European literature.

EVENT HORIZON

What, then, as Sebald asked, is literature good for, especially when it emerges in the entropic late days of European culture? Through their sustained lateness and their melancholy view of history, such a collective of backward-facing novels as those identified and analysed in this study defers the resolution of the tensions that are fundamentally constitutive of European fiction at the turn of the millennium. A vestigial future potentiality thus emerges out of and simultaneously reaches beyond their ongoing sense of ending. Moving forward into the future with its gaze fixed on the past, melancholy late European fiction seems to enter into what might be thought of as a kind of event horizon of European literature: an end ever approached but never quite reached. In general relativity, an event horizon, crudely summarized, is a spacetime region beyond which light cannot fully escape. From the point of view of the observer, an object approaching the horizon will therefore appear continually to move closer to it without ever passing over it. Though teleological in nature, it would be necessary to know the universe's entire past and future spacetime in

---

[11] See Ian Ellison, 'Melancholy Cosmopolitanism: Reflections on a genre of European literary fiction', in *History of European Ideas*, 47:6 (2021), 1022–1037.

order to precisely locate the event horizon, which is to all intents and purposes impossible. Beyond its application in theoretical physics, the term acts as a useful metaphor for the way in which the idea of 'European literature' might, on the one hand, be understood to be continually approaching its end, but, on the other, be sustained into an unknown future yet to come.[12]

In drawing this study to a close, it may be worth considering two recurrent and resonant metaphors from *Dora Bruder*, *Austerlitz*, and *Sefarad*, which encapsulate and illuminate these works' intrinsic tensions. While some might balk at this study's recourse to metaphor in order to illustrate its arguments, particularly in this conclusion, this is justified and retains conceptual potency, not least because the metaphors elaborated here are concrete realities both within and beyond the novels examined in the preceding chapters. In particular, the key ambiguities and potentialities of late European novels are encapsulated in two powerful images that appear frequently in the three novels that have been examined in the preceding pages: trains and twilight.

There is no symbol of European modernity more potent than the railway, with its criss-crossing lines, its monumental station edifices, and, most resonant of all, the steam locomotive thundering ever faster towards its goal along the rails scarring the landscape laid out before it. In *Dora Bruder*, images of trains recur during the narrator's Parisian peregrinations as reminders of Dora's ultimate fate, such that 'en passant au-dessus des voies ferrées, [c'était] comme si j'avais pénétré dans la zone la plus obscure de Paris' (*DB*, 29).[13] In *Austerlitz*, railways and stations link together the travels of both the narrator and the protagonist: the novel opens with that image of the narrator arriving by train into Antwerp, and, later, underground stations act as symbolic places of descent and discovery during Austerlitz's story, while the first meeting and final leave-taking of the narrator and Austerlitz also both occur in railways stations (*A*, 14 and 414). In *Sefarad*, European railways emerge once again as a frequent symbolic touchstone for the narrator's account of twentieth-century exile, persecution, and suffering throughout the novel's seventeen chapters,

---

[12] For further discussion of these ideas, see Eric Chaisson, *Relatively Speaking: Relativity, Black Holes, and the Fate of the Universe* (New York: Norton, 1990), especially 213.

[13] 'On crossing the railway tracks, [it was] as if I had penetrated the darkest part of Paris' (*DB*, 24).

serving as a reminder to the reader that 'la gran noche de Europa está cruzada de largos trenes siniestros' (S, 217).[14] In European modernity, and in modern European literature, the default metaphoric resonance of the train is one of ineluctability, of a single route forward, which is most closely associated with ideas of inexorability, of progress, and of an ultimately inevitable and teleological line of history with all the destruction and calamity that entails. However, it should not be forgotten that equally constitutive of the main line railway is the smaller and less-noticed alternative of the branch line. Largely unacknowledged in the representation of railways in the modern European literary tradition is the metaphorical possibility of steering the train of history onto an alternative track, finding a heretofore undetected or unexpected route. Conceived of in these terms, the resonant metaphor of the railway in the novels examined in this study not only echoes the legacy of European modernity, but also encapsulates the potential of symbolically rescuing trains—and, by extension, the novels in which they act as crucially significant metaphors—from notions of doomed progress, destruction, inevitability, and ultimate obsolescence, recoupling them instead to a future plurality of new directions.

Another recurrent image in *Dora Bruder*, *Austerlitz*, and *Sefarad* that helps elucidate the tensions of late European novels, as well as their latent possibilities, is that of twilight. Often portentously presented in the novels examined in this study, twilight is the melancholy darkness in which much of their narratives, but most especially their endings, take place. From *Sefarad*'s conclusion as 'empieza un anochecer de diciembre' (S, 746),[15] to *Austerlitz*'s narrative ending 'als es Abend wurde' (A, 421),[16] to *Dora Bruder*'s final ruminations on 'les rues vides', which, as the narrator remarks, 'pour moi elles le restent, même le soir' (DB, 144),[17] these novels are saturated with crepuscular gloom. Yet, while twilight or crepuscularity—in French, *le crépuscule*; in Spanish, *el crepúsculo*; in German, *die Dämmerung*—might typically denote dusk and the evening, it might just as equally connote the dark half-light before dawn, the dim glow of future renewal, in which *Erstlinge* might emerge from a melancholy collective of *Spätlinge*. In this sense, an imagined dawn, along with remembered evenings, is better than no light ahead at all. Perhaps, however, the crepuscular

[14] 'The great night of Europe is shot through with long, sinister trains' (S, 29).
[15] 'Night falls at the end of a December day'.
[16] 'As evening fell'.
[17] 'Empty streets' [...] 'for me they are always empty, even in the evening'.

glimmer on the horizon constitutes neither a longer sunset, nor a slower dawn, but rather an ongoing constitutive ambiguity. It is in the strange light of this ambiguous crepuscularity that late European novels emerge, and such ambiguity is inherent to them. Inasmuch as the idea of lateness is predicated on its own overcoming and an implied future, reading European novels published around the millennial caesura in the way the present study has chosen to suggests that through self-consciously late and melancholy aesthetics a collective of works that articulates the possibility of future renewal and restitution for European literature and culture may be perceived. While an ultimate *finis* or *telos* may remain as elusive as ever, European literature moves ever closer towards it. Or so it seems for these melancholy late European novels at the turn of the millennium.

Bibliography

Primary

Modiano, Patrick, *Dora Bruder* (Paris: Gallimard, 1997)
Modiano, Patrick, *Dora Bruder* (Berkeley: University of California Press, 1999), later republished as *The Search Warrant*, trans. by Joanna Kilmartin (London: Harvill Secker, 2000)
Muñoz Molina, Antonio, *Sefarad*, ed. by Pablo Valdivia (Madrid: Cátedra, 2013)
Muñoz Molina, Antonio, *Sepharad*, trans. by Margaret Sayers Peden (London: Harcourt Press, 2003)
Sebald, W. G., *Austerlitz* (Frankfurt am Main: Fischer, 2001)
Sebald, W. G., *Austerlitz*, trans. by Anthea Bell (London: Hamish Hamilton, 2001)

Secondary

Adma, Janneke and Marije Hristova, 'The Exile Condition: Space – Time Dissociation in Historical Experience – A Reading of *Sefarad*', in *Krisis: Journal for contemporary philosophy*, 1 (2010), 62–76
Adler, Hans, 'Herder's Concept of *Humanität*', in *A Companion to the Works of Johann Gottfried Herder*, ed. by Hans Adler and Wulf Koepke (Rochester, New York: Camden House, 2009), 93–116
Adorno, Theodor W., 'Kulturkritik und Gesellschaft', in *Gesammelte Schriften 10.1*, ed. by Rolf Tiedemann (Frankfurt am Main: Suhrkamp, 1977)
Adorno, Theodor W., 'Jene zwanziger Jahre', in *Gesammelte Schriften 10.2*, ed. by Rolf Tiedemann (Frankfurt am Main: Suhrkamp, 1977), 499–506

© The Author(s), under exclusive license to Springer Nature Switzerland AG 2022
I. Ellison, *Late Europeans and Melancholy Fiction at the Turn of the Millennium*, Palgrave Studies in Modern European Literature,
https://doi.org/10.1007/978-3-030-95447-5

243

Adorno, Theodor W., *Gesammelte Schriften 4. Minima Moralia: Reflexionen aus dem beschädigten Leben* (Frankfurt am Main: Suhrkamp, 1980)

Adorno, Theodor W., 'Spätstil (I): Spätstil Beethovens', in *Nachgelassene Schriften I* (Frankfurt am Main: Suhrkamp, 1993), 180–199

Adorno, Theodor W., 'Late Style in Beethoven', trans. by Susan H. Gillespie, in *Essays on Music*, ed. by Richard Leppert (Berkley: University of California Press, 2002), 564–567

Adorno, Theodor W., *Minima Moralia: Reflections from Damaged Life*, trans. by E. F. N. Jephcott (London: Verso, 2005)

Adorno, Theodor W. and Max Horkheimer, 'Dialektik der Aufklärung: Philosophische Fragmente', in Max Horkheimer, *Gesammelte Schriften 5. 'Dialektik der Aufklärung' und Schriften 1940–1950*, ed. by Alfred Schmidt and Gunzelin Schmidt Noerr (Frankfurt am Main: Fischer, 1987)

Alder, Bill, *Maigret, Simenon and France: Social Dimensions of the Novels and Stories* (London: McFarland & Company, 2013)

Anderson, Benedict, *Imagined Communities: Reflections on the Origin and Spread of Nationalism* (London: Verso, 1983)

Anderson, Perry, *The New Old World* (London: Verso, 2009)

Apel, Friedmar, *Die Zaubergärten der Phantasie: Zur Theorie und Geschichte des Kunstmärchens* (Heidelberg: Carl Winter, 1987)

Appadurai, Arjun, *Modernity at Large: Cultural Dimensions of Globalization* (Minneapolis: University of Minnesota Press, 1996)

Appiah, Kwame Anthony, 'Boundaries of Culture', in *PMLA* 132:3 (2017), 513–525

Apter, Emily, *Against World Literature: On the Poetics of Untranslatability* (London: Verso, 2013)

Arendt, Hannah, *The Human Condition* (London: University of Chicago Press, 1958)

Arendt, Hannah, *Vita Activa oder Vom tätingen Leben* (Munich: Piper, 1958)

Assmann, Aleida, *Erinnerungsräume: Formen und Wandlungen des kulturellen Gedächtnisses* (Munich: C. H. Beck, 1999)

Assmann, Aleida, 'The Holocaust – a Global Memory? Extensions and Limits of a New Memory Community', in *Memory in a Global Age: Discourses, Practices and Trajectories*, ed. by Aleida Assmann and Sebastian Conrad (Basingstoke: Palgrave Macmillan, 2010), 97–117

Assmann, Aleida, *Cultural Memory and Western Civilization* (Cambridge: Cambridge University Press, 2012)

Assmann, Aleida, *Ist die Zeit aus den Fugen?* (Munich: Carl Hanser, 2013)

Assmann, Aleida, *Der europäische Traum: Vier Lehren aus der Geschichte* (Munich: C. H. Beck, 2018)

Assmann, Aleida, *Die Wiedererfindung der Nation: Warum wir sie fürchten und warum wir sie brauchen* (Munich: C. H. Beck, 2020)

Auden, W. H., *The Dyer's Hand and Other Essays* (London: Faber, 1948)

Auerbach, Erich, *Mimesis: Dargestellte Wirklichkeit in der abendländlischen Wirklichkeit* (Bern: Francke, 1946)

Auerbach, Erich, *Die Philologie der Weltliteratur*, in *Weltliteratur: Festgabe für Fritz Strich zum 70. Geburtstag*, ed. by Walter Muschg and E. Staiger (Bern: Francke, 1952), pp 39–50

Auerbach, Erich, *Mimesis: The Representation of Reality in Western Literature*, trans. by Willard R. Trask (Princeton: Princeton University Press, 1953)

Austin, J. L., *How to Do Things with Words* (Oxford: Oxford University Press, 1962)

Avni, Ora, 'Patrick Modiano: A French Jew?', *Yale French Studies* 85 (1994), 227–247

Baer, Alejandro, 'The Voices of Sepharad: The Memory of the Holocaust in Spain', in *Journal of Spanish Cultural Studies*, 12 (2011), 95–120

Bahun, Sanja, *Modernism and Melancholia: Writing as Countermourning* (Oxford: Oxford University Press, 2014)

Bal, Mieke, *The Mottled Screen: Reading Proust Visually*, trans. by Anna-Lousie Milne (California: Stanford University Press, 1997)

Barbeito, J. Manuel, Jaime Feijóo, Antón Figueroa, and Jorge Sacido, eds., *National Identities and European Literatures / Nationale Identitäten und Europäische Literaturen* (Berlin: Peter Lang, 2008)

Bartra, Roger, *Melancholy and Culture: Essays on the Diseases of the Soul in Golden Age Spain*, trans. by Christopher Follett (Cardiff: University of Wales Press, 2008)

Bartra, Roger, *Angels in Mourning: Sublime Madness, Ennui and Melancholy in Modern Thought*, trans. Nick Caistor (Chicago: University of Chicago Press, 2018)

Barthes, Roland, *S/Z* (Paris: Seuil, 1970)

Barthes, Roland, *La chambre claire: note sur la photographie* (Paris: Gallimard and Seuil, 1980)

Barthes, Roland, *Camera Lucida: Reflections on Photography*, trans. by Richard Howard (New York: Hill & Wang, 1981)

Barthes, Roland, *S/Z*, trans. by Richard Miller (Blackwell: London, 1990)

Bauer, Karin, 'The Dystopian Entwinements of Histories and Identities in W. G. Sebald's *Austerlitz*', in *W. G. Sebald: History, Memory, Trauma*, ed. by Scott Denham and Mark McCulloh (Berlin: de Gruyter, 2006), 233–250

Baudelaire, Charles, *Œuvres complètes, tome 1*, ed. by Yves-Gérard le Dantec and Claude Pichois (Paris: Gallimard, 1966)

Baudelaire, Charles, *The Flowers of Evil*, trans. by James McGowan (Oxford: Oxford University Press, 2008)

Becker, George J., ed., *Documents of Modern Literary Realism* (Princeton: Princeton University Press, 1963)

Bell, Anthea, 'On Translating W. G. Sebald', in *The Anatomist of Melancholy: Essays in Memory of W. G. Sebald*, ed. by Rüdiger Görner (Munich: Iudicium, 2003), 11–18

Bell, Matthew, *Melancholia: The Western Malady* (Cambridge: Cambridge University Press, 2014)

Benjamin, Walter, *Illuminations*, ed. by Hannah Arendt, trans. by Harry Zohn (New York: Schocken Books, 1968)

Benjamin, Walter, *The Origin of German Tragic Drama*, trans. by John Osborne (London: Verso, 1977)

Benjamin, Walter, *Gesammelte Schriften I*, ed. by Rolf Tiedemann und Hermann Schweppenhäuser (Frankfurt am Main: Suhrkamp, 1980)

Benjamin, Walter, *Gesammelte Schriften I.2*, ed. by Rolf Tiedemann und Hermann Schweppenhäuser (Frankfurt am Main: Suhrkamp, 1974)

Benjamin, Walter, *Gesammelte Schriften II.1*, ed. by Rolf Tiedemann und Hermann Schweppenhäuser (Frankfurt am Main: Suhrkamp, 1977)

Benjamin, Walter, *Gesammelte Schriften II.2*, ed. by Rolf Tiedemann and Hermann Schweppenhäuser (Frankfurt am Main: Suhrkamp, 1980)

Benjamin, Walter, *Gesammelte Schriften III*, ed. by Hella Tiedemann-Bartels (Frankfurt am Main: Suhrkamp, 1972)

Benjamin, Walter, *Gesammelte Schriften V.1*, ed. by Rolf Tiedemann (Frankfurt am Main: Suhrkamp, 1982), 45–654

Benjamin, Walter, *The Correspondence of Walter Benjamin, 1910–1940*, ed. by Gershom Scholem and Theordor W. Adorno, trans. by Manfred R. Jacobson and Evelyn M. Jacobson (Chicago: University of Chicago Press, 1994)

Benjamin, Walter, *Selected Writings, Volume 2, Part 2, 1931–1934*, trans. by Rodney Livingstone and Others ed. by Michael W. Jennings, Howard Eiland, and Gary Smith (Cambridge, Massachusetts: The Belknap Press of Harvard University Press, 1999)

Benjamin, Walter, *The Arcades Project*, trans. by Howard Eiland and Kevin McLaughlin (Cambridge, Massachusetts: The Belknap Press of Harvard University Press, 1999)

Benjamin, Walter, *Gesammelte Briefe VI: 1938–1940*, ed. by Christoph Gödde and Henri Lonitz (Frankfurt am Main: Suhrkamp, 2000)

Bewes, Timothy, 'Reading with the Grain: A New World in Literary Studies', in *Differences*, 21:3 (2010), 1–33

Bewes, Timothy, 'Against Exemplarity: W. G. Sebald and the Problem of Connection', in *Contemporary Literature*, 55:1 (2014), 1–31

Bloch, Ernst, *Gesamtausgabe 5: Das Prinzip Hoffnung: Kapitel 28–55* (Frankfurt am Main: Suhrkamp, 1959)

Bloch, Ernst, *The Principle of Hope, 3 Volumes* (Cambridge, Massachusetts: MIT Press, 1986)

Bonnet, Alistair, *Left in the Past: Radicalism and the Politics of Nostalgia* (New York: Continuum, 2010)

Bourla, Lisa, 'Shaping and reshaping memory: the Łódź Ghetto photographs', in *Word & Image*, 31:1 (2015), 54–72

Boxall, Peter, *Twenty-First-Century Fiction: A Critical Introduction* (Cambridge: Cambridge University Press, 2013)

Boyle, Nicholas, *A Very Short Introduction to German Literature* (Oxford: Oxford University Press, 2008)

Boym, Svetlana, *The Future of Nostalgia* (New York: Basic Books, 2001)

Bracke, Sarah, 'Nostalgia's Violence', in *Forum* 15 (2012), 1–6

Braidotti, Rosi, *Transpositions: On Nomadic Ethics* (Cambridge: Polity, 2006)

Brooker, Peter, ed., *Modernism/Postmodernism* (Oxford: Routledge, 2014)

Brown, Catherine, 'What is Comparative Literature?', in *Comparative Critical Studies*, 10:1 (2013), 67–88

Burgelin, Claude, 'Modiano et ses "je"', in *Autofiction(s)*, ed. by Claude Burgelin, Isabelle Grell, and Roger Yves-Roche (Lyon: Presses universitaires de Lyon, 2010), 207–222

Cahoone, Lawrence E., *From Modernism to Postmodernism: An Anthology Expanded* (Hoboken, New Jersey: Wiley-Blackwell, 2003)

Camallonga, Salvador Orti, 'A "European memory of Jewish Extermination"? Spain as a Methodological Challenge', in *European Review*, 20 (2012), 475–91

Cardwell, Richard A., 'The Poetry of *Modernismo* in Spain', in *The Cambridge History of Spanish Literature*, ed. by David T. Gies (Cambridge: Cambridge University Press, 2004), 500–512

Casanova, Pascale, 'European Literature: simply a higher degree of universality?', in *Literature for Europe?*, ed. by Theo D'Haen and Iannis Goerlandt (Amsterdam: Rodopi, 2009), 13–25

Chaisson, Eric, *Relatively Speaking: Relativity, Black Holes, and the Fate of the Universe* (New York: Norton, 1990)

Chakrabarty, Dipesh, *Provincializing Europe: Postcolonial Thought and Historical Difference* (Princeton: Princeton University Press, 2007)

Chambers, Ross, *The Writing of Melancholy: Modes of Opposition in Early French Modernism* (Chicago: University of Chicago Press, 1993)

Chandler, James, 'About Loss: W.G. Sebald's Romantic Art of Memory', in *The South Atlantic Quarterly*, 102:1 (2003), 235–262

Cheah, Pheng, *What is a World? On Postcolonial Literature as World Literature* (Durham, North Carolina: Duke University Press, 2016)

Codding, Mitchell, 'Archer Milton Huntington, Champion of Spain in the United States', in *Spain in America: The Origins of Hispanism in the United States*, ed. by Richard L. Kagan (Champaign, Illinois: University of Illinois Press, 2002), 142–170

Cohen, Walter, *A History of European Literature: The West and the World from Antiquity to the Present* (Oxford: Oxford University Press, 2017)

Collins, John J. and Michael Fishbanel, eds., *Death, Ecstasy, and Other Worldly Journeys* (Albany, New York: State University of New York Press, 1995)

Compagnon, Antoine, *Les Chiffoniers de Paris* (Paris: Gallimard, 2017)

Cooke, Dervila, *Present Pasts: Patrick Modiano's (Auto)Biographical Fictions* (Amsterdam: Rodopi, 2005)

Cooke, Dervila, 'Hollow Imprints', in *Journal of Modern Jewish Studies*, 3:2 (2007), 131–145

Cosgrove, Mary, 'The Anxiety of German Influence: Affiliation, Rejection, and Jewish Identity in W. G. Sebald's Work', in *German Memory Contests: The Quest for Identity in Literature, Film, and Discourse since 1990*, ed. by Anne Fuchs, Mary Cosgrove, and Georg Grote (Rochester, New York: Camden House, 2006), 229–252

Cosgrove, Mary, 'Introduction: Sadness and Melancholy in German-Language Literature from the Seventeenth Century to the Present: An Overview', *Edinburgh German Yearbook Volume 6: Sadness and Melancholy in German-Language Literature and Culture* (New York: Camden House, 2012), 1–17

Cosgrove, Mary, *Born under Auschwitz: Melancholy Traditions in Postwar German Literature* (Rochester: Camden House, 2014)

Cros, Edmond, *El sujeto cultural: sociocrítica y psicoanálisis* (Montpellier: CERS 2002)

Crownshaw, Richard, *The Afterlives of Holocaust Memory in Contemporary Literature and Culture* (Basingstoke: Palgrave Macmillan, 2010)

Cubillo, Adolfo Campoy, *Memories of the Maghreb: Transnational Identities in Spanish Cultural Production* (Basingstoke: Palgrave Macmillan, 2012)

D'Haen, Theo, 'Introduction', in *Literature for Europe?*, ed. by Theo D'Haen and Iannis Goerlandt (Amsterdam: Rodopi, 2009), 5–9

Dainotto, Roberto M., 'World Literature and European Literature', in *The Routledge Companion to World Literature*, ed. by Theo D'haen, David Damrosch, and Djelal Kadir (Oxford: Routledge, 2012), 425–434

Domínguez, Frank A., *Love and Remembrance: The Poetry of Jorge Manrique* (Lexington: The University Press of Kentucky, 1989)

Eaglestone, Robert, *The Holocaust and the Postmodern* (Oxford: Oxford University Press, 2004)

Eaglestone, Robert, *The Broken Voice: Reading Post-Holocaust Literature* (Oxford: Oxford University Press, 2017)

Eckart, Gabriele, 'The Rereading of Willy Münzenberg's and Margarete Buber-Neumann's Lives in Antonio Muñoz Molina's Novel *Sefarad* (2001)', in *Romance Notes*, 48:1 (2007), 59–66

Eckart, Gabriele, 'Against "Cartesian Rigidity" in W. G. Sebald's Reception of Borges', in *W. G. Sebald: Schreiben Ex Patria / Expatriate Writing*, ed. by Gerhard Fischer (Amsterdam: Rodopi, 2009), 509–521

Edmonds III, Radcliffe G., *Myths of the Underworld Journey: Plato, Aristophanes, and the 'Orphic' Gold Tablets* (Cambridge: Cambridge University Press, 2004)

Eliot, T. S., *The Waste Land other poems* (London: Faber and Faber, 1999)

Ellison, Ian, '"Eine Märchenerzählung, die [...] älter geworden ist mit der verflossenen Zeit": W. G. Sebald's *Austerlitz* as a melancholy *Kunstmärchen*', in *Oxford German Studies*, 49:1 (2020), 86–101

Ellison, Ian, '"Un homme marche dans la rue": Parisian flânerie and Jewish cosmopolitanism in Patrick Modiano's *Dora Bruder*', in *Modern Language Review*, 116:2 (2021), 264–280

Ellison, Ian, 'Melancholy Cosmopolitanism: Reflections on a genre of European literary fiction', in *History of European Ideas*, 47:6 (2021), 1022–1037

Emden, Christian, *Friedrich Nietzsche and the Politics of History* (Cambridge: Cambridge University Press, 2008)

Epps, Brad, 'Spanish Prose, 1975–2002', in *The Cambridge History of Spanish Literature*, ed. by David T. Gies (Cambridge: Cambridge University Press, 2004), 705–723

Eshel, Amir, 'Against the Power of Time: The Poetics of Suspension in W. G. Sebald's *Austerlitz*', in *New German Critique*, 88:1 (2003), 71–96

Eshel, Amir, *Futurity: Contemporary Literature and the Quest for the Past* (Chicago: University of Chicago Press, 2013)

Even-Zohar, Itamar, 'The Role of Literature in the Making of the Nations of Europe: A Socio-Semiotic Study', in *Applied Semiotics/Sémiotique appliquée*, 1:1 (1996), 39–59

Ezine, Jean-Louis, 'Patrick Modiano ou le passé antérieur', in *Les Nouvelles littéraires*, 2501 (1975)

Falconer, Rachael, Hell in Contemporary Literature: Western Descent Narratives Since 1945 (Edinburgh: Edinburgh University Press, 2005)

Felski, Rita, 'Critique and the Hermeneutics of Suspicion', in *M/C – A Journal of Music and Culture*, 15:1 (2012). Available on-line: http://journal.media-culture.org.au/index.php/mcjournal/article/view/431

Figueiredo, Eurídice, 'A Pós-memória em Patrick Modiano e W. G. Sebald', in *Alea*, 15:1 (2013), 137–151

Finch, Alison, *French Literature: A Cultural History* (Cambridge: Polity Press, 2010)

Finch, Helen, *Sebald's Bachelors: Queer Resistance and the Unconforming Life* (London: Legenda, 2012)

Finch, Helen, 'Revenge, Restitution, Ressentiment. Edgar Hilsenrath's and Ruth Klüger's Late Writings as Holocaust Metatestimony' in *German Jewish*

Literature after 1990, ed. by Katja Garloff and Agnes Mueller (Rochester, New York: Camden House, 2018), 60–79

Fisher, Mark, *Capitalist Realism: Is There No Alternative?* (Winchester: Zero Books, 2008)

FitzRoy, Charles, *The Rape of Europa: The Intriguing History of Titian's Masterpiece* (London: Bloomsbury, 2015)

Flatley, Jonathan, *Affective Mapping: Melancholia and the Politics of Modernism* (Cambridge, Massachusetts: Harvard University Press, 2008)

Flower, John, 'Introduction' in *Patrick Modiano*, ed. by John Flower (Amsterdam: Rodopi, 2007), 7–18

Folkart, Jessica A., *Liminal Fiction at the Edge of the Millennium: The Ends of Spanish Identity* (Lewisburg, Pennsylvania: Bucknell University Press, 2014)

Fritzsche, Peter, 'Spectres of History: On Nostalgia, Exile, and Modernity', in *The American Historical Review*, 106:5 (2001), 1587–1618

Fritzsche, Peter, *Stranded in the Present: Modern Time and the Melancholy of History* (Cambridge, Massachusetts: Harvard University Press, 2004)

Fuchs, Anne, *Die Schmerzensspuren der Geschichte: Zur Poetik der Errinerung in W. G. Sebald's Prosa* (Cologne: Böhlau, 2004)

Fuchs, Anne, 'A *Heimat* in Ruins and the Ruins as *Heimat*: W. G. Sebald's *Luftkrieg und Literatur*', in *German Memory Contests: The Quest for Identity in Literature, Film, and Discourse Since 1990*, ed. by Anne Fuchs, Mary Cosgrove, and Georg Grote (Rochester, New York: Camden House, 2006), 287–302

Fuchs, Anne, 'Temporal Ambivalence: Acceleration, Attention and Lateness in Modernist Discourse', in *Time in German Literature and Culture, 1900–2015: Between Acceleration and Slowness*, ed. by Anne Fuchs and J. J. Long (London: Palgrave Macmillan, 2016), 21–28

Fuchs, Anne, *Precarious Times: Temporality and History in Modern German Culture* (Ithaca, New York: Cornell University Press, 2019)

Fuchs, Barbara, *Exotic Nation: Maurophilia and the Construction of Early Modern Spain* (Philadelphia: University of Pennsylvania Press, 2009)

Fuchs, Barbara, *The Poetics of Piracy: Emulating Spain in English Literature* (Philadelphia: University of Pennsylvania Press, 2013)

Fukuyama, Francis, 'The End of History?', in *The National Interest*, 16 (1989), 3–18

Fukuyama, Francis, *The End of History and the Last Man* (New York: The Free Press, 1992)

Gadamer, Hans-Georg, *Wahrheit und Methode* (Tübingen: J. C. B. Mohr, 1960)

Gadamer, Hans-Georg, *Truth and Method* (London: Continuum, 2004)

Garloff, Katja, 'The Task of the Narrator: Moments of Symbolic Investiture in W. G. Sebald's *Austerlitz*', in *W. G. Sebald: History, Memory, Trauma*, ed. by Scott Denham and Mark McCulloh (Berlin: de Gruyter GmbH & Co., 2006), 157–170

Genette, Gérard, 'Proust Palimpseste', in *Figures I* (Paris: Seuil, 1964), 39–67
Genette, Gérard, 'Proust Palimpsest', in *Figures of Literary Discourse* (Oxford: Blackwell, 1982), 203–228
Gillespie, Gerald, Manfred Engel, and Bernard Dieterle, eds., *Romantic Prose Fiction* (Amsterdam: John Benjamins, 2008)
Gilman, Stephen, *Galdós and the Art of the European Novel: 1867–1887* (Princeton: Princeton University Press, 1981)
Gilmour, Nicola, 'The Afterlife of Traumatic Memories: The Workings and Uses of Empathy in Antonio Muñoz Molina's *Sefarad*', in *Bulletin of Spanish Studies*, 88:6 (2011), 839–862
Gilroy, Paul, *After Empire: Multiculture or Postcolonial Melancholia* (London: Routledge, 2004)
Ginger, Andrew, *Instead of Modernity: The Western Canon and the Incorporation of the Hispanic (c. 1850–75)* (Manchester: University of Manchester Press, 2020)
Goldberg, Chad Alan, *Modernity and the Jews in Western Social Thought* (Chicago: University of Chicago Press, 2017)
Golsan, Richard J. and Lynn A. Higgins, 'Introduction: Patrick Modiano's Dora Bruder', *Studies in 20th and 21st Century Literature*, 31:2 (2007), 317–324
Golsan, Richard J. and Lynn A. Higgins, eds., '"Detecting" Patrick Modiano: New Perspectives', *Yale French Studies* (special issue), 133 (2014)
Gorrara, Claire, 'Tracking down the Past': The Detective as Historian in Texts by Patrick Modiano and Didier Daeninckx', in *Crime Scenes: Detective Narratives in European Culture since 1945*, ed. by Anne Mullen and Emer O'Beire (Amsterdam: Rodopi, 2000), 281–290
Graham, Helen and Jo Labanyi, eds., *Spanish Cultural Studies. An Introduction: The Struggle for Modernity* (Oxford: Oxford University Press, 1995)
Greenberg, Judith, 'Trauma and Transmission: Echoes of the Missing Past in Dora Bruder', in *Studies in 20th and 21st Century Literature*, 31:2 (2007), 351–377
Grohmann, Alexis, 'Errant Text: Sefarad, by Antonio Muñoz Molina', in *Journal of Iberian and Latin American Studies*, 12: 2–3 (2006), 233–246
Grossman, Edith, trans., *The Golden Age: Poems of the Spanish Renaissance* (New York: Norton, 2006)
Hagnel, Olle, Jan Lanke, Birgitta Rorsman, and Leif Öjesjö, 'Are we entering an age of melancholy?', in *Psychological Medicine*, 12 (1982), 279–98
Hamburger, Michael, *Late* (London: Anvil Press Poetry, 1997)
Hammond, Andrew, ed., *The Novel and Europe: Imagining the Continent in Post-1945 Fiction* (London: Palgrave Macmillan, 2016)
Harner, Gary Wayne, 'Edgar Allan Poe in France: Baudelaire's Labor of Love', in *Poe and His Times: The Artist and His Milieu*, ed. by Benjamin Franklin Fischer (Baltimore: The Edgar Allan Poe Society, 1990)
Hartog, François, *Présentisme simple ou par défaut?* (Paris: Seuil, 2003)

Hartog, François, *Regimes of Historicity: Presentism and Experiences of Time*, trans. Saskia Brown (New York: Columbia University Press, 2016)

Haustein, Katja, *Regarding Lost Time: Photography, Identity, and Affect in Proust, Benjamin, and Barthes* (London: Legenda, 2012)

Haustein, Katja, 'How to Be Alone with Others: Plessner, Adorno, and Barthes on Tact', in *Modern Language Review*, 114:1 (2019), 1–21

Heine, Heinrich, *Die romantische Schule*, ed. by Karl-Maria Guth (Berlin: Hofenberg, 2017)

Hell, Julia, 'The Angel's Enigmatic Eyes, or The Gothic Beauty of Catastrophic History in W. G. Sebald's *Airwar and Literature*', in *Criticism*, 46:3 (2004), 361–392

Herder, Johann Gottfried, 'Resultat der Vergleichung der Poesie verschiedener Völker alter und neuer Zeit', in *Sämmtliche Werke 18*, ed. by Bernhard Suphan (Berlin: Weibmannsche Buchhandlung, 1883), 134–140

Herder, Johann Gottfried, 'Results of a Comparison of Different People's Poetry in Ancient and Modern Times (1797)', trans. by Jan Kueveler, in *The Princeton Sourcebook in Comparative Literature: From the European Enlightenment to the Global Present*, ed. by David Damrosch, Natalie Melas, and Mbongiseni Buthelezi (Princeton: Princeton University Press, 2009), 3–9

Herzberger, David K., 'Representing the Holocaust: Story and experience in Antonio Muñoz Molina's Sefarad', in *Romance Quarterly*, 51:2 (2004), 85–96

Hirsch, Marianne, *Family Frames: Photography, Narrative, and Postmemory* (Harvard, Massachusetts: Harvard University Press, 1997)

Hodkinson, James, 'Impersonating an Ideal? Islam, Orientalism and Cosmopolitanism in Political, Academic and Popular Literary Discourses of *Fin-de-siècle* Germany', in *Comparative Critical Studies*, 10:2 (2013), 283–302

Hoffmann, E. T. A., *Der goldne Topf* (Stuttgart: Reclam, 1986)

Hoffmann, E. T. A., *Der Sandmann* (Stuttgart, Reclam, 1996)

Hofmann, Gert, Marko Pajevic, Rachel MagShamhráin, and Michael Shields, 'Introduction', in Gert Hofmann, Marko Pajevic, Rachel MagShamhráin, and Michael Shields, eds., *German and European Poetics After the Holocaust: Crisis and Creativity* (Rochester, New York: Camden House, 2011), 1–15

Howell, Jennifer, 'In defiance of genre: The language of Patrick Modiano's Dora Bruder project', in *Journal of European Studies*, 40:1 (2010), 59–72

Hristova, Marije, *Reimagining Spain: Transnational Entanglements and Remembrance of the Spanish Civil War since 1989* (Maastricht: Universitaire pers Maastricht, 2016)

Hroch, Miroslav, *Das Europa der Nationen: Die modern Nationsbildung im europäischen Vergleich*, trans. by Eližka and Ralph Melville (Göttingen: Vandenhoeck & Ruprecht, 2005)

Hutchinson, Ben, *W. G. Sebald: Die dialektische Imagination* (Berlin: de Gruyter, 2009)

Hutchinson, Ben, *Modernism and Style* (Basingstoke: Palgrave Macmillan, 2011)

Hutchinson, Ben, 'The Shadow of Resistance: W. G. Sebald and the Frankfurt School', in *Journal of European Studies*, 41: 3–4 (2011), 267–284

Hutchinson, Ben, 'Afterword', in *Late Style and its Discontents: Essays in Art, Literature, and Music*, ed. by Gordon McMullan and Sam Smiles (Oxford: Oxford University Press, 2016), 235–239

Hutchinson, Ben, *Lateness and Modern European Literature* (Oxford: University of Oxford Press, 2016)

Hutton, Margaret-Anne, *French Crime Fiction, 1945–2000: Investigating World War II* (Farnham: Ashgate, 2013)

Huyssen, Andreas, 'Mapping the Postmodern', in *New German Critique*, 33 (1984), 5–52

Huyssen, Andreas, *After the Great Divide: Modernism, Mass Culture, Postmodernism* (Bloomington: Indiana University Press, 1986)

Huyssen, Andreas, *Present Pasts: Urban Palimpsests and the Politics of Memory* (Stanford: Stanford University Press, 2003)

Huyssen, Andreas, 'Grey Zones of Remembrance', in *A New History of German Literature*, ed. by David E. Wellbery, Judith Ryan, Hans Ulrich Gumbrecht, Anton Kaes, Joseph Leo Koerner, and Dorothea E. von Mücke (Cambridge, Massachusetts: Harvard University Press, 2004), 970–976

Hyslop, Lois Boe, 'Baudelaire on *Les Misérables*', in *The French Review*, 41:1 (1967), 23–29

Itkin, Alan, '"Eine Art Eingang zur Unterwelt": *Katabasis* in Austerlitz', in *The Undiscover'd Country: W. G. Sebald's Poetics of Travel*, ed. by Markus Zisselsberger (2010), 161–185

Itkin, Alan, *Underworlds of Memory: W. G. Sebald's Epic Journeys through the Past* (Evanston, Illinois: Northwestern University Press, 2017)

Jackman, Graham, '"Gebranntes Kind"? W. G. Sebald's "Metaphysik Der Geschichte"', in *German Life and Letters*, 57:4 (2004), 456–471

Jaggi, Maya, 'Recovered Memories', in *The Guardian*, 22 September 2001. Available on-line: https://www.theguardian.com/books/2001/sep/22/artsandhumanities.highereducation

James, David, *Discrepant Solace: Contemporary Literature and the Work of Consolation* (Oxford: Oxford University Press, 2019)

Jameson, Fredric, 'Postmodernism and Consumer Society', in *The Anti-Aesthetic: Essays on Postmodern Culture*, ed. by Hal Foster (London: Pluto Press, 1983), 111–125

Jameson, Fredric, *Postmoderism, or, The Cultural Logic of Late Capitalism* (London: Verso, 1991)

Jameson, Fredric, *The Seeds of Time* (New York: Columbia University Press, 1994)

Jameson, Fredric, *A Singular Modernity: Essay on the Ontology of the Present* (London: Verso, 2002)

Jameson, Fredric, *The Antinomies of Realism* (London: Verso, 2013)

Jamet, Dominique, 'Patrick Modiano s'explique', in *Lire*, 1 (1975), 23–36

Jrade, Cathy L., *Modernismo, Modernity, and the Development of Spanish American Literature* (Austin: University of Texas Press, 1991)

Jurgensen, Manfred, 'Creative Reflection: W. G. Sebald's Critical Essays and Literary Fiction', in *W. G. Sebald: Schreiben Ex Patria / Expatriate Writing*, ed. by Gerhard Fischer (Amsterdam: Rodopi, 2009)

Jurt, Joseph, 'La mémoire de la Shoah', in *Patrick Modiano*, ed. by John Flower (Amsterdam: Rodopi, 2007), 89–108

Kaakinen, Kaisa, *Comparative Literature and the Historical Imaginary: Reading Conrad, Weiss, Sebald* (London: Palgrave Macmillan, 2017)

Kafka, Franz, *Der Process* (Stuttgart: Reclam, 2017)

Kawakami, Akane, *A Self-Conscious Art: Patrick Modiano's Postmodern Fictions* (Liverpool: Liverpool University Press, 2000)

Kermode, Frank, 'The Life and Death of the Novel', in *The New York Review of Books*, 28 October 1965. Available on-line: https://www.nybooks.com/articles/1965/10/28/life-and-death-of-the-novel

Kermode, Frank, *The Sense of an Ending: Studies in the Theory of Fiction* (Oxford: Oxford University Press, 1967)

Kilbourn, Russell J. A., 'The Question of Genre in W. G. Sebald's "Prose" (Towards a Post-Memorial Literature of Restitution)', in *A Literature of Restitution: Critical Essays on W. G. Sebald*, ed. by Jeannette Baxter, Valerie Henitiuk, and Ben Hutchinson (Manchester: Manchester University Press, 2013), 247–264

Kleinberg-Levin, David, *Redeeming words: Language and the Promise of Happiness in the Stories of Döblin and Sebald* (Albany, New York: State University of New York Press, 2013)

Kleinhenz, Christopher and Fannie J. LeMoine, eds., *Fearful Hope: Approaching the New Millennium* (Madison: University of Wisconsin Press, 1999)

Kleingeld, Pauline, 'Romantic Cosmopolitanism: Novalis's "Christianity or Europe"', in *Journal of the History of Philosophy*, 46:2 (2008), 269–284

Kleingeld, *Kant and Cosmopolitanism: The Philosophical Ideal of World Citizenship* (Cambridge: Cambridge University Press, 2012)

Klerman, G. L., 'Is this the Age of Melancholy?', in *Psychology Today*, 12 (1979), 36–42

Klotz, Volker, *Das europäische Kunstmärchen: Fünfundzwanzig Kapitel seiner Geschichte von der Renaissance bis zur Moderne* (Munich: Deutscher Taschenbuchverlag, 1987)

Knott, Marie Luise, *Verlernen: Denkwege bei Hannah Arendt* (Berlin: Matthes & Seiz, 2011)

Kohlenbach, Margarete, 'Transformations of German Romanticism, 1830–2000', in *The Cambridge Companion to German Romanticism*, ed. by Nicholas Saul (Cambridge: Cambridge University Press, 2009), 257–280

Kohn, Hans, 'Romanticism and the Rise of German Nationalism', in *Review of Politics*, 12:4 (1950), 443–472

Koselleck, Reinhart, *Vergangene Zukunft: Zur Semantik geschichtlicher Zeiten* (Frankfurt am Main: Suhrkamp, 1979)

Koselleck, Reinhart, *Futures Past: On the Semantics of Historical Time*, trans. by Keith Tribe (New York: Columbia University Press, 2012)

Kosofsky Sedgwick, Eve, 'Paranoid Reading and Reparative Reading, Or, You're So Paranoid, You Probably Think This Essay is About You', in *Touching Feeling: Affect, Pedagogy, Performativity* (Durham, North Carolina: Duke University Press, 2003)

Labanyi, Jo, 'The languages of silence: historical memory, generational transmission and witnessing in contemporary Spain', in *Journal of Romance Studies*, 9 (2009), 23–35

Labanyi, Jo, *A Very Short Introduction to Spanish Literature* (Oxford: Oxford University Press, 2010)

Larsen, Sven Erik, 'Georg Brandes: The Telescope of Comparative Literature' in *The Routledge Companion to World Literature*, ed. by Theo D'haen, David Damrosch, and Djelal Kadir (Oxford: Routledge, 2012), 21–29

Lebovic, Nitzan, *Zionism and Melancholy: The Short Life of Israel Zarchi* (Bloomington: Indiana University Press, 2019)

Leeder, Karen, 'Figuring Lateness in Modern German Culture', in *New German Critique*, 125 (2015), 1–30

Leerssen, Joep, *National Thought in Europe: A Cultural History* (Amsterdam: Amsterdam University Press, 2018)

Lévi-Strauss, Claude, *La pensée sauvage* (Paris: Plon, 1962)

Lévi-Strauss, Claude, *The Savage Mind*, trans. by Doreen Weightman and John Weightman (Chicago: University of Chicago Press, 1966)

Linhard, Tabia, *Jewish Spain: A Mediterranean Memory* (Stanford: Stanford University Press, 2014)

Long, J. J., *W. G. Sebald: Image, Archive Modernity* (Edinburgh: Edinburgh University Press, 2007)

Long, J. J., 'W. G. Sebald: A Biographical Essay on Current Research', in Anne Fuchs and J. J. Long, eds., *W. G. Sebald and the Writing of History* (Würzburg: Königshausen & Neumann, 2007), 11–29

López-Quiñones, Antonio Gómez and Susanne Zepp, eds., *The Holocaust in Spanish Memory: Historical perceptions and Cultural Discourses* (Berlin: Leipziger Universitätsverlag, 2010)

Lorenzo, Patricia Fernández, *Archer M. Huntington: El fundador del Hispanic Society of America en España* (Madrid: Marcial Pons, 2018)

Lukács, Georg, *The Theory of the Novel: A Historico-Philosophical Essay on the Forms of Great Epic Literature*, trans. by Anna Bostock (Cambridge, Massachusetts: MIT Press, 1971)

Macaulay, Rose, *Pleasure of Ruins* (New York: Walker, 1953)

Mandrell, James, 'Realism in Spain: Galdós, Pardo Bazán, Clarín and the European Context', in *Spanish Literature from 1700 to the Present*, ed. by David William Foster, Daniel Altamiranda, and Carmen Urioste-Azcorra (London: Garland, 2001), 99–128

Marcuse, Herbert, 'Über den affirmative Charakter der Kultur', in *Zeitschrift für Sozialforschung*, ed. by Max Horkheimer (Paris: Librairie Félix Alcan, 1937), 54–94

Marcuse, Herbert, 'The Affirmative Character of Culture', in *Art and Liberation: Collected Papers of Herbert Marcuse, Volume Four*, ed. by Douglas Kellner, trans. by Jeremy J. Shapiro (London: Routledge, 2007), 82–112

Marías, Javier, *Todas las almas* (Barcelona: Anagrama, 1989)

Marías, Javier, *Negra espalda del tiempo* (Madrid: Alfaguara, 1998)

Marías, Javier, *Tu rostro mañana I: Fiebre y lanza* (Madrid: Alfaguara, 2002)

Marías, Javier, *Tu rostro mañana II: Baile y sueño* (Madrid: Alfaguara, 2004)

Marías, Javier, *Tu rostro mañana III: Veneno y sombra y adiós* (Madrid: Alfaguara, 2007)

Marino, Nancy, *Jorge Manrique's Coplas por la muerte de su padre: A History of the Poem and Its Reception* (Woodbridge: Tamesis, 2011)

Marsella, Anthony J., Norman Sartorius, Assen Jablensky, and Fred R. Fenton, 'Cross-cultural studies of depressive disorders: an overview', in *Culture and Depression* (Berkeley: University of California Press, 1985)

Martin, James R., 'On Misunderstanding W. G. Sebald', in *Cambridge Literary Review*, 4:7 (2013), 123–138

Maury, Pierre, 'Patrick Modiano: Un Cirque passe', in *Magazine littéraire*, 302, September 1992, 102.

Mayer, Mathias and Jens Tismar, eds., *Kunstmärchen* (Stuttgart: Metzler, 2003)

McHale, Brian, *Postmodernist Fiction* (London: Methuen, 1987)

McMullan, Gordon, 'The "Strangeness" of George Oppen: Criticism, Modernity, and the Conditions of Late Style', in *Late Style and its Discontents: Essays in Art, Literature, and Music*, ed. by Gordon McMullan and Sam Smiles (Oxford: Oxford University Press, 2006), 37–38

McMullan, Gordon, *Shakespeare and the Idea of Late Writing* (Cambridge: Cambridge University Press, 2007)

Minden, Michael, *Modern German Literature* (Cambridge: Polity, 2011)

Modiano, Patrick, *Dora Bruder*, trans. by Elisabeth Edl (München: Hanser, 1998)

Moretti, Franco, *Atlas of the European Novel, 1800–1900* (London: Verso, 1997)

Moretti, Franco, *Modern Epic: The World System from Goethe to García Márquez*, trans. by Quintin Hoare (London: Verso, 1996)

Morgan, Peter, 'The Sign of Saturn: Melancholy, Homelessness and Apocalypse in W. G. Sebald's Prose Narratives', in *German Life and Letters*, 58:1 (2005), 75–92

Morgan, Peter, 'Literature and National redemption in W. G. Sebald's On the Natural History of Destruction', in *W. G. Sebald: Schreiben Ex Patria / Expatriate Writing*, ed. by Gerhard Fischer (Amsterdam: Rodopi, 2009), 213–229

Morris, Alan, '"Avec Klarsfeld, contre l'oubli": Patrick Modiano's *Dora Bruder*, in *Journal of European Studies*, 36:3 (2006), 269–293

Morris, Alan, 'Patrick Modiano: A Marcel Proust of our Time?', in *French Studies Bulletin*, 36:134 (2015), 1–3

Morse, Jonathan, 'English Literature of the Twentieth Century', in *Antisemitism: A Historical Encyclopedia of Prejudice and Persecution: Volume 1: A–K*, ed. by Richard S. Levy (Santa Barbara, California: ABC-CLIO, 2005), 206–209

Moser, Walter, 'Mélancholie et nostalgie: Affects de la *Spätzeit*', in *Etudes littéraires*, 32 (1999), 83–103

Muñoz Molina, Antonio, 'Eine unmögliche Liebe', trans. by Maralde Meyer-Minnemann, in *Literaturmagazin 23: Auch Spanien ist Europa*, ed. by Martin Lüdke, Delf Schmidt, and Hans-Jürgen Schmitt (Rowohlt: Reinbek bei Hamburg, 1989), 66–70

Naqvi, Nauman, *The Nostalgic Subject: A Genealogy of the "Critique of Nostalgia"* (Università di Messina: CIRSDIG, working paper 23, 2007)

Navajas, Gonzalo, 'The Curse of the Nation: Institutionalized History and Literature in Global Spain', in *New Spain, New Literatures*, ed. by Luis Martín-Estudillo and Nicholas Spadaccini (Nashville, Tennessee: Vanderbilt University Press, 2010), 165–182

Nettelbeck, Colin, 'Novelists and their engagement with history: some contemporary French cases', in *Australian Journal of French Studies*, 35:2 (1998), 243–257

Nietzsche, Friedrich, *Unzeitgemäße Betrachtungen* (Stuttgart: Alfred Kröner, 1964). DLA Marbach: WGS:8 Geistes- und Kulturwissenschaften (einschließlich Geschichte, Psychologie, Philosophie etc.)

Nietzsche, Friedrich, *Nietzsche Werke III.1: Unzeitgemäße Betrachtungen I–III*, ed. by Giorgio Colli und Mazzino Montinari (Berlin: de Gruyter, 1972)

Nietzsche, Friedrich, *Nietzsche Werke IV.2: Menschliches, Allzumenschliches I*, ed. by Giorgio Colli und Mazzino Montinari (Berlin: de Gruyter, 1967)

Nietzsche, Friedrich, *Nietzsche Werke VI.1: Also sprach Zarathustra*, ed. by Giorgio Colli und Mazzino Montinari (Berlin: de Gruyter, 1968)

Nietzsche, Friedrich, *Nietzsche Werke VI.2: Jenseits von Gut und Böse*, ed. by Giorgio Colli und Mazzino Montinari (Berlin: de Gruyter, 1968)

Nietzsche, Friedrich, *Human, All Too Human: A Book for Free Spirits*, trans. by R. J. Hollingdale (Cambridge: Cambridge University Press, 1996)

Nietzsche, Friedrich, *Untimely Meditations*, trans. by R. J. Hollingdale (Cambridge: Cambridge University Press, 1997)

Nietzsche, Friedrich, *Beyond Good and Evil*, trans. by Judith Norman (Cambridge: Cambridge University Press, 2002)

Niekerk, Carl, 'Romanticism and Other Cultures', in *The Cambridge Companion to German Romanticism*, ed. by Nicholas Saul (Cambridge: Cambridge University Press, 2009), 158–177

Novalis, *Novalis Werke*, ed. by Gerhard Schultz (Munich: C. H. Beck, 1969)

Novalis, *Novalis: Werke, Tagebücher und Briefe von Friedrich von Hardenberg Vol. 2.*, ed. by Hans-Joachim Mähl (Munich: Carl Hanser, 1987), 311–424

Novalis, *Heinrich von Ofterdingen* (Stuttgart: Reclam, 1987)

O'Donoghue, Samuel, 'Errancy and alterity: Antonio Muñoz Molina's search for lost time', in *Journal of Iberian and Latin American Studies*, 19: 3 (2013), 211–232

O'Donoghue, Samuel, 'Negotiating Space in Literary Representations of Holocaust Trauma: Jorge Semprún's *Le grand voyage* and Antonio Muñoz Molina's *Sefarad*', in *Bulletin of Hispanic Studies*, 93: 1 (2016), 45–61

O'Donoghue, Samuel, 'The "Truth" of the Past: Fiction as an Alternative to History in Contemporary Spanish Narratives of the Civil War and the Holocaust', in *Hispanic Research Journal*, 17: 4 (2016), 322–338

O'Donoghue, Samuel, *Rewriting Franco's Spain: Marcel Proust and the Dissident Novelists of Memory* (Lewisburg, Pennsylvania: Bucknell University Press, 2018)

Omlor, Daniela, 'Death and Desire: Memories of Milena Jesenská in Jorge Semprún and Antonio Muñoz Molina', *Modern Language Review*, 116:3 (2021), 387–407

Ortega y Gasset, José, *Obras de Ortega y Gasset, Vol. 26: Europa y la idea de nación*, ed. by Paulino Garagorri (Madrid: Alianza, 2003)

Pamuk, Orhan, *Istanbul: Memories and the City* (London: Faber & Faber, 2005)

Patten, Alan, '"The Most Natural State": Herder and Nationalism', in *History of Political Thought*, 31:4 (2010), 657–689

Paulsen, Lasse-Emil, '"The great night of Europe is shot through with long, sinister trains": Transnational memory and European identity in Antonio Muñoz Molina's *Sepharad*', in *Forum: Edinburgh Postgraduate Journal of Culture and Arts*, 4 (2015), 1–13

Payne, Stanley G., *The Franco Regime, 1936–1975* (Madison: Univeristy of Wisconsin Press, 1987)

Pearson, Ann, '"Remembrance … Is Nothing Other than a Quotation": The Intertextual Fictions of W. G. Sebald', in *Comparative Literature*, 60:3 (2008), 261–278

Perriam, Chris, Michael Thompson, Susan Frenk, and Vanessa Knights, *A New History of Spanish Writing: From 1939 to the 1990s* (Oxford: Oxford University Press, 2000)

Prager, Brad, 'The Good German as Narrator', in *New German Critique*, 96 (2005), 75–102

Prange, Martine, 'Cosmopolitan roads to culture and the festival road of human-ity: The cosmopolitan praxis of Nietzsche's good European against Kantian cosmopolitanism' in *Ethical Perspectives: Journal of the European Ethics Network* 14: 3 (2007), 269–286

Preston, Paul, *The Spanish Holocaust: Inquisition and Extermination in Twentieth-Century Spain* (London: Harper, 2012)

Preuschoff, Nikolas Jan, 'Schreiben als Restitution der Sprache', in *Mit Walter Benjamin. Melancholie, Geschichte und Erzählen bei W. G. Sebald* (Heidelberg: Universitätsverlag Winter, 2015)

Radden, Jennifer, ed., *The Nature of Melancholy: From Aristotle to Kristeva* (Oxford: Oxford University Press, 2000)

Rasch, Wolfdietrich, 'Zum Verhältnis der Romantik zur Aufklärung', in *Romantik: Ein literaturwissenschaftliches Studienbuch*, ed. by Ernst Ribbat (Königstein: Athenäum, 1979), 7–21

Reynolds, Matthew, *The Poetry of Translation: From Chaucer & Petrarch to Homer & Logue* (Oxford: Oxford University Press, 2011)

Ricoeur, Paul, *Freud and Philosophy: An Essay on Interpretation* (New Haven: Yale University Press, 1970)

Riley, Kathleen, *Imagining Ithaca: Nostos and Nostalgia Since the Great War* (Oxford: Oxford University Press, 2021)

Ríos-Font, Wadda C., 'National Literature in the Protean Nation: The Question of Nineteenth-Century Spanish Literary History', in *Spain Beyond Spain: Modernity, Literary History, and National Identity*, ed. by Brad Epps and Luis Fernández Cifuentes (Lewisburg, Pennsylvania: Bucknell University Press, 2005), 127–147

Roberts, Gayle, *Modernism and the New Spain: Britain, Cosmopolitan Europe, and Literary History* (Oxford: Oxford University Press, 2012)

Rosaldo, Renato, 'Imperialist Nostalgia', in *Representations*, 26 (1989), 107–122

Rose, Sven-Erik, 'Remembering Dora Bruder: Patrick Modiano's Surrealist Encounter with the Postmemorial Archive', in *Postmodern Culture*, 18:2 (2008), 1–37

Rothberg, Michael, *Multidirectional Memory: Remembering the Holocaust in the Age of Decolonization* (Stanford: Stanford University Press, 2009)

Safranski, Rüdiger, *Romanticism: A German Affair*, trans. by Robert E. Goodwin (Evanston, Illinois: Northwestern University Press, 2014)

Saglia, Diego, *Poetic Castles in Spain: British Romanticism and Figurations of Iberia* (Amsterdam: Rodopi, 2000)

Said, Edward, 'Reflections on Exile', in *Reflections of Exile and Other Essays* (Cambridge, Massachusetts: Harvard University Press, 2000), 173–186

Said, Edward, *On Late Style* (London: Bloomsbury, 2006)

Santner, Eric L., *My Own Private Germany: Daniel Paul Schreber's Secret History of Modernity* (Princeton: Princeton University Press, 1996)

Santner, Eric L., *On Creaturely Life: Rilke, Benjamin, Sebald* (Chicago: University of Chicago Press, 2006)

Saul, Nicolas, 'The Reception of German Romanticism in the Twentieth Century', in *The Literature of German Romanticism*, ed. by Dennis F. Mahoney (Rochester, New York: Camden House, 2009), 327–359

Schlegel, August Wilhelm, *Poetische Werke 2* (Heidelberg: Mohr und Zimmer, 1811)

Schlegel, Friedrich, *Kritische Schriften*, ed. by Wolfdietrich Rasch (Munich: Carl Hanser, 1958)

Schlegel, Friedrich, 'Versuch über den Begriff des Republikanismus (1796)', *Kritische Friedrich Schlegel Ausgabe*, Vol. 7, ed. by Ernst Behler, Jean-Jacques Anstett, and Hans Eichner (Paderborn: Schönigh, 1958), 11–25

Schley, Fridolin, *Kataloge der Wahrheit: Zur Inszenierung von Autorschaft bei W. G. Sebald* (Göttingen: Wallstein, 2012)

Schmitz, Helmut, *On Their Own Terms: The Legacy of National Socialism in Post-1990 German Fiction* (Birmingham: University of Birmingham Press, 2004)

Schulte-Sasse, Jochen, 'The Concept of Literary Criticism in German Romanticism' in *A History of German Literary Criticism: 1730–1980*, ed. by Peter Uwe Hohendahl (Lincoln, Nebraska: University of Nebraska Press, 1988), 99–178

Schulte Nordholt, Annelies, '*Dora Bruder*: le témoignage par le biais de la fiction', in *Patrick Modiano*, ed. by John Flower (Amsterdam: Rodopi, 2007), 75–87

Schulte Nordholt, Annelies, 'Photographie et image en prose dans *Dora Bruder* de Patrick Modiano', in *Neophilologus*, 96:4 (2012), 523–540

Schwartz, Lynne Sharon, ed., *The Emergence of Memory: Conversations with W. G. Sebald* (New York: Seven Stories Press, 2007)

Sebald, W. G., *Die Beschreibung des Unglücks: Zur österrichischen Literatur von Stifter bis Handke* (Salzburg: Residenz, 1985)

Sebald, W. G., 'Die Zerknirschung des Herzens. Über Erinnerung und Grausamkeit im Werk von Peter Weiss', in *Orbis litterarum*, 41 (1986), 265–278

Sebald, W. G., *Nach der Natur* (Frankfurt am Main: Fischer, 1989)

Sebald, W. G., *Die Ausgewanderten: Vier lange Erzählungen* (Frankfurt am Main: Fischer, 1994)

Sebald, W. G., *The Emigrants*, trans. by Michael Hulse (London: Vintage, 1996)

Sebald, W. G., *Luftkrieg und Literatur* (Frankfurt am Main: Fischer, 1999)

Sebald, W. G., 'Zerstreute Reminiszenzen: Gedanken zur Eröffnung eines Stuttgarter Hauses', in *Stuttgarter Zeitung*, 18 November 2001

Sebald, W. G., *Campo Santo*, ed. by Sven Meyer (Munich: Carl Hanser, 2003), 128–148

Sebald, W. G., *Campo Santo*, trans. by Anthea Bell (London: Penguin, 2005)

Sebald, W. G., *On the Natural History of Destruction*, trans. by Anthea Bell (London: Vintage, 2011)

Sebald, W. G., 'Wildes Denken', in *Auf ungeheuer dünnem Eis: Gespräche 1971–2001*, ed. by Torsten Hoffman (Frankfurt am Main: Fischer, 2011), 85

Semprún, Jorge, *Le grand voyage* (Paris: Gallimard, 1963)

Semprún, Jorge, *L'écriture ou la vie* (Paris: Gallimard, 1994)

Semprún, Jorge, *Le mort qu'il faut* (Paris: Gallimard, 2001)

Seyhan, Azade, *Representation and its Discontents: The Critical Legacy of German Romanticism* (Berkley: University of California Press, 1992)

Seyhan, Azade, 'What is Romanticism, and where did it come from?', in *The Cambridge Companion to German Romanticism*, ed. by Nicholas Saul (Cambridge: Cambridge University Press, 2009), 1–20

Sheppard, Richard, 'Dexter-Sinister: Some observations on Decrypting the Mors Code in the work of W. G. Sebald', in *Journal of European Studies*, 35:4 (2005), 419–463

Silverman, Max, *Palimpsestic Memory: The Holocaust and Colonialism in French and Francophone Fiction and Film* (Oxford: Berghahn Books, 2013)

Sontag, Susan, *On Photography* (London: Penguin, 1977)

Soulsby, Marlene P. and J. T. Fraser, eds., *Time: Perspectives at the Millennium (The Study of Time X)* (Westport, Connecticut: Bergin and Garvey, 2001)

Spector, Scott, *Modernism without Jews? German-Jewish Subjects and Histories* (Bloomington: Indiana University Press, 2017)

Sperber, Richard, *The Discourse of Flanerie in Antonio Muñoz Molina's Texts* (Lewisburg, Pennsylvania: Bucknell University Press, 2015)

Steiner, George, *After Babel: Aspects of Language and Translation* (Oxford: Oxford University Press, 1975)

Steiner, George, *Grammars of Creation* (London: Faber & Faber, 2001)

Steiner, George, *The Idea of Europe: An Essay* (New York: Overlook Books, 2015)

Stewart, Susan, *On Longing: Narratives of the Miniature, the Gigantic, the Souvenir, the Collection* (Durham, North Carolina: Duke University Press, 1992)

Stewart, Susan, *The Ruins Lesson: Meaning and Material in Western Culture* (Chicago: University of Chicago Press, 2019)

Strozier, Charles B. and Michael Flynn, eds., *The Year 2000: Essays on the End* (New York: New York University Press, 1997)

Su, John J., *Ethics and Nostalgia in the Contemporary Novel* (Cambridge: Cambridge University Press, 2005)

Suleiman, Susan Rubin, '"Oneself as Another": Identification and Mourning in Patrick Modiano's *Dora Bruder*', in *Studies in 20th and 21st Century Literature*, 31:2 (2007), 325–350

Taberner, Stuart, 'German Nostalgia? Remembering German-Jewish Life in W.G. Sebald's *Die Ausgewanderten* and *Austerlitz*', in *Germanic Review*, 79 (2004), 181–202

Tennyson, Alfred, *The Works of Alfred Lord Tennyson*, ed. by Karen Hodder (London: Wordsworth Editions, 1994)

Tieck, Ludwig, *Kritische Schriften* (Berlin: de Gruyter, 1974)

Tieck, Ludwig. *Der blonde Eckbert/Der Runenberg* (Reclam XL: 2018)

Tomka, Béla, *A Social History of Twentieth-Century Europe* (London: Routledge, 2013)

Traverso, Enzo, *The Ends of Jewish Modernity?* (London: Pluto Press, 2016)

Traverso, Enzo, *Left-Wing Melancholia: Marxism, History, and Memory* (New York: Columbia University Press, 2017)

Ungar, Steven, 'Modiano and Sebald: Walking in Another's Footsteps', in *Studies in 20th & 21st Century Literature*, 31:2 (2007), 1–25

Valéry, Paul, *Regards sur le monde actuel et autres essais* (Paris: Gallimard, 1988)

Valéry, Paul, *Cahiers/Notebooks* vol. IV, trans. by Paul Gifford, Robert Pickering, Joseph Rima, Norma Rinsler, and Brian Stimpson (Frankfurt am Main: Peter Lang, 2010)

Van Straten, Giorgio, *In Search of Lost Books: The forgotten stories of eight mythical volumes*, trans. Simon Carnell and Erica Segre (London: Pushkin Press, 2017)

Van Ziegert, Sylvia, *Global Spaces of Chinese Culture: Diasporic Chinese Communities in the United States and Germany* (Oxford: Routledge, 2009)

Vanderbosch, Dagmar, 'Transnational Memories in Antonio Muñoz Molina's *Sepharad*', in *European Review*, 22:4 (2014), 613–622

Vermeulen, Pieter, *Contemporary Literature and the End of the Novel: Creature, Affect, Form* (Basingstoke: Palgrave Macmillan, 2015)

Vilarós, Teresa M., *El mono del desencanto: una crítica cultural de la transición española (1973–1993)* (Madrid: Siglo XXI, 1998)

Vilarós, Teresa M., 'The Novel Beyond Modernity', in *The Cambridge Companion to the Spanish Novel: From 1600 to the Present*, ed. by Harriet Turner and Adelaida López de Martínez (Cambridge: Cambridge University Press, 2003), 251–262

Walkowitz, Rebecca L., *Cosmopolitan Style: Modernism Beyond the Nation* (New York: Columbia University Press, 2006)

Warner, Marina, *From the Beast to the Blonde: Of Fairy Tales and their Tellers* (London: Vintage, 1995)

Warner, Marina, *Once Upon a Time: A Short History of Fairy Tales* (Oxford: Oxford University Press, 2014)

Weiß, Peter, *Die Ästhetik des Widerstands* (Frankfurt am Main: Suhrkamp, 1975, 1978, 1981)

Weller, Shane, *Language and Negativity in European Modernism: Towards a Literature of the Unword* (Cambridge: Cambridge University Press, 2019)

Weller, Shane, *The Idea of Europe: A Critical History* (Cambridge: Cambridge University Press, 2021)

West, Rebecca, *Black Lamb and Grey Falcon: A Journey through Yugoslavia* (London: Penguin, 1941)

Wheeler, Duncan, *Following Franco: Spanish culture and politics in transition* (Manchester: Manchester University Press, 2020)

Williams, Raymond and Michael Orrom, *Preface to Film* (London: Film Drama, Ltd., 1954)

Williams, Raymond, *The Year 2000* (New York: Pantheon Books, 1983)

Wilkins, Catherine, *Landscape, Imagery, Politics, and Identity in a Divided Germany: 1968–1989* (London: Routledge, 2013)

Wolff, Lynn L., 'W. G. Sebald: A "Grenzgänger" of the 20th/21st Century', in *Eurostudia – Revue Transatlantique de Recherche sur L'Europe*, 7:1–2 (2011), 191–198

Wolff, Lynn L., 'Zur Sebald-Forschung', in *W. G. Sebald – Handbuch: Leben, Werk, Wirkung*, ed. by Claudia Öhlschläger and Michael Nichaus (Stuttgart: Metzler, 2017), 312–318

Wood, James, 'W. G. Sebald: Reveries of a Solitary Walker', in *The Guardian*, 20 April 2013

Wu, Fusheng, *The Poetics of Decadence: Chinese Poetry of the Southern Dynasties and Late Tang Periods* (New York: State University of New York Press, 1998)

Wührl, Paul W., *Das deutsche Kunstmärchen: Geschichte, Botschaft und Erzählstrukturen* (Baltmannsweiler: Schneider, 2012)

Yacavone, Kathrin, *Benjamin, Barthes and the Singularity of Photography* (Bloomsbury: London, 2012)

Zilcosky, John, 'Lost and Found: Disorientation, Nostalgia, and Holocaust Melodrama in Sebald's "Austerlitz"', in *Modern Language Notes*, 121:3 (2006), 679–698

Ziolkowski, Theodore, 'Ruminations on Ruins: Classical versus Romantic', in *The German Quarterly*, 89:3 (2016), 265–281

Zipes, Jack, *Breaking the Magic Spell: Radical Theories of Folk and Fairy Tales* (Austin: Texas University Press, 1979)

Zipes, Jack, *The Brothers Grimm: From Enchanted Forest to the Modern World* (Basingstoke: Palgrave Macmillan, 2002)

Zipes, Jack, *The Enchanted Screen: The Unknown History of Fairy-tale Films* (London: Routledge, 2011)

Zipes, Jack, *The Irresistible Fairy Tale: The Cultural and Social History of a Genre* (Princeton University Press, 2012)

WEBSITES

www.etymonline.com/word/nostalgia

www.theguardian.com/books/2014/oct/09/nobel-prize-literature-winer-patrick-modiano-hailed-modern-marcel-proust

https://www.nobelprize.org/prizes/literature/2014/summary/

INDEX[1]

---

[1] Note: Page numbers followed by 'n' refer to notes.